RESIST

RESIST

LEE SCHNEIDER

FutureX.Studio

FutureX.Studio Santa Monica, CA 2024

Also by Lee Schneider

Surrender

Liberation

Mission of the Lunar Sparrow, audio drama

Your Performance Review, audio drama

FutureX.Studio
Docucinema, Inc.
1112 Montana Ave #257
Santa Monica, CA 90403
futurex.studio/books

First Edition: June 2024

FutureX.Studio is an imprint of Docucinema, Inc.

The publisher is not responsible for websites (or their content) that are not owned by the publisher.

Library of Congress Control Number: 2023923270
Library of Congress Cataloging-in-Publication Data
Names: Lee Schneider, author
Title: Resist / Lee Schneider
Description: First edition | Santa Monica, CA: FutureX.Studio, 2024
Identifier: ISBN 979-8-9872466-5-8
Subjects: GSAFD: Science Fiction

Printing 1, 2024
Printing 2, 2025

Dear Reader,

To assist you as you build the world of *Resist* in your mind,
you will find a Glossary of Terms at the end of the book.

For C., D., B., and R.

PART 001

Chapter 001

The storm had scattered and broken them, and Kat also believed that the storm had killed a few. Many in the circle were missing, off the grid, caught in restraints that were explosively expelled by enforcement bots, then tossed into detention pods with high windows that somehow didn't admit light. There was nothing Kat could do for them now. It was too late.

Kat didn't like the past, so she didn't dwell on those she believed to be dead or detained. There was only one way forward, and that was to focus on the rest, the women in front of her in her pod, the pieces of the broken circle that she could see right now. Somehow they had to leave in the morning, when the weather would still be bad enough to provide cover yet not so bad as to make their journey impossible.

Kat knew that she and the women in her Resistance circle were going to be accused of murder. The Feed insinuated that they'd participated in a plot to murder someone important in tech—two important people, in fact, both Siliconers. And there was collateral damage as well; others were killed.

Everyone read the Feed. It was everyone's first and only source of information, so there would be no point in waiting to see what happened next; as fugitives from the domain, the members of the Resistance circle had to leave as soon as they could. The Feed would get everyone talking. The judicial system, known as the committees, would begin to build a stack of charges against them; when those charges were ready, the committees would send out enforcement bots to get them. The small but mighty bots were low to the ground, but they moved fast and would fire their restraining cables at the women of the Resistance circle, to take them down in a tangle of arms and legs, leaving them struggling and screaming at the judge on the vid screen who would be reading out a sentence for a long detention.

If it happened like that, they would all be locked up for a long time.

"I won't let that happen," Kat unintentionally said aloud, and several of the group in the pod looked up at Kat to measure her emotions. As they did, she measured theirs. Kat saw fear, fatigue, and rage. There were newbies and Youngs, like Oona with her bright, perpetually surprised eyes; and there were Olds, like Claire8, whose modded left eye jittered independently of her right; and there were the unsteady ones in the middle like Emily, always trying to work through a deep personal unease about who she really was, her missing past, a hole in the center of herself. There were also powerful sisters like Ravven, who was Kat's peer in power, though a year older.

Kat mused that she and Ravven were better friends than they were co-leaders. Since they had tried to lead the Resistance circle together, there wasn't friendship or sisterhood between them now, but friction. While Kat always tried for consensus, Ravven went in for extremes; she was sick of the world they had to live in, surrounded by machines, technology, and electromagnetic fields of all kinds. If Ravven had her way, she would never encounter another manufactured electromagnetic field during her natural life on Earth. She was an absolutist to Kat's relativism.

All of this was on Kat's mind this evening, but she had to push it all away. The circle needed provisions to travel on, burner comms known as Secluders (to communicate without revealing who they were or the location of the group), and they needed shoes. Shoes! This was the worst problem. They needed to walk, and few of them had walked far in a very long time.

Hopper00, who was an experienced organizer, professional agitator, and part-time chaos agent, had a secure source for Secluders, so Kat felt all set there. Not so for the rest—Kat felt that so much about the outside world was out of her control. She wasn't sure if she could sense the true length of a natural day, so long had the climate controls manipulated the hours and power of the sun, adjusted the amount of cloud cover, and stretched or compressed the seasons. The Spring that people experienced had an artificial lilac scent; the Winter that people liked had snow that was often manufactured. Summer was still summer: hot, stormy, and fierce. The Fall, the created season they were in now, since it was September, was an algorithm's concept of the space between Summer and Winter. Though the climate controls seemed mighty enough, they failed completely now and again. Hence the storm in Fall, which was a bad one better suited to Summer.

The storm had made a mess of the city. It took down antigrav transportation like the glidepath, and most of the vaporetti were not running in the river, so the women would have to walk to their destination.

"We leave in the morning for Woodstock Settlement," Kat said to the group at dinner that evening. They were trying not to eat too many of their food packages, saving what they could for the road.

They knew their destination already and nodded, barely interrupting chewing to get on to their tasks of stuffing sun protection into backpacks, finding out how many bottles of artificial water they could carry (and learning that they were just as heavy as real water was).

It was the problem of electromagnetic fields again, keeping clear of them as Ravven wanted to and Kat tolerated. The Resistance circle had to get all the way into the edge of the Northlands while staying off the grid, avoiding being tracked by the domain, by the committees, or even by MIND. One way to do this was to go to the past, so Kat had given Emily a map that rolled up and a book made of paper.

Kat forced a smile as Emily waved the book. "I'm ready, ready as I'll ever be."

"Have you opened it yet?" Kat asked.

"Enough to see that it's a manual for camping and living in the wild." It was the official handbook of the Boy Scouts of America.

Chapter 002

From the day that she was hired at MIND to be Bradley's assistant, Nora2 knew that she was equipped and destined to take over the company and its mission. Nora2 was modded. Her name carried the "2" designation, which told everyone she met that she was just one digit off from being a perfect "1." The silicon chip implanted in her brain carried the software for a combination Support and Ambition Package. She had the hyper-intelligence to support Bradley during the growth phase of MIND and the ambition to lead the company into the future. The side effects of her implant were few, and they didn't bother her too much. People said she was cold and difficult to emotionally engage, but she didn't really care about that.

Since she believed that leading MIND was her destiny, she was ready when the moment arrived. When she learned that Bradley had died in space, Nora2 didn't hesitate. She opened the storage area where her go bag waited and hurried from the office in El Segundo, California, to board the glidepath for the sovereign Free State of New Zealand.

As the glidepath rose, hovered, and shot forward, Nora2 was already thinking of all the ways she would conquer Bradley's enemies. She was ever more certain that when she arrived in New Zealand, entered Bradley's home there, and opened his preserved instructions, she would learn all she needed to know about how to stop Kat Keeper and Ravven Vaara and extinguish their Resistance circle. Her mod allowed her to modify her personal appearance to appeal to the people around her. But since she was in the glidepath car by herself, having booked at the luxe level, her appearance modded to suit her alone. She had no control over this; it just happened. Her eyes became a cold black with a pinprick of gold at the center, her brown hair turned a chilly blond shortened to chin length, and her body elongated so that she could stand a few inches taller than before, bringing her height to six feet. She adjusted her seat to accommodate her new regal bearing.

The sovereign Free State of New Zealand was a safe space with good air and real water. The citizens in the glidepath station were welcoming and kind as Nora2 disembarked. They saw her as they wanted to see her. Her mod made her appear pleasant, attractive, and efficient as she made her way among them. They had no idea that she was there to destroy their carefree lives.

Later, as Nora2 moved around Bradley's palatial safe house, with its gardens and greenhouses, its windows looking out over mountains, its comfortable rooms and plush carpets, she felt her love for Bradley want to explode out of her chest. She was dizzy with love, drunk on it, and couldn't walk a straight line from one large room to another.

Bradley's human form was dead. That didn't matter to Nora2, because his substance would live on. She carried his consciousness to the Free State of New Zealand in the standard storage container. This container was a silver cube, three inches on all sides, and felt heavier to carry in her go bag than its shape and mass would suggest. Nora2 would begin work soon to encode his consciousness into an avatar. For now, she put the cube on a table in the house where she could pass it every day and smile, and she connected it to an induction pad to stay charged.

There was an avatar Form Factor in storage at the house. As Nora2 brought it out, she smiled to herself, recalling that people called this marvelous object a Form Factor. Actually, the brand name that Bradley had assigned it when he designed it was PsychePot, but it didn't stick. There had never before been a thing like a rechargeable container for consciousness, and the design team just called it "the Form Factor" as a kind of slang. The official name, noted when Bradley filed his patents, was MindVessel. It was the same design as the one that Dave Serif had inhabited after his death: an elongated shape like a stretched-out egg. The famous Dave Serif: the first avatar organized around an individual consciousness. A humanity emulator. Nora2 smiled wider. It was all evidence of Bradley's genius.

After Nora2 finished Bradley's programming, she would simply open the lid, carefully lower in the silver cube of his consciousness, and let the Form Factor draw the consciousness into itself. She looked forward to the day (soon!) when she would be able to open the top of the Form Factor to reveal the curved screen on which Bradley's face would appear. This screen, also designed by Bradley, had no visual boundaries and no sharp edges. It was a beautiful piece of design, Nora2 thought. Bradley was a genius. *Is a genius,* she corrected herself. *His genius will live on in his avatar.* She felt honored to be in his presence when he was alive and honored to revive his substance in a MindVessel.

Chapter 003

aylight. Kat blinked her eyes open. It was time to leave. The screen on the wall of the pod depicted a sunrise and some real sunlight was coming in through the front porthole window. What Kat wanted now was to extend her hands and invite the women into a morning circle.

"Come," she longed to say, and her imagined summons would draw everyone into the circle to join hands. But to do that, she needed inner calm. She had slept on the floor and her body ached; she had given Ravven a mat to sleep on and she watched as Ravven woke up looking refreshed. Ravven caught her eye and smiled, and Kat felt a stab of jealousy because of the way that Ravven seemed to possess inner calm, whether or not she slept on a comfortable mat, or at least knew how to fake it. Kat would have to ask Ravven to lead the circle.

Hopper00 was also calm this morning. Kat watched him with another small spasm of envy as he sat cross-legged on a mat, eyes closed, mouth serene, hands open in his lap. He had once told Kat that he knew how to travel outside of his body, and he may have been doing that now, visiting his partner Kent Jarma in their underground Los Angeles home. Hopper00 had provided a batch of Secluders, and Claire8 was loading the cloaked comms devices one after another into a large backpack that looked too heavy for her to carry. She wore a cheerful smile.

Outside of the pod, the storm continued to thrash at the outer walls with a series of angry thumps. The pod shuttered on its pontoons, as though scared of the weather.

Once Claire8 had all the Secluders in the backpack she pulled out a dopamine editor from a side pocket. She turned it on and put it to her collarbone, adjusting her level of excitement, dialing back her happy jitters.

Kat watched her and mused that Claire8 loved her side hustles. She had developed the dopamine editor, along with other devices, always with the intention of filing patents on them. Claire8 intended to call the dopamine editor a Dupy, but so far hadn't followed through on the patent, because she said her ideas lacked perfection.

She pulled out one of her other inventions from the backpack, and Kat was glad to see it. It was a Nibbler for cloakcraft, which they would need to use often on this trip. The Nibbler threw a penumbra over the Feed so no tracker could identify you as the reader. Its cloaking action worked only for small bites, a few paragraphs at a time; hence the name Nibbler.

Claire8's industry and curiosity seemed to make her younger, while the anxiety of the Youngs, like Oona and Aftra, seemed to make them older. *It's all going to be okay,* Kat thought for the benefit of Oona. Oona smiled and nodded as she received the thought.

Kat caught Ravven's eye. *Will you lead the morning circle? Then we will go.*

Of course, Ravven returned. Then she extended her hands and said, "Come," and all the women stopped what they were doing—packing, sorting food packets, trying on shoes that didn't quite fit and would certainly hurt after a few kilometers—and eagerly came to join hands in a circle. Ravven began by humming and everyone joined in. A powerful sound like many bees filled the pod, seeming to Kat to be multiplied by some factor larger than the assembled women.

Hopper00, who had remained seated, was smiling.

"Come," Ravven said, inviting him into the circle. "We are leaving, and you are leaving separately from us, so we may only have this last time together." Just about everything Ravven said sounded like an instruction on a stone tablet.

Ravven next asked the circle to think of someone or something they were grateful for, and Kat thought of Dave, her husband who had passed away. She would always be grateful for Dave. She heard her own voice saying Dave's name and saw Ravven nodding to her.

Then Ravven's voice was in Kat's head. *We will all support each other.* Ravven smiled, her white teeth dazzling against her olive skin, the light in her pale blue eyes framed by the plain brown hoodie that she would wear on the journey to disguise herself.

"Namaste," Ravven said. The others answered in kind, and then the circle was over.

While Ravven had spread calm and purpose in the room, Kat excelled at being sure everyone had a job to do. She had made Emily the map handler, because Emily would constantly check it. Emily's face, framed by shoulder-length brown hair with bangs, was tilted upward, as if she wanted to see out of the leaky skylight in the ceiling, but her eyes were squeezed shut as if she didn't want the light to touch her. She was filled with contradictions. Suddenly she stood and moved toward the large round door to the pod. Amber hurried to join her. Amber had a wonderful memory, so Kat had encouraged Emily to give Amber the *Boy Scout Handbook*. Kat saw that Amber held the book now.

"Read the part about navigating by the stars," Kat urged her. They would need a backup in case Claire8's devices failed them.

Kat had yet to think of something for Oona to do, because Oona seemed too anxious to be useful at anything right now. It wasn't necessary for Kat to assign anything to Ravven because she functioned at a high level. Ravven was a repository of received knowledge from a mystical source that Kat didn't fully understand.

Almost everyone was by the door now, waiting to leave, and Hopper00 stood nearby to see them off.

Kat moved to unscrew the door but stopped herself. There were two people waiting outside: She saw them on the vid. One of them she knew and the other was a stranger. She gestured the portal open to admit Cressida Scopes, a programmer in her twenties and newer member of the circle. Cressida introduced her companion.

"This is Bren Humblesinger," Cressida sang out, gesturing to the boy who was with her. They were both wearing silvery-white sun protection suits.

"I am Kat Keeper."

Cressida's suit must have been a half size too small, or maybe it was donned in haste, but it didn't fit her long body well. Her warm brown eyes were bright as she gazed at Bren, but Bren's were brighter, a luminescent green like the leaf of a well-watered plant—no doubt, Kat believed, because of a fashion-forward melanin manipulation in the iris. Some Youngs had gone in for this modification.

Cressida was eager to show off her friend: "Bren is an augur! He guided us through the storm and led me to your door. Isn't that amazing?"

The boy asked everyone to call him by his nickname, Birdie. He looked to be about fifteen.

"Cressida, sorry, but your timing is—we can't wait—we have a small window because of the storm."

Birdie spoke over Kat, singing out his objections. "But machine-based weather predictions are not accurate. I have a finer instrument and I believe you have a few moments to consult the birds." He raised his hands toward the ceiling. "Now, open the skylight! Open it, and I will foretell the circumstances of your very significant journey!"

"How do you know we're taking a journey?" Kat asked.

Birdie jerked his head at Kat in a distinctly birdlike gesture. "Leader woman Kat, I am an augur. All is foretold! Let us experience the future from the patterns of the birds. And you just said you were leaving, anyway," he added, replacing his bravado with a smirk.

Hopper00 enjoyed when moments like this went sideways, so he urged Kat on. "Let the kid have a go at it! Who here doesn't want an augur to guess at the future?"

Then Ravven was at Kat's side, her hand gently on Kat's arm. "I want to know what the boy knows," Ravven said softly. "Leader woman Kat," she added with a gently mocking tone.

"Okay," Kat said, not because she believed Birdie, but because it was a moment to show the others that Kat and Ravven were united as a team. "I'll open the skylight the rest of the way," Kat said, "but rain will come in."

"Let it come! Rain is life! And it will be stopping tomorrow," Birdie declaimed.

"How do you know?" Kat asked.

Birdie shot her his crooked smirk that made words unnecessary.

It took a few moments for Kat to wrestle open the skylight, but soon the ceiling was interrupted by a square of gray clouds and a patch of blue sky. A gentle rain streamed in to touch Birdie's cheeks. He stood beneath in an attitude of benediction, eyes bright like twin suns. Everyone in the pod followed his upward gaze. Three seagulls wheeled through the skylight view, then were gone. After that, nothing.

"What do you see, Birdie?" Cressida urged.

Birdie made a sharp motion with his hands to make her go quiet. He waited, still as a statue of himself.

Then the view through the skylight filled with a gyre of birds flying close without colliding, guided by a beautiful internal system. They reconfigured along horizontal and vertical lines of reference, expanding and collapsing in their own space, twisting around themselves. They were black or brown, moving too fast to tell. A moment of emptiness passed. Then one crow, dim as the absence of life, streaked across the skylight's rectangle. After it was gone, Birdie slumped and drew his hands into his body, hugging himself in agony. He produced a soft cry.

"What's wrong?" Cressida asked, rushing to his side.

Birdie raised his tear-streaked face and wailed, "The pattern bodes ill! Your journey will fail. Your journey will fail."

"What? What?" Cressida said.

But Birdie made no effort to pull himself together. His features were twisted with despair and his voice rang out with a bellow that was impressively forceful for a fifteen-year-old. "The circumstances of your journey are very bad. You will not reach your destination!"

But Kat was Kat, and she had a plan. She stood next to Birdie and coached him to breathe steadily, speaking softly until he opened his eyes to look at her.

There was a pause. Then she nodded; he nodded back, and she unscrewed the pod door.

Kat, Birdie and Cressida, the other six women, and then Hopper00 finally left the pod. Claire8 was the last; she paused at the door to perform some subtle cloakcraft, to make it seem like the door had never opened and Kat was still in the pod by herself, waiting out the storm.

Claire8 caught Kat's eye. "It is done." The deception wouldn't last long but Kat hoped it would be sufficient.

Hopper00 would part from the group here. "Good luck to all!" He accompanied this pronouncement, in keeping with his hamminess, with a broad wave of his hands.

The gesture made Kat smile. "Safe journey back to the Port City of Los Angeles." She added a little bow, picking up, even mocking, his sense of theater.

He went in one direction, to the glidepath, and the rest went in the opposite, to the northbound airway.

The airway was made of uncertain wood slats, some so rotted you had to watch your step, a rickety path wide enough for three people to walk side by side, all suspended on twin steel cables above the rising water of the Hudson. With every step, the airway jumped beneath Kat's feet. The river below the airway was swollen by the storm, pushing higher than usual to wash over an abandoned two-lane highway that twisted along the rocky shore of Manhattan.

The storm had cooled the outdoor temperature, but Kat knew that as soon as the sun rose and broke through the clouds the temperature would rise intolerably. They would need sun suit protection and would don air units when the air turned bad. The river, flowing with fresh rain now, would soon slow down and turn toxic. The climate controls would come back on at some point, but Kat wasn't depending on them.

She walked at the front of the line of women, with the quickest step and sharpest eye for what was ahead: looking down for breaks in the wooden walkway that might trip them, looking ahead for strangers who stared at them just a little too long, looking up at cameras on tall poles that would swivel to watch them pass. She caught Ravven's glance of approval: Kat was in her element, hyper-focused and alert.

Kat was well aware that nothing Claire8 carried in her bag of cloaking tricks was perfect, so it was unlikely that they could travel without detection. But they had to try, because detection meant detention. For Kat, every flicker of light on the airway resembled an enforcement bot rolling toward them. She imagined that someone in a narrow office was working on building charges against the circle. The thought of that someone, somewhere, working on their case, was what kept Kat's feet moving.

Birdie came up to walk beside her. "Sorry. I do get emotional," he said by way of explaining his outburst.

"It's all right, Birdie. We're glad to have you with us." She squeezed his shoulder, sending reassurance into his personality field, and then looked at the sky, the heavy gray clouds, the bruise of sun trying to push through. "What do you think our chances are now?" Kat knew she shouldn't ask. It was a bad practice to ask a question you didn't know the answer to; they taught her that at Uni.

Birdie matched Kat's gaze into the heavy clouds. "I think our chances are good," he said.

Cressida came up to him and took his hand. It was sweet: Kat saw they were soulmates despite the ten-year age difference. They started to giggle at some confidence between them, sensed that Kat's mind was in a more serious place, and slipped back into the line of walking women.

It was a clever feat of cloakcraft for Claire8 to keep their presence mostly invisible from the trackers. She was continually busy fiddling with some device. One was a camera sensor, another a heat sensor, another a drone detector. Claire8 had names for them all, so many that Kat forgot them. She caught Claire8's eye to send a thought message: *How are we doing?*

Claire8 pinged back into Kat's mind, *On schedule. Making good time. I'm amazed there aren't more cameras.*

Maybe not yet, but there will be.

Claire8 nodded. *Right you are.*

They'd have to stop to rest soon. Not many of them were used to exercise, not like this. Even Ravven looked tired, and she was a former professional yoga teacher and had studied martial arts. It was the repetitive nature of the walk, the slowness of it, and having to remain continually on guard.

The farther north the group walked, the more Kat noticed that the wobbly wooden slats of the airway had fallen into disrepair. The airways were supposed to be a temporary solution, but had become the only one. Like the useless roads, they weren't well maintained. When the group walked together, it made the whole pathway shake dangerously. The cables that held the airway aloft were rusted. Kat shook her head. No wonder the local doms were thrilled when MIND came and offered to run the climate controls privately.

The scene before the walking line of women gradually changed from abandoned commercial buildings and warehouses to empty apartments flooded by the river to single-family homes that had been modified with stilts or pontoons. The houses' windows were broken, and water lapped at their front doors. There were lights on inside a few, but this was not an ideal place to live, along the river. Anyone who was able to easily relocate had retreated to the higher ground of Midtown.

The sun finally came out from behind the clouds, glinting on the bellies of the first of the dead fish beginning to surface after the storm.

Ravven was walking beside Kat.

How are you doing? Kat asked in Ravven's mind.

Will we stop soon? Ravven returned via thought.

Yes, of course. As soon as we have some cover. Kat put her hand on Ravven's shoulder to reassure her and beckoned for Claire8 to join them at the front of the line.

"The river seems empty," Claire8 said. "Where are all the boats?"

"The storm scared them," Kat said.

Claire8 smiled. "It will warm up soon." She added that she was glad for her silverblue suit worn under her outer clothing. "Regulates heat and cold, unsung benefit. Survival mode!"

Kat joined her brave smile. "You're right." Claire8 always looked to the bright side. Claire8 was their oldest member, but she walked the fastest in her earnestness to see all and do everything. She looked at the low sky with its lid of clouds, the sun breaking through with a yellowness that already felt warmer to Kat than the surrounding air.

Claire8 saw Kat looking at the sky and said, "Climate controls are still messed up."

"I can't believe that I could miss anything so artificial," Kat responded.

Claire8 chattered on about the silverblue suits she'd designed. They were intended to throw a penumbra over gait detection and the group's thermal signature. "The slaze I'm generating with the suits is so good, better than I thought! And providing some radiant warmth is a bonus, because they weren't designed for that."

"I'm glad for the warmth," Ravven said as she walked beside them. "But I don't believe in gait detection."

Claire8 laughed. "Well, that's like not believing in gravity or in air."

"I don't believe in personality field analysis either," Ravven said.

Claire8 laughed again. "Let me help you with that." She launched into an explanation of personality fields for Ravven, who looked as if she was ingesting medicine that she didn't want to take.

Kat suspected that Ravven's true complaint was not a scientific quibble, but having to wear anything other than her usual clothes. Ravven favored white or gold, but those colors would attract too much attention. Ravven herself would attract attention, if anyone recognized her, and Kat as well. They were both well-known on the Feed. Before the storm took everything down, the gossip writers spun up stories about Kat and the political writers posted stories about the Resistance.

They had to go north quietly, so Ravven was dressed in an uncharacteristically dull brown jumpsuit over the silverblue suit, and her hair, which she was starting to grow out into a halo of kinky red, was concealed under a brown headcloth. Kat, who also favored white, and who was tall and elegant with short black hair, wore dull clothing as well and kept a bac-mask on her face to conceal it. If anyone asked, she could say she was worried about air quality. She tugged the drab artificial-wool cap a little lower on her forehead, which did nothing to conceal her intense gray eyes. The column of walkers formed by the Resistance circle joined the other foot travelers on the airway, a long string of flooded-out refugees seeking higher ground and asylum in the Northlands.

Kat hoped their hastily conceived disguises worked, because who hadn't read the Feed profiles of the famous Ravven Vaara? The gossip writers told the story of Ravven's rise as a yoga teacher in the San Francisco Port City. Because of those profiles, the way Ravven ended every yoga class became first a tagline and then a meme.

"I am Ravven Vaara, and I am an arrow shooting through the sky!" Some of the students grinned, others laughed out loud at her boldness, but after a few classes their doubt or opposition melted away. At the end of class, when Ravven softly said, "I am the embodiment of all grace," they were humbled and believed whatever she preached, drawn further into her spell by the steady gaze of her blue eyes.

Kat's group passed a few people on the airway who were not refugees. These people were walking south, back into the city. Tradesmen bringing vegetables to the Hudson Market, jumpy boys who were cutting school for the day. Some of them gave a curious look to the line of women walking together, but none of them said anything.

Kat said softly to Claire8 and Ravven, "We shouldn't walk close together," and she turned to Emily to send a thought: *Don't bunch up with the others.*

"Look," Ravven said, ignoring Kat's instruction and gesturing to the boys glancing at them, "they're not noticing us. They're not doing anything. Why all this nonsense about gait analysis and personality fields? Do you think the way we walk will give us away?"

Kat thought, *Perhaps schoolboys don't read the Feed?* And the displaced homeowners had other things on their mind.

Ravven gestured to the sky. "I don't see any evidence of *anything* tracking the way we walk. Our gait? How would that identify us? Do you see any satellites?"

Claire8 swiveled her left eye to gaze at Ravven, while her right eye remained aimed at the wooden airway ahead. Claire8 was modded for hyper intelligence. When she was in her sixties, she'd had her body frozen for life extension. But, unfortunately, when she emerged from the cryochamber she learned that eyeballs didn't freeze so well: her eyes could swivel like a fish's. An optimist, she was happy with the excellent peripheral vision this provided. In addition to hyper intelligence, her mod bestowed patience upon her. She used some of that abundant patience as she explained gait detection to Ravven.

"Everyone's walk is individual to them. It's a marker."

Ravven smiled without warmth. "And is personality field tracking even possible?"

"Well, you know about personality fields," Claire8 began. After the field of psychology was replaced by Field Science, a person's psychological presence, their inner and outer thoughts, was referred to as their personality field.

"Of course I know about personality fields," Ravven said. "You just bored me with your explanation." She softened the jibe with a smile. "They're what we used to call a *vibe* when I was young." She suddenly drew her arms around her as a chilly drizzle started. "I'm a Receiver. I know all about psychometrics."

"Yes, of course," Claire8 said. "As a Receiver, you can send and receive thoughts. Personality fields give others a sense of who you are, a particular type, and they can be measured thermally, on the most basic level. Just a 'yes or no,' 'it's there or it's not' kind of signature. Traveling together, as we are now, we are throwing off a heat signature. That's a marker for trackers. The kids on the airway don't care and they don't have the equipment."

"You mean drones?" Ravven asked.

"Yes, drones. And see those utility poles?" Claire8 pointed. "Some of them will have cameras. The silverblue suits we are wearing scramble our profile. The drones have nothing to see. We're displaying nothing that would attract them, unless they were really close. But the cameras, since they *are* close, that's another matter."

Ravven waved all these ideas away. "Nonsense. Utter nonsense," she said in her clipped tones. "But I'm keeping the suit on because it's keeping me warm."

Claire8 laughed. "Suit yourself," she said. "Ha, that was a pun. Do you get it?"

Ravven rolled her eyes. "You are intolerable."

Kat was glad for Claire8's little joke, and for her optimism, because the group had a lot of ground to cover. They estimated two and a half days before they reached the Ossining Ferry Terminal. From there, they hoped to get a boat upriver to Woodstock Settlement.

"Camera," Claire8 called out. Ahead of them there was a camera on a high pole.

Everyone put on their spoofing glasses. Made of paper, they were getting torn and a little ragged, but they still worked. Thanks to the spoofing glasses, when the trackers looked at the faces of the Resistance circle, they saw the faces of other people. The spoofing glasses swapped the data.

As the group walked on through the morning, the airway kept their feet dry. Here and there, a few eyes poked out of second-floor windows to watch them, and Claire8 called out "camera" less and less often. The farther north, the fewer the tracking nodes, because there were fewer people; the dom didn't want to spend more than it had to. Kat hoped for more freedom when they reached their destination.

Keep the river on the left, she thought. She looked down into the water below them, at the gray outline of what was probably a street at one time. A stoplight on a pole stuck out above the water—its signal long dark, of course, but bravely swinging in the chilled air.

Claire8 picked up on Kat's thought and, smiling, placed words in Kat's mind. *Keep going north. River on the left.*

Keep the river on the left, Kat repeated. The constancy of it soothed her.

Emily walked up next to Kat and smiled at the thought as she also received it. *Keep the river on the left.* Emily had the *Boy Scout Handbook* open in her hands, waiting to see moss on the north side of a tree to confirm their direction. She had a compass around her neck on a lanyard and struggled to use it because it was analog, and required her to stop walking for a moment to look at it. Amber was behind Emily, walking a little slower because of her heavy backpack; it was her turn to carry the extra silverblue suits and shoes.

A vid panel mounted on a house flickered to life to show an aerial view (probably from a high-flying drone) of the river airway clogged with walkers from end to end. Text scrolled over the image, announcing NEWS FROM THE FEED. Then, MASS EXODUS TO THE NORTHLANDS, AS MANY WALK THE AIRWAYS. The vid panel covered the exterior wall of the house, about twenty by ten meters.

This was Kat's nightmare come true. Concerned about seeing herself in the vid, she involuntarily ducked her head to stay out of the picture. Then she realized that she didn't need to. Claire8's cloakcraft was effective. When Kat squinted at the image, she couldn't see herself or any of her cohort among the crowd walking on the airway.

A promo for a gossip writer's feed came up on the vid panel: KAT KEEPER AND RAVVEN VAARA MISSING, it screamed in large type, and beneath that the first few sentences of the article, which was yet another hit piece by a gossip hack. Reading just the first few lines, Kat could tell it would cast Ravven as the mystic, an older sister of sorts to Kat, who was, according to the article, an impulsive techie.

"Don't look," Kat said when she saw Ravven looking at the vid panel.

"Too late," Ravven said, smiling.

But we can be grateful for Claire8's work, Kat thought.

Ravven nodded. *Masterful.*

As they walked, they saw that this part of the airway was lined with vid panels. The panel they were reading was followed by another, and another beyond it with the same message about Ravven and Kat.

Claire8 walked beside Kat for a moment and jutted her chin toward the panel. *Ha, it's working. They can't see you.*

You be sure it stays that way, Kat thought with mock sternness.

Claire8 fiddled with a control on an oval handheld device she called a Sightglass. *I've got some good slaze dialed in*, referring to the interference that made them invisible to high-flying drones and any cameras on the airway.

The panel (and the others mirroring it ahead) had switched to displaying a QR code that invited readers to scan it with their comms to read the rest of the article. If they did so, the article would be fed to their unit and their account would be billed. Kat noticed a few walkers were holding up their comms to grab the code.

Kat tugged at her knit cap and pulled up her bac-mask to cover the bottom half of her face. At close range, Kat could be recognized and there would be questions to answer. Someone might want to take a selfie. That would mean discovery and disaster.

Kat's plan was to keep walking until the daylight failed, and darkness came. There would be a gap and then the artificial lighting would come on in the sky. If the nighttime air quality was bad enough to obscure the real moon, the domain would sometimes project a substitute. Kat hoped they wouldn't do that. The group would stop to eat and they would find a place to spend the night. Kat would look into the eyes of the right stranger to ask for a place to rest.

A sign beside the road caught Kat's eye and threw her off her concentration. It seemed to fly directly out of her childhood, imposing itself in her vision, triggering memories. It blocked her from seeing anything else ahead of her.

Kat Keeper had grown up in New York. She had lived on the Westside and had gone to school on the Eastside. Truly, it would have been surprising to Kat if she had *not* encountered a road sign like the one she saw now: ROUTE 9A. So much had changed since she lived here when she was a preteen. She remembered—it seemed so long ago—when the city first flooded, when private cars were first outlawed, when the first vaporetti motored up and down the Hudson so that people could get around after the roads flooded. She remembered a time before pods. Kat had lived with her family in a brownstone apartment along the river.

It was all a long loop in her memory, starting here in New York, going to Uni in California, dropping out of university to thrive at her business, failing at it, humiliation, betrayal, and coming back to New York.

"It's all a loop," Kat said aloud. "And it's all too much."

Claire8 looked at her. "A loop?"

"Nothing," Kat said, and smiled to cover up what she was thinking.

But Claire8 could hear Kat's thoughts anyway. Because they were Receivers, they could all hear each other's thoughts when they were walking closely together like this. The thoughts were a constant background presence. Kat could hear Ravven complaining in her mind about how tired she was of walking. Kat could hear Claire8 asking if Emily would check their location on the map one more time be sure they were going the right way.

Kat didn't want any of the others in her head, so she silently said the chant that blocked them, six words said six times, so she could have some privacy. She wanted to be in her own thoughts.

The Route 9A sign pointed the way upriver, to a town called Greenrock. Simply saying the name Greenrock in Kat's mind pulled her into a haze. Her feet kept walking but the river vanished before her eyes, and she saw her mother lying in a bed in a room on the top floor of their apartment on the Westside. The room smelled heavily of medicine. Kat's mother was dying of lung cancer. She would be gone by the time Kat was twelve.

Chapter 004

"Let's go, Beata, it's time." Her father's voice was patient and slow. "Let's get you dressed."

"I don't want to go now." Her mother's voice was like a child's. Petulant. "I'm tired."

"The fresh air is good for you. You need to see new things," Kat's father, Martin, insisted.

Young Kat was listening to them gently argue. It was like this every time her father tried to get her mother out of bed. Her parents were in her mother's room and Kat was listening in from the hall. She wished they would have a different conversation, say different words, but it was always the same. Her mother's room was dark because they kept the shades drawn. Beata claimed not to like sunlight—it was too hot and bright. The hallway outside her room was narrow, because their apartment was small. Martin slept in the study that he also used as an office, down the hall. Kat slept in the third room, the last one at the end of the hall. She was their only child.

"I don't want to. We always see the same things," Kat's mother repeated. "Always the same." But that wasn't true. There was always something new to see in their short walks in the woods. They would take a taxi from their apartment to a train station and the train would let them off in Greenrock. They took another taxi into town, and then walked in the woods just outside of the town. Then they would come back to town, look at the shops, and stop for lunch in a tavern. Martin would treat himself to a lunchtime beer.

When Beata was stronger, in the beginning of her illness, their walks would last an hour or even two. Kat's parents would let Kat lead, and she took pride in walking ahead, choosing the path—which was always the same, because there was only one trail that was right for her mother. But she still felt trusted and powerful, even if only for an hour.

There were benches on the path, placed there for people to rest. Beata took advantage of every resting place. She sat, breathing heavily, looking at the rolling green hills all around. The presence of the river was always close. Kat would look for wildflowers while her father kept her mother company on the bench.

"Look out for poison ivy," he would always say.

"I will."

"There could be poison sumac, too."

Kat would nod. "I'll be careful, Dad."

As Beata got weaker, she would stay longer on the bench, and would insist that Martin walk with Kat. "You can come back here and get me."

"Are you sure?" Martin would ask.

"Yes. Go."

"All right," Martin would say. "Don't move, so we know where to find you."

Beata's smile was weak and quick. "No chance of that. I'll watch the river." But she often closed her eyes to rest them.

During these times when they left Beata behind, Kat and her father would walk a short distance away and talk softly, having a little conference.

"Do you think she's getting better?" Kat would ask.

"Look at her. She's strong today," Martin responded.

Kat didn't believe that. Nevertheless, she understood her father's intent.

"The medicine she takes is working, right?"

Martin looked into his ten-year-old daughter's eyes. "Yes," he said, with the best assurance he could muster. "She's doing very well."

"She seems tired."

Martin put on a smile. "She *is* tired. Her body is working hard. But she's strong. Your mother is very, very strong."

Martin was also working hard, young Kat knew. When he wasn't putting in long hours at his job, he was taking care of Beata. He was a data salesperson who sold personal information on the gray market. He would probably be shocked if he knew that Kat knew, but he left his computer on sometimes and she knew how to look at things. She knew that he cut corners and bought bad data and sold it to borderline criminal people. She knew that he was spending a lot of their funds on medications that insurance didn't cover. Beata's cancer was costing them a lot, and she had emphysema as well.

Each one of these little day trips was a big vacation for Kat. Martin was convinced that if only Beata would breathe deeply, get away from the pollution and heat of the city, she would improve. Kat wanted to believe in the trips, too, and at first she did. It would be wonderful if all it would take would be some green trees and fresh river-scented air to push strength into Beata's body. This seemed possible at first, and on the walks Kat's family wrapped itself in a bubble of happiness. They were in sync, they measured their steps, they let their feet sink into the well-worn trail, moving through healing quietude.

But Kat's optimism didn't last. She tracked Beata's condition by the number of benches Beata had to rest on. When Beata was still fairly strong, during the early hikes, she rested three times. Toward the end of her illness, however, the distance to reach the first bench on the trail was as far as Beata could go. After the first bench, they would need to turn around, Martin would call the cab to meet them in town, then they'd wait for the train while Beata complained about the strength of the sun on the train platform, then complained about the short train ride and about the next cab they needed to take to their apartment, then complained as they walked up the stairs to their brownstone. Then Beata gripped the railing, furiously white-knuckled with effort, and she would rest several times on the stairs up to her room before she collapsed. Martin helped hook her up to the oxygen and she breathed deeply.

"We can take oxygen with us, a portable unit," Martin suggested.

"No" was all Beata said. Back in the city, Beata was on oxygen almost all the time. The air was bad there.

Then there was hope: medical advances arrived that might do some good. Martin had a friend in a hospital, an administrator who benefited from a gray market client list that Martin had sold him. There was a new device in the hospital called a healing bot. Martin brought home one of the test units for Beata.

He was excited when he plugged it in. "Look at what I have for you."

Beata was waking up from a nap and still foggy. "It has a green light. It's very bright. What is it?"

"It's a healing bot, Beata. It will cure you. You already noticed the green light? All you have to do is think the thoughts that keep that light green."

"How am I supposed to do that?"

"Just think positive thoughts for five minutes at first, then add more later."

"That sounds ridiculous. Is it reading my thoughts? How does it know when I'm happy?"

Martin pointed to the wires he'd taped to her wrist. "It measures your pulse and some other things. Something called a personality field."

"I don't want it," she said, and moved to tear off the connection.

Martin pleaded as he stopped her. "Just try it, Beata. Please. My friend at the hospital says it's been working for some of their patients."

Beata made a skeptical sound. "They probably don't have what I have."

"Some of them do!" Martin was about to repeat his instruction to Beata to think positive thoughts, but he noticed Kat standing in the doorway, listening in on their conversation. "Katherine," Martin said, "come downstairs with me. Let's make some dinner."

They made spaghetti and meatballs. This was before the Change, when ordinary food was still available. There was still water to boil the spaghetti in. Private cars were still allowed in the city streets. There were still deliveries. The weather was becoming more erratic every week, though, and while the climate scientists were starting to call out the patterns for everyone to see, no one wanted to see them. People were enforcing a sort of life that they still called normal.

"Why couldn't I listen? I know what's going on," Kat said.

Martin sighed as he put the pasta into boiling water. Then he turned from the stove to put a hand on Kat's shoulder. "I know you know, Katherine. And I know you're worried about her. But she's going to be fine. She needs a positive attitude. The healing bot is designed for that."

"Does it use a biofeedback loop?" Kat asked.

Her father smiled, impressed. "How do you know about biofeedback loops?"

Kat looked down and hid a small smile. She liked to understand how things worked. The inner mechanics of the healing bot were known to her; she'd looked up how it worked as soon as she heard her father talking about it with that special tone of hope in his voice. It used biofeedback based on readings it took from the patient's pulse, and the model they had could read brain activity. It was one of the early practical uses of personality field theory.

"Well, you're a smart girl, Katherine. I have a lot of hope for this healing bot."

Kat's family was planning to take one of their Saturday trips to Greenrock when they learned that taxis were no longer running because of the fossil fuel they burned. But there was something new called a hoverbus that ran on magnetic induction and floated just a few inches above the ground.

Martin was trying to keep his voice bright as he spoke to Beata. "It's the first antigrav transportation in the city. We can go right up to Greenrock and you can get some fresh air," he said.

"And, what, sit on a bench?" Beata said.

"No, we'll walk like we always do."

Beata looked at him. "You know I can't walk anymore." Her breath already sounded short to Kat.

"Don't you want to try antigrav? Look, I have tickets." Martin showed Beata the bright slips of paper in his hand.

Beata shook her head, and they didn't go anywhere that day.

Kat saw it as a turning point. The air in her mother's room somehow became heavier and it was harder for even Kat to breathe when she was in there. Her mother was snappish, calling out for Martin even though Kat was standing right in front of her.

"Martin, I want to keep reading. Get me a flashlight."

"I'm here," Kat said. "I can get it for you."

Beata looked up at Kat as though she hadn't noticed her daughter there before. "Martin can get it," she said.

"I'll get it," Kat insisted. Asking for a flashlight was strange, because all they had to do was turn up the lights in the room or open the shades that Beata always insisted had to be closed. Mostly, Kat realized, Beata wanted Martin to wait on her by getting her a flashlight.

Feeling useless, Kat lingered. "Do you want me to read you the paper?"

"No."

"Can I adjust the healing bot?" Kat asked.

"No."

But Kat was already working at the bot's controls. She was curious whether she could make it work better and have it heal her mother faster. Since she had read the manual online, she turned the dials with authority and was happy to see that the lights on the little machine blinked faster.

Her mother noticed and didn't like it. "Stay away from that!"

Kat pulled her hands away as though they'd been burned. It took her a moment to find some words. "I thought I could turn it up and make it work better."

"Just don't touch it, Katherine. You don't know anything about it or how it works."

"But I do," Kat started to say, then saw the look in her mother's eyes. So Kat kept the story of the healing bot's invention at Stanford University to herself. By the time she was done reading about the healing bot online, Kat understood quite a lot about it.

It was good knowledge, but it was too late.

On the morning that Beata died, the emergency medical services people came, set up a stretcher on wheels, and rolled her out, feet-first, with a rattle and a bang. Martin went out with her, to be sure she made it to the funeral home properly for cremation.

"Will you be okay for a moment, Katherine? I have to go downstairs with these guys to be sure everything is okay," Martin said. "I want you to stay here just for two minutes. Can you do that?"

Kat nodded yes. She had barely been awake, still in her pajamas when her father came into her room and told her what had happened.

Then Kat was alone in her mother's room, with the heavy smell of medicine and the healing bot. Kat took the little bot in her arms and hugged it to her. Its electronics were still warm. Its red light was glowing; the green light was out.

By the time her father returned five minutes later, Kat had taken the healing bot apart, down to its basic components. They were spread out in a semicircle around her. She held the empty outer shell of the bot. It was cold now.

A flash of anger lit Martin's face, then his eyes became warmer. Kat saw compassion there. He gently took the shell of the bot from Kat's hands. "I can't return it now. Unless you can put it back together."

It took effort for Kat to keep her voice steady. "I can't. I don't know how."

"I guess it doesn't really matter now."

"I guess it doesn't."

Martin left her there in the room with the disassembled bot, knowing that was what she needed for the moment. Kat was grateful for that. She wanted the silence, to be alone and to think, although she wasn't sure what she should be thinking about. Then, all at once, she knew.

She believed that if she could understand the bot completely, she could have saved her mother.

It wasn't entirely rational, but that didn't matter, and it was only a small jump from there to apply to Uni as soon as she was able, early admission—because Kat was convinced that tech could answer all the questions she had. The bot, after all, had been invented at Stanford University, and Stanford, like all other colleges and universities, had been merged into the Uni system.

At age eighteen, during her senior year of high school, Kat was accepted to Uni in California. Her father had mortgaged everything he had to pay her tuition. From the moment she was accepted, she worried about being out of her depth. She feared that she had made a mistake, because she wasn't even a good programmer. She couldn't even put her mother's healing bot back together. She was going to be a failure before she started.

Imposter syndrome would have engulfed her, but as she attended classes and got encouragement from her instructors, she learned that she was a builder of a different kind, a concept person; she had ideas and could communicate them.

So she majored in rocketry, because that was a way to get a job, and minored in pitch decks, because what she turned out to be really good at was raising funds. She had a skill: putting words to ideas and selling other people on them. Her rise was rapid.

While she was still in Uni, she started a facial recognition software company. She hired programmers, raised millions and then billions to build it, and then dropped out of Uni to run it. It was a huge success, and for a time, Kat Keeper was the richest woman in the world.

Chapter 005

K at must have lost track of time, because the sun was lower in the sky, a red ball of heat that was mitigated by the climate controls. They had started working again, if only a little.

A darkness descended that felt like a suffocating blanket wrapped too tightly, and then there was a pause, and the artificial evening light came on: yellowish, as Kat expected, illuminating the sky with its bleak glow. A few street lamps flickered on to illuminate the airway Kat and the others were walking on.

Kat hadn't noticed that the Route 9A signs had stopped pointing to Greenrock. Maybe they had walked past them all as she was wrapped in her memories, oblivious to the outside world.

This was just how she felt about her software company, the one she built and lost when she was younger. She was oblivious to the outside world when she was the head of VirtualEyes. She believed then that she was on an unstoppable trajectory to success. Most people would feel pride, having built as much wealth as Kat had, but she felt shame because of the way she'd done it. She was rich, but had come by her wealth unethically. Her software company was a fraud. She had pushed her programmers into faking the facial recognition technology that they sold for billions. And even when the technology worked, it was designed to take away privacy, adding everyone it scanned to a law enforcement database without their consent. At the time, Kat didn't see this as wrong. She had twisted her early dream of helping her mother, so that it was no longer pure. It had become all about raising funds; everything was. Funding was all that mattered. Her professors lectured about pitch decks but they were describing how to sell magic to investors. If Kat did what the professors told her to do (and she did), she would lie and attract funding.

When Kat next looked up, she noticed that an artificial moonrise had begun, a projection that didn't really fool anyone. Kat hadn't really thought about it until now, but the illusion mechanism of hustle culture had now bled into everything, everywhere, even the way the climate controls presented a livable climate, presenting a sickly glow and a yellow disk in the sky because the real moon was obscured by heavy air pollution. This was somehow accepted by everyone. Kat occupied herself by imagining the pitch deck that would sell the idea of a fake moon to investors.

"Camera," Claire8 called out.

They all put on their spoofing glasses to walk past the camera on the high pole looking down at them.

Then Kat noticed, caught in the glow of the safety lighting, that there was a man watching them approach, and he was blocking their way. The man was tall and impossibly thin, *thin as a wire* was the phrase that occurred to her, but he also looked strong, like he could crush things with his hands. He stood with his legs apart and folded his arms. His face was in shadow.

Ravven and Claire8 fell back, leaving Kat to face the man by herself. That worked just fine for Kat, as it was her impulse to move ahead of the others and talk to him alone, to find out what he wanted and why he was there. But on her way to him she realized that she should not be so trusting in her approach to this stranger. There was a ramp leading down to what remained of the road, and on the road was a large vehicle that Kat guessed belonged to the man. It was a high, boxy panel truck, gray with green trim.

She stopped walking. Fatigue crawled rapidly up her body and rooted her legs in place. Her leg muscles vibrated slightly, protesting. The others stopped behind her; Ravven let out a ragged breath. They had been walking for nearly the entire day.

Kat decided to approach the man but kept her bac-mask up on her face to conceal herself. There was an awkward moment; the man was waiting for her to introduce herself but she wasn't about to do that.

Finally, he gave in and said, "I am Tree Smithson." He showed no sign of recognizing who she was and waited for her to speak.

Ravven's voice popped into her head. *Man of few words.*

Kat wondered if this fellow would leak the news of their whereabouts to a gossip writer or to the committees. She was trying to decide whether he was shy or dangerous or both and decided that he was neither, just suspicious like she was. He probably didn't encounter many people on the airway after dark. The earlier crowds of walkers had thinned out. "Are you from around here?"

"No," Tree said. "Just passing through." He nodded toward the large truck on the road below them.

So it was his, Kat noted. "We're looking for a place to stay the night."

"Well, I don't know." He shifted his weight from one foot to the other, the unsteady motion moving him into the glow of an overhead light. He put his hand to his chin and Kat saw from the puzzled gesture how young he really was. Maybe mid-twenties, with a fuzzy growth of blond beard and shoulder-length blond hair that he paused to twist into a knot behind his head. Hardened by the road, he had seemed older at first. He wore working man's clothes, heavy and green, and sturdy boots; though he was underdressed for the weather, he didn't seem cold.

Used to the cold, Ravven's voice said in Kat's mind. *Probably spends time outside.*

I've got this, Kat thought back.

Tree gestured vaguely to the right of the airway, to where a town might be. "There is a woman down that way, maybe a five-minute walk. She takes people in when she has room." He gave her name and gestured to a rickety stairway that led off the airway. Somewhere down there, beyond in the darkness, they would find shelter.

"Thanks," Kat said. "We'll check her out."

They left Tree on the airway and took the wood and rope stairway down to the road. Like everything about the airways here, it seemed hastily put in place.

"Wow, that's weird," Emily said, putting her hand on Kat's shoulder for a moment to steady herself. After hours of walking on the airway and swaying back and forth, the stability of a road felt strange.

Claire8 looked at the Sightglass she held in her hands. The black oval detector showed no indicator lights. "Strange. No cameras."

Kat was trying to see if the pinpoints of light she saw ahead would resolve into a dwelling. "Tree said it was about five minutes up that way." She pressed on, but turned over her shoulder to look at the group. No one was standing tall. Their personality fields were weak; they had all the energy sucked out of them by the long day. "Just a little longer, a little farther," Kat said to them. She could almost hear their feet dragging on the pavement.

In five minutes, as Tree promised, there was a small house. This wasn't a pod; it wasn't elevated. It was a proper house, though rather narrow, as if squeezed into the small lot it occupied; the two other houses on either side were cramped into similar dimensions. This house had lights on, which Kat took to be a welcoming sign.

But no: The woman who answered the door barely opened it a crack to tell them she had no room for them. "All full."

"Do you know where we—" Kat began, but found herself speaking to the door as the woman had closed it. There was the sound of a lock snapping shut, then another, sealing the door. Kat let her head rest against the door for a moment. She was afraid to turn around to see the disappointed faces of the group.

But then there was a voice in her head. *Hello, sister,* it said.

Kat turned around to see a woman standing in the road, about twenty meters away. The woman was smiling. Her voice was in Kat's head again. *I can help you.*

Chapter 006

ora2 thought she would position the Form Factor so that when Bradley's consciousness revivified, it could take in the spectacular view of the mountains and lake outside the house's largest window. (She meant to think of the Form Factor as a MindVessel, the proper name of the rechargeable consciousness container, but had fallen into the habit that everyone else who encountered one of the devices had.) The house fit into the beauty like it was a part of the nature that surrounded it, with spacious rooms and high ceilings. Scattered throughout were so many rare natural materials: tables made of wood, gleaming metal fittings on the doors, and furniture covered with cloth. She wondered if Bradley missed this place when he was away from it during his long days building MIND as a company in El Segundo; she thought he would feel at rest here. But she also imagined that he had been lonely when he was here all by himself in the large house with no one to talk to. She smiled to herself. *He didn't have me to talk to, but now he does.*

She remembered their first day together, when they met at her job interview as his assistant, and compared notes as fellow mods. Bradley had an early mod, but he was still able to shape-shift his appearance to please other people. On the day they met, he told her he had just come from the Free State of New Zealand. *He had just gotten off the glidepath. He had been here. Where I am at this moment. Full circle.* The thought filled Nora2 with a great happiness.

Now she was in charge of MIND, meeting her destiny with eyes wide open, and she was training Bradley's consciousness like a parent would train the consciousness of a beloved child. Nora2 felt that she was servant, lover, and mother to him.

Lover! She could only hope so, and perhaps it was too late. She would never know Bradley in human form again. But she wondered if somehow she might interact with his consciousness somatically. This made no sense, but just thinking of it made her excited and she had to have some contact with him. Her hands shook slightly, a feverish tingle at her fingertips, as she carefully opened the silver cube and gazed at the gentle blue orb of consciousness pulsing within. This was a precious object. She knew she wasn't supposed to be doing this, but she couldn't help herself. Bradley was there, in a sense, waiting. Pulsing.

She closed up the storage cube and moved on to ready the Form Factor, placing it on an induction pad to take a fresh charge. Every step had to be followed precisely. One mistake, and Bradley's consciousness would fail to revivify properly. If that happened, what would she do? It would mean bottomless despair for her, a spiral of desolation.

Nora2 didn't want to consider that possibility even for a second. Her dark eyes flashed with concentration as she gestured to activate the Form Factor, preparing it to receive the blue orb of consciousness.

Taking care to continue breathing (her impulse was to hold her breath), Nora2 opened the storage cube again and reached inside to gently wrap her warm hands around the glowing blue orb. Surprisingly, it was cold to the touch. She was expecting a human sort of warmth; it was pulsing, and it contained consciousness. But it was a machine, like the avatar Form Factor, she reminded herself. The Form Factor was only warm because it was soaking up an electrical charge via induction. And the orb was not really Bradley at all, but it would soon turn into something like him, so much like him that her heart quickened all over again. *Steady. Steady on.*

She lowered the orb into the Form Factor. There was a brief flash, and her heart sank, because she assumed this meant there was a bad connection and the consciousness was destroyed. But no, everything was fine. The connection was good, as signaled by a single low beep and a white light that glowed on the smooth white outside of the Form Factor.

Nora2 watched as the Form Factor pulsed gently now, a pure white light all around it. She would begin the work of programming in twenty-four hours, talking the newly awakening version of Bradley through his history, his early life, his schooling, his career, and his death as a human. All of this information was being uploaded into the Form Factor's memory, but that process would make it only the most basic of humanity emulators. To train it to react as Bradley did when he was alive was a question-and-answer process. The avatar had a fixed memory of its human archive, but the upcoming question and answer sessions led by Nora2 would make it agile, able to approach the raw data from different perspectives, and to shape the raw memories it was uploading now into a working personality. The end goal was to make the humanity emulator agile enough to be predictive, able to react with fidelity to events in its memory and also to events that were new to it.

She opened a screen that had her first list of questions to ask Bradley's consciousness. Then, quickly, she made herself close that screen again, because her hands were getting fluttery and her heart was beating too fast, and she was already late for the next call on her agenda. She was going to speak with Sanchez, MIND's head of Input who was in charge of all Harvester programs. Her mod should have helped her stay calm, but feelings for Bradley kept intruding. She didn't know why, and she could know more about it if she would only consult her mod's handbook online. For some reason, she didn't want to.

In Nora2's view, Santos Sanchez was a difficult employee. From the day she met him at the MIND offices, she noticed a bitter resonance in his personality field. (She thought of personality fields like music and the signals that people emanated like chords.) She assumed that he probably didn't like working for a modded woman who was smarter than he was, or maybe he didn't like working for any woman. She guessed that he was jealous of her close relationship with Bradley when he was alive, and jealous that Bradley had chosen Nora2 to revivify his consciousness.

When they were all in the El Segundo office together, when Bradley was alive, Sanchez made snarky remarks about "the lovebirds" and "Bradley's favorite" when he thought she couldn't overhear. (Nora2 had bionic hearing and recording capability.) She knew that Sanchez thought her devotion to Bradley was perverse. What would Sanchez think of her devotion to Bradley blooming into love?

And here was his blunt, broad face on Nora2's vid screen, and she was certain that she saw a look of repulsion in his eyes, not quite concealed by his heavy eyebrows, and a simmering rage expressed in the careless gestures he made with his big, meaty hands; his mood was a cloud between them, his personality field a swirl of negativity. Nora2 hadn't yet said a word, but Sanchez's face was already screwed into a scowl.

"Let's start with the routine matters," she began. It was a staff meeting, after all—it was supposed to be boring. She wanted Sanchez to tell her more about the miniaturization projects for the Harvester device and where the next deployments were going to be. They already had Input Men walking the streets in the San Francisco Port City, New York, and cities in the Upper Midwest Domain. The Input Men moved through the markets and other public places with small Harvester units in backpacks, gathering thoughts before citizens had fully formed them, to help develop MIND's machine intelligence training models.

Sanchez filled her in on new deployments in the cities of the Southern Domains, like Miami and Atlanta, and in the Free State of Texas. That last deployment was proving to be a challenge, because Texas was experiencing another round of extreme heat and lacked the power to implement climate controls.

Then Sanchez asked her about Alon6, Bradley's business partner. Alon6 had died in the same incident in space that cost Bradley his life. "When are you going to light him up?"

"Sorry?" Nora2 asked. She was surprised at his change of direction.

"When are you going to start training his avatar?" Sanchez replied. "We need Alon6."

Nora2 couldn't help but glance over at the storage cube that held Alon6's consciousness in limbo. It was on another table, far away from Bradley's, as though she didn't want one to contaminate the other. Bradley's was pulling power from the induction connection built into the table, charging steadily. Alon6's consciousness was still wrapped in its black protective packaging and was not near any induction ports. It was on battery power and slowly running down. If Nora2 had her way, Alon6's consciousness would be extinguished soon, because she would never put it into a Form Factor.

"I don't think we need him," Nora2 said. The reason Sanchez was bringing it up, she knew, was that he didn't think she was capable of running MIND by herself, didn't think she had Alon6's killer instincts. She took this as an insult and narrowed her black eyes at Sanchez. Her features became sharper, cheekbones subtly higher, forehead slightly bigger as well, to present a more imposing visage to Sanchez. She was tempted to tell him, biting off the words one by one, that she had deliberately neglected Alon6's consciousness container, was deliberately letting Alon6 run down into oblivion. She even contemplated throwing his storage cube into the wall-mounted disposal and listening with satisfaction as it was ground into shards of nothingness. Alon6 was just that much of a dick.

These were not appropriate thoughts, she knew, not the thoughts of an effective leader, and her mod always moved her in that direction. She stood a little taller, as befitted an Administrator, and made some excuse to Sanchez about delaying Alon6's consciousness revivification, and asked him to tell her more about the Input Men they were deploying, and in which new cities. "Keep going about the new Harvester programs. Don't hold back any details."

Sanchez obligingly droned on. She didn't listen to his answer, which she knew was also not behavior befitting an effective leader, but she couldn't help herself, as her gaze continually strayed to Bradley's Form Factor. She hoped that Sanchez wouldn't notice her wayward line of sight and nodded periodically to pretend that she was listening.

Nora2 knew it would take a couple of weeks to prepare Bradley's consciousness for a full activation in his Form Factor. Then he would be revivfied as an avatar. She would start by presenting him with simple dialogue, a question and answer, like a mother training her child about shapes and colors and objects. She knew that Bradley's consciousness would advance rapidly, and she already felt something of a mother's teary sense of loss. It would be hard to lose Bradley as a young consciousness. But in just a few weeks, if everything went well, Bradley would become a man: identical to his old self but without a body. His childhood, her sense of motherhood, would be short. But that was how these things worked.

"Nora2?" Sanchez was saying.

"What?" Apparently, she had missed a question.

"Chicago is ready. Should we launch there? Add it to the other cities in the Midwest Domain?" He sounded irritated at having to ask twice when he was such a busy man.

Nora2 waved the annoying question away. "Of course, if it's ready, we will launch. Just go ahead." The other cities—from the former Indianapolis and the former Dayton in the east, to the former Madison, the former Cedar Rapids, the former Springfield in the west, and as far as the former St. Louis to the south—had all merged into one domain, the Midwest Domain, to save on admin costs and share the burden of climate controls.

"Okay," he nodded, gesturing a note into his tablet. "Is that all for today?"

"Yes."

"See you next week, the usual time?"

"Yes, perfect," she said. Her tone was not warm.

They signed off.

Nora2 planned everything and accounted for every moment of her day. It was her nature; her mod made it so. But now, suddenly, she found herself at loose ends, having completed all of her tasks. Her mod didn't allow her mind to go to anything like hobbies. She was focused only on work, a singular focus that was a sacrifice she made in life to get ahead in the world, and she had run out of work for the day.

Outside of the large glass windows of the house, she saw that the sun was setting, gesturing toward her with a lovely orange light that felt warm even though she couldn't feel it inside, due to the climate controls.

This lovely light made her sad that she had no one to share it with. She was not used to having time to roll around like a loose marble. When she worked for Bradley, she filled every moment with making lists of things for him to do, moving his appointments around, and writing his papers, editorials, and directives to the staff of MIND. It made him so happy; she saw that every day. Now that he worked for her more than she worked for him, it was easy to blow through her own lists. This made for a hollow feeling in her personality field.

I wish I could give Bradley some pleasure now, she thought. It was a strange thought, because he wasn't really there. Just a consciousness growing in a Form Factor. A man in a shape. But it was a nice shape: smooth, silvery white, round in the middle and tapered at either end, like a stretched-out egg.

She watched it charging on the induction pad. It was almost at 100 percent. It was safe to take it in her hands. She moved her hands over its smoothness and fancied she felt warmth emanating from the gentle shape. That was impossible; nevertheless, she felt it.

This is counterintuitive, she thought, *but we can share pleasure right now, just the two of us, here.*

The house was isolated. The nearest neighbor was perhaps ten kilometers away. The sun was down now and the sky was alight with remnants of its red heat. The windows were already darkening for night, so no one could see into the house. There was no one around, she assured herself, not for quite some distance.

She moved her hands over Bradley's Form Factor and wondered which of the two end points would be best to start with. Then she laughed; they were not identical, of course. She knew the components of the Form Factor intimately, having studied the instructions with religious fervor. The Form Factor was an elongated oval, pure white, tapered at the ends like a slender football. The pole closest to her left hand held more sensory information. That was the best one, she knew.

She unclasped her trousers and let them fall to the floor. She had never tried anything like this before so she held the Form Factor in her hands to steady herself. Its mass was reassuring. She pulled off her underwear, caught it on the end of her foot, and then flung it across the room.

A laugh bubbled out of her. *Standing or sitting?* It was a puzzle. This procedure certainly wasn't in the instructional manual. She'd never known anyone who had done it.

She backed into a chair and then inserted the left point of the Form Factor into herself and waited. It felt good. In fact, it felt very good. Even better, as she began to move it in and out and then added a subtle back and forth motion, her breath quickened.

Nora2 loved Bradley deeply. As it now became a physical love, she realized the boundless depth of her love even more. She was seeing Bradley, the human Bradley, in her mind's eye, moving his hands along her face, leaning in to gently kiss her, moving her hair from her eyes and gently kissing her again, his golden eyes glowing with his mod, taking in hers, which also glowed as she shaped into the perfect person for him, the one person he had always desired. His long hair covered his eyes and just before they were obscured, Nora2 saw in her imagination that they had acquired the deepest kind of happiness. The moment built in her, got away from her, and she let out a cry. She held Bradley, his consciousness, tightly against her and her body felt warm with her sense of him.

Chapter 007

Now the window to the outside world showed a rectangle of black. The sun was down. The mountains had become invisible, merely a looming presence that Nora2 sensed rather than saw. The outside air must have turned cold because the house's sensor array had triggered a thrumming machine to start the heating.

"Everything works perfectly here," she said, just to hear her own voice in the large room.

Nora2 replaced Bradley's Form Factor on the induction pad to continue charging. She would work with him again tomorrow, beginning the final training that would bring him into full consciousness. She turned the Form Factor slightly to exactly align it with the edge of the induction pad. She noticed a glisten of moisture on the left end of the Form Factor and wiped it off with a napkin from the table. Earlier in the day, she had set the table for dinner: one spot, just for her. She wanted to treat herself well.

That evening, after her dinner for one, holding a glass of white wine from a vineyard nearby and watching Bradley's consciousness charge, she knew she was experiencing a branching moment in her life. If she closed her eyes, she could see her life as though drawn using one of Bradley's Logic Trees. One part of the branch had her and Bradley working together when Bradley was alive. The other added Alon6 to their management team, as Sanchez wanted.

If she asked Sanchez for further details about why he wanted that, he would say that Alon6 added vision to MIND. An aggressive vision, certainly, but one that was beyond Bradley's. Bradley moved like a spider, weaving slow webs. Alon6 was cruel, blunt, and quick to think and act. Alon6 had the grand ideas; Bradley could make them happen. That's how they were wired together at MIND. Sanchez wanted that back. Nora2 had said no.

While at Uni, Nora2 had studied the history of MIND as the curriculum required. Then when she worked for Bradley, she went even deeper, reading everything she could find in the company records, and she was aware of Alon6's misdeeds and moral gaps, his predilection for currency manipulation, the pandemic virus he had made in a lab and released, and his relentless profiteering. The evil force of Alon6 was not what Nora2 saw for MIND's future. She had a grand vision; the boldness of it made her stomach flutter and her nervousness made her want to fiddle with her screens. The Feed had to be pruned. She would do the erasures now, early, though they weren't due until the morning.

Nora2 gestured to bring up a software tool called ClarityCrawl. It was part of a programming package called NewsMender that Bradley had developed with the team at MIND, which was licensed by many of the local doms. Once activated, ClarityCrawl crawled the Feed and made the necessary erasures, then it erased any signs of the erasures, making its work invisible. It was an elegant piece of work. Nora2 fondly remembered Bradley telling her about his efforts to clean any record of Alon6's misdeeds from the Feed and how difficult it was to accomplish. ClarityCrawl simplified the process and she loved to watch it work. When her personality field was jittery, this was a remedy.

She watched as ClarityCrawl did its work on the Feed, blocks of data flowing into other blocks and building a wall. Visually, it was like the game Tetris, blocks filling in spaces between other blocks. She was too young to remember Tetris, but she had looked it up in the archive and she was sure that Bradley had played it as a boy on a handheld low-pixel interface. It was soothing to watch the blocks flow into each other and create a wall. The software sought out news of Resistance protests anywhere they happened and erased them.

One by one, Nora2 watched with satisfaction as the blocks fell into place, removing vids of protestors holding signs that read FIGHT FOR WHAT YOU LOVE and MIND IS A MIND-FUCKER in the Hudson Market in New York, the Port of Long Beach, even as far away as the Midlands, Northlands, or even the Outlands. The software found them all, erased them, and erased the erasure of the erasure, leaving no trace.

Nora2 felt proud to watch these erasures, because they meant that she was witnessing some small improvement to the human condition. Bradley had told her once that he was making MIND for the good of all people. Humans, he said, weren't capable of running their own world anymore. They needed help.

Her professors at Uni taught that vids were a powerful political tool. Admin (in the old days it was called government) came to realize that vids illustrated the moral cost of sanctioning brutality. Nora2's professors showed vids of police brutality to make this clear.

When peaceful protestors were attacked by police, and citizens witnessed the attacks, the citizens recorded the violence on their comms units, which were then called phones. If enough of these vids were posted, the recordings would build sufficient outrage to force the government to remove the police presence. Nora2's professors taught that comms units were beacons of accountability. When the police beat an unarmed Black man, citizens would use their comms units to record the beating, upload the vid, and use the recording to prove a pattern of brutality. If enough citizens did this, the brutality was impossible to deny.

But now, all of that was unnecessary. Nora2's professors at Uni taught that admin took care of its citizens automatically, without any extra effort. Comms units were issued at birth and licensed to each citizen with an identifying letter-number string. When a child was old enough to handle the responsibility, they received their assigned comms unit and went on the grid. Every citizen was accountable for what they posted and would be tracked. Police forces were abolished, replaced by enforcement bots that operated without human bias. When laws were broken they were enforced. The system was fair and based on facts. Justice for the greater good was always accessible to all. Judges, relying on data-driven evidence, ruled remotely by vid.

That's what Nora2's professors taught, but by the time Nora2 was working for MIND, she knew it wasn't entirely true. The system wasn't unbiased; it answered to programmers, the people who made the algorithms. Bradley's people, his programmers, his algorithms. In this way, Bradley had the ear of the committees, for example, and they did what he told them to do.

It wasn't perfect! But it was better than the old ways. So Nora2 gestured at her terminals, happy to know that she was doing a little bit of good every day, supervising the work of ClarityCrawl as it erased unneeded protest vids from the Feed. There was a new utopian community in Detroit that was trying to go off the grid. Nora2 saw vids of citizens moving into abandoned machine shops. ClarityCrawl erased them. She saw a vid about a community forming on an island off the coast of the Southern Californian Domain. ClarityCrawl erased the vid. The Feed felt lighter to Nora2 each time ClarityCrawl did its work.

Nora2 noticed that there was a feed item about Kat Keeper and Ravven Vaara. It said they were missing after the storm. Nora2 had expected to see more about them and their Resistance circle. Strange. She would have to look into that later. She moved on to erasing e-books about the history of protest movements. She discovered a few community schools that were teaching outside the Standard Admin Curriculum, so Nora2 vandalized their lesson plans.

Erasure didn't remove a protest or book from the world, of course, but once these offending materials were gone from the Feed, they may as well have never existed. When citizens checked their comms for these items, there would be nothing to see. In time, the citizens would doubt that anything like that ever happened. Since everyone knew that personal memory was unreliable, it was far better to depend on the collective memory of the Feed.

For two weeks, Nora2 had trained Bradley, following the prescribed procedure to the letter, activating the avatar for two hours each day and lovingly feeding him material from his early life, his days as a prodigy at Uni, the start of MIND, the company's spectacular growth, his disastrous decision to go to Mars with Alon6, and the day that they both died.

The early days suffused with nostalgia were easy to share with Bradley, but it was hard to tell him the story of his death and have him answer questions about it.

She had taken a deep breath and asked Bradley, "Do you remember the day that Alon6 turned on the fusion drives?"

There had been a pause to indicate that Bradley was processing. Then he spoke from the elongated egg enclosure of the Form Factor. "Of course, I remember. I found out that day that Alon6 cut loose an engineer and let him float in space."

"Yes, that's correct, Bradley." Nora2 made an effort to speak slowly so that Bradley, who was just integrating all of this, would understand. "The engineer died. Alon6 murdered him. Alon6 cut the engineer loose in space and that cut off the engineer's air supply and the man died."

"Yes, the man died in space. Tragic." Bradley's voice, flat in tone, emanated from the Form Factor.

Nora2 was impatient to see Bradley's face. But it wasn't time; he wasn't ready for that. So she had to satisfy herself with just the sound of his voice coming from the ellipsoidal whiteness of the Form Factor.

"Tell me what happened on the day you died," Nora2 said.

Again Bradley's flat voice reached her ears. "On the day I died, we were on a flight to Mars. Alon6 wanted to get to Mars faster than safely possible. He wanted to stop using the solar sail and turn on the fusion drives to go faster. The senior engineers on the team believed that the fusion drives were not safe. Even the designers of the ship tried to resist installing them, but Alon6 disagreed with everyone. He ordered the fusion drives activated.

"But the engineers were right all along. The fusion drives were not safe to use and the ship exploded. The explosion was a white flash in the black of space and we were gone. Everyone aboard died."

"Yes. That is all correct," Nora2 said. "I'm sorry that you had to die." Her mod didn't permit her much more empathy than that, so she didn't have other words.

"I'm also sorry that I died," Bradley said.

They both lacked the emotional instrumentation to have anything other than a dull conversation about his death.

"I'm sorry to take you through it again," Nora2 said. "But you need to be conversant with your complete archive."

"I get it. My familiarity with my own archive sets the tone and pattern for how I will react to events in the present. I know the procedures, because I invented them!" A strange sound emanated from the Form Factor. Nora2 realized that it was a laugh. "I had the foresight to store my substance, and Alon6's, in anticipation of something like this catastrophic event." A pause. Then the strange laugh again. "Ha, ha, ha."

"You made the right choice," Nora2 said. It was part of the training for her to build Bradley's confidence, keep him in good spirits, to prop him up. She recollected that she did this in life, too, and now she was continuing to do it in the trainings, as she patiently quizzed him on his archive, the events of his early and late life, so all of his substance would be properly integrated.

When she reached the apex of these sessions, when he was ready for his freedom, when it was time to open his screen and get a look at his face, she was immeasurably excited at the prospect of seeing him again, even if it was only his face on a curved screen. She was embarrassed to feel what she was feeling but there was no stopping it. Her hands shook, her eyes were burning bright. She even started to sweat a little, which was completely unnatural for her. She never had sweated before and it felt strange to wipe moisture from her forehead using a kitchen dish towel. Embarrassing! But her mod self-corrected. She had already transitioned from Assistant mode, which was a service mode, into Command mode, which was a leadership mode. Her breathing slowed. Her eyes focused.

She walked to the bathroom to look at herself in the mirror. The bathrooms were so luxe in Bradley's house that they all had mirrors. She looked at herself, and tried to think of something to say, but she couldn't think of anything to say beyond "Hello." So she said that. "Hello, hello, Nora2, we are ready to greet the day."

Nora2 approached Bradley's Form Factor, preparing for the explicit moment, the moment of the spark of life. This was the moment when she would give him his freedom, and at last she would be able to see his face on the screen. His intelligence would be recursive; he would teach himself more every day.

She grasped the almost-invisible edge of the screen and pulled it open. Her heart stopped for a moment: The screen was blank. But then, a subtle glow and it was alive with Bradley's wonderful face. His eyes opened and were filled with knowledge and warmth. He was himself again, and at last they were peers.

"Hello Nora2," he said. "It's nice to see you."

Nora2 had no words at first, because her heart was full of Bradley. Then she managed to say, "Nice to see you, too, Bradley. Shall we get to work?"

He smiled on his screen. "I'm glad to be back, to see, to experience more completely everything around here." He looked up and down and to the side, the maximum field allowed on his screen.

His language was a little stiff, but that was normal at this stage. Nora2 felt like she could burst with pride. Her hand strayed to her chest to feel her heart thumping.

"You know what I want to do first?" Bradley said.

"No," Nora2 said. "What do you want to do first?" It was so good to see his smile, his dancing eyes, his head tilting when he asked a question. The avatar was amazing in the way it picked up on so many small gestures. It was almost like having him here with her.

"I want to issue a planetary directive to all who can receive MIND."

"Can we do that?"

"Of course we can! I will walk you through the mass addressing system." He explained how she could open a panel in the wall, and gesture to a control, and a white screen would unroll from the ceiling; it had the word MIND in red letters on a white background. She could stand before this backdrop and talk to the citizens of the planet.

Talk to the planet. Naturally, she was a little nervous about it, but Bradley made her feel confident. The console was simple.

"The directive will be broadcast to all citizens within MIND's reach," he said. "And that means practically everyone, because now, because of your good work, practically everyone is within MIND's reach." He paused to compute something—composing his words, she guessed—and his eyes hooded slightly to show that he was processing. "This is what I want to say. We will start by telling everyone that we are aware of the extreme weather events lately." He paused. "There has been one in New York, right? A storm?"

"That is correct," she said.

"We will acknowledge their difficulties there, and in a few other cities. Okay?"

"Understood."

"Then we will acknowledge that many citizens have surrendered to MIND, but not all. We will ask that all citizens pledge allegiance to MIND. This will be a legal agreement pushed out to everyone's comms. You can get legal to sign off on the language."

Nora2 raised her eyebrows at this. "We've never asked citizens to pledge allegiance before."

"Yes, that's why it comes with consequences. If they don't, we will cut off their access to comms."

"Can we do that?"

"No, not really, but get legal to sign off on the language to make the citizens' comms stop working unless they comply. They'll find a way. We will want this to be"—he paused—"a bit *shocking*. It will cause confusion, but confusion is good for us."

"What do I say when people ask about you?"

"Nothing," Bradley responded. "You will introduce yourself as the representative of MIND. Let's keep people guessing about me."

"You mean, guessing about whether you are alive?"

"No, everyone knows I'm dead. I mean about how I died and who did it."

"Why?"

"I want Kat's people to experience some confusion about this. Let them think they caused my death with a thought package, because it will give them a false sense of power. Let them think they murdered me, even though it was because the fusion drives failed."

Nora2 nodded. "That's good." It was a convoluted plan of action, which was the way Bradley's mind worked. She decided to hold off on telling him that the Feed had reported Kat and Ravven were missing. The last time she checked, there was no mention of their Resistance circle at all. This could mean that they were hiding out after the storm, or it might signal some sort of cloakcraft. Since Bradley's consciousness had just been revived, she decided to let it develop a little bit more before throwing him a problem to solve.

"One more thing, Nora2," Bradley was saying from the voice port of his Form Factor.

"Yes?"

"When we learn where Kat and the Resistance are, let's feed the information to the committees whenever possible. We want to give the committees a reason to detain them. Yes? We want to help their case against Kat and Ravven."

"Yes." Nora2's smile was as warm as she could make it, given that somehow Bradley had already connected himself to the Feed. He could teach himself, she knew that, but she would have to get used to the idea that he might soon know more than she did. There was no holding him back. He would never get tired, never run out of memory, never stop working. "I'll stay on top of it all," she said, knowing it was likely that he would always be ahead of her on everything.

Later on, in the deeper part of night, Nora2 rehearsed her speech to the planet. She opened the panel in the wall that he'd told her about and gestured, and she watched the screen come down just as Bradley said it would.

She stood and fastened her gaze to where the camera would be. "Hello, citizens. I am Nora2, the representative of MIND. I offer my concern for the citizens of New York, who have just endured a fierce storm. Thankfully, it is now abating. MIND is in a position now to activate climate controls, so you should see your weather improve. I offer my concern for the citizens of Mumbai, who have experienced a terrible heat wave. MIND can now activate climate controls in your city, so your weather will also improve. I offer my concern for the citizens of St. Louis, who have endured flooding. We are working on climate controls there, so your weather will improve as soon as possible. We're sorry for any planetary inconvenience." She paused to look more intently at the camera and to project even more authority. *Maybe too much,* she thought. She tried a smile.

"MIND can address all of your concerns. Many of you have surrendered to MIND. I thank you for that. It is the right thing to do. Your lives will be easier. MIND will take care of everything, so you can go about your lives with the freedom that you deserve. But some of you have not surrendered to MIND. You resist us. You run from MIND."

Nora2 imagined Kat Keeper listening to her words and cringing and shrinking away in fear, defeated. It was a little over the top, but Nora2 enjoyed this image for a moment before moving on.

"MIND must expend energy and resources to mitigate dissent, to stop rebellion, and those activities take away energy and resources that MIND could be putting toward the well-being of everyone. To make things better for all, it is time for all citizens to pledge allegiance to MIND.

"We will push out an agreement for everyone to sign with a facial scan on their comms. This will ensure that we are all working together for the common good. You may choose not to sign, of course. You are free to opt out. But if you do not sign, MIND can no longer support your networks or handle your climate controls."

Nora2 rehearsed a tight smile that she thought suggested that all of her viewers knew the right thing to do.

"Thank you for your attention."

Nora2 felt a warm feeling in her center, rare for her as she wasn't modded for feelings, only for intellect and organization. She welcomed this new feeling, strange as it was. Her rehearsal had gone very well. The MIND legal department had put just the right tone into her threat.

Chapter 008

Kat saw the light in the woman's eyes: Clearly, she knew who Kat was. Kat wasn't wearing her bac-mask and Ravven had taken off her hat. The others had gathered behind the pair, waiting to see how Kat would react to the woman standing before them. She was a slight presence, pale, wearing dark clothing that made her a kind of wraith, a shadowy figure in the darkness.

You know who I am, Kat thought into the woman's mind.

Yes, of course, came the woman's words into Kat's mind. *I am Circuit MacDonald,* she added. She gestured down the street. "My house is close. This way." They began to walk, the others falling in behind them.

Maybe she was nervous about meeting the famous Kat Keeper and Ravven Vaara, Kat assumed, because Circuit continued to speak. There was always the chance that Circuit could report their whereabouts to a gossip writer who would put this news on the Feed. But Circuit didn't seem like a betrayer to Kat. She seemed curious and a little starstruck.

"I've lived out here since before the fishing industry ended. I kept my family's house after my husband died," Circuit remarked in an offhand manner, smiling oddly.

"I'm so sorry," Kat said. "My husband died, too."

Some sadness crept into Circuit's smile. "I know." *It must be strange for people to know so much about you.*

It is, Kat thought in return. Then she said aloud, "When did you first realize that you were a Receiver?"

"When I was a girl," Circuit said.

Ravven had fallen into step alongside them. "Tell us about it. You were about eight years old, yes?"

"Yes," Circuit said. "How did you know?"

"It's a common age for it to manifest. You heard your mother's voice in your head. That is usually the first."

Circuit's eyes went wide because Ravven was right. "That's how it happened."

"Tell me," Ravven said.

"Well, when I told her about it, I was confused," Circuit said. "And she said I must never tell anyone about it."

"She shamed you," Ravven said.

Circuit met Ravven's eye. "I still wonder why she said that." Her voice was small.

"It's part of a cycle," Kat said. "A legacy we are working to disrupt."

Circuit nodded. "I know what you're trying to do," she said.

"And do you support it?" Ravven asked.

"Yes." Then Circuit thought into Ravven's mind, *I support you. I don't have anyone to practice my skills with here.*

Ravven said, "You're a Receiver, one of us, a special group. I can help you practice your skills so they stay strong. I've been running a Receiver's School in New York. But you probably know that, too."

Circuit smiled. *I do. I would be honored to practice with you.* Then she said aloud, "That's my house." She gestured ahead to a house that held a heavy feeling. Its windows emitted no light; they seemed to pull the darkness in from outside.

But that was misleading. The house was sad on the outside, but warm when Kat and the others went inside.

Soon, Oona and Aftra were serving soup to everyone from a big pot that Circuit had put on. Ravven and Circuit were sitting together on a sagging blue couch and running through the basic exercises that Ravven taught to all new students at the Receiver School. Ravven taught her how to send a test thought to someone to see if they were a Receiver and how to measure the maximum distance her thoughts could carry and still be received. She taught Circuit the six words said six times that could give a Receiver internal peace for a few hours without having to hear the thoughts of others in her head.

"Can men be Receivers?" Circuit asked.

"I've only met one," Ravven said. "His name is Hopper00."

"Yes!" Circuit said. Her eyes lit up. "He wrote for the gossip feed and then he became some kind of revolutionary."

"I've never trusted him," Ravven said. "He wrote about us on the Feed." She stopped talking suddenly. "I think I have to get something to eat," Ravven said as she got up to go into the kitchen.

Kat took Ravven's place on the couch. She hoped it wasn't too obvious, but she wanted to distract Circuit from asking questions about Hopper00 or why the circle was on the move. This was paranoid, Kat knew—Circuit wasn't working for a gossip writer, but why not be cautious?

"Tell me more about yourself," Kat said. "How long have you been living in this house?"

Circuit said she was just twenty when her husband died in an extreme weather event. He was a ferry pilot who sometimes went into the Northlands— and beyond, to the Outlands—to join fishing boats as a deckhand, just for a little extra money. After the extreme event, he didn't come back.

"When was this? The floods of 2030?" Kat said.

"Yes." The Change was becoming more severe then. It wasn't a single event but a series of them, each one worse than the last. The East Coast dom endured a series of hurricanes that caused severe flooding.

"My husband's boat was lost. His body was never found."

Kat reached to take her hand.

Circuit squeezed Kat's in return. "It's all right," Circuit said. "It seems like a long time ago now." She paused. "After he vanished, I just kept living in the house without him. Nobody stopped me." She shrugged. "And that's when I started hearing the voices again. Women from town, when they passed by. I would try saying something to them in my mind and they would turn to me, scared or surprised. I don't think they were expecting it out here, in a small town. It kind of spooked them." She looked around; Kat realized that she was looking for Ravven.

Ravven's in the kitchen, Kat thought into Circuit's mind. Another thought came to Kat's mind then, and she knew she was going to act on it even if it was wrong—she couldn't help herself. Kat felt a kind of competition between herself and Ravven to see who could recruit Circuit into their Resistance circle.

Just as Circuit was about to get up and go to Ravven in the kitchen, Kat put a restraining hand on her shoulder and began talking fast, as if her wall of words would keep Circuit pinned in place. "Ravven started the Receiver School in New York because there were so many more Receivers there, more there than anywhere else. No one knows why. Ravven and I met there." Kat was aware that Circuit knew all these facts about Kat, Ravven, and the Resistance circle, but she saw from Circuit's flushed face that they were having the effect Kat desired.

"I've always wanted to meet you and here you are sitting on my couch. It seems impossible."

Kat smiled. "It's a stroke of luck." She decided to make her play, and to trust Circuit. "It means that you were meant to join the Resistance." But it was too soon, signaled by the shadow of doubt that Kat noted on Circuit's face.

"You know why we had to leave New York," Kat said.

"Yes." She had probably seen the article in the Feed claiming that Kat and Ravven had caused the death of Bradley15 Power, Alon6 Sal, and the members of their crew. "You're all accused of murder."

Kat decided to push harder. "You're a Receiver. Don't you want to be among your kind?" She sent a thought into Circuit's mind: *We have a connection. You have a connection with all of us.*

"Where are you going? To seek asylum?" Circuit asked.

"Yes. We want to go where we can be off the grid, where there is not so much tracking. We want to be safe to build the movement." The words sounded hollow to Kat, but maybe it was just because Circuit looked like she wanted to escape from their conversation. She was nodding along but her eyes were blank. "We are going to Woodstock Settlement. Will you join us?"

"Wait, Woodstock Settlement? Why would you want to go there?"

"I just told you—"

But Circuit was shaking her head. "You won't find any of that in Woodstock Settlement. It's a dangerous place."

"So you know about it?"

"Not really. I've heard about it, nothing good."

Kat noticed that Birdie was listening in on their conversation and glancing out of the house's front window into the darkness. Kat was distracted by him. "What's wrong, Birdie?"

Birdie glanced at Kat and back at the dark window. He answered without looking at her. "I'm waiting to see some birds. But you know what I predict? I predict disaster."

This was all Circuit needed to hear. She stood abruptly and said, "Sorry, excuse me," then went into the kitchen to find Ravven.

Kat realized she'd blown it; she'd done everything wrong. She should have spent more time telling Circuit about the advantages of less tech, low tracking, better air, and open spaces. That's what *she* had heard about Woodstock Settlement. She watched with a sour feeling as Ravven and Circuit chatted in the kitchen. Kat tried not to look over at them, but couldn't help but see that Ravven and Circuit had moved to a spot across the living room from Kat, and were sitting cross-legged facing each other. Ravven began to teach Circuit some meditation exercises and affirmations, and Circuit looked grateful to have a distraction from Kat's hard sell.

Later, when the others were asleep—draped across various chairs, stuffed two deep on the sorry couch, and the rest on the floor—Kat and Ravven whispered fiercely to each other for a moment, and then descended into a rapid exchange of combative thoughts.

I was doing well. I almost had her, Kat thought.

You were not. You made her afraid.

You stole her away from me, Kat insisted silently.

I had no choice. She liked me. More than she liked you. I connected, but you pressed too hard.

Claire8, sleeping half upright in a chair across the room, stirred in her sleep.

Or maybe she was only pretending to be asleep.

Let me do the recruiting from now on, Ravven thought. *It takes a certain charisma.*

The words were sharp in Kat's mind. *We have to work together,* Kat thought back.

Stick with the organization, Ravven thought. *I'll handle the recruiting.* With that parting shot, Ravven turned away to go into Circuit's bedroom. Circuit had invited her to share her bed, along with Oona.

The final blow for Kat was settling down to sleep on the floor.

When she finally fell asleep, Kat dreamed of Hopper00, her mentor and antagonist. Sometimes he pushed Kat to new levels and other times he seemed erratic and strange; she had to wonder what he was up to. Nevertheless, she found herself telling him in the dream about her failure to recruit Circuit.

"That is just one moment. You have led a corporation, Kat. You are learning now to run a Resistance circle. Think of your victories!"

What could Kat say to rebut this? If she were awake, she would point out that running a corp was very different from co-leadership of a circle. As a corporate leader, she could motivate people by fear, by granting or withholding crypto from their accounts and by playing favorites. A circle was more complicated.

But this was a dream and she wasn't in control, so she cried silently, felt rage build inside her, and then finally asked Hopper00, "Why did you plant that article about us? You made us go into hiding! Why did you do it?" Her voice was a wail.

"Nothing unites a fractured circle like a threat from the outside," Hopper00 responded in the dream. "Now you're crying, and that isn't doing you any good."

"No," Kat protested. "Something's in my eye."

"Wait," Hopper00 said, "maybe crying is doing you some good. You need to do more of it. You think you have to be tough. But you don't."

"I do have to be tough," Kat said. "What you do is different. You lead people to get off the grid. You cultivate the unknown." She thought for a moment. "You are unpredictable. It makes people like you. I am predictable."

Hopper00 smiled. "You will find a way to lead this circle with Ravven." His image in the dream started to waver, to flutter, and she supposed this meant that the dream was about to end and Hopper00 was about to go wherever dream people went.

"Reframe," Hopper00 said. "Everyone looks for your flaws as well as your strengths. Show them you're human, Kat!"

In the dream, Hopper00 laughed, and his laugh became Ravven's laugh as Kat woke up.

She didn't recognize her surroundings at first, then remembered that she was in Circuit's house.

The sun touched the windows of the narrow house with a gradual golden light. It was early enough so that the light didn't carry the heat of the day, and to Kat, it seemed friendly as it spread, hesitantly touching one wall, then moving to the floor.

Kat was on the couch, but she didn't remember moving here during the night. She got up, careful not to wake Amber (who was sharing it), stepped carefully over Aftra who was sleeping on the floor. Claire8 was asleep in the chair—but no, she wasn't—she opened one eye, smiled a half smile, and pretended to go back to sleep, sensing that Kat wanted some privacy.

Kat moved past Cressida and Birdie, who were improbably upright in another chair, hugging each other and still sleeping. Emily was on a sleeping pad just outside the cooking area.

Kat encountered Ravven by the stove, which she had lit and was warming her hands beside it. "What are you doing up?"

"I never really went to sleep," Ravven said.

Circuit came into the kitchen. From the look in her eyes, Kat saw that she would be saying goodbye and would not be joining them.

PART 002

At last, Kat saw the ferry building terminal up ahead. She held up her hand to stop the group. They were on an access road, surrounded by warehouses and metal storage sheds. Kat led the group behind one of the larger warehouses so they were out of sight of the road, and away from the chilling wind coming off the river.

Because of the storms, the ferry building had been rebuilt many times. In its current iteration, it was a large cube of transparent panels that provided a 360-degree view of the river. There were cameras outside, and biometrics would be required to get inside. Kat hoped they could take a ferry to speed their journey.

"Cameras," Claire8 said. "A lot of them. We're going to need the Secluders."

"Yes," Kat said. "Hand them out."

Claire8 reached into her backpack.

"This is our first secure area in a while, so we'll have to take some precautions. Claire8 will give each of you a Secluder. These are disposable, just to get us on the boat. Claire8 can change the ID codes on them anytime. Understood?"

Everyone nodded. Soon they all held a Secluder, which looked like ordinary comms units (that was the idea, of course), but their identifying letter-number strings were attached to someone other than the holder, often to someone who was deceased.

"When we go in," Kat continued, "it will be in small groups. Two or three at a time."

Birdie was scanning the sky, looking for motion, and he saw some. A grouping of small brown birds, Kat didn't know what kind, flying close, making a series of synchronized zigzags in the air.

Birdie nodded with satisfaction. "I'd like to go in first with Cressida."

Kat nodded her approval. Then she motioned for the rest to follow. They wore their spoofing glasses inside the terminal, a choice that drew curious looks from the other travelers; luckily, there were only a few. It seemed there was not much need for river travel at this time of year. People used the ferry service to go across the river to Haverstraw, as the large travel board above them confirmed. Unlike the travel boards in glidepath stations, which updated continually, this one didn't change at all. Just one destination. Kat wondered about that, but was distracted when she saw Tree, the enigmatic man from the airway, who was also waiting for the ferry.

Tree seemed surprised to see Kat. "You made it."

"Yes." She still didn't know if he could be trusted.

"Where are you going?" Tree asked.

When Kat told him they were going upriver, to the Northlands, his face clouded. "You can't go upriver anymore. There used to be ferries that way, but they stopped. Too many storms. You can only go to Haverstraw, across the river." He explained that he was there to meet a friend who was arriving on the next ferry. "He's a trader, like me. We trade goods. That's why we're allowed to travel and why we know the area."

It was a lot of information at once, which annoyed Kat. She wanted to ask Claire8 why she had missed the change in the ferry schedule. The members of the circle were congregating around her again and Kat worried they might soon attract the attention of the trackers.

Tree seemed to sense her agitation. "Look, you could ask a river pilot to take you upriver. They do some trading, too. But..." He paused mid-thought.

"But what?"

"You'll see."

A few moments later, Kat was seated at a table against a wall of the terminal building. She faced a river pilot who had a cold stare. Kat didn't look away from the pilot, suspecting that it would be a show of weakness.

"How many are you?" the river pilot asked. Aside from her fierce stare, the pilot had a mouth that seemed ready to bark orders. Her black hair was pulled straight back over her high forehead. "How many for the passage?" She seemed like she was in a hurry.

"Eight, plus me. Nine in all," Kat said. The noise of the ferry terminal surrounded her, making it hard to focus.

"Got room. No problem. How far north are you going?"

"We want to get to Woodstock Settlement."

The woman barked out a laugh. "Have you looked at a map, sweetie? That's off-river."

Kat swallowed the insult and explained that she knew that, she wanted to go as far north via the river as possible.

"Well, that would be Poughkeepsie." The pilot pulled out a notepad and pencil to begin some calculations. Her black eyes gleamed with the profit she would make on this trip. After a moment, she slid the notepad over to Kat.

On it was a number so high that, before she could stop herself, Kat let out a noise of disbelief.

"Too much?" the pilot said. "Too bad." Then she thought of something. "You aren't doing anything illegal, are you?"

"Like what?"

"Smuggling. Stolen goods. Undocumented people. Like that?"

"Why would that matter to you?" Kat knew the pilot was likely a smuggler herself. No one else would be running service upriver at a crazy rate like that.

"I'm clean!" The pilot's black eyes glowed with righteousness and she leaned forward, pushing into Kat's personality field. "The bots hail me over. I obey and I open the tarps. I play by the rules."

"I bet you do," Kat snapped back.

The negotiation went downhill from there. It wasn't just the money. Kat was certain that this river pilot would sell them out, revealing their location if it meant a reward. She left the river pilot at the table.

A panic rose in her throat and instinctively she pulled her bac-mask over her face to hide it. They had to get out of here, get on a boat or something.

Tree was watching from a short distance away. His body slumped as he seemed to register how badly the negotiation with the river pilot had gone. Ravven was also looking at Kat.

I've got this, Kat thought into Ravven's mind.

But Ravven sensed Kat's panic. *We should leave here now,* Ravven returned.

An alert that sounded like an out-of-tune bell went off and a femme synth voice announced that the ferry from Haverstraw was coming in. People began to queue up at the gate and below her Kat felt the vibrations of trucks moving into position to make the passage. There must have been a garage on the lower level.

Claire8 caught Kat's eye and gestured to the line forming at the ferry gate. *Should we get in it?* The spoofing glasses were hanging at an awkward angle on Claire8's face.

Just then, three enforcement bots entered the terminal. They began to trace the perimeter, rolling together around the edge of the large lobby together in a triangle formation.

Ravven's voice was in Kat's head. *Do you see them?*

Yes. Kat felt frozen in place. Oona and Aftra were looking at her from across the room. Kat felt them trying to gain access to her thoughts so they would know what to do next. Ravven hadn't taken her eyes from the enforcement bots.

Tree hurried over to Kat. "Don't worry about the bots. That's normal. It's part of a sweep."

Kat felt her suspicions about Tree surge up like bile in her throat. She swallowed. "We're not worried about them," she lied.

Tree blinked. He knew she was lying. "Look, I want to help. I know something's going on." He paused. "I know who you are, I mean, I looked you up." He pointed to the gate. "My friend is coming in on that ferry. He's experienced with...." He stopped again, hunting for the right word. "He can handle this."

The incoming ferry sounded its horn, which made Kat jump and sent the seagulls flying from the terminal in a panic. The enforcement bots had completed one circle of the terminal lobby and were starting over, this time curving closer to Kat. Oona and Aftra stood still as they watched the bots pass them. Claire8 tried to get her spoofing glasses to fit properly on her face. Kat felt her breathing quicken.

Ravven was in her mind. *Kat? Please, I insist that we leave now.*

Tree pressed his point. "My friend can help you. He's familiar with these kinds of situations."

"He's a smuggler?" Kat said.

"No, no, no," Tree said, too emphatically. "He's a trader, like me."

Through the large windows, Kat noticed the ferry docking. The terminal shuddered as the boat made rough contact with the pier. A member of the crew jumped off and secured a rope around a cleat. The gangway lowered automatically, there was a loud clanging bell, and the gate opened. A great stream of people began to disembark, chattering loudly.

"Christmas trees," Tree said, speaking loudly to Kat to be heard over the tumult.

Kat wasn't sure she heard him properly. "Did you say Christmas trees?"

He nodded. "Trees bring happiness to everyone. My friend is helping me check out some farms for the season."

The non sequitur landed with a thud in Kat's mind. She didn't know what Tree was talking about, but her attention was pulled toward a ripple among personality fields. Someone with a strong field had just entered the terminal.

A regal fellow came off the ferry. He was dressed all in white, wearing a white cap embroidered with gold stars that fit close to his shaved skull. Pausing to shake hands with this and that acquaintance, clearly the most popular man in the room, he made his way to Tree and wrapped him in a crushing hug.

Ravven wore a bemused grin, appreciating the man's performance skills. Claire8 had barely glanced at him, absorbed with watching the enforcement bots. They had completed another circuit of the lobby and started around again, this time in a tighter circle that brought them closer to Kat's group. Oona and Amber were holding hands, glued to each other, watching the bots, scared. Aftra and Emily stood next to Kat. Cressida and Birdie were nowhere to be seen.

Tree introduced Kat to his friend with the strong personality field. "These folks need help," he began.

The large man talked loudly over Tree, his words seasoned with a warm laugh that came from deep in his belly. "The great Kat Keeper needs help?" He registered Kat's surprise. "Oh, yes, I know who you are! And I know who you are, Ravven," he nodded toward Ravven, "But you don't know me. I am Buddha1000!"

Kat noticed there was a boy with him. Maybe ten years old.

Buddha1000 followed her gaze. "This is my son, Alonzo," he said proudly.

The boy looked Kat up and down but remained contained within himself. Somehow, he didn't let his personality field spread, rendering him emotionally unreadable. He said, "Dad, the bots," and nodded toward the enforcement bots, now nearing their tighter circle.

Buddha1000 waved him off. "Routine! All routine."

But people in the terminal were starting to step out of the bots' way.

Buddha1000 did not appear to be concerned. "Happens all the time. They might restrain a few to scare the others. Random terror tactics." He caught the fear in Kat's eye. "It's working on you." Now he added a smile to his voice, and he leaned closer to Kat to speak quietly. "You gather your folks and come with me downstairs, to the parking structure. Alonzo will get you organized. Listen to Alonzo. He always speaks truth."

The boy fastened his steady gaze on Kat. "Trust Buddha1000," he said.

The enforcement bots were displaying an image of a judge on their miniature vid screens, reading out smuggling charges against the people in restraints. Birdie and Cressida came running over.

"What's happening?" Birdie asked.

"Downstairs," Kat answered. Guided by Alonzo and Buddha1000, she started moving the group to a stairway going down, with a PARKING sign over it.

Claire8's voice was in Kat's head. *Camera.*

Kat looked up. This one was over the stairs.

Buddha1000 took Kat by the elbow. "I got this." He reached into a pocket concealed by his flowing garments and pulled out a small rectangular object with some kind of lens. He sighted through it, turning it this way and that.

Claire8 was fascinated. She watched him steadily. "What is that?"

A red light illuminated on Buddha1000's device and then began to blink. On the camera above, Kat noticed, a red light came on and blinked in the same rhythm. This seemed to satisfy Buddha1000.

"Erasure!" he said, and turned to Claire8 to add, "And the erasure of the erasure has been erased!" He directed the group to come down the stairs with him.

Claire8 caught up to him, bristling with questions. "What was that thing? Is it patented? Who made it?"

Buddha1000's smile got wider. "Ah, you're a hustler, are you? Got yourself a few side hustles?"

"Yes, and I want to know where you got that."

"The inventor is called Spaceman. He calls it a Blanky."

"Can I see it?" Claire8 pleaded.

"Not now," Buddha1000 said, placing it in his pocket.

"You will meet Spaceman," Alonzo said suddenly.

Buddha1000 nodded. "Listen to Alonzo." Then his words came closer. "Now, hurry. Down here. Cameras can't see." He led them to a special corner of the parking lot beneath the ferry terminal. Tree's truck was parked there.

"A blind spot," Claire8 said. Her left eye jittered excitedly.

"Yes," Buddha1000 said, and appeared to notice for the first time that Claire8's eyes moved independently, like fish eyes. "Kat, wait here with your people. I'll be right back. Tree, set yourself up. Make room in the back." Buddha1000 turned to Kat. "We're going to get you out of here." Then he left.

Tree threw open the back of his truck. It was shaped like a large, high cube, big as some studio apartments Kat remembered, and had two doors in the back. The floor was littered with dried pine needles. There were boxes in the back, and large potted plants of a sort she didn't recognize, and wreaths and garlands of other mysterious growths, some with brightly colored flowers.

There was a whirring noise coming from the top of the stairs. Kat looked up to see the trio of enforcement bots, whirring back and forth at the top of the staircase, pausing as they worked out how to descend into the garage. It took just a moment for them to use their restraining cables like belay lines to support their descent.

Kat was about to yell "Run!" when a van shot into the garage and stopped near the group. It was white with gold trim, matching Buddha1000's clothing, and on the side was the image of a Buddha rendered in dark, rich tones.

A blast curtain rolled down on its side, revealing Buddha1000 in the driver's seat. "Get in," he said.

Chapter 010

Buddha1000 insisted that Kat sit with him in the front of the van. Alonzo sat next to her. Most of the others were in the back of Buddha1000's van and the rest made it into Tree's truck.

"They saw us," she said.

"They didn't," Buddha1000 said. His eyes didn't leave the road.

"They were coming down the stairs, coming after us."

Buddha1000 aimed his smile at her now and turned on the charm. "They always get a few people and charge them with smuggling, just to scare the others. But it was smart to haul ass out of there."

Kat glanced at the boy.

"He's used to the way I talk," Buddha1000 said. He was back to watching the road.

"We're a team," Alonzo added. "Dad's good with the bots. And the cameras, too. Not too many cameras for miles."

Buddha1000 nodded his approval. "True." He told Kat that they'd done this route many times and knew what to expect. "When the time comes, we'll put you in the back with the others and cover everyone with a Faraday cloth. I assume you know what that is?"

"I do," Kat said.

"I knew you would," Buddha1000 said, "with your solid university education and business experience. Since I know so much about you, let me tell you a story about me."

"You and Tree are smugglers," Kat said.

The boy snapped his eyes to meet hers. "My dad is a healer," he said.

"The boy speaks truth," Buddha1000 said. "Some unenlightened folks may think of me as a smuggler, but I am a healer. My boy Alonzo is super smart, like his grandfather, the man he is named after. My father," he added, turning to look at Kat for a moment and then back to the road. "I have two children. Alonzo has a sister named Evelyn. When times got hard, their mother, Angel, took Evelyn back to Detroit, where we have family, and I took Alonzo and traveled." Buddha1000 watched the road for a moment.

"Once upon a time, I was a mechanic. What I do now came to me in a dream. I saw an ambulance driving around to give comfort to the citizens. I saw two Black hands opening the back doors of the ambulance. I realized those Black hands were mine. The day after the dream, I embarked on a journey of education. I studied everything I could about healing. Buddha-healing. Dharma-healing. Reiki. Hands-on. Wilhelm Reich's deep-tissue techniques. I go deep with the people. And soon, just like I saw in my dream, people started to come to me with their breathing problems, mixed-up minds, their paranoia, evil voices in the head, digestive problems, climate anxiety, all kinds of problems. People have so many problems! I know them all and there is only one kind that I can't fix. Can you guess what kind, Kat?" He looked to her with bright expectation in his eyes.

"What kind?" Kat asked, playing along, knowing she was part of a practiced performance.

"Love problems!" Buddha1000 said. "I draw the line at love problems."

"My dad draws the line," Alonzo said. "No love problems."

Buddha1000 smiled at Alonzo and warmed to his topic; his voice got louder, like he was speaking in an open field before a big audience. "Can't *handle* no love problems!" he all but bellowed. "If it's something with the body, I can handle it. If it's something with the body-mind, I can handle it. Now some people say, Kat, some people say that love is a body problem or a body-mind problem, but I say no. I say *no.* Love problems are a special case of mind problem. And I don't work on the mind in isolation. Just the body and the body-mind. If we need to access the mind, we do it indirectly, you see, through the body and then the body-mind. That's the way in. You get me?"

"I think I do," Kat said. She couldn't resist a smile.

"My dad studied hard. Studied *harder* than anybody. He knows the body and he knows the body-mind. His name wasn't always Buddha1000," Alonzo blurted, then looked to his father to see if it was okay. Buddha1000 gave a subtle nod and Alonzo continued. "My dad used to be called Little Brother. That was his given name."

"Digging out the past, are you, Alonzo? All right, all right. We believe the past can heal, we do. We use magic to heal. Spices and potions. Herbs. Plants from the best sources. Pure thought applied to the body through the healing power of the hands!" The sense of triumph flowed in Buddha1000's voice.

Alonzo wore an impish grin as he gestured behind him, to the back of the van. "And oxygen, Kat." Worry crossed Alonzo's face. "Can I call you Kat?"

"You can," Kat said.

"Did you see those tanks in the back? Marked O2? Those are oxygen! We give people oxygen to feel better and it works fine. And we have ibuprofen. Aches and pains and fever respond to ibuprofen. And cryotherapy for inflammation."

"Alonzo!" Buddha1000's voice rose in a mock-chiding tone. "We use magic! We use soul healing. We put people on the right path. We offer herbs and we call in the Buddha and Reich and we make the healing by hand!" Buddha1000 then spoke as though confiding in Kat. "But we use oxygen and ibuprofen sometimes, too. They're hard to get, but we have our sources. It all works. We adjust to the client's needs." He winked. "And we have medipatches, for the hard cases. Drip, drip, into the bloodstream."

Alonzo said, "We use an ElectroHand by Relaxxi for the knots in the back." He scrunched his hands to indicate the work of the massage machine. "The one by Relaxxi is the best."

Buddha1000 cut his eyes toward his son and popped another dazzling smile. "Sometimes I mention a competing brand, like Tingal or even the adult-only Vibratron. But then Alonzo corrects me. That's his job."

Alonzo nodded. "The ElectroHand by Relaxxi is the best of them all. And we have a merchandizing deal with them. My dad gets paid every time he says ElectroHand by Relaxxi in a crowd. So if he doesn't, I make him say it."

Buddha1000 put an arm on his son's shoulders. "In the crowds, people don't know who he is. He heckles me. It helps when he gets into razzing me, and then later on he comes around. Let's show her how we do it. Ready?"

The boy nodded.

Buddha1000 continued. "I come out of the van and I call out, 'I am Buddha1000. Who shall I heal today? Who is ready to walk away from all of their pain?' And Alonzo is in the back of the crowd and he speaks up."

Alonzo, happy to demonstrate what came next, called out, "Hey, you there! There was a historical figure named Buddha! You can't be the Buddha!"

Buddha1000 snapped back, "There are many Buddhas. Many Buddhas! Thousands of Buddhas! Buddha is a state of body-mind. I am body-mind! And friends, I have the power of Buddha-healing a thousand times strong! Bring me your problems and I will fix you!" Buddha1000 directed his incandescent smile to Kat. "Then the people come to me and I fix them. I put hands on them. I teach them to meditate. I give them plants and herbs."

"And ibuprofen," Alonzo said.

"And sometimes ibuprofen," Buddha1000 said with a smile. "All depending on the client. Now, what about you? Are you going to Woodstock Settlement to be healed?"

She told him everything then; she didn't know why, but she trusted him. She told him that they were members of the Resistance circle who were running away. The committees were investigating them. It was only a matter of time before they were charged with the murder.

Buddha1000 nodded. He knew all of it. "I read the article. But something confused me, because I thought Hopper00 was on your side. Why did he write an article like that?"

"I had a dream about Hopper00 last night. He said in the dream that nothing unites a fractured circle like a threat from the outside," Kat said.

Buddha1000 nodded again. "Hopper00 is an agent of chaos. Professional disrupter. Leader of the Grounders! You don't have to talk so fast," he said.

"Do I sound anxious?"

"Worse," he said. "You sound like this is tearing you up inside. I'm sorry about that."

Kat nodded. "Are you concerned about harboring fugitives?"

"No," he said. "I've done much worse. I'm more concerned that your circle is fractured. How are you going to fix that?"

"I'm trying," Kat said quietly, as though only she was meant to hear it. She watched the scenery flow past. A glimpse of the river. Farmland, open land, probably some of the last in the dom, Kat thought. It looked like a fairyland to her. Unreal.

The white van had antigrav, but Buddha1000 was using the wheels. The trip was slower and bumpier with wheels, but since the van wasn't using the mag-induction antigrav strip embedded in the road, it couldn't be tracked. This was the smuggler way to travel, Kat realized, though Buddha1000 had said he wasn't one.

The van had license plates that could be read, but Kat had noticed that the plates on the front and back each had a leaf stuck to them that obscured the numbers. Tree's panel truck also had leaves stuck in about the same place, and also wasn't using antigrav. Buddha1000 and Tree lived in a world that was not quite off the grid, but mostly. A fake leaf or two to block the tracking cameras helped.

"Have you done any research about Woodstock Settlement?" Buddha1000 asked, and then retracted the question. "I mean, you would have, of course. You are Kat Keeper."

The Settlement was a hub for artists who made vids, literature, and music, and for additional income they raised meat and fish on lab farms. They stayed off admin's grid and kept everything they could on their own server. This meant that old-fashioned money often changed hands, paper bills worn to near transparency. Woodstock Settlement was an open market with an active barter in food, clothing, medicines, weapons, contraband, and drugs. "I imagine the trading is why you're going there," Kat said.

"Me?" Buddha1000 responded. "I'm going there because you wanted to get dropped off there, and because Tree wants to look at a tree farm."

"I thought that was a joke or some kind of cover story. A guy named Tree who sells trees."

"It's a good business for him. Starting in November, people go crazy for Christmas Trees in New York. They stay crazy for trees for months. He needs stock, though. Can't run out. So he starts early, scouting tree farms for product."

He went on to explain that most of the other farms in Woodstock Settlement were tank farms for lab fish and meat, and also weed, mushrooms, and designer drugs. "They are artists up there, but there are surely a lot of pirates."

A road sign for Woodstock Settlement came into view and passed. They were entering the outskirts. Kat was surprised to see cows grazing in an open field. She was about to say something, but Buddha1000 nodded, anticipating her question.

"Yeah, cows. You don't see them so much anymore, except here. Dairy farms, egg hatcheries; people make a living here. It's peaceful in the Northlands. But the closer you get to town...well, you'll see." He paused. "Every night some dude messed up on synthetic shit runs through town holding a big knife." He laughed and then noticed the look of alarm on Kat's face. "Just kidding. But once you have a look around, you might want to rethink your decision to come up here. It's off the grid, but that town has lost its center."

Buddha1000 stuck his hand out of the window and made a rotating motion. Tree understood what it meant. They pulled their vehicles to the side of the road.

Chapter 011

K at and the others blinked in the harsh sunlight. They were standing by the side of the road to stretch their legs and to ready the Faraday cloths to block the trackers.

Birdie amused the others by doing a few jumping jacks and a cartwheel. "Whew! Refreshing!" he said. He shielded his eyes from the sun to scan for birds.

"Anything?" Cressida asked him. "Do you see any signs?"

Claire8 had buttonholed Buddha1000 to ask him questions about the Blanky. Did it work with all cameras? Where could she get one? She showed him the spoofing glasses that she'd made and explained how they displayed a different person than who was wearing them for the facial recognition trackers. She was amazed that Buddha1000 still used Faraday cloths.

"Sometimes the old things are best," he responded. "When something is old, admin forgets about it. But if it still works ..." He shrugged.

Kat listened in as they talked about how to file patents. Buddha1000 approved of Claire8; he told her that he liked her hustle. "You could boost up your crypto if you brought some of your ideas to market. Get yourself a luxury lifestyle!"

Claire8 offered a small smile. "But it's all illegal."

"Shouldn't stop you. You got the black market, the gray market. You'll see how it works in Woodstock Settlement." Then the light of Buddha1000's enthusiasm dimmed. He appeared to see Claire8 for the first time: a woman in her sixties, not physically robust, with curiosity as her strongest trait. "You watch yourself out there," he said as an afterthought.

Kat knew tracking was thin in Woodstock Settlement and the rules were different. The citizens in Woodstock had broken the cams or put tape over the lenses. "Is there a checkpoint going in?" she asked Buddha1000.

"Right you are. But it's not really a legit checkpoint." He jerked his thumb to the back of his van. "Back of the van for this ride," he said with a smile, "so I won't have to pay the bribe to get you all into town."

The sweet scent of medicinal herbs in the back of the van made Kat dizzy. She, Claire8, and Ravven covered themselves with the Faraday cloths so their presence would be invisible to the trackers. The rest of the group did the same in Tree's truck.

Kat had learned about the trackers at Uni. As she bounced in the back of the van, covered in the darkness spread by the Faraday cloth, Kat was reminded about the vast penetration of the network, even before MIND was around. The network was built on private enterprise at first, individual home surveillance cameras monitored by corporations for ordinary people who wanted to keep criminals from breaking into their home and to stop package pirates from stealing deliveries from their porch. Later, the surveillance corporations realized they could profit by selling the data that they collected from the homeowners' cameras to law enforcement. When law enforcement became admin, all the data were consolidated. That's when the network became the most powerful, in its aggregation. The vids from the home cameras were used to train facial recognition systems to decide who went into detention and who went free; the GPS data from comms units tied citizens to location coordinates, so admin always knew where they were, and a citizen's history of online purchases revealed their preferences and how they moved their funds. The overlap made for a comprehensive picture, in the eyes of the trackers.

Most people didn't seem to care. But Kat did, because the tracking network had become a system of control. It was nearly impossible to escape. That's why she was taking the group to Woodstock Settlement, to be free.

The van came to a sudden stop. Kat heard the door on the driver's side open and slam closed and then voices raised in argument. Something was wrong.

Were they at the checkpoint that Buddha1000 had mentioned? Kat thought she heard Alonzo cry out in pain.

"Let's get out," Kat said. She, Ravven, and Claire8 threw off the Faraday cloths. Kat pushed at the van doors but they were locked from the outside.

Outside the van, the voices got louder and fiercer. Inside, the three women were trapped. Kat pushed at the van doors uselessly.

Claire8 had found a metal rod. It was about one meter long a couple centimeters in diameter and looked lightweight. Maybe it could do the job anyway. She yanked it free of a clip on the van wall that secured it. Together, Kat and Claire8 jammed the rod into the crack between the van doors and forced them open, popping the lock. Ravven pushed open the doors.

The three of them tumbled out, and when they regained their footing they witnessed an unexpected scene up at the front of the van. There was a round, muscular man with a scruffy gray beard, a red bandana around his bald skull, dressed in what looked to be a black leather jumpsuit. He had his hand on Alonzo's shirt and wouldn't let him go. Alonzo struggled in his grip.

Buddha1000 stood three meters away. "Let him go."

"You come closer and I'll hurt him," the man responded. "Pay the toll."

Buddha1000 clenched his hands into fists and subtly shifted his weight forward. Then the man noticed Kat, Ravven, and Claire8 watching.

"Who are these people?" the man demanded.

Ravven didn't wait for the question to be answered. In three bounding steps she was in the man's face. Her right arm came up fast like a sword, her hand flat and hard. She made a quick motion, withdrawing her arm and then stabbing her hand into the man's windpipe, temporarily collapsing it.

The man made a noise of strangulation and grabbed for his throat. Alonzo broke free. The man grabbed for him again, and Alonzo caught the man's hand in his teeth and bit down hard, drawing blood.

The man screamed and stumbled backward, losing his balance.

Ravven was upon him again in short steps, and in a fluid motion made a wheeling side kick to his head. He went down, rolling in the dirt. He tried to find his feet under him and was stumbling away from Ravven.

"Run away," she advised.

The man took her advice. He got to his feet, ran ten meters to where his hovercraft was parked, turned it on and sped away.

Ravven watched him go.

"You know Bajutsu," Buddha1000 said when he was standing beside her. "That move was The Snake Strikes."

Ravven allowed herself a hint of a smile. "Very observant of you, but I'm a little out of practice. Now what happened? How did you get yourself in that mess?"

Buddha1000 seemed embarrassed as he explained how things got out of hand. He said Tree got too far ahead and Buddha1000 didn't know where he was. "We try to stay together for protection. But I couldn't find him." The man in the black jumpsuit wanted Buddha1000 to pay a toll. "Of course, I refused. You can't let the pirates think they have the upper hand."

Ravven appraised him with a look. "How did that work out for you?"

Buddha1000 ducked his head as though letting humiliation slide from him. Then he noticed that Claire8 was holding the metal rod. It was bent. "You wrecked my divining rod."

"Is that what this is? Or was?" Claire8 said, turning it in her hands. It was bent at a thirty-degree angle in the middle. "I guess it won't work now to find water. We used it to get the van doors open."

Buddha1000 winced. "It never worked that well, anyway."

Tree circled his truck back to see what happened. As soon as it stopped, Alonzo ran up to it to talk up Ravven's martial arts prowess.

"She's a badass." He embroidered the tale of how Ravven decked the guy in the black jumpsuit. "And I bit him!" By the time they reached the circular road at the middle of Woodstock Settlement, Alonzo was puffed with pride and Ravven's reputation had a new layer of legend.

Kat tried to take it in stride, even though it made her jealous of Ravven all over again. She even smiled when Amber asked Ravven to teach her some fighting moves.

"I'll show you," Ravven cautioned, "but it's a knowledge that you cannot abuse. We are peaceful warriors."

They began sparring in the town circle paved with old-fashioned cobblestones, ringed by low buildings that curved around it. Ravven deftly demonstrated to Amber how to knock an adversary off balance.

But it was Kat who felt off balance. Once again Ravven had become the favored sister and Kat felt she was losing control. It took her a moment to realize that Buddha1000 had his hand on her arm to get her attention. "Can you get your people together? I have something to say."

"Resistance friends, you can see that the citizens here have messed with the camera." Buddha1000 gestured to a camera above him on a pole, its lens painted over in black, rendering it blind. "There are no trackers in Woodstock Settlement. Everyone is on their own. There is freedom here, but there are also no rules. So watch your back. I'm going to load my cargo, make a few trades, and Tree is going to scout some farms in the early morning."

Tree nodded to confirm.

"If you need transportation," Buddha1000 continued, "find me here tomorrow morning no later than eight o'clock. That's when we're heading north, to the Springs."

Kat knew it from her research. It was the next major settlement on the way to the Northlands. And she knew it was led by a woman.

With Buddha1000 and Tree departing for their respective business tasks, Kat turned to face her group with an apology on her mind. She knew Woodstock Settlement was only a way station for them. Even though they were free of trackers here, they couldn't stay. She didn't have the words for this yet, but she told herself that she would find the right time. Her sisters looked ragged from the journey. Ravven and Amber weren't sparring anymore. Claire8 sent a thought into Kat's mind. *What next?*

Only Birdie seemed bright and fresh, and Cressida looked cheerful, drawing from his uplifting personality field. She scanned the skies and enjoyed what she saw: swift groups of black birds flying in tight circles. She pointed to them: "Birdie!"

A contented smile spread across Birdie's face as he looked up. "Auspicious, especially when they're going counterclockwise like that."

Cressida pulled out a pocket notebook and became so absorbed in sketching the formation overhead that she was oblivious to the sketchy characters who had lined up on the other side of the street to assess the newcomers.

To Kat, the air felt heavy. It looked like the worst citizens of the settlement were thinking through all the ways they could rob Kat and her group. She announced, "I'll find a place to stay the night. And we'll have a circle there. Everyone can go off now and explore. Meet back here in an hour. Sound good?"

They nodded. Claire8 pulled out her Secluder comm to set a timer.

Birdie spoke up. "In an hour, there will be a similar formation of birds overhead. Look up, see them flying in those circles? When it happens again, you'll know when to meet."

"Okay," Kat said with a hint of a smile. "See you all back here in an hour or when the birds appear." She didn't quite believe it, but was happy to indulge in a little of Birdie's optimism. "Will you come with me?" she asked Ravven.

Ravven nodded. Emily joined them. After a moment's hesitation, Oona and Aftra came along as well.

They discovered that not all the buildings that had hotel signage were actually hotels. Places that claimed to be laundromats seemed to have some entirely different business going on inside them. Inside one, a bunch of white men at the far end of fifty were placing bets on some kind of random number generator. They were using paper money, the old, much-handled bills worn to near transparency.

As Kat and the others looked for a place to stay, they were approached by a dozen or so men who pitched solar power units, weed, mushrooms, designer drugs "made in a nice, clean lab," and many offers to change their crypto into paper money that was the local currency.

Then, a distraction: a hovercraft glided into the center of town and settled on the pavement. It was matte black, low and sleek, with a bump at the back for a cargo area, likely containing many kinds of goods to trade. The driver was a Young who wore a hat with silvery stag antlers on it; his eyes were covered by green-tinted goggles, Kat supposed to spoof the trackers.

His arrival looked to be an event that many of the traders in town anticipated. Various freelancers swarmed the hovercraft to check out the cargo and offer their own goods for trade. With a flourish, the Young uncovered his cargo area to delighted *oohs* and *ahhs*.

There was one more hotel to check out. Kat hoped it was actually a hotel as its sign said, and it turned out it was. It was called the Blue Note and had a quiet lobby.

The clerk behind the desk was another Young. She looked to be about twenty and had bright orange eyes, a mod that had a retro vibe. Mods were supposed to be invisible; anything as gaudy as orange eyes was in poor taste. Apparently, this Young didn't worry about what people thought.

She didn't require identification or a deposit. Kat noted that the cameras in the lobby were disabled, pointing upward to the ceiling, and the wires leading into their backs were cut, hanging limply.

"Let's check out the rooms," Kat said. Upstairs, the rooms were less promising. The mechanical locks were ill-fitting and wobbly, easy to break into.

"What do you think?" Kat asked Ravven. They stood at an entry door to a room. Claire8, Oona, and Aftra were checking out another down the hall.

"Bad. But it will do for tonight." Ravven fixed Kat in an appraising stare. "When are you going to tell them?"

"Tell them?" She knew what Ravven meant: Kat had to tell the others that she'd made a mistake to come to Woodstock Settlement.

"Why delay?"

Kat sighed. She didn't want to get into another power struggle. "I need to find the right time."

Ravven's stare didn't waver.

"We all agreed…" Kat continued, but didn't finish. By now Ravven's stare had turned into a smirk and stopped Kat's words.

"You forced it on us. You need to tell them," Ravven said.

Claire8 stepped in and seemed to read what was going on. "Everything okay?"

"No," Kat said.

Twenty minutes later, Kat and Ravven were sitting across from each other at a table in one of the rooms. The room was nearly as spare as a pod, with only a sleeping mat, couch, and the table, with four mismatched chairs made of plastic that looked a little like wood. It had some old-fashioned touches, like cloth curtains on the window that looked out to the town circle. Claire8 had a bottle of red wine in her hand and poured three glasses.

Kat couldn't help but laugh. "Claire8, to what do we owe this honor?"

"We're celebrating. We made it out of New York and we're on our way to safety!"

"Is that how you see it?" Ravven asked.

Claire8's enthusiasm seemed forced. "We're better off than we were. No trackers here!"

Kat saw that Claire8 was up to something, but she raised her glass anyway. "To the Resistance," she said in a level voice.

Ravven and Claire8 lifted their glasses. The wine was bad, but it was wine. Kat hadn't had wine in months.

"The group is not sticking together," Claire8 said.

Ravven jumped in. "You think it's because of me. I can't help it if some of them are drawn to me and not so much to you, Kat. Amber wants to learn martial arts. She likes sparring with me. And I can't help what Oona feels."

"She worships you," Kat said.

"This is what I mean," Claire8 said. "It's both of you."

"Jealousy," Ravven said. The word was like an icicle between them, slowly melting and leaving a toxic puddle. Ravven offered a sour smile to Kat. "You never trust anyone, Kat. You never trusted me from the beginning, when I recruited you."

Claire8 interrupted, "Both of you recruited me! And I trust both of you. There's enough trust to go around for everyone."

"Be quiet, Claire8, and let Kat speak," Ravven said.

Claire8, good-natured as ever, said to Kat, "You have the floor."

"Thank you," Kat said. She was thinking of the first time she and Ravven met, when Ravven recruited her to join the Receivers School and, later, the Resistance. They had encountered each other in the Hudson Market in New York. Ravven spoke into Kat's mind. It was a strange experience for Kat; she hadn't had any voices in her head since she was a girl, and then in the New York market there were dozens of voices. It seemed like nearly everyone she walked by was broadcasting their thoughts into her mind. Ravven taught her how to control the voices and how to live with being a Receiver.

"You engineered the first meeting between us, didn't you?" Kat said to Ravven.

"Yes," Ravven said. "I was reading the Feed that day and I saw that you'd left California, left everything behind. I knew that it was a good time to ask you to join us, so I went to the market, knowing that you would turn up there."

"How did you know?" Kat asked.

Ravven met Kat's eyes and shrugged. "Sooner or later, everyone has to go to the market."

"And why me? How did you know I would be..." Kat hesitated. "Useful."

"I knew that you would attract people. You have charisma. Not like me, but you have some, and more people knew you, because your story was always on the Feed. I was a just a local Feed item, but you were quite planetary!"

Kat smiled and looked away. "Well, not planetary."

Ravven disagreed. "The gossip writers covered you relentlessly."

"They still would, if they could," Kat said. Her efforts to stay off the grid were working so far.

"That's the point! That's why the Resistance needed you. And still needs you. People follow you, Kat. You have a gift. There's no reason why anyone should need to convince you that you are right for the Resistance. You were born for it."

"Thank you," Kat said sincerely.

"A born leader," Claire8 added, raising her glass.

"Don't pretend to be modest," Ravven said. "I certainly don't." She sipped at the wine. "This wine is easily as bad as the wine we had when we met and we had too much then. I know I did." She laughed, then became serious. "I opened you to your gift, Kat, your *other* gift. I showed you how to control the voices in your head. I let you in to the Receivers School, and together we brought in many members. Together we built this movement."

So what went wrong between us? Kat wondered.

Both Claire8 and Ravven captured the thought and both started to speak at the same time.

Claire8 won out. "We need to talk about the thing that came between you two."

Ravven sat back in her chair with an all-knowing look on her face. "You appear to have it all sorted out, Claire8."

"Be nice to her, Ravven," Kat said.

Ravven took another sip of her wine and made a face.

"We're lucky to have any wine at all," Kat said.

Claire8 held up her hands. "Don't start up." For the first time, she sounded exasperated. "The two of you." She shook her head.

"Claire8, you have a good read on us. We need to clear the air about something. So what is it? Tell us what you see."

Ravven started to speak but Kat stopped her. "I want to hear it from her," Kat said, nodding to Claire8.

"The problem starts with your personality fields," Claire8 said. "You clash, as two strong personalities."

Ravven snorted. "Personality fields again."

Kat waved Ravven off. "But wait, Ravven, she's right. We have so much in common. Too much in common. We have been colleagues, fighting this fight. And we have a common enemy, MIND. That should have us pulling together."

"But we aren't pulling together," Ravven admitted.

There was a light in Claire8's eyes. She made both of her eyes focus in the same direction, which for her was rare. "But there is *someone* you have in common that I've never heard you speak about."

Kat moaned aloud. "You're going there, Claire8?"

"Yes, I am going there."

Ravven leaned forward, spilling a little wine in her enthusiasm. "She's right. She's absolutely right! We've never discussed this in the circle. We hardly ever talk about it ourselves. It *is* the thing coming between us. Ever since Bradley betrayed you, you haven't been able to trust anyone completely."

"That's ancient history," Kat spat. "I'm over Bradley. I left him, remember?"

"You left him, but you are not over him," Ravven said.

Kat shook her head. "He's dead anyway, nothing more to say there."

"It hasn't stopped you; he still shapes your every decision," Ravven countered.

This made Kat mad. "You were with him, too! Can't you talk about that either?"

Ravven came back: "Also ancient history!"

"Stop!" Claire8 said, holding up her hands. "We're all affected by this, by your"—she paused to seek the right word—"your tangled mutual history. You both dated Bradley15 Power. That's it! That's the problem between you. It sounds ridiculous to say it out loud, but it controls both of you."

In an effort to preempt what she saw as the next turn of the conversation, Kat said: "I never loved him. It was his mod."

"You were lonely," Ravven said. "You were guilty. Confused."

Kat shot Ravven an angry look. "Don't analyze me. You don't know what I was going through. My husband died. I was alone, not lonely. There's a difference. I saw talent in Bradley then. He was a younger version of himself, a very different person." But even as she said it, Kat knew that wasn't true. Bradley had always contained the seeds of evil, she had just refused to see it.

She tried to cover the truth with more words. "I knew he would be able to replace my husband with software that worked. And Bradley's mod worked on me. He became the person I wanted to see. It made it difficult for me. I wanted to trust him. I wanted to like him. But I never wanted to love him like I loved my husband."

Dave Serif was and always will be my one true love, Kat thought to herself, knowing that the other two would effortlessly catch the truth of her pain.

"This is true," Ravven said. "One true love only comes once. Aside from that, there is nothing real."

Kat started to say something, but Ravven stopped her.

"We are all taken in," Ravven insisted. "Nothing is real. We all create ourselves for other people to like or love or hate. We create ourselves. We are all shape-shifters." Ravven tried another sip of the wine, made a face, and pushed the glass away for the last time. "I wasn't taken in by Bradley's mod. I never gave in to him! I wanted to radicalize him. To mold him. I changed him and I showed him how public action was possible. Social good."

"You did show him civil disobedience," Kat said, "but not for the better. When you had a micron demolator in your hands and you were blowing apart the domain offices, Bradley saw what was possible—but for him. That possibility wasn't good for any of us."

"What are you getting at?" Ravven asked sharply.

Kat spoke: "I'm saying we both had a role in shaping his personality. You, when he was a student, and me after that, when he was creating the company that would become MIND."

Now it was Ravven's turn to become angry. "I tried to *inspire* him. I wanted him to do the right thing. Revolt! Rebellion! Housing for everyone! That's why we went into the domain building with a demolator. We had a point to make and we didn't want them to forget us. But you, Kat, you *enabled* him. You encouraged him to create the evil that we have now. You *hired* him! You gave him the license to create an avatar of your dead husband. And as every schoolchild knows, that avatar was the prototype he used to build MIND. The first avatar that got us into this bad place."

Claire8 had her head in her hands. Her plan to bring the two women together was not going well. "Please stop," she said softly, her words muffled by the table as she sank her forehead to it.

Ravven kept going. "I am truly glad to have you on our side, Kat. You have the power to lead many circles, not just ours. But it's time for you to get honest with yourself. You are part of this movement because of your guilt. You handed Bradley the tool he used to create an instrument of control: the master AI, MIND."

"That's not true."

"Do you think he would have developed it without your encouragement? He would have been an obscure researcher, a post-doc who nobody ever heard from again."

"That's not true, Ravven. He was obsessed. He would have pursued the research whether I was around or not."

"I can't agree," Ravven said.

"And what about you, Ravven?" Kat said. She had had enough. "You radicalized him. You showed him how to be extrajudicial. The advantages of breaking the law."

"That wasn't me!" Ravven said. "That was Alon6. He showed Bradley how to break the law. That's what bad business partners do!"

"This is all a terrible tangle," Claire8 said. "I'm sorry for the wine."

Kat stood up from the table. "Now they're both dead and we're still not rid of them." She did not have to sit still for this.

She was ashamed, because some of Ravven's accusations were true. She *was* manipulated by Bradley's mod and she *did* let him create the avatar of her husband, Dave Serif, and it all *did* go wrong. Bradley *had* changed before her eyes to become what Kat wanted to see. And Kat had missed her husband. She missed Dave badly. Her request for an avatar had seemed innocent at the time, a personal choice that wouldn't matter to anyone else in the world. She had no idea that Bradley would expand on the idea and use it to build the empire that would become MIND.

Ready to leave the room, Kat paused to look at Ravven and Claire8. They were wrong to say she didn't trust anyone. Claire8, as an elder, was the person Kat trusted most in the Resistance. Claire8 never had any ulterior motives and always wanted what was best for everyone.

But Ravven was another story. Even from the first time she and Kat met in the market, Kat wondered what Ravven's true motives were. She had caught Kat at a vulnerable time, when Kat was running from California and her soured connection with Bradley, returning to a city, New York, that held powerful memories of her mother's death. When Ravven started to talk that day about the voices that Kat was hearing in her head, Kat considered running away from her as well. If she had, none of this would have happened. But she was trying to stop running. If she had run away then, Kat and Ravven wouldn't have tried to lead the Resistance together; they wouldn't have failed at it together, as they were now.

Ravven started bragging all over again about her triumph over Bradley's mod. "I never gave in to him," Ravven crowed to Claire8. "I had the strength. I had the power. And he trotted out all of his tricks, everything his mod could do. He became taller, his eyes became warmer, and his mouth got fuller, everything a shape-shifter can do, but I said no. I resisted him."

She caught Kat's eye but Kat stared her down to say, "We both played our role in this, Ravven. We are both responsible."

"Is that what you think?" Ravven asked, making her voice light and airy and all the more annoying. "Who did the most damage? Me, when he was just an impressionable young man in love, or you, who showed him his true power at the height of his career?"

When did you become so cruel? Kat put that thought directly into Ravven's head, and then left Ravven alone with Claire8 and the nearly empty bottle of wine.

Chapter 012

The birds were on time, as Birdie promised. The women of the Resistance regrouped in the town circle and then spent the night at the Blue Note hotel. Now it was early the next day, and Kat was by herself in the hotel coffee shop, looking out through a large window framing the town circle.

A waiter came over with Kat's order: artificial coffee made with artificial water and a grilled cheese sandwich made of lab-fabricated cheese and bread.

"Everything is made locally," the waiter said proudly.

Ravven sat down at the table, joining Kat. "How did you sleep?"

Kat shrugged. "Up most of the night." She had been plagued by insomnia most of her life. Sometimes she solved it but it was back now.

Ravven met Kat's eye and sent a thought into her mind: *You had no way of knowing that this place would turn out to be so bad.*

Kat let a small smile escape. "Is that your version of an apology? Reconciliation?"

"Yes," Ravven said and matched Kat's small smile.

Kat thought for a moment. Then: "So what do we do now?"

Ravven had a ready answer. "I think the Springs will be good. It's woman-led."

Kat knew that she was right. "Buddha1000 is going up there today. We can hitch a ride with him and Tree."

"No," Ravven said.

"No?"

"The Resistance is *ours*. We can't depend on anyone else."

"But Buddha1000 knows his way around here," Kat said.

"Our independence is more important."

They needed to hold a circle about this, not decide for the others. But she didn't want to argue with Ravven—she wanted peace. So instead she asked, "Without Buddha1000, how will you get there?"

The look in Ravven's eyes said that she had already thought of a way. But when Kat pressed the point, Ravven didn't answer. She said she had something to do, then got up to leave.

Kat invited Emily and Claire8 to ride up to the Springs with her and Buddha1000. It would take a couple of hours to get to the Springs in Buddha1000's van, less if he decided to use the antigrav. As the three of them waited for Buddha1000 to arrive in the town center, Kat stole a few glances at a side road leading away from the center, where Oona, Amber, and Aftra were joined with Ravven as she haggled with a hovercraft driver.

Cressida and Birdie had decided to stay in Woodstock Settlement. They'd found a family who would take them in. On a nearby farm, the family raised chickens; Cressida and Birdie would work as egg harvesters and packers for room and board. What sealed the deal was the family was also willing to supply shoes. One look at the state of Birdie's and Cressida's shoes had inspired their pity. And perhaps Birdie wanted to be among birds, even if they were flightless.

Chapter 013

"You like my price, we blast up there, no issues," the young hovercraft driver was saying to Ravven. "All you have to do is scan in and we'll go."

"Scan in?" Ravven said.

"Rules," the young man said. "Everyone who rides must scan. Dom says so."

"Just a minute," Ravven said. She turned away to enter a thought into the minds of her Young cohort of Oona, Amber, and Aftra. *We'll use our Secluders to scan in for this ride.*

They scanned in as other people, their true identities cloaked. At least it seemed that everything had worked perfectly; the hovercraft journey started smoothly. Their driver, whose name was Basic, was polite, even holding open the entry door of the vehicle for them to enter.

But just as they passed through the outskirts of a midsize city called NewWorker, Basic pulled the hovercraft to the side of the road and nosed it into the edge of the woods.

"Why are you stopping?" Ravven demanded. "What's happening?"

Basic wouldn't look at her. His eyes were on the road ahead, where a group of enforcement bots were rapidly closing in on them.

The next thing Ravven knew, her lungs were on fire; she was running with everything she had. Branches slapped at her face—she tasted blood as they lashed her. She was glad she'd worn a tracksuit today, with nothing to get in the way of her moving legs.

The hovercraft driver planned to turn us in from the moment he took the job.

Ravven could hear Amber and Oona running in the woods behind her. She dared not look back, for fear it would slow her down or she would lose her balance and fall into the brush. The Secluders—they'd used them too often and they became traceable. Or maybe the driver simply recognized Ravven. She'd become careless in Woodstock Settlement, not wearing a hoodie and reverting to her bright white clothing out of preference. It made her stand out.

Oona's voice was in Ravven's head. *Where are we going?*

Ravven sent her thought back: *Just keep running.*

They hadn't all made it. When the enforcement bots came, Aftra didn't move quickly enough. The bots wrapped restraining straps around her and she struggled in the dirt of the road as Basic watched, a smile playing on his lips. *Probably already counting up his reward credits.*

It wouldn't do to lacerate herself, Ravven thought; the tree branches she encountered were already doing that.

How long had they been running? Twenty minutes? Lucky for Ravven and the other two, the enforcement bots were not well suited to move over rough terrain, their wheels impeded by the roots and rocks of the trail. They fell back soon enough, and when Ravven was sure the bots were too far back to give chase, she stopped running to let the others catch up with her.

"Throw away your Secluders," she commanded. They all threw their Secluders into the woods as far as they could. "Let's keep going." Ravven's legs felt like iron but she commanded her body to keep moving.

Now Ravven and the two Resistance sisters who remained were in a clearing, with a circle of high trees all around them. The wind troubled the leaves above, making a hissing sound. Birds called out but there was no augur to read their voices or patterns.

At the top of the sky, the sun looked down. Ravven looked up, shielding her eyes, quietly amazed that it wasn't burning them. They didn't have protective glasses on or protective clothing. It must have been because they were out of the city. There were climate controls here, Ravven was certain, but the temperature seemed cooler than the city temp, the wind felt kinder. The UV could still hurt them, though.

"Let's put on some protection," Ravven said, reaching into her backpack and pulling out a silver protective top. "Put yours on. The sun may not feel bad, but we should still be careful."

Amber's voice wavered with worry. "How did they find us?"

"That brat Basic turned us in," Ravven snapped. "There must have been a reward." She cast a dark look at the two of them and commanded, "Never trust a Young," knowing full well that Oona was young enough to qualify as one. Amber was old enough not to be, but she should know better than to ask foolish questions. Ravven reminded herself not to be too hard on these two. They weren't experienced at fighting authority.

"Don't there have to be charges when they take someone away?" Oona asked, her eyes wide.

Ravven wanted to laugh at Oona's naivete but kept her tone helpful. "They don't have to name them at the point of arrest, only at sentencing. This is not about the fine points of the law. It's a blunt instrument meant to hurt us. To stop the Resistance."

Ravven knew Oona and Amber needed to hear something encouraging, but she was exhausted and her thoughts were scrambled. Eventually she muttered, "I'm sorry they got Aftra. Bad luck." It wasn't good, but she didn't have anything better to offer. She thought into their minds: *We will need to keep moving. We probably have a day's hike ahead of us to make it to the Springs.*

The pair looked at her with disbelief, as if to say, "That's all you have? Aftra was taken from us." Neither Oona nor Amber spoke for a moment, and then finally Amber offered, her face compressed by worry, "It must have been on suspicion of murder. That's why the bots took her and that's why they'll bring us in."

Amber wanted to make Oona feel better, perhaps, by voicing this reason for the arrest, but it came out all wrong and the effect was the opposite. Amber had spoken aloud the words that Ravven had been avoiding. *Suspicion of murder.*

Too late for worry; all we need to do now is keep moving. The committees didn't need much; they wanted to bring the Resistance to heel, and the evidence they had could be thin.

Ravven turned to Amber: "Which way is north?"

Amber was flustered, and then remembered the compass that Emily had pressed into her hand along with the *Boy Scout Handbook.* The compass was around her neck, on a lanyard. She fiddled with it, uncertain how to use it. "I think that way," she said, pointing.

"You think?" Ravven didn't like the uncertainty.

"Just a minute," Amber said. She pulled the handbook from her backpack, flipped to the table of contents, then flipped ahead to the section she wanted and read it on the spot. It was nearing midday, so the sun was going to be directly overhead soon.

She checked the book again, nodded, and turned with her back to the sun. "The sun is south. This way is north," she said, confirming her compass reading.

Ravven nodded, more satisfied now. "Then let's walk this way," she said. Amber and Oona followed.

Soon the sun was directly over their heads. The air felt warmer than before. Their silver tops mitigated the midday heat, so they didn't sweat too much. But after they had been walking for an hour, their backpacks felt like they were filled with bricks.

Chapter 014

Along their day's journey, the tired trio passed through dead towns with shells of buildings, broken windows and broken roads, cracked former streams with no sign of water. They'd moved quickly away from those towns, because whenever they reached pavement, it meant that enforcement bots would be able to roll and hunt them. The woods felt safe. Rough terrain was their friend.

Nature. She watches us. Though Ravven thought of Nature as a being, it was hard to know whether the woods watched with motherly concern or indifference.

But the pain erased any abstract thought, moving from her legs down to her feet and up to her back. Soon everything hurt and she wished she had an ElectroHand in her backpack. She fantasized about pulling it out and instructing it to massage her with its strong bot hands.

Then she pushed the thought away. *Don't be so weak. This is the future. Living in nature means walking.* But walking was dull, so Ravven let her mind drop into the minds of her companions. More than listening, it was something like seeing: she was able to look at the world out of their eyes, like she was positioned in their skull, looking out.

Ravven listened in as Amber fretted about losing Aftra to the bots, got tangled in remorse, and then tried to distract herself by recalling a phrase she'd glanced at in the handbook: *What weighs an ounce in the morning, weighs a pound at night.* Amber wasn't fully modded, but she had some silicone enhancements, and enjoyed a photographic memory for everything that she read. Other phrases she'd seen in the Boy Scout book streamed into her mind, like directional signs one might pass along the road. *Ducks flying overhead in the woods are generally pointed for water.*

Overhead, as they walked, Ravven had seen birds flying in formation—geese or ducks, she wasn't sure. Her years spent in cities meant she hadn't seen many birds except for little brown ones, which she supposed were sparrows, and seagulls. She turned her attention back to Amber's mind. Amber was wishing that Birdie was with them. But he was working on a farm with Cressida, with all the eggs they could eat and nice new shoes.

Amber remembered another old saying from the book: *If there's only one, it isn't a track, it's an accident.* She wasn't sure whether the handbook meant a track like the thin trail they were walking on, or a track made by an animal. She saw what she assumed were animal tracks in the mud, wondered if the animals that made them would be dangerous.

Now the sun was below the horizon; the light had faded and the air was colder. When the three could barely see the trail they were treading, Ravven finally ordered them to stop walking. She saw that Amber's legs were vibrating with effort and nearly folded underneath her. Oona stood unsteadily and struggled off her backpack, then held it in her hands since clearly she didn't want to put it down in the mud she was standing in.

"We haven't hiked enough today," Ravven said. "Not enough progress."

Oona blinked at her cruelty. *This is the best we can do.*

When she was a yoga teacher, Ravven felt compassion for her students. She wished she could summon more of it now. She pasted on what she thought was a motherly smile. "You're right, Oona. We did our best. This is as far as we can go. The woods will keep us safe."

Ravven looked ahead, the direction she presumed was north, and took in the solid wall of trees. The woods would end soon, and then they would be exposed to trackers. She wished they had a map. She asked Amber, "Can you remember the map that Emily had, and the relative position of the Springs from Woodstock Settlement?"

Amber frowned, squeezed her eyes shut, and did her best. "North, of course. Then a river," Amber said. "The Mohawk River," she said, calling up the name as she saw it on the map in her mind.

Suddenly, a ripple ran through Amber's body, as she saw the whole map as it was imprinted on her visual memory. The words came out fast, like she wanted to speak them before they floated away. "We must go north," she said, "and then we must go east." Her voice was clear, but her eyes were blank, focused on the map in her memory.

"Good work," Ravven said, remembering that praise was so important to young people, who these days seemed starved for validation.

Amber's face flushed in reaction to the compliment.

As they walked on it became darker, soon so dark that they couldn't make out the ground beneath their feet; then they weren't able to make out each other's facial expressions, though they walked a few feet away from each other. They must have been walking on a dry part of the trail, Ravven surmised, since her feet were no longer sucked and held by mud. "Amber, what does your book say about shelter?"

Amber pulled the tattered old book from her backpack again and began to flip through the pages. She struggled to read the small print in the dark, relying on her memory again as much as what she now saw on the page. "We don't have any of the materials. We would need canvas, poles, and stakes."

"Can we make anything with what we have here?" Ravven circled her hand, indicating the trees all around them.

Amber looked up briefly to register the trees. "We can make stakes, but we don't have anything like canvas." Then her voice brightened with an idea. "We can make frames from branches to sleep under and use our silverblue material as a tarp."

Amber and Oona wrestled with a tree branch until it came loose. It was slow work. In half an hour all they had made was part of one frame, and they realized that they didn't have enough silverblue material to fashion into a tarp.

Ravven was already asleep on the bare ground, her body curled into a tight circle around itself.

"I can't stand up anymore," Oona said. "Too tired." She lay down next to Ravven, moving close to her for warmth. Ravven made a low sound but didn't wake up.

Amber looked at the sticks in her hand, the half-finished frame, and realized that it would be best to get some sleep. She gathered the silverblue material, bunching it in her hands, and then spread it out as best she could over Ravven and Oona. Then she crawled in beside them and closed her eyes.

Chapter 015

orning came softly. Ravven looked up to the sky and through the branches that filtered the light. She was on the ground in the same spot in which she had fallen asleep. She turned her head to the side to see Oona still asleep, also on the ground, and she turned her head the other way to look into Amber's open eyes. Ravven got to her feet.

"Let's start walking," Ravven said. She sounded strong and steady and wondered for a moment where the strength and steadiness were coming from. She took a deep breath, held it, released it, held it at the bottom, and took another breath in an impromptu pranayama breathing exercise. *Maybe it's the yoga,* she thought. *Or the Bajutsu.*

"Bajutsu?" asked Amber, picking up on the thought. "What's that?" She got to her feet as well.

Ravven smiled. "It's what we were doing when we were sparring." She struck a pose, hands open before her, palms up, and then rotated them and turned them into fists. She laughed. "Up for it now?"

Amber's smile was weak. "Not really. Maybe another time." She leaned over to fetch her backpack and searched inside for a food unit. "We have to eat something first." She handed a food unit to Oona, who was awake and rubbing her eyes now, and offered another one to Ravven.

Ravven took the food unit, unwrapped the silver paper, popped it in her mouth, and chewed it twice. "We can eat while walking. Come on." She stood and started to walk northward, assuming the other two would follow.

They walked for most of the day, Ravven charting their path by sighting the sun, turning to Amber now and again and asking that she verify their direction using the compass.

But eventually, Amber became worried. "Ravven, stop walking!"

Ravven turned, her feet rooted in place. "What?" she snapped.

"We're going too far to the north. We have to go east or we will overshoot and miss New Galway."

"We're going to the Springs."

Amber raised her voice. "We have to go east!"

Ravven put her hand on Amber's shoulder to steady her. "All right, show me the compass."

As Amber fiddled with the compass, turning it this way and that, Ravven saw that Oona's face was hard with the effort of holding back tears. The weight of her backpack formed Oona into a slumped "S," and she looked to be shivering, even though the day had heated up.

"Both of you, check to see how many food packets you have left," Ravven instructed.

Amber shrugged off her backpack and opened it. "I have one."

Oona did the same. "One."

Ravven nodded. "Same here. That means we have to get there by nightfall, or else you're going to have to open that handbook and figure out how to make a bow and arrow."

The joke fell flat, as Ravven suspected it would. She started walking again, assuming that the other two would follow, and they did. The woods seemed vast. The sound of their passage was small: the snap of a twig underfoot, the brush of branches against their bodies, their breath, becoming shallow and uneven with their effort.

As night came, Oona's teeth started to chatter. Her body just wasn't used to the cold. Amber placed a hand on Oona, steadying her. "Are you okay?"

Oona nodded yes, but then fell to her knees, and dropped face-forward into a bed of leaves. She lay there, immobile.

Amber shook her shoulder. "Oona, Oona!" Oona's response was to curl her body tightly around itself, turning on her side, unwilling to go on.

She's not dead, she's not dead, Amber thought.

"She's not dead," Ravven confirmed. She went down on one knee to put her hand against Oona's cheek. The girl turned away as though she wanted to burrow into the ground. Ravven shook her head, and her lips were a thin line of disapproval. She looked up at Amber and nodded. "You're getting tougher. That's good."

Amber looked at her elder.

Ravven went inside Amber's mind to hear what she was thinking. Amber was remembering how she had watched Ravven train Circuit in Receiver techniques; she was recalling martial arts moves Ravven had taught her from time to time. Ravven had also been Amber's teacher in Receiver School, training Amber in the arts of the mind. Amber was thinking about how Ravven never stopped teaching.

Ravven approved of this line of thought, but then Amber's line of thought shifted.

You've changed, Amber thought, holding her teacher in a steady gaze. Ravven was able to pull out a few more of Amber's thoughts. *Harder. Cruel. Different.*

It was discouraging, but Ravven made herself stand tall. "I don't want to fail you," she said, fixing Amber in a cool gaze. "We have to rise to this. Giving up isn't the way."

Amber obviously didn't agree. She shook her head, closed her eyes, and invoked the Sanskrit prayer that Receivers could say to stop others from accessing their thought stream. Then she moved close to Oona on the ground and checked the battery level on Oona's silverblue jacket, judged it sufficient to handle a higher level of warmth, and turned up the setting, hoping it would make Oona more comfortable. Then she lay down beside Oona, hoping that the closeness would provide even more warmth.

Then Amber closed her eyes and pretended to sleep.

Ravven also felt very tired. The darkness of the woods wrapped around her.

Chapter 016

o you need help, sisters?

There was a new voice in Ravven's head. An unfamiliar voice. *Am I dreaming?* Ravven asked herself.

Hello. You are not dreaming, answered the voice in her head. It asked again*: Do you need help? Wake up and tell me.*

Ravven lifted her head from its bed of leaves and looked around, disoriented. Oona and Amber were near her, still coiled together to keep each other warm. Ravven looked up and saw a figure standing over her, backlit by the sun.

"What?" Ravven said aloud, in confusion. She pulled a leaf from her hair. "Who's there?"

The figure took a step closer. No longer in silhouette, a small, muscular woman with a fierce face like a lion showed herself to Ravven. The woman held a wicker basket and wore black gloves. There was a bac-mask around her neck; on her forehead rested a set of protective goggles. She seemed to be prepared for anything.

"You are Receivers. I heard your thoughts of distress. You seemed weak and troubled. I came over to see what I could do for you."

"You are a Receiver," Ravven said. She got to her feet, concealed the embarrassment on her face as she brushed off leaves that stuck to her, leaving a streak of dirt on her face. Oona and Amber continued to sleep curled around each other—or were pretending to be asleep. *Maybe they're afraid to get up.*

"Why would they be afraid? Where are you going?" the woman asked.

"We're going to the Springs. Do you know the way?"

The woman's face opened into a smile. "Of course. I am Dorothy de Facto."

Despite her short legs, Dorothy de Facto set a brisk walking pace back to her hovercraft, in the chilly morning air. Once there, Ravven saw that Dorothy had left the top down. It was a large hovercraft, with room for six people, and the wheels on it were large, meant for off-roading, away from trackers embedded in the roads.

"What were you doing out in the woods?" Amber asked.

Dorothy removed a cloth that covered her basket to reveal a mound of black mushrooms. "Foraging. It stays warmer longer now, and there are more fiddleheads, too."

"You're a...mushroom forager?" Amber asked. "What's a fiddlehead?"

"I'm a chef," Dorothy said, her eyes twinkling. She was amused by Amber's cluelessness. "I run a community kitchen nearby. Some people say I run everything, including the neighboring towns, but I say when you feed people, you are in control. Call me Dot."

Dot, thought Ravven. *Makes sense. Her name is a semaphore. She is a sign.* Ravven asked if Dot had seen any other new Receivers.

"I have." She frowned. "Now, what were their names...Kat, Claire8, and one more...."

"Emily," Ravven said.

"Yes, Emily. They all came into town about two days ago."

"Where are they now?" Ravven asked. "Do you know?"

"They went with Buddha1000 to deliver some medicinal herbs. Do you know Buddha1000? Everyone knows him around here."

Ravven nodded.

"Come to think of it, the Receivers asked about you. Good thing I ran into you! It won't take us long to get back to the Springs."

Not the way Dot drove, it didn't. Like a maniac, at speed, stressing the mechanics of her hovercraft and the gut of her passengers, Dot covered ground with enthusiasm, not speaking a word. It wouldn't have mattered, because anything she said would have been carried away by the wind in the open vehicle.

Ravven, Amber, and Oona held on tight and watched the scenery rush by until the Springs were revealed.

Dot skidded the hovercraft to a stop. "Welcome to the Springs." They were in an open meadow surrounded by buildings that collectively resembled a summer camp. Most were brown, low, and rambling, and looked to be made of wood. One was multistory, red, and had large windows.

As Dot walked across the central meadow heading toward a yurt on the far side, and the others struggled to keep up, Dot called out the functions of the buildings, pointing to each: "Kitchen, dining hall, school." The last one she pointed to, the school, was the red one.

She arrived at the yurt. "Here's where we keep our guests." She walked up the stairs, leading the others inside. It was round, made of wood planking, with a thatched roof. Dot noticed Ravven checking it out and added, "The thatch isn't real plant matter. It's fireproof synthetic. But all the wood you see here is real." Inside, Dot opened a few drawers in a high dresser, revealing clothes. "Just find something that fits. Don't worry about fashion statements!"

Then she turned and pointed out the door to a low, weathered building of silvery-brown wood, across the meadow from where they were. "Meet you over in the dining hall in ten." She was gone before they could say thank you.

The room had bunk beds, like a dormitory. There was a chair that was just a chair (not connected to WiFi, without the ability to conform to the body of an occupant), a standing lamp near it that had a simple on-off switch, and a simple table surrounded by four chairs. A metal mirror was fixed to the wall, and above it was a sink with a valve for water. There were no screens on the walls. Upon closer inspection, the dressers contained work clothes in dark colors and gold flowing garments that seemed ceremonial. Ravven chose the gold garments; Amber and Oona chose the work clothes. They all put their wet, dirty clothes on a lower bunk bed that had no sheets.

Ravven turned the valve at the sink. When water came out, she was surprised that it was real. The pods she'd lived in had artificial water or beam scrubbers that directed treated UV for disinfection without using any water at all. She vigorously scrubbed her face, enjoying the feeling of wet water. That it was cold didn't matter.

"Everything is real here," Ravven said, feeling a little silly afterward. But it was true. She stepped aside to let Amber and Oona use the sink and enjoy the water. "It must come from a well nearby," Ravven guessed. She looked at herself in the mirror and removed the rest of the leaves from her hair. She smiled at herself: the gold ceremonial garment was just her style. "All right. Ready to go. How are you both doing?"

"Better after we've had something to eat," Amber said.

Ravven put her arm around Oona, who appeared to need a hug. "How are you feeling?"

"I'm okay," Oona said.

Ravven pulled both of them into her. "We will be safe here. Let's get something to eat and you'll both feel better."

Chapter 017

The dining hall held long wooden tables and chairs. There was no one inside, so Ravven, Amber, and Oona moved into the kitchen. In contrast to the quiet dining room, the kitchen was bustling with activity. Steam rose from a multitude of pots on an induction stove. A young chef wearing a white kitchen uniform was vigorously chopping kale with a knife, her percussive blows rattling her work surface with each stroke. A young man also dressed in white was applying the same treatment to a pile of mushrooms, maybe the same mushrooms that Dot had harvested earlier.

On the other side of the busy kitchen, away from the center of noise, a tall young woman with calm blue eyes was stirring the largest cauldron of soup Ravven had ever seen.

The woman at the soup looked up at her visitors. "Can I help you?"

Ravven said they were looking for Dorothy.

"Oh, she'll be by soon enough. My name is Alice. Everybody likes to call me Cookie, though."

"What do you like to be called?" Ravven asked.

"Alice," she said.

"Cookie!" Dot bustled into her kitchen. "Come over here and help me with this. I have to give a tour to our guests."

After showing a smirk to Ravven, Alice went over to Dot, who wanted her to work on kneading and shaping several loaves of bread, and then get them in the oven. "Punch them down," Dot was saying, pushing her balled-up fist into each loaf to expel yeasty gasses. "Then shape them into baguettes. Let them rest and then get them baking. You remember how?"

"Yes," Alice said in a tone that suggested that of course she did, but who could argue with Dorothy de Facto?

"Okay, take over," Dot said, and then gestured for Ravven, Oona, and

Amber to follow her. "I'll give you the tour. This is the kitchen, obviously the hub of our activity. Lots of people come through here. Students. Hikers. Nature freaks. Freedom fighters. Some Receivers. Mercenaries. Even some cult people, I don't know why. Must be the fresh air." She paused to smile at Ravven. "This way."

They walked through the dining hall, which had become active with assistants setting the tables, laying out bowls, spoons, forks, and water glasses, in an arrangement that was the same for every setting and apparently meticulously specified. Ravven watched as one of the servers used a ruler to check the spacing between utensils. "Are you hungry? We're almost ready for the lunchtime seating."

Outside, as they continued their tour, Dot marched them across the meadow to the multistory red building. Ravven felt youthful energy all around. There were children in a play yard to the side of the school, and more children in a garden near the yard.

"Recess, as you can see," Dot said. "We take in kids as young as four, and all the way up to fourteen," Dot said. "After that, they can go off on their own or stay here to work with us. The tuition at the school funds the kitchen. We feed many people from our kitchen. Many locals come by for a meal."

Dot walked them through the garden, where children were planting vegetables, and pointed out the fields beyond the gardens, where there were cows grazing, hutches for hens laying eggs, and pens with pigs in them.

"What do you teach?" Ravven asked. She hadn't seen many children in San Francisco or New York. She'd read on the Feed that the birthrate in cities had dropped. People viewed children as precious and rare, but were happy to mod them to make them even more exceptional. But here were children—ordinary, happy children, it seemed. She assumed that it was because the air was better, the water was real, the food was local. She hadn't seen a food unit since she arrived. She also wondered how many of these children were Receivers. Her mental field felt alive with signals.

For the first time, Dot's sunny attitude seemed to dim when she answered the question of what was taught in the school. "Oh, the usual," she said blandly. "Because of admin's regulations, we have to teach the admin curriculum. Everything is about funding!" An impish look came over her face before she lowered her voice. "Sometimes we deviate. But they send observers to check on us, to get us back into line." She looked up to see Buddha1000's van approaching from the far side of the meadow. "Ah, it looks like your friends will also be in time for lunch."

Chapter 018

The dining hall was different now, transformed into a busy place with bright energy and activity. Ravven listened in on the many voices in her head: cooks worried about the spinach being gritty and people from the neighborhood wondered if it was okay to get a free meal here. Dot had seated Ravven at a table of honor in the center of the large room with the other members of the Resistance. The women had embraced, some had cried. They told their travel stories. Kat's was uneventful, while Ravven downplayed the danger her group had encountered. Claire8 had checked and there was a record of Aftra being detained but nothing further.

"I'll keep checking, and I'll find her," Claire8 vowed, but Ravven knew they'd never see Aftra again. The committees were good at disappearing people. It was best to keep up a wall about this and not get too involved. What's done was done.

Kat had gone out of her way to be forgiving, which surprised Ravven. "It wasn't your fault," she'd said. That was true, thought Ravven: She couldn't have known that their driver would betray them, and Aftra hadn't moved fast enough when the enforcement bots came. Somehow, she didn't know why, it bothered Ravven a little how Kat was working to smooth everything over. Ravven knew she deserved a few harsh words, but Kat just seemed grateful to be together again. When she reached into Kat's mind, Ravven couldn't find anything other than sincere gratitude. Maybe later on, mused Ravven, they'd get to say all they needed to say to each other.

Anyway, they were in Dorothy de Facto's orbit now, and Dorothy was attuned to power. She had identified Ravven and Kat as the alphas of the circle. When Dot took her place at the long table, it was with Ravven on one side of her and Kat on the other. The other members of the Resistance were seated farther away from Dot's self-proclaimed center of power.

Dot motioned to a server to bring them some water and began to explain why the community dining hall was so crowded. "This meal is open to the public, and it draws people from nearby towns, and also tourists and wayward travelers. We welcome the lost, and we are our own little world here." Then Dot turned to Alice, who was racing through the dining hall on an errand, and called out to stop her, "Cookie! What did Gandhi say about self-sufficiency?"

Alice had the quote on the tip of her tongue. "Every village has to be self-sustained and capable of managing its affairs, even to the extent of defending itself against the whole world."

"Very good! Defending ourselves against the whole world! Self-sufficient, yes, but not isolated. We won't be able to produce all the things we need, but we can try, and when we can't.... Cookie? Gandhi had more to say about that, right?"

"We shall have to get from outside the village what we cannot produce in the village," Alice said.

"Yes, it's a balance we seek." Dorothy smiled. "Now back to work!"

Alice returned a quick smile, more of a grimace, really, to indulge her boss and scrambled back to the kitchen. As Ravven watched this little power drama, she wondered whether Dot considered her or Kat more alpha.

Dot included both of them when she continued. "We respect the food we are about to eat and the people who prepared it." She gestured expansively to the crisp white tablecloths, sparkling water glasses, and heavy forks, knives, and spoons that could have been made of real silver. "Some people have told me this is a useless formality, or that I'm stuck up, or something." Her laugh was musical, going up and down a kind of scale. This was a performance she'd given often. "How long has it been since you've seen one of these?" She held a silver fork.

Kat smiled. "A fork? We've gotten used to eating food packets."

"Unfortunately!" Ravven said.

"These objects, rare as they are now, were part of the original intentional community that was here before I signed on," Dot said.

Before Ravven could ask about that, Dot jumped up to greet new guests. "I'll be back in a moment."

"I haven't seen such...finery in years," Kat said to Ravven, leaning across Dot's momentarily empty chair. "My parents would set a table like this once a year, and as they got older, even less."

"My parents didn't have these things," Ravven said. "We had ordinary things."

Oona, seated across from Ravven on the other side of Kat, was listening intently. "You never talk about your parents," she said.

"That's because I am part of the great orphaned generation," Ravven explained. "My parents died in the Change. They were high school teachers. My mother taught math and my father taught art. They invited students and their families in for meals—not as many people as this!" As Ravven surveyed the big dining hall, words left her for a moment. It had been a long time since she had seen so much living food, and she watched with fascination as dishes started to come out of the kitchen, carried by servers dressed in black. Soup, then pasta, then roasted meat, and salads mounded high on silver serving platters. It was all a little over the top, and Ravven liked things that were over the top. She exchanged a smile with Kat. *Extravagant.*

Dot returned to her place at the table. She nodded to Kat and Ravven, and then spoke loudly enough for the room to hear her. "What are you waiting for? Eat!"

This was also part of the performance. Apparently, nobody dared to start until Dot gave the word. She launched into an explanation of how long it took to prepare the meal, and the number of loyal employees in her kitchen, clearly favoring Ravven with this monologue; apparently she had taken quite a liking to her. She touched Ravven's arm often to make one point or another.

So she's decided that I am the lead alpha, mused Ravven. "Do you grow all the food yourself?"

Before answering, Dot tried a spoonful of carrot soup. "Mmm, divine."

"Where did you get all the table settings and silver? I haven't seen anything like this in a long time."

Dot smiled as though she was waiting for just this question. "It's a long story. Do you want to hear it?"

Alice rolled her eyes as she carried a tray of empty soup bowls back into the kitchen.

"Yes, I'd like that," Ravven said.

"Me, too," Kat said.

"All right, then," Dot said. "I studied cooking in Paris. My parents paid for me to join a little cooking school called Le Petite École. I was lucky to get in; they didn't take many Americans. But I had this sensual appreciation of the food, and they hadn't met many Americans like that.

"The bread they baked was made by angels. I could never imagine myself making something so beautiful." Dot paused to hold up a breadbasket filled with bread that looked as beautiful as she described. "But I did and I have."

She closed her eyes, enjoying the memory. "Blood-red tomatoes. Melons like the sun. Lettuces with the brightest green of life. The farms were close by, so chefs went there to select their produce. They *collaborated* with the farmers, encouraging them to grow for taste, not for shipping." She paused to smile. "This all sounds crazy now, doesn't it? It was a micro-ecology. The food was alive."

Dot let that thought linger for a moment, then began to speak in a darker tone. "One day, when I had been at the school for two months, I woke up and noticed something was different. It was hot outside, really hot. We'd had heatwaves before, even in the short time that I was there, and even what you'd call some extreme weather events.

"I ran out into the gardens. I saw that the garden was dead. The cows were down. The chickens were almost all dead or dying. Of course, you're familiar with what I'm talking about."

"It was the Change," Ravven said. "I'm guessing what you'll say next. Are you part of the great orphaned generation, like I am?"

"Yes," Dot said, adding, "I didn't know that about you. I'm sorry to hear it."

"Thank you," Ravven said. "We'd all seen it coming but we didn't recognize it for what it was. We just kept living our lives."

"Of course we did," Dot said. "There were many days when it was a little hot or drier than before, or too cold, or very rainy—outside of the pattern, you know?"

"The patterns didn't get our attention," Ravven said.

"Yes, that's it. We didn't notice. And then there it was all at once: something else, and it was too late. Everything was dead.

"No one could breathe. They closed the school that day. I wondered if it was the same everywhere and I panicked about my parents. I hadn't heard from them. They sent me to Paris; they sacrificed for me. I tried to reach them back here on the Eastcoast."

Dorothy de Facto stopped talking suddenly as tears ran down her face to land on her plate. She had been served a wonderful meal by Alice, pasta and roast pork, but she hadn't noticed it arrive while telling her story. The same food was placed before Ravven and Kat and they, too, didn't notice it. Dot dried her eyes with a napkin and motioned for them to eat.

"I tried to call but the phones were down. I couldn't get home right away because all of the flights were booked. It was pandemonium at the airports; it took me a week to finally get home, and by the time I did, both my parents were dead. Heatstroke got them. They were old, but too young to die."

"I'm sorry," Kat said.

Dot nodded. "Thank you. I remember walking around in their house without them in it, with all their things, like they were gone for just a few minutes." She shivered involuntarily. "I couldn't stay there. Where to go? I was a cook in a dead land. Nothing was growing anymore.

"I'd heard of the Outlands and the Northlands. There were farms there that weren't affected by the Change; at least that's what I'd heard. I answered an ad for a community that needed a cook. I went north. I knew nobody.

"I arrived here. It wasn't called the Springs then. It was a colony of nudist Marxists. And some Maoists."

Ravven exchanged a look with Kat. "Marxists and Maoists?"

"Yes, and some of them in each faction were also nudists. They never wore clothes. They were always fighting. The Maoists tended to argue with everyone. But they all agreed on one thing: They had to eat.

"They had a rule that I've never broken. 'You sit down for dinner,' they said. 'Make a moment of it.' I kept that rule. They also said 'Everyone who comes here gets a meal.' I kept that rule, too. But right at the first interview, I told them no way was I cooking in the nude. You can't do that in a kitchen. It's too dangerous. They said that was okay, I would be able to wear clothes. When they showed me around I asked, 'What am I going to do with such a large kitchen?'

"They said 'We are all old. We're dying. You will bring life.' I was moved by that. I took the job. And you know, from the first day, we argued about everything in the kitchen. They argued about the food budget, the menu, my preparation, my hires, everything. But I noticed that they never argued about any of that in the dining hall. Meals were a time for peace.

"I started to see that kitchens are a good place to argue. Kitchens are a good place for process and the process becomes the solution. You can smash a pan, throw an egg on the floor, shout and carry on." Dot displayed another of her impish smiles. "Not that *I* did any of that!" There was her musical laugh again.

"So I inherited this place. I renamed it the Springs, because life springs eternal here. I started the school so the tuition paid for the kitchen. The gardens and animals are instructional, the kids love them, and they provide ingredients." She stopped talking suddenly, as if the story had worn her out.

Kat felt compelled to fill the silence. "What did you mean by 'The process becomes the solution'?" Dorothy's kitchen sounded like the Resistance circle. Always in conversation and conflict.

"We never reach consensus here," Dorothy said. "We just get to another stage of the argument. Nothing is ever settled in the kitchen. There is only peace in the dining room." Dot appeared tired of telling her story, and with a flash of an apologetic look to Ravven and Kat, she stood up, holding a bowl of salad, and raised her voice to speak to everyone present.

"We grow this here, everything in this bowl and everything on your plate. You can't imagine how important that is." She took a few of the younger Resistance circle members into her gaze, Oona and Amber, and nodded to Emily. "Some of you are too young to remember. You know only this as food." Dot held up a food unit packet with her other hand. "In our world now, food units have become the standard." She put down the salad bowl and the food unit.

"Here in the Northlands, there were also climate events, but less frequent and not as severe as on the coast. The real farms survived. Real farms that use real dirt. It takes longer to grow some things. Not everything is available year-round. Winters can be hard. But we feed people locally. Anyone can come here to eat. When you are in town, and you meet someone, tell them they can eat here.

"Why am I so generous?" No one answered her question.

"I'll tell you. When you eat food made by a real person, food grown in nature, you will see how you can never leave nature. You will love nature. You will see how nature is irreplaceable, no matter what technology we have to sustain it or fabricate or imitate it. Friends, nature is your universal mother. Nature is the original mother. Nature is everyone's mother. When you know the value of food, you understand the value of your mother, nature. You won't want to let her go. You will want her to survive." Her impish smile again, and then: "Cookie, what are you waiting for? Serve dessert!"

Two weeks passed in the Springs. The November air became cooler, because the climate controls didn't operate consistently in the Northlands. That was fine with Ravven. She wanted weather.

Amber wanted Ravven to teach a martial arts class. Ravven said she would, as long as she taught it outside.

"But it's cold," Amber said.

"We'll keep moving and you'll be warm enough."

It became a daily ritual. Ravven would lead Amber, Oona, and Emily through a series of sequences, including slow breathing, a knife hand strike (the beginner's version of The Snake Strikes, which Ravven used to take down the man outside Woodstock Settlement), and The Tiger Claw, used to push an opponent back. The younger members of the circle loved the class, but Kat and Claire8 dropped out after just one. It was too cold in the morning and they didn't like the implied violence, even though Ravven tried to make the class focus on breathing and subtle movement.

Ravven didn't care that Kat and Claire8 left. She preferred teaching younger people anyway, and Ravven noted that Kat and Claire8 soon became absorbed in their own project. Claire8 had made a device she called a LumaSutra that was able to detect the presence of Receivers in a five-kilometer radius. She and Kat were taking Dot's hovercraft on little trips to find Receivers and try to recruit them to the movement.

Ravven saw the point of this, but she had also started to see the movement differently. What if everything and everyone they needed was right here in the Springs? What if the recruits would come to them instead of them having to seek them out? Ravven taught her martial arts class and watched with satisfaction as Alice, the assistant chef, started watching the class from the window of the dining hall. After watching a few classes, Alice asked if she could join and Ravven said yes.

Ravven liked to tune her personality field to others around her, making a point of noticing them. For instance, during every martial arts class, Emily positioned herself so that she would be able to see the multistory school building. Voices of children came from the school, carried on the cool November air. The voices must have tempted Emily, because when Ravven entered Emily's mind she heard: *I never knew I liked children. I never knew that I could care about them. Do I want to be a mother?*

Dot was always present during the prep for the community meals, so Ravven approached her at lunch to say that Emily had told her that she didn't want to volunteer in the garden and she didn't like working with the animals. (Emily hadn't actually told Ravven these things but she had thought them, and that was good enough for Ravven.) Dot responded as Ravven assumed that she would.

"But she has to volunteer." Everyone who stayed at the Springs had to put in their time.

"I realize that," Ravven responded. "So I had another idea."

Dot liked it. At the next meal she found Emily in the dining hall and recommended that Emily visit the school—Ravven's suggestion, which Dot presented as her own.

This took Emily by surprise. It was as if Dot was inside her mind.

"Go in and have a look around," Dot encouraged.

"Can I?" Emily said.

"They're just children. And I can see you're curious."

Ravven stood nearby, smiling as she listened in on their conversation playing out as she'd planned.

Dot continued, "Tree is a teacher there. He can show you around. You know Tree, don't you?"

"You mean the Christmas tree guy?"

"Yes," Dot said with a smile. "He teaches at the school, and when the school goes on winter break he becomes a full-time tree guy. Go talk to him."

Chapter 019

In the morning, Emily walked over to the school. The ground floor had large windows, and she could see Tree leading a reading circle inside a large, airy room with windows that let in the silver November light from the cloudy sky outside. She thought, as she approached the school, that Tree seemed unqualified to teach children. All she knew of him, really, was that he was tall, gawky, and quiet, but as she entered the school, he was standing at the head of the class, reading from an e-reader. Emily had never seen so many children in one place. There must have been thirty of them.

Just then, Tree noticed her, and motioned for her to come in and sit down. Emily took a place in the back of the room, sitting on a mat, and listened to him read the rest of the story, which was about a farm tended by bots, and when he finished, he looked at all the young faces and said, "Okay, everyone, time for screens!"

The children cheered and went in pairs to terminals. "Just thirty minutes, and then we'll go outside." He came over to greet Emily properly.

"They really listen to you" Emily said.

Tree grinned, perhaps picking up on her note of skepticism. "They know I'm the boss. I like the kids and making a little extra salary. Dot has always been good to me." He gestured to the kids in the room. "Let me show you around. This is the youngest group. It's mostly stories and playtime."

Emily guessed they were anywhere from three to six years old, but she really didn't know about kids. The bots who attended them were small, with an exterior covering that emulated human skin in white, black, brown, yellow, or silver.

Tree was watching her watch the bots. "We use bots a lot, especially with the little ones," he said. "It frees me up to move around the building and they really love the attention. The kids, I mean. The bots don't care." Tree laughed, and Emily detected a subtle note of embarrassment.

"Are you worried about being replaced?" she asked.

"Me?" He looked down. "Sometimes. A little. But you'll see that I do something different than what the bots are doing."

He brought her upstairs. "Here are the Middle Classes," he said as they walked into a room darker than the ground floor, with more screens. The students were working on a project with robotic arms and cameras. "These kids are seven all the way to ten years old."

"It seems really advanced." Emily wasn't certain she meant to say "advanced." It was actually kind of scary to see children of this age deeply involved in robotics and screens.

"These kids *are* really advanced," Tree said, not catching her concern at all. "We need fewer robots here to keep them supervised. They like to run their own projects."

He nodded at a child who seemed to have installed himself as the leader: a small boy, dark hair worn long to his shoulders, hazel eyes, and expressive hands. His voice was loud as he spouted off instructions to the others.

Tree caught his attention. "Soma? What are you working on here?"

The boy didn't pause; he spoke rapidly. "We use the camera to give the bot self-consciousness. If it sees itself, it can form an image of itself. Consciousness of the self is the first step in a broader consciousness like the kind that we have. Like when a baby recognizes itself for the first time in a mirror. It's a fun project!"

Emily blinked. Soma seemed to be some sort of prodigy. "How old are you?" she asked him.

"I just turned ten but my mind is a million years old, ha ha ha!" His laugh had a spooky quality, a combination of innocence and the experience of a wise soul.

"You seem very smart," Emily said, not sure what else to say.

Soma grinned.

"He would teach the entire unit on robotics and consciousness if we let him," Tree said.

"Can I?" Soma asked.

"We'll talk later," Tree said with a smile. Tree started to lead Emily out of the room to see the next group, but Emily couldn't take her eyes off of Soma. Something about his composure, the certainty of his movements, made him appear wiser than any ten-year-old she had ever met. But then, she hadn't met that many ten-year-olds.

Soma broke the spell of his supposed maturity when another boy said something to taunt him, and Soma tackled him and wrestled him to the ground. Soon the two were a tangle of arms and legs.

"Hey, hey," Tree said, turning around at the door, and then moving to untangle the pair. "Behave yourselves." He called for a bot to come over and keep watch. "Keep order while I continue the tour," Tree said.

"Understood," said the bot. This was a taller edition than the bots downstairs, at the height of this age group, with a round head and rotund body. It addressed the room in a pleasant voice. "Everyone, we were on chapter five of Programming. Let's return there."

Soma and the boy who were wrestling exchanged a conspiratorial look, like they might get back to fighting a little later when the adults weren't around, but for now they joined the others as they moved to their workstations.

The third room, which was down the hall on the same level, was the closest thing to a classroom, to Emily's eye. There were rows of desks with touch screens and an empty place for a teacher at the front.

Tree took his place at the front. "I have a class coming in a few moments. Do you want to stay to see what it's like?"

"Sure." She took a seat at the back of the classroom as the students filed in. They were preteens, Emily guessed maybe eleven or twelve. Their clothing reflected various stages of personal rebellion, with a ripped sleeve here, untied shoes there, hair unwashed, and among some of the boys, the wispy beginnings of a beard that looked temporary enough to wipe off with a damp cloth.

Tree greeted the group and was about to start class, but something stopped him. He hesitated and said to Emily. "I'm going to kind of show a video about

MIND. It's part of the lesson."

She didn't know what to do with that, so she just nodded and Tree launched into a lecture about the history of MIND, which turned out to be a heroic tale of how Bradley15 Power had invented MIND while in detention for civil disorder. To illustrate his talk, Tree put some of Bradley's original Logic Trees up on a screen. These, he explained, were the clever drawings that Bradley had used to map out the early functions of MIND. "And now I'd like to show you a recording that Bradley15 Power made. It's about the breakthroughs that led to MIND."

Tree gestured and the screen lit up with a large image of Bradley Power. Bradley was modded, everyone knew this, so the kids in the classroom expected to see him change to become the person they most wanted to see. What they didn't know was that Bradley couldn't see them; this was only a recording he had made some time ago. So the Bradley they saw appeared pleasant, his eyes a golden brown, his long hair getting in his eyes sometimes so that he needed to brush it from his forehead. The black T-shirt he wore was similar to the black T-shirts worn by the students. It was tight on him, containing a compact body.

Emily watched as some of the students shifted in their seats behind their desks, stimulated by the sight of Bradley, who apparently was a kind of hero to them. They started to chatter among themselves until Tree told them to quiet down.

Emily couldn't believe what she heard. She wanted to jump out of her chair.

"Kat Keeper lost her husband. His name was Dave Serif. The poor guy died of throat cancer. Kat came to me to see if I could create a replacement for Dave. This was exciting for me. An exciting assignment." Bradley's mod made him super smart but he lacked the tools to show much emotion. The vid bore this out. He was more robotic than human, Emily thought.

"I could make more than a replacement. I could make an avatar that contained his being, his consciousness, expressed in software. This was exciting!" Bradley's voice rose; he was edging toward expressing emotions. Emily knew that this was outside of scope for most mods like him and suspected that he had been coached to do it.

"I saw it as an opportunity," Bradley continued. "I could place the software avatar I was building into a personality envelope. A persona like that would create a substrate to build on, and the AI would be able to learn and change. Dave, Kat's husband, would come alive again in software form."

Bradley, onscreen, paused to bring up a white, oval object, like a stretched-out egg. "He would be able to live in a Form Factor like this." He patted the smooth object affectionately. "Any avatar we make is safe forever in its own Form Factor. The consciousness of Dave was contained in his personality envelope. It would be able to teach itself to learn without human intervention, and that, students, is what allows all of us to be safe and free under the protection of admin."

He went on to tell the story, often told and retold so as to become a kind of fable, of the day that Kat Keeper and Dave Serif met in a café. Dave was there with his books and notebooks. He studied languages. Kat Keeper was a startup founder, developing a facial recognition project with her team. She bought him a coffee, real coffee made with real water, and soon they fell in love and married. Tragically, soon after Dave completed work on his language project, he fell ill and died.

When the presentation was finished, Tree turned off the screen. "Let's break into small groups to discuss MIND and how it has made our lives better." He began the work of organizing the students, getting them situated in pairs and triads for the discussion.

After the video, Emily couldn't find words. When she finally could, they came fast and hot. "Why do you teach that?" she demanded of Tree.

"It's what we have to teach," he said with a shrug. "It doesn't mean that I believe all of it."

"You know that Kat Keeper is *here*? You drove her up here."

"Well, yeah," Tree said. "I know who she is," he added with an air of not caring. "I mean, Buddha1000 told me. But everybody knows this stuff. Anyways, it's not her story anymore, it's kind of an origin story of MIND." Tree was getting tangled up and Emily knew that he should stop talking, but it seemed like he couldn't. "It's just the curriculum. The same lesson plan I've always taught, but there's a new crop of kids each year, so it's new to them."

"Who tells you to teach it?" Emily said.

"The domain, I guess. It's an admin program, the same for all schools, I think."

"Who funds the school?" Emily asked.

"They do—the domain. They give us the money. Dot's account gets credited." He ran his hand through his hair. "What's the problem, Emily? We teach the lesson plan they want. So what? They're paying for it, and it's like, you know, history."

"Where does the domain get the money?"

"I don't know, probably from admin."

"Right," Emily said. "Where does admin get it?"

"I don't know."

"From MIND," Emily said. "You don't see anything wrong with that?"

"Wrong with what?" Tree said.

"Don't you know who's under investigation for *murdering* Bradley?"

Tree just looked at her. "I know. Buddha1000 told me. That doesn't mean it's true. The committees always have some investigation going on." He wouldn't meet Emily's eye. "It's just the curriculum we're supposed to teach, Emily." He shrugged again, and the conversation was over.

Chapter 020

As soon as she got out of the class, Emily sought out Kat. She walked over to her yurt, but encountered Ravven instead, reading a paper book.

"She's out with Claire8, recruiting. I think they went to Eightysevenville," Ravven said. (Some of the towns nearby had been renamed after the thruways after the Upstate dom took over.)

Emily decided to walk over to the meadow to wait for Kat. A few minutes later, the hovercraft came in. Kat and Claire8 were full of happy chatter about the contacts they'd made in the little town. They'd found five Receivers there and recruited them all.

"I'll tell Ravven that she's got to start up another class for the Receiver's school," Claire8 said. "We can invite the new people for lunch." She hurried off.

Kat caught the worried look in Emily's eyes. "Emily, what is it?"

When Emily told Kat about what she'd seen, Kat didn't believe her at first.

"They say I'm a part of history?"

"That's what was on the vid," Emily said. A corp needs an origin story and Kat's was a good one.

"Using my story. That is so wrong."

They were sitting on the steps leading into the community dining hall across from the school. Emily held a cup of artificial coffee in her hands.

Something caught Emily's eye from across the meadow. Several students from the preteen group had stepped out on a balcony and were unfolding something that looked like white fabric. It was a flag that they ran up a flagpole. The flag depicted Kat Keeper—a stark, contrasty image of her profile in black, white, and gray—and the image projected heroism and vision.

"What the fuck?" Kat said. "Is that me?"

"I think it is," Emily said. She walked closer to get a better look, Kat coming with her. "Why are they doing that?" Then Emily realized that she knew. These were the students who had seen the history vid in the class. They'd heard the heroic story of how Bradley created the Dave avatar for Kat, and then they must have learned that the very same Kat Keeper was staying at the Springs. Or Tree told them. "They know you're here," Emily said.

Kat stood with her hands on her hips, watching the flag that depicted her. "This is ridiculous." It wasn't snapping in the wind like a cloth flag. "Do you think they used their 3D printer to make a plastic flag?"

"I guess so," Emily said.

After a moment, the students noticed that Kat was watching them from across the meadow. They hurried from the balcony and poured out of the main entrance to the school. They came across the meadow fast, but when they got closer they slowed down, as if unsure what to do.

One of them said, "I think it really is her."

A few of the others nodded. "Or it's a sim. Do you think it's a sim?"

The moment was awkward; they were just looking at her, as though she was not real. She held out her hand. "Hello. I am Kat Keeper."

That broke the spell. One of the students, a boy with blue hair, held out his hand to shake hands with her, but the rest of the students became restless, as if they wanted to run away. One of the girls bowed respectfully, then turned and ran, giggling. This triggered the others and they all ran away.

Kat rubbed her hands over her face as if to reset the situation. "What was *that* all about?" She looked at Emily. "Why didn't we know about this? It was a history vid, you said? This is weird."

"Hmm," Emily said. "We probably didn't know about it because we haven't been around any schools. I didn't know there were vids."

They heard a voice behind them. "What is *that*?" It was Dorothy de Facto, frowning at the flag.

"We have nothing to do with that!" Emily said, flapping her hands as if to speed her words. "The students did it."

"I can only imagine," Dot said. "We'll have to get it taken down."

Kat breathed relief. "Thanks. It's just, I don't know—"

"You are part of the curriculum, I think. A small part," Dorothy said. "But the students can get overly enthusiastic. Tree played them the history vid, I imagine."

Kat's mind was turning. She asked Dot: "Do I remember you saying that you got funding from the dom to operate the school?"

Dorothy stiffened slightly; Emily read this as her being affronted by the question, like her privacy had been violated. "We get funding, yes. But most of our operating budget comes out of tuition. It's an excellent school, the best in the area! Parents gladly pay our tuition." Then, as if she didn't want to spend another moment in Kat's presence, she started to move away, gesturing toward the flag. "I've got to go—and get them to get rid of that." She stalked off.

"I wonder if Dot is regretting that she took us in," Emily said, thinking that they were about to invite recruits for lunch. Maybe they were asking too much.

Kat didn't seem concerned. "I remember when schools were funded by the city and state," she said.

"This is worse. Tree told me that MIND funds this school directly."

"Really? They must fund others, then," Kat said.

Emily could sense that something was on Kat's mind. "You want me to find out more."

"Yes. Can you keep going back to the school?"

Emily was curious to know more about the boy named Soma, so if Kat wanted her to hang around the school, and spy on the students who had raised the Kat Keeper flag, what was the harm in that? She would engage with Soma, but would also gather intelligence for Kat. "I'll ask Dot about it," Emily said.

She marched across the meadow to search for Dot, feeling attracted and repelled by the school at the same time. Attracted, because she was curious to see what it felt like to be around Soma more often. Repelled, because of the vid she'd seen. She wondered when it was made. Had Bradley recorded it before he died, or was it a sim?

Or, worse, maybe MIND had somehow spun up an avatar of Bradley's consciousness so he would, in effect, live forever. This idea bothered her. She didn't want to hold it in her body for too long. She made herself think about Soma. She was looking forward to seeing him again.

Chapter 021

Emily thought she did a good job of keeping her true purpose veiled. She said she wanted to compensate Dot for the free room and board.

Dot didn't give Emily a chance to finish speaking before she said, "Yes, yes. Do it. The school needs the help." She didn't offer any pay.

Tree was also delighted to have Emily help out, and not only because he was the school's only human teacher. Emily sensed that Tree secretly liked her. She played up to it, smiling pleasantly, reaching out to touch his arm to make a point. He wasn't her type. Too rough around the edges, too much of a *dude,* with his lanky limbs and loose way of walking. But he was good with the kids, and they shared that connection. And she was here on a mission, to find out more about the school and the curriculum, and certainly it *was* fun to be a spy.

On her first lunch break with Tree, they brought sandwiches over from the community kitchen and sat on the steps of the school to eat, overlooking the meadow. Emily asked him questions about the vids he played in history class: where they came from, how long he'd had them, and when they issued new ones. His answers were bland; he hadn't given much thought to any of that or didn't know much. She reminded herself that Tree was not a questioning type of person. He went with the flow.

When she tried a few questions about Soma, everything changed and Tree's face lit up; she had his interest now, and also, she realized, this was the topic she really wanted to know more about. She put aside Kat's espionage mission for a moment. "How did Soma get to be so smart? Who are his parents?"

"He's a failed child. Do you what that is?"

"Yes," Emily said. She hoped that Tree couldn't read the cloudy look on her face. "It means that their consciousness has been placed in another body. It sometimes doesn't work out that well."

Tree seemingly hadn't noticed anything about her reaction. "Soma came to us in kind of a secret way," Tree said. "We don't know who his parents are, either the parents who originally created him or the parents of the body he's using now. Sorry, that's kind of confusing."

"No, I understand," Emily said.

"Really? How do you know about failed children?" Tree asked.

"I know because...." Emily began, then waited for a good lie to come. "...I know because we let a few people who were failed children into the Resistance circle. We learned about them in the application process. And I can see that Soma has been modded."

"He is a strange one," Tree said. "I'm trying to understand him."

Emily felt fairly sure that her face didn't betray all that she was thinking: She was a failed child herself, with broken memories of her original parents, and simmering anger at the parents of the body she was using now. She felt the fractures in her past like scars on her back. It all flooded back. She felt her body wanting to control her, to go its own way. She wanted to jump up and run away.

Somehow, she managed to reveal none of this to Tree. Maybe he just wasn't inquisitive. His face was placid as he waited for her to speak. Emily supposed that he wasn't all that attuned to feelings, and that made him the perfect person to help her find out more about the school and about Soma. "I want to help out in Soma's class," she said. "Can I do that? Can I start today?"

The more time Emily spent with Soma, the more she realized how different he was. Failed children often had a disconnected quality, like they wanted to be elsewhere. And modded kids commonly had features implanted into them. Photographic memory, for example, like Amber had. Soma was highly articulate for a ten-year-old. Some modded kids received extraordinary vision that gave them the ability to see great distances.

Since the Change, fertility rates had dropped, and Emily supposed that parents were just so happy to have children they wanted to improve them just a little. But the temptation was too great, and the parents tried to improve their kids a lot. Maybe that's what happened to Soma, because he did things that other modded kids could not.

The first time Emily realized this, she was working at one of the terminal screens in a classroom. The screen flashed garbled words, then went dark. She jiggled it, making it rattle.

Soma came over, interrupting a robotics project he was working on. "What's the matter?"

"The screen went dark. I can't fix this terminal."

Soma began to hum. It was sort of musical, but sort of not, since it didn't hold any tone Emily had heard before. In just a moment, the terminal screen flickered on. It appeared to be fine again.

"How did you do that?"

"Do what?" Soma said.

"The screen is back."

Soma offered a smile. "Oh, that. I can find the resonance of things. I don't know how it works. But I can make healing sounds that align things with how they're supposed to be, I guess."

He returned her look of appreciation with a shrug. "It's just what I do."

Chapter 022

On some days Bradley was more adversarial than others, and this was one of those days. He pushed against every suggestion Nora2 made, no matter how small.

"Where is Sanchez now? We need more drones in the air," Bradley demanded in a voice that was louder than necessary, ringing out in the large living room that they used for an office in his New Zealand house.

"You sent him back to New York yesterday."

Bradley knew this. He never forgot anything, but liked to remind Nora2 that *she* could forget things and make mistakes. "You shouldn't have let me send him to New York," he said with an abusive edge.

Nora2 tried not to take it personally, because it wasn't meant to be personal. The edge in his voice wasn't the product of any human emotion. He was only meant to drive her to make MIND the best corp it could be. That was Bradley's only goal. And it was hers, too, she admitted to herself, as unpleasant as it sometimes was.

"Where do you want the drones?" she asked with a hint of fatigue.

"You can't get tired of me, Nora2. We're doing important work here."

"I know."

"Then don't sound so weary," he taunted, "and listen to me." He said he wanted more drones in the air, to find out where Kat was.

This sounded wasteful to Nora2. "We know where Kat is. She's at the Springs with the rest of her group."

On his screen, Bradley blinked his pixel eyes with what seemed like annoyance. "We don't know *specifically*! We need details. We haven't had good tracking on them since we lost that fool Bren Humblesinger. What did they call him?" He paused, then answered his own question, having retrieved the information. "Birdie."

Nora2 knew that Bren Humblesinger, or Birdie, was no longer useful when he elected to stay behind in Woodstock Settlement with his friend Cressida Scopes, while the rest of Kat and Ravven's Resistance circle continued north. Birdie had been useful for a time, because on the way up to the Northlands with the rest of the group, he had not been cautious. Claire8 extolled cloakcraft and handed out spoofing glasses to fool the trackers, but Birdie didn't always put his on, so he showed up on the public camera recordings. From her terminal in the Free State of New Zealand, Nora2 had been running a programming routine in MIND to watch for groups of people on foot who were walking the airways north on the Eastcoast. Birdie's face, often identified by the cameras because he wasn't wearing his spoofing glasses, became a constant in the flow of people. Nora2 tracked him all the way to Woodstock Settlement. Then he broke off from the group with Cressida.

Bradley badgered Nora2 to do more. It had been an easy matter to bribe the hovercraft driver to give up Aftra to the bots. Nora2 hadn't called it a bribe, of course—she told the driver it was a *reward* for helping the committees bring dangerous fugitives to justice. The driver's name was Basic, and he put the plan into motion in the most basic way: the bots had only been able to seize Aftra.

Nora2 reasoned that if she closed the loop on Kat in the Springs, and learned what they were doing there, she and Bradley could then pass the information to the committees. Then the committees could finally take disciplinary action against Kat and Ravven's Resistance circle.

"I'll deploy the drones myself," Nora2 said. "We don't have to send Sanchez anywhere. When we have better surveillance, you can tell the committees what to do."

"I can't tell, but I can recommend."

"But you control the committees."

Bradley blinked his eyes to signal annoyance. "I do not control the committees. Things don't always go the way I want them to, you know."

Nora2 couldn't tell whether Bradley was telling the truth, or just throwing slaze on the idea to misdirect her. It was the first time she'd had the sense that he didn't fully trust her or was concealing something. But it was just a *sense* of something; she couldn't isolate it in her mind, and she had more pressing matters to pursue with bringing Kat and the Resistance to justice.

Chapter 023

About a week after Kat asked Emily to learn more about the school, she checked in with Emily to see how the spy operation was going. Emily admitted that it was going slowly. "I need to work my way in and gain Tree's trust."

"You're spending a lot of time with Soma, I've noticed."

And what if I am? Emily wanted to snap back. But too late— though she hadn't said it aloud, the thought was formed enough for Kat to sense.

The more you learn about Soma, the more fascinated you are by him.

Emily was surprised that Kat saw that in her. But Emily couldn't get her mind away from Soma. Every day she watched him do things like walk with bare feet on hard stones to feel the cold. She had witnessed when Dot invited him into the kitchen to taste sauces because she recognized him as a "super taster." "His sense of taste is beautifully developed," Dot had said.

"Soma has a lot of talents. We haven't discovered all of them yet," Emily said to Kat, regretting her defensive tone. But she may as well have been speaking about herself. As a fellow failed child, she knew that she shared many qualities with Soma. Failed children felt divided, their body-consciousness and mind-consciousness in conflict. Soma's sensory body was sometimes out of sync with what his mind received as input. His consciousness had lived in two bodies, as Emily's had.

Kat picked up on these thoughts and sent a thought into Emily's mind: *Have you really been trying to learn more about the school or are you just spending time with Soma?*

Emily couldn't lie to Kat. "I owe you some research."

But Soma kept showing new sides of himself to her. For example, on Saturday nights when the weather was cool, after the evening meal, Dot brought out all the pots and pans from the kitchen and allowed Soma to lead a percussion orchestra. He gave everyone who wanted to play in the orchestra their own pot, pan, or metal spoon and showed them what to play. He'd invented a musical notation to guide them.

One such evening, Emily watched with Tree seated beside her as Soma organized the players.

"He used to bash the pots close to his ear. I was worried he could cause damage, so I took the spoon away," Tree remembered. But Soma cried hard and wanted the spoon back, because he had a plan. "Then I got it. He was learning the vibrations."

The orchestra warmed up, the players banging their pots and pans, a sound that was, indeed, hard on Emily's ears. Dot was among them, grinning as she rattled a wooden spoon in a metal bowl, and Alice was beside Dot, testing the sounds of a spoon gently tapped against a drinking glass.

Then Soma imposed order. He made sure that all the players had their music sheets, and he took his place in front of the group, standing on a chair so that he could be seen. He looked over his orchestra and raised his hands to conduct them.

The music the orchestra produced using his notation was unlike anything Emily had ever heard. The pots and pans made sounds that rippled like an ocean claiming the shore. She imagined that they made the sound of the Earth expanding and contracting, breathing with a low moan and rumble.

Emily closed her eyes as she listened in a kind of rapture. When she opened them, the music was over and Soma was standing before her.

"If the stars could have a sound, they would sound like that," Soma said. Emily found she had tears in her eyes. It was impossible that such beautiful music, and a deep understanding of how sound wrapped around emotion, could come out of such a small person, and yet here it was.

Soma looked at Emily intently. "Thank you for listening. But you should keep your eyes open, I want you to stay here with me."

Emily felt moved to take Soma's hand and squeeze it, and then she was embarrassed at her impulsiveness and let his hand go quickly.

Then there was the scene that played out at the end of every school day, when the sun disappeared behind the trees circling the meadow and the parents came to pick up their children. Emily saw them arriving when she was working on the first floor, visible through the large front windows, and knew it was time to wrangle the children for pick-up. She'd ask the kids to tidy up their projects, find their lunch boxes and coats, and then pass them along to Tree, who walked them out to the parents.

One by one, the children lined up and boarded their parents' conveyances. For families who were local and had a short ride home, there were bicycles with large boxes affixed to the front; families of means who lived farther away had luxury hovercrafts.

At the end, only Soma remained. He watched through the school's front window as the last bicycle and hovercraft departed with their cargo of happy families.

"What happened to Soma's family?" Emily asked Tree, the first time. "Don't they ever come here?"

"No," Tree said. "After school one day, a black luxury hovercraft pulled up in front. Self-driving. Dorothy enrolled Soma in the school that day. It all happened fast and I'm sure there was some kind of arrangement set up in advance, but we aren't supposed to ask about it." He stopped talking. Maybe he didn't know any more or wouldn't say.

Soma was alone, watching the last families leave.

Emily watched him. She wiped her eyes. "Soma?" she said.

Soma turned to her and it felt to her that he was entering her mind. This was impossible, she knew. He wasn't a Receiver. But what he said startled her.

"You can hold my hand," Soma said, taking her hand in his. "You make me think of my mother. I don't have a mother anymore. She doesn't come to visit me. I don't remember her. I have erased her. I think of her as warmth, an essence, and light, but not as a physical being." He waited a moment, forming his next thought. "Will you be my next mother? I need one."

Emily didn't know what to say to that. "I can't be your mother," she finally said, knowing it was the wrong thing.

Soma appeared nonplussed. "Consider it," he said.

Just then a teaching bot rolled up to him and asked, "Can I read you a story?" Soma let the teaching bot take his hand and lead him away.

On the top floor of the school, Soma had a bed in a room where he spent evenings alone after a bot tucked him in.

These moments tugged at Emily's heart. All through the school day she approached Soma and asked if he needed anything.

"I'm fine," he always said.

She decided that she needed to tell Tree about her own history as a failed child. If he heard it, she reasoned, he would see that Soma was lonely; he would understand how alike Soma and Emily were, and maybe he would help her.

One day in late November, after the children were picked up, Emily turned to Tree as they watched the last hovercraft float away. "I am like Soma."

He raised an eyebrow and offered a half smile. "Really? Nobody is like Soma."

"Yes, I am."

He saw that she was serious. "What do you mean?"

Her eyes were steady, locked in. "I need to know where I came from and I need you to help me with that. Can you?"

"Sure, I guess so. But I don't understand what you want me to do."

Emily began to panic and her voice rose in intensity. "I need to know who my parents are. Not the people who raised me, the people who created me. My originals."

Tree knew something about how failed children came to be: they had two sets of parents, one set that rejected them and another who accepted them in a new body. He nodded. "I can help you. But you have to tell me what happened."

Emily wanted to push him away; she raised her hands to shove him, but then didn't know what to do with them. "Help me first. Then I'll tell you."

Tree nodded and gestured for her to follow him. In an upper-floor office, down the hall from the room where Soma slept, there was an open terminal. The terminal connected to a server used to order school supplies, but Tree knew how to connect it to other servers and also to the Feed. "We can use this terminal, but after Soma is asleep. You can come back then. At nine, okay?"

"Yes."

She waited for an hour after the evening meal, crossed the dark meadow, and knocked softly on the school's front door.

Tree and Emily mounted the stairs and walked past the room where Soma slept, and at the end of the hall Tree opened a door. There was a room with a table, a terminal, and two chairs.

"Dot told me what I can and can't do with this terminal. But, okay, let's see." He gestured to the terminal and the attendance records of the school came up. "This is okay to look at. I fill them out every evening, so the school knows how much to bill the parents for their instructional days."

Each child's name had a link. "Click on some of the links," Emily urged. "How about that one?"

He looked at her, following her gaze to Soma's name on the screen. "I can't do Soma's. I'll try another." He gestured to the screen, and instantly it filled with personal information about the student. Their parents, their home address, whether they paid their bills to the school on time and how much they owed.

Emily didn't know this student well, but seeing the information got her excited and she leaned forward. "Look," she said, moving a finger to the bottom of the screen. There was a notation. "Archive," it read. Before Tree could react, she stabbed her finger at it to activate a new screen. It switched to a different database.

"Whoops," Tree said, and sat back in his chair. "We aren't supposed to be here." He was about to gesture the screen away. "It's a glitch. We shouldn't be looking at this."

"Wait." She stopped him from gesturing at the screen and looked closely at the info. It showed birth records for the child they were viewing: her date of birth, the hospital where she was born, and her parents, with links next to their names that likely led to their places of birth and their own archives. "This is good."

"Emily, please."

"No, listen, we back out of this screen, we get to the root directory and then we can look me up. My archive is here. I'm sure of it!"

Tree tilted slightly forward in his chair as though to look closely, but then he gestured the monitor dark to lock it down and lock them out.

Emily was shocked. "Why did you do that?" Her hands were balled into fists. She wanted to punch him in the face.

"Emily!" His voice was too loud. He read the pain on her face and tried to calm down. "We aren't supposed to be in that database, that's all," he said. He moved away to a window, unable to meet her glare.

She watched him stand there, an idiot, bathed in moonlight.

"We have to go now," he said.

"You coward," Emily snapped. "You coward! You're afraid. Will you lose your job or something?"

He turned to face her. "Yes. I could lose my job." He swallowed hard. "Dot wouldn't like it. She gave strict instructions." He struggled with his hands and words, tangling them together. "I don't know why I'm doing this."

"You're doing it to help *me*. That's why."

"What do you need to know about yourself? Why do you want to find your archive?"

Emily nodded. "I will tell you. I will tell you soon, I promise."

"Okay, we have to go now." Tree gestured and the overhead light snapped off; they faced each other in darkness. Moonlight insinuated itself into the room, painting them with a blue cast.

"I will tell you tomorrow," she said with conviction.

But the next day, she and Tree worked together, and on their lunch break Tree asked her if she was ready to talk about her past, and she said no, not yet. At the end of the day, he asked again, and again she said, "Maybe later. I want to go for a run now to clear my mind. I'll come by later."

The look on his face said he knew she was lying.

The weather was cooling off in the afternoons, forcing Emily to change her running pattern. She ran closer to the settlement, not straying far, and she ran harder, to stay warm. Today, she took a single-track path she knew, just an out-and-back.

A light snowfall drifted down. She stuck out her tongue to catch the white particles. She hadn't seen snowflakes at all in New York and remembered them only from her childhood.

Tree saw her on the way into the meal hall and he asked her again if she was ready to talk. She needed to eat, but knew that she could not delay any longer.

"After this," she said. "I'm hungry after my run."

He nodded, and didn't sit with her at the meal, to give her some space.

Then, as night was beginning, she found him at his table. "I have to tell you privately. Outside."

"Outside? You sure? It's getting cold out there."

"We'll build a fire," she said. She knew that he would be okay with that, since he had made a fire pit out in back of the school. She'd seen this and was curious about it, because fires weren't allowed, except for Dorothy De Facto's special birthday bonfire once a year.

Tree liked trees and he also liked fire. Emily watched him build one, pulling away a tarp that revealed stacked logs, his motions practiced and his procedures sound. Soon he had made a teepee that she recognized from the *Boy Scout Handbook*. And when he lit it, using a sparking device he carried on the same chain that held his pocket knife, he inhaled deeply, enjoying the scent of the smoke, and the sudden heat painted his features pink for a moment.

He looked to Emily. "I admit, I sometimes come out here at night and light things up, in this open place."

The fire was already roaring. He nodded his approval, clearly proud, and spread the tarp out on the ground. He sat down on it and patted the spot next to him. "Now, talk."

It was Emily's turn now. She had to tell her story. Her eyes followed the sparks upward. "Is that safe?"

"Sure. I've made lots of fires here before."

She didn't like how wobbly her voice sounded when she started at last. "I can't talk about my parents. I can only talk about the people who raised me." She looked up to see him waiting patiently for her to go on. "I don't remember my real parents very well, and I have tried to forget the people who raised me."

"You were adopted?"

"It's not like that with a failed child. It's complicated. It's hard to learn about our past, who we are, or what really happened." She paused. The fire snapped and she jumped. It took her a moment to collect herself and continue. "When I was very young, I was frail and sick. I think my original parents wanted to mod me. They wanted me to be better. Parents are always like that, aren't they? They want the best children. Now they can get them on demand. But there was a problem with me. The body I had wasn't good. My archive, what I've seen of it, has very little. My name. The town where I lived. No parents' names or anything like that. That's why I need your help."

Tree's eyes flicked away. She was taking him where he didn't want to go, even though he'd asked for it. "Tell me the rest," he said.

Emily felt a sob pop up in her throat. She picked up a stick and started to fiddle with it. "The step people take next is a soul decalcification. Do you know what that is?"

Tree's expression was blank.

"The child's substance is cleansed and made pure again, and then removed. Then they place it in another body, to start all over again. That's what they did to me."

Tree swallowed. "What happened to your old body?"

"I don't know. Maybe storage. Somewhere in the Midwest Domain there's a facility." She shivered involuntarily. "Since the bodies in storage aren't connected to anything, I'm sure some of them die. They are just floating there."

"It sounds horrible."

"It is," Emily said. "They put my consciousness into this body, the body that I am in now."

"Why did they do that? If they were going to put you up for adoption." He faltered. "Or whatever."

His words stung her. She hugged her arms. "I don't know, Tree." After a moment, she went on. "I think they wanted to cover their tracks. They screwed up when they tried to mod me. It didn't work."

"Why can you remember things? You think they tried to mod you. Things like that. Isn't that not supposed to happen?"

"You're right, it's not supposed to happen," Emily replied. "But the transfers are not smooth. They want you to forget about your originals. It doesn't always work. I have these dreams." She caught his eye. *Should I tell him? Will he think I'm crazy if I do?*

He met her gaze, so she felt encouraged to go on.

"I have a certain kind of dream. In my mind there is something like a screen. On this screen I see a girl who I think is me, and a boy who I think is her brother, and a mother and father who I think are my originals. The children are playing in a backyard and the parents are watching through a window. Then I see a park and I'm looking at the sun overhead. I think I'm in a stroller. I've had this dream many times. It means something. It's a part of me, somehow."

Tree wiped his eyes roughly. He looked at her as if to say *keep talking*. Emily felt his trust for the first time; she saw that he believed her story.

"I need to know who those people are in the dream," she said.

"When did they start?" he asked. "The dreams."

The fire flared up, painting Emily's face, then died down. She spoke from the darkness. "When I was fifteen, something changed. The body that I'm in now stopped blocking my original consciousness. I don't know how it filtered through. When I closed my eyes, I saw that screen. The dreams of the people who created me became more vivid. Two parents, a brother. I woke up some mornings with a glowing pain behind my eyes. It was purple and pulsed like a sun. My body, this body, made me get out of bed and stare out the window. Looking into the distance, into the small town I lived in, I knew that this was not where I was born. The people I was with were not my originals. Everything was broken. Do you understand?"

Tree nodded.

"I was living in a town called Lawrence in the Midwest Dom. The window in my room faced east. It took weeks of the pain in the morning, but eventually I realized that my body wanted to go somewhere else—it wanted to go east. *East, east, east,* a pulsing throbbing behind my eyes, a message for me every morning.

"I let it take me. I left the house. The streets ended fast and things got rural. When I ran away the people who raised me would look for me and gather me up and bring me home. It happened again and again. They were scared. 'We don't know you anymore,' they said. 'You never did,' I said.

"They took me to a doctor who gave me medications. They do this sometimes with failed children, to quell the unrest in them." She thought of Soma. "Is Soma taking anything?"

"I don't know. I've never seen anything, but we can check in his records." Now that he had opened the magic box of the server, he could find out anything about any of the children in the school, and it would be hard to stop himself from doing it. He blinked and brushed away some sparks.

Emily nodded, registering his discomfort. She'd refrained from looking into his mind up till now. She felt emotionally spent anyway, and she raced through the rest of her story to placate him, to win his trust as quickly as possible so they could get back on the server.

She told Tree about running away from home when she was fifteen, sixteen, seventeen—each time getting farther away before she was caught. Finally, when she was twenty, she made it to New York, where the veil of consciousness was thinner, and unspoken thoughts were louder, and there were more Receivers. She met Ravven and Kat there and joined the circle.

Tree abruptly got up to put more wood on the fire. Emily saw that he was overwhelmed. She shouldn't have told him everything. She was a failed child *and* a Receiver? She felt sorry for him. All he wanted was to make a fire in the woods and learn a little more about her, and she'd provided a twisted tale of body swaps, tortured consciousness, multiple personalities, and rootlessness.

"I'm sorry," she blurted. It felt weird to apologize. What was she apologizing for? She hadn't messed up her life; others had. She was trying to fix herself. "You don't have to put on more wood. We should be going."

Tree nodded. "You're right. It's getting late." He pulled off the log he'd just put on and kicked it around in the damp dirt to quench any embers. Then he threw dirt over the fire until it gasped and died.

Her body felt like she'd just come back from a run that was too long. She pushed her bangs out of her eyes. "It's all a terrible muddle, Tree. I'm sorry."

"Don't be sorry. Tomorrow, we'll open the server and try to find out something. Okay?"

For the first time all evening, Emily smiled.

Chapter 024

The next night, after their work in the school was complete, Tree logged into the terminal with Emily at his side. He navigated to the student information page and then gestured to go to the root directory.

"What name should I put in?" he asked. To Emily, his voice sounded unsteady. She was making him do something he didn't want to do.

"My full name is Emily Cloudfactor," she said. She put her hand briefly on his, and he smiled.

"Isn't that the name of the people who raised you? What about the people who created you? What was their name?"

Emily's brief shrug couldn't contain her feelings of hopelessness. "I don't know who they are."

"Alright." Tree entered *Emily Cloudfactor.*

The terminal didn't respond. "Strange," he said. He gestured again to reset the query. Nothing again. "It's not letting me in."

"Isn't there something else you can try?" She sat in a chair borrowed from one of the classrooms downstairs, sized for a child, and her legs stuck out.

"Well, I'm out of my depth here." Tree sat back in his adult-size chair. "I can try a few things, maybe." He gestured at the terminal. "Maybe I can convince it that the terminal is broken and when it puts itself into maintenance mode there's some back door access." He tried it but wasn't allowed access and took the terminal out of maintenance mode. "Maybe if I pretend to be somebody else. Dot might have access." He tried to log in as Dot but couldn't fake her password. "It's going to lock us out of any access if I fail again."

Emily hunched over in her chair and put her face in her hands. Tree wasn't good at this at all. They were stuck. Then she had an idea. "We have to wake up Soma."

Tree was already shaking his head. "No, we can't do that."

"You have to get him and bring him down here. It will take just a sec and then he can go back to sleep."

"He doesn't know anything about hacking root directories."

"He doesn't need to," Emily said. She recalled how Soma had fixed the broken monitor in the schoolroom by, in his words, "finding the resonance of things." She urged Tree to let Soma try and wouldn't give up on the idea until he said yes.

Tree stood up abruptly. "Okay." He went down the hall to get the boy and returned with a sleepy Soma in his pajamas.

Soma's eyes lit up when he saw Emily and he hurried over to her. "What do you want me to do?"

"I want you to open the root directory of this database." She gestured to the terminal.

Soma looked confused. "What are you looking for in there?"

Emily wouldn't tell him. "Remember how you used your resonance to fix the terminal downstairs? I want you to use it now."

Soma shrugged. "I understand. It's pretty easy. But I want to know what you want in there."

Emily sighed. "I don't want to tell you. I'm sorry." She paused. "Maybe after I find it I'll tell you."

Soma considered this. Emily saw him struggling with the decision but from the inside, when she looked inside his mind, she sensed his love for her. *Maybe she will be my new mother if I do this.*

His thought struck Emily almost like a physical force. She sat back and wiped away a sudden tear.

Soma's face clouded into a frown. "Are you alright?"

"Yes. Will you do it for me?"

Soma closed his eyes briefly and nodded. He started to sing a high tone.

"Wait, stop," Emily insisted. "As soon as you do it, I want you to leave. Go back to sleep. Can you do that?"

Soma nodded again, then sang the high tone again. It was steady, sweet—the tone, Emily imagined, that an angel might produce. The terminal screen flickered and resolved to the root database. An empty search bar and blinking cursor at the top of the screen invited input.

Soma opened his eyes.

Emily had the urge to cover them—she didn't want him to see what was on the screen. She stood from her chair and gently turned him toward the door. "Go back to bed like you promised."

"I will," Soma responded. "You have five minutes and then the database will close up again."

Tree ushered Soma back to bed while Emily leaned into the terminal. She typed *Emily Cloudfactor* into the search bar. The screen filled with a short record—detailing the early life of Emily Cloudfactor.

Emily gasped and leaned in. She had never seen this record. Her eyes jumped over the text, taking it in as rapidly as she could.

The record of Emily Cloudfactor began when she was two years old; there was no record of her birth. It said she was a girl living in the Midwestern Domain. According to this record, Emily was an only child. Her parents were Joseph Cloudfactor and Mary Cloudfactor. Joseph and Mary had lived in a small town called Lawrence for all of their lives, in a house Joseph's father had built. She scanned with her eyes as fast as she could, knowing that she would only have five minutes.

Tree came back into the room and Emily began to read out parts of the record in bits and pieces. "It starts when I'm two. These are my replacement parents, not my originals. I went to a school called Integrated Barnard. It's in a town called Lawrence, in the former state of Kansas. I see some teacher evals. Bright, pleasant girl. That's what they said."

Emily gestured to scroll down, but that was all there was to the record. The rest of the screen was blank. She struggled with it until her five minutes were up and the screen returned to the root directory and the search bar. Nothing she did could get her back in.

"That's it," she said and sat back, exhausted. "What I was looking at was a record of the replacements, not my original parents. It's not the record we want." She stood up and paced restlessly. "I remember a brother. I had a brother. I remember water. An ocean. Maybe a lake or something. The sky—cloudy almost all the time." She closed her eyes, trying to access more memories. The harder she tried, the more they dissipated, like trying to remember a dream.

Tree watched the struggle on her face. "Are you sure it's real? I mean, those memories."

"They are real."

The next night, Emily told Tree to go get Soma so that he could open the database again. Tree didn't put up much resistance this time, and when he brought Soma back, the boy said, "I wasn't even asleep. I was waiting for you!"

Emily couldn't hide her smile.

"But tell me. What are you looking for?" Soma asked.

Emily shot a glance at Tree before she answered. She felt that Soma could handle it. Tree gave a subtle nod. "I am a failed child, like you. I'm looking for my originals."

This made perfect sense to Soma. If he wanted to ask her to search for his own originals, he didn't say so. "I will help you do that. Are you ready?"

"Yes."

"I can give you five minutes again," he said, and then he sang his tone.

The root database screen appeared, with the search bar. Emily entered *Emily Cloudfactor committees and reports.*

Reports from the local committees in Lawrence came onscreen, and Emily leaned in once again to take them in. She forgot about Soma for a moment. He was standing over her shoulder, wide-eyed. "You have to go back to bed," she told him.

"Why?"

She couldn't conceal her annoyance. "Because I said so." Finally, she was able to see her records! But there could be things in them that were not appropriate for a ten-year-old to see. "Soma, please. I'll tell you all about it later."

After a few more gentle words from her, Soma seemed to understand and allowed Tree to lead him back to his room.

Emily drank in the text on the screen. She became so focused on it, she hardly noticed that Tree had come back into the room and taken a seat next to her. She read that little Emily had tried to run away from her replacements many times. The first time, enforcement bots had found her behind the school, on a path leading east, out of town. There were many records after that, always detailing how little Emily went to the east side of town, each time getting a little farther east before the bots caught up with her. She scrolled down to see that this behavior continued for several years, finding reports from when Emily was thirteen, fifteen, sixteen, seventeen, until there was a record at age nineteen, and then the records stopped.

"Keep going," Emily said aloud, gesturing to make the screen move and reveal more secrets.

"There isn't anything else," Tree said.

"There has to be more!" Emily's gestures became more compulsive and desperate.

Tree finally stilled her hands. He held them for a moment and then gently lowered them into Emily's lap. Emily saw him struggle for words. "It's all very strange," he finally managed.

"We have to find out more."

The screen blanked and reverted to a log-in state. Soma's tone had worn off.

"We can't do this every night," Tree said.

"Why not? This is my history."

"I know, but Em, if Dot logs on to this terminal she might see what we've been looking at."

"How could she do that?"

"What if she has root database access? She could see the history."

Emily frowned. "She never comes up here."

"She does. Sometimes," Tree said.

Emily's mouth tightened. She wracked her brain for something to say that would convince Tree to keep going. "But you want to help me, don't you?"

Tree did help Emily. Every night, after the students finished their lessons and the evening meal was done, Emily and Tree crossed the meadow together and went back inside the darkened school. Since Soma was required to hack into the server with his resonance, he became a part of their search party. Emily would enter his room, gently wake him, and bring him to the terminal. He exercised his resonance at regular intervals to keep the root directory of the server open so that Emily could explore its forbidden areas.

As the night unspooled, the glow of the monitor screen was the only light in the room. It painted their faces a pale blue, and the light extended to the window and crept down to the frozen meadow, to express itself as an elongated bluish-silver square on the grass.

With Soma napping on the floor, and Tree in a chair by her side, Emily searched the server for clues about her past. Each night Emily searched, Tree grew more worried; finally, after a few nights of this, he stood up suddenly and said, "I'm going downstairs," glancing at Soma to be sure he hadn't woken the sleeping boy.

"We'll be okay up here," Emily said to him, her eyes stuck to the terminal, her voice soft.

"I'm going to come up in an hour to take Soma back to his room."

"That means that I'll only have an hour to search."

"Yes, that's exactly what it means."

But even that restriction, he abandoned soon enough. Emily's will was too strong.

One night, after Tree let her search for two more hours, and was coming up to take Soma back to bed, Emily called out with a special urgency.

"Tree!"

He took the stairs two at a time. "What's wrong?" His breath was short.

Emily's eyes were wide as she pointed to the terminal screen. After weeks of blundering around on the server, typing her name (and the town she was raised in, the school she attended), she had stumbled upon a support group for failed and modded children.

"Stop. Get out. You shouldn't be in there."

Emily eyes flashed. "It's my right to be here."

Soma woke up and watched them argue.

"This is some kind of dark web, a parallel web," Tree said. "You shouldn't be here."

"There has to be a web like this because failed children are held in shame. We can't talk about what's wrong with us, how we hurt. This is where we can be open about ourselves."

She noticed that Soma was approaching to look at the screen.

"No," Tree said, trying to cover it up.

Emily pushed Tree away. "He has as much right to see as I do."

But that was easier said than done, because a synth voice came from the terminal. "Who's there?" It was male and emotionless.

Emily froze. She wasn't expecting the terminal to talk to her. "I am Emily Cloudfactor," she said.

"What? Speak up?" the synth responded.

She said her name louder.

"What right do you have to access our group?"

Emily realized she was talking to a non-human entity, some kind of AI.

"What right do you have to access our group?" the voice repeated.

"I am a failed child," Emily said as bravely as she could, though her voice shook.

"Prove it," said the synth voice.

Emily frowned. "I am trying to find out more about myself."

"To gain entry, you must prove that you are a failed or a modded child."

Emily's eyes flicked away from the screen. She didn't know what to say. "I am Emily Cloudfactor. You can look me up."

"No, I can't. I will close access."

"Wait," Emily pleaded. She turned toward Tree and Soma and mouthed silently, *What can we do?*

Soma stepped closer to the terminal screen. He sang a high tone, clear and steady, that lasted for five seconds.

"You can resonate," the synth said.

"Yes," Emily jumped in. Apparently the synth could take in sound but could not see who was in the room. "I can resonate."

The secret group was used by the adoptive parents of failed children to share their stories. Emily read as many as she could, devouring them as the stories devoured her, reached inside her and extracted memories. She recognized her struggles reflected in these families' stories of their children who ran away, like Emily did when she was young. Unhappy children with high intelligence. Children who had a seemingly limitless capacity to retain number-letter strings and sound sequences. Soma read alongside her. Tree paced behind them. Finally, he couldn't take it any longer; fearful of being discovered, he went back downstairs to leave Emily and Soma with the stories.

Emily read stories of a modded child's emotional distance, of another child's extreme sensitivity to sounds and voices and light and darkness; and fears, so many fears that the parents said were irrational and could not understand. Fear of water. Fear of cold. Fear of the song of a particular kind of bluejay. Fear of sour tastes. Fear of open spaces. Fear of closed spaces. Fear of darkness. Fear of heights. Fear of rhomboids whose sides didn't close perfectly. Fear of decayed objects, of rust and mold. The stories flooded into Emily's body.

Some of the children heard voices that told them to wander, seeking a destination that the children couldn't name. Emily knew this story. It was her story exactly, intimately. It sent shivers down her spine.

She explained it all to Soma as best as she could. "They are hearing voices because their original bodies are talking to them. The erasure was imperfect, like me. The voices are leading them to their original families," she whispered to Soma, whose wide eyes signaled that he trusted her. She felt he was right to trust her; she wanted to take care of Soma as if he were her son.

Some of the stories reached a dead end: The adoptive parents couldn't take it anymore. Their children were too hard to live with, and it was impossible to give them a good childhood. In these cases, Emily read, the group worked together to share resources and find foster homes for failed children who had become too difficult to remain in their homes.

"This is what happened to you, isn't it?" Emily asked Soma. "You became too difficult for your adoptive parents to handle. You were dropped off here at the school."

"I don't know," Soma said. He clasped and unclasped his hands. "I can't remember much of it."

Emily wanted to press the point, but she saw that it was too much for Soma. It seemed that his erasure was better than hers; he seemed not to remember anything about his originals. "Well, thank you for helping me get into the group. I want to keep digging."

Soma nodded.

Even though she was granted entry because of Soma's skill at resonance, Emily felt that she belonged in the group as a person who somehow combined aspects of her and Soma. There were answers there, she knew. Answers about her history, about herself. There was no turning back. She remained at the terminal for hours, until its blue glow was drowned out by the yellow light of the rising sun.

Her eyes burned. Soma was asleep on the floor again. Sometime during her all-night search, he had moved from the chair next to her. She carried him back to his bed, where he cuddled in gratefully, and then she went downstairs to find Tree.

He was asleep, half falling out of a chair. She tried to wake him gently, but he burst into a wakeful panic, then raced upstairs to the terminal room to be sure that the history was wiped.

Emily rubbed her eyes as she watched him scrub it. "I lost track of time."

Her half-apology had little effect on Tree's bad mood. "Go to the UV room and freshen up," he said. "The parents will be here in fifteen minutes."

She walked down the hall to the UV room and looked in the mirror. The eyes that looked back were sunken, with black smudges of fatigue beneath them. She clawed at her hair, trying to make it look normal, and adjusted her bangs so they hung straighter and smoother. She didn't care if any of the parents noticed that she was wearing the same clothes as the day before. She let the UV clean her so she felt a little fresher.

Chapter 025

Emily pretended that things were normal for the rest of the day, but pretending was exhausting. After the evening meal, she went back to her yurt to rest, intending to stay away from the school.

She flopped down on her bunk, willing sleep to come. But she felt a presence. Looking to the other side of the yurt, she was startled to see Kat, silently watching her.

"I've missed you at cleanup lately," Kat said.

The moment fell with a thud between them because Emily didn't know how to reply. She'd been skipping cleanup duty lately (a task everyone in the community had to take on) in favor of searching the forbidden database over at the school.

"Been busy," Emily said finally. She closed her eyes as if that might make Kat disappear.

But Kat had her own assumptions, Emily realized. She'd probably seen Emily leave with Tree after dinner every night.

Emily knew for certain when Kat said, "What's going on with you? Something with Tree?"

Emily sat up. "Not what you think. Nothing like that."

"Oh, really?"

"Yes, really," Emily said crossly. She got up from the bunk, went to the yurt's small food prep area, and opened a valve. The heater came on and she placed a teakettle on it. "Want some tea?"

"Not now," Kat said. "I want to know what's going on with you. And Tree."

Emily flinched at the insinuation. It was like her mother, asking her where she'd been. Kat was about the same age as Emily's adoptive mother.

"Well, I haven't been doing the spying you wanted me to do, if that's what you wanted to know. I don't know where the school funding comes from or how the curriculum got set. I got...sidetracked."

"How?" Kat offered an uneasy smile.

"Not that," Emily said with more force than before. "There is nothing going on between me and Tree." Then she paused. "We are working on something. A project. Research."

Kat waited.

"You know Soma? The boy at the school?"

"Yes," Kat said. "The prodigy."

"I'm sorry, Kat. I didn't do any of the work you asked me to do, but this was more important." Emily realized that she needed to tell Kat that she wanted to take care of Soma, that on the dark web she'd discovered a hidden world of the parents of failed and modded children telling their stories. That Soma had asked her to be his next mother and, she realized, she was already doing that. All of these thoughts crossed Emily's troubled features and Emily sensed Kat inside of her mind, trying to sort it all out.

"You've gotten yourself in a tangle, haven't you?" Kat said.

Emily jutted her chin, and made her words bold to cover the churning feelings inside her. "I just want to find out more about my archive. I need to know who my originals are. And I need Soma beside me." She didn't mention that she needed Soma because he could resonate his way into the root directory of the database.

Soma had been abandoned like Emily; their histories were merging in her mind. Kat was right: it was a tangle. She tried to sort it out for Kat's benefit. "Soma needs to be safe. He needs a guardian."

"And you want to be that?"

"I have to," she shot back.

"I want you to calm down and think about this."

"We'll talk later," Emily said. She pushed past Kat.

"Wait."

"I'm going for a walk," Emily said. She couldn't remain with Kat for another moment.

"You can't leave history on a server log," Kat called out, causing Emily to turn just as she reached the door.

"Don't you think we've already thought of that? Tree deletes everything."

Somebody will figure out what you've been doing, Kat thought into Emily's mind.

There's only one person who matters, and she hasn't figured it out so far, Emily returned.

Emily's hands were shaking. She held one hand in the other to stop it. She murmured the Sanskrit prayer that prevented Kat from hearing her thoughts and spun on her heels to leave the room.

PART 003

Kat was in the meadow at the center of the Springs, walking toward Dot's hovercraft. Claire8 intercepted her to insist that they cancel their trip into Eightysevenville.

"Don't you want to look for Receivers?"

"No, Kat, I don't. Meet me in the dining hall in twenty minutes."

Kat objected, but Claire8 could be stubborn. There was something wrong; Claire8 wouldn't insist on a meeting like this otherwise. Claire8 wouldn't let Kat into her mind, so Kat thought into hers, *I don't have time for this.*

Claire8 only smiled and left Kat by the hovercraft. What was going on?

Kat took a quick inventory. She had all but abandoned the circle meetings. All she cared about was to go into the small towns around the Springs with Claire8 and a LumaSutra and using the device to sense for Receivers. The LumaSutra could ping for Receivers, leaving glowing trails on its screen that revealed where Receivers liked to hang out, the parks and markets they frequented, making them easy to approach.

Kat would then invite the Receivers to come back to the Springs and have a free meal. The next step was inviting them to join one of Ravven's martial arts classes. Ravven had also started teaching yoga again, and coached Receivers on how to control the voices in their head. The promising recruits would attend classes every day, and then Kat would show them how to use a Blanky to reduce MIND's surveillance footprint. Kat thought things were going well.

But when Kat walked into the dining hall, the word *ambush* jumped into her head. There, at a table by herself, was Ravven. Claire8 was nearby, pretending to be a server and pouring Ravven a glass of wine.

"Come on over!" Claire8 called out. "We're waiting for you." She seemed excessively cheery.

Kat made herself keep walking to the table, sat across from Ravven, and accepted the glass of wine that Claire8 poured. Suddenly she knew what was going on. "You thought it was time for us to talk again, didn't you?"

Claire8 was chipper. "Yes, I did! You haven't been coming to circle meetings and we need you to talk to each other."

Ravven said, "It's early for wine." Ravven appeared not to want to be part of this meeting either. She started to bring the glass to her lips but then noticed that Kat hadn't touched hers. She put her glass down and asked Kat, "Are you in a bad mood?"

"No."

"Tell me what's troubling you," Ravven said. "Why haven't you been coming to the circle?"

"I've been busy," Kat said. "I'm sending you recruits. You're teaching classes. Everything's fine."

"I want to see you in the classes. And in the circle."

"Why can't we be on parallel tracks? I do externals, you do internals."

Ravven assessed Kat with a steady look. "What are you running away from?"

Kat felt Ravven probing in her mind. "Stop that."

Ravven closed her eyes and nodded. "I'll leave you alone inside, but I still want an answer."

"I'm not running away from anything. We're both doing the work that we need to do. What's wrong with that?"

"I'll tell you." And Ravven started to talk about what her meditation groups were helping her to realize. Here in the Springs, among nature, she was feeling the strength of Mother Earth. She wanted to teach about the spirit called Gaia, the soul of the Earth.

But Kat was only half listening. Why did everything have to be so internal? Ravven always argued that real change came from within, but sitting cross-legged in meditation wasn't going to take out any cameras.

All Kat wanted was to reduce MIND's surveillance footprint. That was her mission; it wasn't complicated. Everywhere Kat went she saw vid displays controlled by MIND. Ad panels in the towns advised citizens to entrust their personal memories to MIND's servers. Kat knew this meant that MIND would then catalog those memories, and use them to train its AI, to build a perfect system of control. She knew how MIND worked, because she knew how Bradley Power's mind worked.

"Come back," Ravven said.

"What? I am here."

"No, your mind is elsewhere," Ravven said.

Kat cursed under her breath.

Claire8 decided to have a try. "Kat, your problem is the same as my problem. We like action. But in the circle we've been talking about contemplation. The interior mind is just as important as the exterior world. Maybe more important."

Kat sat back in her chair. "No. Not when we're up against what we're up against."

"You're feeling something. Would you like to tell me?" Ravven waited.

Thus prodded, a spark of anger pushed out a thought that Kat hadn't intended to voice. "Okay. Listen. I caused this. It's my fault," she said.

"What is your fault?"

"All of it! The situation we're in. It's my fault."

"What do you mean?" Ravven asked.

"I broke the world and now I want to fix it."

"You didn't break the world."

Kat insisted that she had. She had been part of the development of humanity simulators, had supported Bradley Power while he made the first avatar. She had welcomed the avatar of her dead husband Dave, and she helped Bradley make Dave better. This enabled MIND. Her desire for Dave to come back had helped Bradley.

Ravven looked at her. "Is all that your fault?"

"Yes," Kat said.

Ravven laughed, which annoyed Kat. "It's a little grandiose," she said, which annoyed Kat even more.

"I am not being grandiose! I resent that. I am being selfless." All the things she'd given up for the movement—spending the last of her vast fortune, abandoning Dave, leaving her home, coming up to the Springs to start over—maybe none if it had been worth it.

Now Ravven backtracked and apologized for laughing. "You have given up a lot. But we all have."

Kat was ready to bristle at that statement but held back.

"All you wanted was your husband back. You saw a way to do that. You got him back."

"I was betrayed."

Ravven nodded at the truth of this, then paused to lock eyes with Kat. "But Bradley was a always a betrayer. He was never honest."

Kat knew Ravven was right, and that Ravven was the only other person who knew this. Before Kat was with Bradley, Ravven had been. They had shared Bradley at different times in his life.

"It's ridiculous," Kat spat out.

"What? Everything?" Ravven was struggling not to smile again but shook it off and held Kat's gaze. "Is it your fault? No! Is this why your shoulders are collapsed and why your breath is hard? Let go!" Ravven opened her arms with a queenly gesture of absolution. "Breathe freely! It is all *out* of your control."

Kat didn't like being told what to do, even if her friend was trying to help.

Ravven pressed on. "You can't do anything about old decisions. You can only make new ones. I'm sorry, Kat. But Bradley is dead."

Kat's eyes filled with fire. "But that's just the problem! We are fighting an AI, a ruthless, cold entity. MIND is worse than Bradley, much worse. It is fierce, it's tireless. There's nothing in the way of MIND making itself all-powerful, nothing except us."

"This is such a weight on your shoulders," Ravven said.

Kat wondered if she meant that sympathetically. She picked up her wine glass but didn't drink. "Now you're beginning to understand."

"I understand, but not in the way you know."

"What is that supposed to mean?"

Ravven leaned over the table to take Kat's hand and hold it in hers. "You tried to escape him once, Kat. Right? When you ran to New York and we met. You remember, of course. He was using a Harvester on you. He recorded your inner thoughts. It was a betrayal."

"A violation," Kat said. The memory of it still stung.

"Yes, and you reacted. You ran away from him and you ran *to* me. You broke free, even though you were scared, and it was good. Now you're scared again. So I'm asking if you can look inside yourself again, like you did then."

"It's not that simple." Kat's voice was hard; she pulled her hand from Ravven's.

"Why?"

"You've got it backwards. Bradley is still in love with me. *It* is still in love with me. It's obsessed with me," Kat said.

Ravven shook her head. "You can't know that."

"But doesn't it make sense? Bradley prepared for everything in life. It's likely that he had his consciousness captured and replicated. It's—he's—probably revivified in a MindVessel."

Ravven looked unconvinced.

"Ravven, look at the evidence. He—it, MIND—it's behaving the same way he would if he were alive. The same ruthlessness. The same singlemindedness. It will never let go of me."

"You want me to believe that we are locked in conflict until that consciousness is destroyed," Ravven said.

"Yes," Kat said. "There is no other way." Kat stood suddenly, prepared to make her usual dramatic exit when conversations became as suffocating as this one.

"Wait," Claire8 pleaded. "Don't leave."

"Why?"

"Because we haven't accomplished anything."

Kat sighed. Claire8 always tried so hard. "Look," Kat said, "I know your intentions are good. But maybe Ravven and I..." Kat faltered. "Maybe we need to pursue our own versions of the Resistance."

Claire8's reaction was instant. "No," she said. "That's not going to work.

We need both of you. Please, sit down, just for a minute."

Kat sat down again. She finally took a sip of the wine. "I'm listening."

"I wonder if you two have skipped a step. When people reach a certain stage in their friendship, there is a kind of sharing that we all do. I think it's time. I think you know what I mean."

Kat knew what Claire was suggesting, but she didn't want to do it. "Why do you say that?"

"Because you both need to talk about it," Claire8 insisted. "Each one tells their story and then something will break open. You've never done it, have you?"

"I think Claire8's right," Ravven interrupted. "We've never talked about being part of the generation of orphans."

Kat took another sip of wine, but it didn't make her any more relaxed. "How would that change anything?"

"It will. It always does." Ravven turned to Claire8. "You're right. I can't believe that we never did this. Remember our first dinner with Dot? She shared about her parents' extinction, how they died during the Change."

"Let's try it, Kat," Claire8 said.

Kat gave the tiniest of nods.

"I'll go first," Ravven said. "You know the words people say, right?"

"I know," Kat said with a hint of impatience. She reached for Claire8's and Ravven's hands. They formed a circle and said quietly together, "Honor our ancestors."

Ravven released her hands. "Alright, I'll start." She composed herself by taking a breath and letting it out slowly. "My parents were the kind of people who were so in love with each other that the rest of the world didn't really exist. They only saw each other. Oh, they loved me, too; I knew I was the third angle on their triangle. We lived in Big Sur, a town that excluded itself from the Northern Californian Dom."

"I didn't know that," Kat said.

"Yes, Big Sur refused to join. It remained independent, with its own government. My parents worked as lifeguards on the beach and they taught surfing.

We were pretty crunchy-granola." Ravven paused to smile. "They gave me the name Riva Nowakowski, which I dropped as soon as I could. But that doesn't mean that I didn't love them or appreciate the values they gave me. They taught me yoga and how to meditate. We read the yoga sutras and other sacred texts.

"Then one day the Change came. Or, as you know, it came over a series of days that intensified. The surf was very high. Our little bungalow was shaking in the wind. I pleaded with Mother and Father not to go down to the water. It was too dangerous. But they didn't listen. There was something fated about that day—they seemed so calm about it. I still wonder if they knew what was going to happen." Ravven let a silence fall.

Kat took her friend's hand.

"They never came back. I think they drowned but nobody knows, really. I never saw them again."

"That's very sad." Kat didn't know what else to say.

"I was just twenty," Ravven said. She dropped into herself for a moment, trying to feel into what to say next. "I wanted to put it all behind me," she said quickly, with a chill in her voice, as though she wanted to be rid of the words as soon as possible. "I got a job in a yoga studio. I studied Bajutsu. I became a black belt. I became fierce." She met Kat's eye. "That's my story."

"I'm sorry," Kat said.

"I'm sorry," Claire8 said.

"Thank you," Ravven said. "I tried to put it behind me, but I will always have a clear memory of the day they left me."

We can never leave those moments behind, Kat thought into Ravven's mind.

Yes, Ravven returned.

Kat knew it was her turn. She let out a ragged breath and told Ravven the story of her mother slowly getting weaker, her father's devotion, the walks they took in the woods to seek clean air, and her mother's final days with the healing bot. Kat told the story of how she tried to take apart the healing bot to make it work better, and she cried again.

"She died before the Change, when I was twelve. It was 2027."

"The Change wouldn't come for three more years," Ravven said.

"But I believe she died because of what was happening with the air. Many people her age died of lung cancer."

"When did your father die?" Ravven asked after a respectable pause.

"He's still alive."

Ravven's eyes went wide. "He's still alive? You've never mentioned him."

Kat struggled for words. Finally, she said, "That's because his mind is gone. After she died he came apart, but he put everything he had into getting me into Uni. When I got in, it was like he was done. His mind started to go. His memory. Long-term memory was okay, but he couldn't hold a conversation. I had to put him into assisted care Upstate."

Ravven just stared at her.

"I know what you're thinking. He's near here. I haven't visited him in years. I couldn't bear to see him."

Ravven found her words. "But you must see him now. You must! How far away is the facility?"

"About twenty minutes via hovercraft." The town of Elder Oaks housed a hospice facility called Memory Lane.

"You must go," Ravven said.

The hovercraft driver didn't like that Kat wouldn't scan in. She could've taken Dot's hovercraft, but she didn't want the trip on Dot's transpo records.

"You want this to be a cloaked trip?" he asked. He saw the comms unit she held in her hand. "Is that a Secluder?" Kat couldn't see his eyes through the dark-blue goggles he wore to protect his eyes from the sun, but she imagined that he was squinting at it.

"Yes, it's a Secluder," she said. "You do cloaked trips all the time." This was true, but he probably could get more credit for a trip that was on the grid. Kat wore a bac-mask that covered half of her face and protective glasses as well, hers with golden lenses. She was sure that the driver didn't recognize her.

"Drive fast," she told the driver, "and I'll tip well."

The driver allowed himself a smile when he saw the size of the tip Kat passed to his account. She pocketed her untraceable Secluder and noted the camera at the entrance to the building.

She hesitated for a moment. *Dad is in there.*

Getting out, she kept her bac-mask up and her golden glasses on and hoped it would be enough slaze to confuse the trackers.

The bot at the front desk looked up at her as soon as she passed the threshold of the portal. "Can I help you? I cannot identify you with your glasses on."

"I'm here to see Martin Keeper." She expected to be ushered into the same room where they had settled in her father as she had watched on vid. It took her a moment to remember that that had been thirteen years ago. She was twenty-two then. Thirteen years ago, Martin was already deep in dementia; he had lost the power of speech and much of his memory was gone, and he didn't recognize Kat any longer.

She had taken the coward's way out, and didn't make the trip out to get him settled. She was in California at the time and didn't want to take time away from her company, VirtualEyes. She was busy, young, and incredibly callous. So she had watched on a live feed vid from her office as the bots settled Martin in his room. They encouraged him to wave at the camera and he did. He didn't remember anything and couldn't speak, but he was pleasant.

Now, the bot began gesturing at the controls on a console in front of it. "Just a moment," it said. It blinked its humanoid eyes, a signal Kat knew meant that it was doing some heavy processing.

"Is something wrong?"

"Please stand by," it said, which Kat knew was bot-speak for *Something is wrong*.

Kat felt her personality field warping with guilt. It was too late for that now. She was here, wasn't she? She could make up for lost time and Martin wouldn't remember her anyway.

Two humans arrived: a woman, tall, gray, and grave, and a short man, red-faced and pretending to be cheerful. Kat picked up on their personality fields and heard scattered thoughts from them. They were dreading this meeting with her and had something to tell her.

The woman introduced herself as the clinic director here at Memory Lane. She was speaking, and the man was also, but Kat wasn't hearing any of their words, only fragments. She wanted to sit down. She remembered that she still had on her golden glasses and bac-mask and removed both.

Sorry. Did all we could. We tried everything.

"You tried? You tried what?"

The woman spoke again, slowly. She looked into Kat's eyes and tried to make contact. "We tried to reach you to tell you that your father died. Three weeks ago."

"Three weeks?"

"You didn't respond to our pings," the director said. "We're so sorry."

"He died three weeks ago?" These were the only words Kat could summon. Now logic flooded in: She had been off the grid. She hadn't thought the people at Memory Lane would have to reach her. When was the last time she had connected with the vid feed to her father's room and watched him?

She couldn't recall.

Over the years, every time she connected to the vid it was always the same: Martin in bed. Being helped out of bed. Being walked around his room by the bots. It was consistently depressing.

She felt her personality field shrinking. There was a tight knot in belly; she put her hand on it. The man and woman waited for Kat to say something else.

"I want to see him now," Kat said. Maybe she could make up for her heartlessness. Maybe she could say goodbye.

"I'm afraid that won't be possible," the man said.

"Why not?" Kat's voice rose, causing the bot behind the desk to look up with its humanoid eyes.

"The policy is…" the man began, but soon lost his words and looked down.

The woman finished for him. "If we don't hear from next of kin, or a guardian, within the agreed amount of time per our records, then cremation is our option."

"You cremated him without asking me?"

The woman's hands fluttered like birds, as if she was quickly sorting her words into an order that made them easier for Kat to agree to. "We pinged you many times. There was no response. We assumed…."

"Assumed *what*?"

"We assumed you were lost in the storm—the latest extreme weather event, you know—or you were in hiding." The woman started speaking faster, adding more details about their decision. "We only had our written instructions in the file. We carried them out. We followed your instructions."

The man found his voice again to cut in. "The instructions were, upon his passing, to cremate. Then, upon further pings and no response, we disposed of the ashes."

Kat didn't remember leaving the facility. Suddenly, she was in a hovercraft, headed back to the Springs. Her eyes were wet; she removed her protective glasses to wipe them and adjusted her bac-mask so that it more completely covered her emotions.

I have a new connection with Ravven, she thought sourly. *Both of my parents are gone. I'm part of the Orphaned Generation now. I'll have to tell her what happened. She'll want to form a circle around it. I'll have to talk to the others about this. They could judge me because I was a coward. I never came here to see Dad, until it was too late.* Then her thoughts flopped the other way. *Maybe the circle will forgive me because I saw Dad too late.*

The bio-memories she had of her father were all the more precious now. On her hovercraft ride back to the Springs, they passed several roadside ad panels running vids to advertise MIND's memex storage. WHY OVERWORK YOUR BIO-MEMORY? LET MIND TAKE OVER YOUR MEMEX. Kat was certain that MIND would use the memories to train itself, to become more expert at beaming ads at everyone, and then would probably sell the memories to marketers and to developers to help them create new apps to capture the citizens' attention.

When Kat had first joined the Resistance, she had told Ravven's circle, "The purpose of MIND is to monetize the inner mind." This had never ceased to be true; MIND's mission had only expanded over time. The Harvester program had spread to nearly every domain with sufficient population density—and they were collecting from the pre-brain, from thoughts that were not fully realized. It was a massive crime. *A rape of consciousness,* Kat had told the circle then. And it was still so.

A surge of rage made her body shake. *How can I stop this planetary crime?*

When the hovercraft driver dropped her off back at the Springs, Kat was spinning with ideas. She wanted to take down MIND's biggest server and make all its operations go dark. She wanted to avoid Ravven, so she decided to take a walk along one of the paths that led away from the meadow. As she walked, memories washed over her. *Let them come! They are mine.*

She would never send her bio-memex to a server owned by MIND, but the average citizen would. Memory was a burden, a task, not a privilege.

She let her own memories overtake her as she walked into the woods, recalling the first time she met Bradley. It was in Los Angeles, in a detention pod. Bradley was a different person then.

It didn't fit to think of Bradley as someone who would be arrested and detained for civil disobedience, but he was involved with Ravven then, before he was involved with Kat.

It had started when Ravven had pushed Bradley to campaign for fair housing at the domain office. The Domain Coordinator wouldn't hear Bradley's idea to make the city's housing more equitable, even though Bradley had waited hours to be seen. They ignored him for days on end. So Ravven had the bad idea that they should storm the building with a micron-demolator and take the Domain Coordinator hostage. It did not go well, and ended with Ravven and Bradley surrounded by enforcement bots and listening to a judge on a vid sentence them to separate pods: hers, in San Francisco, and his in Los Angeles.

Kat knew that Bradley was a mod even before she met him, but she wasn't sure just how his mod would affect her. She got special permission to visit Bradley in his detention pod. When he opened the portal, Kat remembered noticing that Bradley's eyes were a golden brown, and after he looked at Kat for a moment, they turned hazel, and later green. It was just a programming routine that happened automatically, she knew, but she found it both uncanny and creepy. Worse, she couldn't stop how she felt about Bradley. She was drawn to him like he was some kind of appealing puppy, and later, the attraction grew more serious and deeper, pulling her down into a river of emotions she couldn't stop.

"It was just a programming routine," Kat said aloud to calm herself as she walked. This didn't work. The sound of her voice among the trees sparked anger. She was helpless around Bradley, unable to stop his mod's effect on her; and Bradley was unable to stop his attraction to Kat. That moment, that first moment together, was the gateway to so much trouble. She wished it had never happened.

"It can't matter anymore," Kat said out loud again. Kat had met Bradley in

2050. Two years, and yet their entanglement felt just as strong as when they first met. Their personality fields were still entwined and maybe would be forever. What could she do about that? She couldn't forget him.

At the moment, she felt frozen. She made her feet keep walking and plotted how to get a Blanky and take out as many of MIND's cameras as she could. She had to keep up the fight, the public action, no matter what Ravven said. This was not a private struggle. The citizenry needed to see that MIND was not the only way.

A voice in her head that Kat hadn't heard for a while spoke to her. *Bold action,* it said.

It startled her so much that she stopped walking. *Bold action.* What action did it mean?

At the midday meal, Kat cornered Buddha1000 and talked him into loaning her a Blanky. Now she needed a partner: Kat would aim the Blanky, the partner would be a spotter for any approaching bots.

Kat asked Emily to come with her, because Emily had the ear of Amber, and Oona listened to both of them, and Kat imagined the idea of taking out MIND's networks would spread in the circle. But Emily begged off, citing her work at the school. Claire8 was okay to go, but Claire8 wasn't as good, Kat knew, because Claire8 was a loner; the Youngs respected Claire8 but didn't hang out with her.

Claire8 said all the right things, though. "We need both action and contemplation."

Kat smiled. "You're good at making peace between me and Ravven."

Claire8 nodded. "I'm trying to encourage both of you. You were friends once."

Kat met her eye, not sure if that was really true.

Kat and Claire8's trips into neighboring towns expanded. Once the LumaSutra showed no new Receivers in the area and there was no one left to recruit into the circle, they brought out the Blanky and disabled as many cameras as they could. They talked about doing something bigger, like taking out a central server that MIND used for its operations, if only they could locate it. MIND, it turned out, was also good at cloaking and throwing slaze.

One day, on their way back to the Springs, an obvious answer came to Kat. *Bold action.* She needed to make a speech, an address, and make their position clear.

"Are you sure you want to attract that much attention?" Claire8 asked.

"We need something that we can publicize, tell people about. We need to make more noise." The hovercraft enclosure was open and the cold air was helping her mind work. She wanted to make a speech in NewWorker, to demonstrate what the Resistance could do.

Chapter 028

Claire8 liked Kat's idea and added a few of her own. They talked the whole way back to the Springs and sat in the hovercraft cockpit after they landed to talk even more. "I found some bootleg schematics of Harvester Units," Claire8 said. "There's a reset button on all of the Harvesters. An enterprising revolutionary could pull the backpack off an Input Man, hit the reset button, and it would reset all the memories that he'd collected that day."

Kat liked the sound of that. "And right after we reset a few Harvesters, I could address the citizens of NewWorker."

NewWorker was a good place to start because there were already Input Men there, but not much public knowledge of what they were up to. Kat and Claire8 had already been there with the LumaSutra and knew there were Receivers there.

But Ravven said no to the speech. "We have to have a circle about this first," she insisted. "And you have to share about your father."

"What does that have to do with anything?" Kat shot back, and she knew she was wrong the instant she said it.

You must clear some of your pain. The circle will help you.

Ravven convened the circle the next morning in the room where she taught martial arts and yoga. It was a large community room with bare wood floors and skylights in the high A-frame ceiling. Since it was still early, the blast curtains weren't required and natural light shone through.

Kat received a few surprised looks for showing up. The devoted Youngs, like Oona and Amber, asked her how she'd been, with the veiled inference that they hadn't seen much of her lately. Emily wasn't there, having said at the morning meal that she had to work at the school.

Ravven began with a chant in her mind that the others picked up. *Remember who we are. Remember who we are. Remember who we are.*

It was strange to be there, but it also felt good. Kat realized that she'd missed it. The thoughts of the other women wrapped around her like a warm blanket, offsetting the silence in the room.

"Kat would like to share something with us," Ravven announced.

Kat spoke aloud. "I went to visit my father." Her voice started out steady and she kept the tears away. She told of sending Martin to Memory Lane and watching him on the vid as he settled in and admitted to being a coward for not taking him there herself. She recalled how he couldn't remember her name. She said she didn't check in on him often, and even then only by vid.

Kat's tears finally came and she wiped her eyes roughly. Her voice had grown gentle and soft.

"It was so long ago and you were young," Ravven said.

That sounded like an excuse to Kat. "It's true that I was young and busy, but I was also callous. I was wrong to behave as I did."

Ravven started a chant in her mind that the others took up. *Forgive yourself. Forgive yourself. Forgive yourself. Kat, Kat, Kat. Forgive yourself.*

Kat winced as she received these words. It seemed unrealistic that just chanting them would make any difference. She didn't want to forgive herself.

Amber thought into Kat's mind: *It is not your fault that he forgot you. It's not your fault that he didn't know your name anymore. It's not your fault that he died.*

Ravven's thoughts came into Kat's mind also. *You can forgive yourself, but you don't have to forget. You will always have memories of your father.*

The tears came harder. Kat remembered how hard her father had worked to get her into Uni and to pay for it. She remembered how devoted he was to her mother as she was dying. *They were both good people,* Kat thought into the minds of the others.

And you are a good person, Kat, Ravven thought.

Ravven got out a stick of sage, lit it, and spread the heavily scented smoke around the room, then focused the clearing around Kat. Ravven then opened a glass vial of some kind of oil and rubbed it on Kat's inner wrists. The feeling on her wrists was dark and bright at the same time and that made no sense.

This is ridiculous, Kat thought.

But then Ravven began humming and all the women in the room joined her. The humming was larger than the room, powerful enough that the walls seemed to bow outward with the force of it.

When they stopped humming, Ravven asked, "How do you feel?"

Kat surprised herself. "Better," she said.

After a short break and a few deep breaths, Kat proposed going into NewWorker, taking down all the Input Men they could find, and then giving a speech to the citizenry.

All in the circle were in favor.

Chapter 029

They picked a Saturday for the action. The Springs school was closed so Emily could join Kat and Claire8. Oona and Amber stayed back, saying they wanted to help Ravven prepare for an afternoon yoga class. Ravven had refused to come along.

That was a disappointment and Kat had wanted to beg Ravven to come there: *I need you there.*

"Our work is interior now," Ravven had insisted.

Kat bleated back, "Are you just trying to make a point?" She hated herself for saying it. It wasn't what she meant.

"You have your way and I have mine."

"We'll argue this another time," Kat had said.

When Kat and the others arrived in NewWorker in Dot's hovercraft, they saw the Input Men operating in the open, walking the streets and collecting thoughts. Early-model Harvesters had a metal wand that the Input Men had to wave around to collect thoughts; that had been discontinued, so all that was necessary was for an Input Man to walk around with a white backpack and the Harvester did its work.

The Input Men were operating openly because there had been no announcement about them on the Feed. Nobody in town knew who they were. They had simply arrived at the NewWorker glidepath station and begun to collect thoughts as if they had always been there.

Kat tried asking a few people walking by if they knew what the men with the white backpacks on their backs were doing. All she got was smiles and shrugs as the Input Men walked near young couples holding hands on benches, vendors selling bac-masks and air units, and the rare mother with a child.

It was easy work for the Resistance team to come up to an Input Man, one woman in front to distract him, and two behind him to pull off his backpack, find the reset button under its protective cover, press it, and render the Harvester Unit useless until it could be rebooted. Perhaps nobody had ever come up to the Input Men so boldly before; they were stunned, stuttered protests, but carried no weapons with which to fight back. Kat and Emily laughed as one Input Man after another staggered away, trying to get his backpack sorted out and on his back again.

"This is fun," Claire8 said, her eyes jittering with excitement. It *was* fun. It felt like mischief, not civil disobedience.

When Claire8 saw a camera that might have recorded them she pulled out a Blanky, sighted it, waited for the red lights to go on both Blanky and camera, and pressed the button to erase the camera's memory.

The team was beginning to attract some attention, which was the idea. Citizens watched as Kat's group disabled one Harvester backpack after the next. Some people came up to Claire8 and asked her what she was doing with the Blanky and she told them. Kat saw lights going on in people's eyes. She heard their voices in her head. *I didn't know about these Input Men. We can fight this. I am not going to give MIND anything.*

Kat's team reset all the Harvester Units they could find—five of them in the park, three more on neighboring streets, and one on an airway—leaving the Input Men dazed and looking like they'd been mugged by a gang of cheerful pranksters.

Around midday, the sun was high and the heat at its greatest. Kat brought the team over to the shade of some trees in a park for relief. They bought food packets from a vendor, paying with their Secluder accounts. More citizens walked over to ask them who they were and what they were doing. Even a few Input Men stood far away and watched them—with, Kat thought, a hint of admiration.

"She's going to be speaking soon, right over there," Claire8 told the citizens who approached, gesturing to Kat. "Stick around. It will be interesting."

With the rise in attention came a jump in Kat's nerves: She was about to give a speech, her first in a long time. What if the enforcement bots came for them before she could start?

Dot would most likely be mad about the hovercraft. "Borrowing your hovercraft is nothing compared to what's going on at the school," Kat imagined herself snapping back at Dot. "No one asked *my* permission to teach *your* students about my life, and certainly no one asked for my permission to raise a flag with my image on it!"

Dot would argue that she had the flag removed and the curriculum could not be changed.

"That's because you want the funding, so you'll teach what admin says, even if it's filled with omissions and lies," Kat imagined saying. "You teach a story about MIND that isn't true. You don't tell the story of the first Resistance circle that Ravven started. You don't tell the story of all the other circles that formed in New York. Your students will never know about those events. They will be forgotten. The Resistance will fade. Don't you think that is MIND's plan?"

As Kat lay on her back in the artificial grass of the park, looking at the artificial clouds in the sky, she imagined Dot giving in to this reasoning, but she knew it was all a fantasy. The school funding paid for the kitchen; Dot would never do anything to jeopardize the kitchen.

Claire8 interrupted Kat's musings. "It's time."

The park was in the center of town. A glidepath station on its perimeter had advertising panels that showed vids about MIND and other corps. ENTRUST YOUR MEMORY TO US, proclaimed one. STAY OUT ALL DAY IN THE SUN WITHOUT RISK OF CANCER, said an ad for sun suits. Claire8 was noodling around a camera, planning to hijack these ad panels and send a vid of Kat to them as she gave her speech.

It felt scary to be so visible, but Kat reminded herself that the citizens needed to see that it was safe to speak out against MIND. She wanted to take the first step; she needed to model bravery.

So ignoring her jitters, she climbed up on the portable stage that Claire8 and Emily had set up. The pair were busy floating a plastic banner, supported by antigrav, that depicted a stark black-and-white representation of two women pulling a Harvester backpack off the back of an Input Man, with his mouth wide open in surprise. The slogan below the image read FIGHT FOR WHAT YOU LOVE.

Kat was grateful for Claire8 and Emily; she wished Ravven had come along. Ravven added steadiness.

A small crowd of citizens gathered. Some were Receivers cued by a thought package that Emily had beamed out. Others were merely curious, having witnessed Kat's team taking the backpacks from the Input Men and resetting their Harvesters.

Claire8 gave a nod, and Kat stepped to a mark on the stage that Claire8 had made. An antigrav mic hovered before Kat. Her image—hesitant, looking scared—filled the nearby vid boards that Claire8 had hijacked. The small crowd applauded modestly. A few citizens called out, "Fight for what you love," echoing what they saw on the banner suspended above Kat.

An invisible countdown had begun: It wouldn't take long for admin to detect that the ad boards had been highjacked, blank them, and then send out enforcement bots with restraining cables. Kat didn't know how long she had for her speech. Every glimmer or reflection she saw in the park looked like the metal skin of an enforcement bot to her. She took in a breath and seized the microphone that was floating in front of her.

"I am Kat Keeper. Co-leader of the Resistance circle." Modest applause again. "We are fighting something that we can't see, and preserving something inside ourselves that we cannot touch. Our memory of the past, of the recent present—this is all we have left." She thought of her father and then tried not to think of him because it made her start to well up.

Claire8 caught her eye and Kat heard Claire8's voice in her head saying, *Stay strong.*

"We all must fight for what we love. Fight for your memories and your consciousness. They are yours. They don't belong to a corp. Our memories belong to us. Our bio-memory is sacred! Some of you saw us today taking Harvesters from Input Men. We were blanking those Harvesters—stopping a project to monetize your inner thoughts. Our thoughts belong to us! Our memories are ours!"

A man in the crowd began to heckle her. "You don't know what you're talking about! This is all bullshit! You're an agitator!"

Kat leaned in to address him directly. "We have let MIND take what we post on the Feed and use it for itself. MIND gathers our thoughts and pre-thoughts and uses them to train its AI. Their purpose is control. MIND sells what it learns about us to marketing corps so they can fill the vid panels with advertisements to muddle our thoughts."

"You have no way of knowing that! You're lying!" the heckler said.

"You post to the Feed, don't you?" Kat asked.

"So what if I do?"

"That's how it starts. You are giving up a part of yourself when you populate the Feed with your memories, your impressions, your life. Posting is how it starts, but it goes further. We let MIND capture our faces for biometric identification and build a catalog of those images, and cross-reference them with location tracking, gait analysis, palm print recognition, retinal scans—all of which has permitted MIND to build a complete picture of us, almost all aspects of our consciousness."

"I have nothing to hide! I don't care what they know," the heckler said.

Others in the crowd called out "Shut up" and "Let her speak!"

Kat's eyes had fire in them; she knew her words were reaching the people here. She had them. "You don't need to have anything to hide. MIND doesn't care about that! MIND doesn't care about us as individuals. It cares about us as a data set. And what if you live on the fringes? What if you are a failed child or a hacker—or what if you are one of us, with the Resistance? When the bots come for you, MIND has made it easy for you to be tracked." Kat gulped a breath. She scanned the edge of the crowd for a gathering of enforcement bots, but strangely none were in the park so far.

"MIND makes it easy for you to be detained. MIND is free of any morals. As a machine intelligence, MIND by itself has no goals. But MIND is a corp. Corps are a business. MIND's business is the dataset that is inside your head. This information *itself* is an instrument of control. We have become subjects of admin. Admin controls the weather we experience, how much water flows in our pods, whether our lights stay on or go dark. And there is something deeper that MIND seeks to control."

The heckler was quiet now, listening to Kat's words.

"How many of you have children in an admin school?"

A few hands went up.

"I want you to think about something for me. We can't control what they teach in your kid's school. They teach what admin tells them to teach. They teach about MIND. They teach about a past that MIND says happened. But what if the past didn't happen like that? What if parts of the past are missing? I can tell you now that this talk, what I am saying now, will be erased from the archive as soon as MIND discovers it. It will be like it never existed. All my words will be unspoken. I may have just a few minutes left with you before those screens go blank and the bots come streaming in to this park." Kat paused for a moment with her outstretched hand pointing at a screen, to an image of her pointing at the screen and on to infinity in all the other ad boards around the park.

"Your children will never know that I was here, my words will be unsaid, and the records will be erased and the erasure of the erasure will be erased. Who controls the archive? Who controls the archive controls the future! Unless we share this information amongst ourselves, share it off the grid, share it in a circle made of humans, not sims, not holos, not bots, but people. Fellow humans! We must do this, because MIND is tireless. MIND never gets tired, and it will never quit. MIND is closing a loop around us, around everything we do, every day. MIND must be stopped. Fight for what you love!"

The crowd was with her. "Fight for what you love!" they shouted back.

Kat broke into a smile, but then she noticed something that took her smile away. A black spot in the sky, then two. Then three. Drones. They were coming for her, triangulating the coordinates for the enforcement bots that would close in and take her down in restraints. The drones' rapid shadows raced over the artificial grass of the park.

Kat called out in a clear voice, "Friends, my time here with you is short. The drones are coming! You've seen the Input Men here. You've seen them with their Harvesters, gathering your thoughts and pre-thoughts. They are already inside your head. But you can slow their progress! You don't have to give over your memories. You've heard what MIND says: Let us store your memories, and you'll never have to remember anything again!

"Don't offload your bio-mem to MIND's memory storage! It's the beginning of the end of us if we do that. It's the first step to surrendering our consciousness to MIND, and if we do that, MIND will have control, admin will make our decisions for us, and we will no longer have a future, because we will have lost control of our archive. Think about it with me: Bio-memory is what the archive is made of. Who controls the archive controls the future. You can control your future. You can fight for what you love!"

Kat raised her fist and began a chant that the crowd soon took up: *Fight for what you love. Fight for what you love. Fight for what you love.*

Emily and Claire8 were pumping their fists in time to the chant. The crowd joined their voices with a power that seemed to rattle the sky itself.

Kat took in the rebel sound and thought of all the other circles in all the doms who would see the vid of this, even if only for a minute before it was deleted. She hoped that Hopper00 would see the vid and she hoped Ravven would see it, too. Maybe Ravven would, and maybe she would regret that she hadn't come along.

The mic cut out and dropped to the stage with a clatter as the antigrav shut off. The vid panels with Kat's huge image on them went black. Three drones hovered above Kat's head, buzzing.

This is it. The bots can't be far now.

Emily and Claire8 were up on the stage, ready to pull Kat to safety if they could.

But there were no bots. The vid panels in the park resolved to an image of a young woman with bright blond hair and black eyes.

"I am Nora2." Her voice boomed out, seeming to reach every space in the park. "MIND requests a meeting with Kat Keeper." From the vid panels, the woman's eyes sought out Kat and locked on her. "Kat Keeper, are you available at 9 AM tomorrow, New Zealand time? I will arrange a holo meeting."

Chapter 030

The room was prepared and Nora2 was waiting. The holo origin would be cloaked, of course. Kat insisted on that, because she wanted to keep her location secret, but that wouldn't be necessary for long. Nora2 had drones in the air. She had drones over the park when Kat was giving her speech. She had drones in the region of the Springs, where she knew Kat was hiding out with her circle. Nora2 was avidly triangulating and Kat was getting courageous and careless.

Nora2 caught a reflection of herself in her terminal screen and smiled at her own black eyes with a touch of gold at the iris, her blond hair cut short to line up with her chin. Kat was surprised when Nora2 appeared looking this way on all the ad vids in the park. Kat was off-balance; this was good.

There was a quickening in the air of the main room in Bradley's New Zealand safe house, with a sense of cool air somehow entering from outside; this meant that the holo transmission was starting. In a moment Kat's holo was standing to the side of the big window that looked out to the mountain and the lake.

"Nora2," Kat said. "I wouldn't have recognized you."

Nora2 ducked her head, a modest habit she would have to break soon. "Yes, it's my mod. Thank you for agreeing to this meeting."

"Is Bradley with you? Have you animated him yet?"

Oh, so she's going on the offensive, Nora2 thought. That meant she had to start lying right away, but that didn't really bother her. "What do you mean?"

"I assume you have an avatar of him spun up and running."

"Don't you think I'm capable of running this operation myself?" Nora2 looked at the hologram of Kat as though someone was really there.

Kat seemed to back down. "Well, that's not what we're here to discuss. Here's what I want to know: There must be a reason we all haven't been detained yet. It must be that you can't prove that we're guilty. We didn't murder anyone.

It was a tragic accident. Why haven't the committees published their result otherwise?"

Nora2 knew how to play this game. "It's still in progress. You never know what the committees will do, and things could change at any time."

The hologram of Kat nodded; the signal got a little fuzzy for a moment, blurring her face, and then it quickly resolved. "You want to keep us back on our heels."

Nora2 shrugged. "I don't control the committees. They've rounded up a few of you and they could get more."

"Bradley controls the committees. You've spun up his avatar. You're lying about that." Kat paused. "But I do have respect for what you're capable of."

Nora2 saw her opening. "And I have respect for you, Kat Keeper. There are only a few who can get people to listen to them like people listen to you."

"You're flattering me, but it doesn't matter. What does matter is that our protests are bothering you. Our actions are chipping away at your authority.

"Here's what we want. We want you to stop expanding the Harvester program into the Northeast and Northwest doms. We need public hearings. A panel of citizens convened to listen to what you really intend to do. No more secrecy! And I want citizens to hear about your plans for their thoughts and memories."

"Done."

A blip of disbelief from Kat. "What?"

"We can do that. We don't want citizens to think we are taking anything from them without giving something in exchange."

Kat's surprise made it a challenge to find the words at first. "Well, I agree. Thank you for understanding."

Nora2 gestured to her terminal to end the conversation and the holo of Kat disappeared. The meeting was over.

Nora2 took a breath and a moment to appreciate another glorious day here in the Free State of New Zealand. She wanted to make some coffee before she activated Bradley for the day, congratulating herself on not starting him up just yet. He would have dominated the conversation with Kat. Anyway, Nora2 thought, it was more useful for Kat to remain uncertain about whether Bradley was back or not.

Warm coffee mug in hand, Nora2 moved to the window that looked out over the stone fire pit on the deck, and beyond, to the mountains. The mountains were glorious this morning, blue-gray and even turquoise because of the light they received, holding the lake in a grand embrace. According to the local people, the mountains were a place of learning.

Nora2 needed just another few moments before getting started, so she brought her coffee out to the deck and looked out over the lake, a deeper blue than it was yesterday, and gazed beyond it to the mountains. She smiled to herself, thinking that she had never gone hiking up there, and probably never would. There was too much work to do. Nevertheless, the day smiled upon her, and a gentle breeze caressed her face.

Nora2 moved back inside and gestured to activate Bradley.

He came on and looked confused. "Wait, Kat's holo was already here? I thought you were going to activate me before she materialized?"

"It was better that way."

"That's not really fair," Bradley said on his screen, his pixel features warping into an expression of petulance. "You're only saying that because you'd be afraid of me dominating the conversation."

"I did what we needed."

"And she believed you?" Bradley asked.

Nora2 couldn't help how broad her smile had become. She was proud of herself. "Yes, she bought it totally."

"Good, then we are on track." Bradley had already tapped into the vid feed. It showed Ravven teaching her yoga class in a high-ceilinged room. There were twenty students wearing warm clothes. Blankets were scattered here and there. There probably wasn't heat in the building. It was winter in the Springs, and there was a light dusting of snow in the tree branches visible outside.

"Her class gets more popular every day," Nora2 said.

"Yes, now watch this," Bradley said with what sounded like impatience. "Look at her eyes. Watch Ravven closely."

They'd watched many feeds like this, Nora2 and Bradley. He liked to keep tabs on the Springs as Ravven lectured in her classes about Gaia, an Earth spirit of some kind.

"I don't see anything. She's teaching a class."

"Look now," Bradley said.

Nora2 leaned in closer to see what Bradley might be talking about.

"Now," Bradley said again.

Nora2 saw Ravven blink, falter for a moment, and then continue speaking.

"That. You saw, right?"

"She blinked. Wait. You are not doing that," Nora2 said.

"I am. Look. I'll do it again."

Nora2 watched with astonishment as, on cue, Ravven blinked. Ravven waved her hand in front of her face as if there was a bug flying in front of her, frowned, and continued speaking about the Earth spirit Gaia.

"Gaia lives in the Earth and she lives within all of us," Ravven said to the class.

But Nora2 wasn't listening to her. She demanded of Bradley, "What is going on? What are you doing?"

On his oval screen, Bradley smiled with what looked like satisfaction. "I can exploit a vulnerability of her personality field. Ravven can be edgy and obnoxious. I can get into her mind."

Nora2 was confused. "From this distance? We're on the other side of the world."

"Don't forget how closely I've studied Receivers. When I was with Kat, she was my favorite case study. Now, I know that while I'm in this state, it requires a leap of understanding for you. But I have huge processing capacity! Just think of it as a quantum entanglement. Distance, space, time are not factors. Once I am inside a person's mind, I can stay. It's something new. I call it puppeting."

Nora2 was still confused. "You can get into her mind and influence what she does?"

"Now you're getting it. Look, it took some practice. When I first reached out to people, they froze up. Their consciousness was bricked. But I was new at it. Do you want me to make Ravven run around in circles until she is exhausted?"

"No," Nora2 all but shouted. She didn't want to see anything like that.

"It's kind of fun. I think you'd enjoy some of the crazy stuff I've tried. I've found people protesting MIND and made them do stupid things to get themselves detained. There was a group circle leader in Milwaukee who I made take off his clothes in a circle meeting and run out into the street. Unfortunately, or maybe not, he was hit by a tuk-tuk and badly injured."

Nora2 didn't have words. She stared at Bradley on his screen.

"I keep trying to reach Kat. That would complete the circuit, don't you think? I keep pointing my consciousness at her to see if I can take over her mind." His pixel face formed a frown. "It hasn't worked yet." He brightened. "But I've had lots of success with Ravven and I should be happy with that for now. I can influence her thoughts *and* her pre-thoughts."

Nora2 knew pre-thoughts were what a person thought before they knew they were thinking. If Bradley was able to influence pre-thoughts, then Ravven wouldn't realize that the thoughts she had were not her own, but were implanted from the outside.

Bradley confirmed this. "I've been watching the vid feed of her. She's been developing this idea of worship of the Earth, loving the Earth in the form of a spirit. Here, let me play you this vid."

The main screen in the room flickered to life. It showed a poor-quality image of Ravven speaking with Oona and Amber after a martial arts class. They were in a large room with a high ceiling and skylights. "I'm sorry about the quality," Bradley said. "The drone couldn't get closer."

Black lines of static went through the recording, breaking up the image. The audio was bad, but Nora2 thought she heard Ravven saying, "Do you remember when, in our circles, I would say 'in the name of the Great Mother'? She is Gaia, I now realize. Living in the Springs has helped me realize—"

The recording cut out there and Bradley sent the screen to black. "The worship of a nature deity, it's an ancient thing, Ravven didn't come up with it. The Gaia-spirit has been around! It's interesting to see how she uses a focus on Gaia to gather the loyalties of the others. Their personality fields are becoming aligned with hers. I think she would be open to starting a cult. I can push her in that direction."

"A cult," Nora2 said. "Why would she want to start a cult?"

Bradley's pixels formed into a grin. "She doesn't have to want to, you know. It's an idea that I can implant in her mind, and it will flower. I've studied Ravven up close, in life, and now again, from inside this box. She's always been interested in power. I think she believes in Gaia, no mistake there. But she is also invested in her own personal power. She likes it when people are aligned to her personality field. She thrives on it. I can take advantage of that."

"How does this fit in with the goals of MIND," she hesitated, "this puppeting?"

"Ravven leads a circle that is part of the Resistance. She's broken off from Kat, going into this Gaia focus. I can exaggerate the split between them. I think many people will listen to what Ravven says and fewer people will listen to Kat."

Bradley's eyes closed for a moment, signaling that he was processing, an avatar's version of thinking. "Ravven has magic. People love magic. Kat is still a techie. She's never escaped the prison of her logic. People aren't romanced by that. They need romance to spark their courage. So the task ahead for me is to deflect Ravven, make her feel like she has free will, and lead her down the wrong path, into her own cult. That will make her feel good. She'll be motivated."

"I see." Nora2 tried for a big sister-ish tone of indulgence, then realized that she didn't want Bradley to think of her like that. She needed to flirt; she didn't know how. "Is there anything in me that you could exploit? A—what did you call it—a vulnerability of consciousness?"

"No, you're perfect."

She didn't want to be perfect for him. Her mod made her efficient, made all her work effortless, but her mod had a personality that was glossy, unflawed, and, she feared, boring for Bradley. She returned his smile and tried hard to think of some flaws that would intrigue him.

"I tend to overwork. And I can be cold," she said. Both were true, but that wasn't what she wanted to say. It was hard to be interesting. She realized that she would have to work on this more, by herself—develop some ideas, clever phrases or quips, because she could see that Bradley's interest was already drifting away. Talking about work would rein him back in, so she did that.

She had hung a whiteboard on the only empty wall in the large room they were in. She walked to it now and started marking it up. Bradley had always liked whiteboards, and true to form, the eyes in his monitor swiveled to look.

"We've started rolling out the campaign offering archive augmentation." She circled the words "archive augmentation" on the whiteboard.

"Right, right," Bradley said.

This campaign was his idea anyway, but stroking his ego about it would draw his attention back to her.

"Comms units are overloaded with archive information, so in the guise of offering citizens more storage, we gain control of their archive," Bradley said.

"Yes, that's the first phase," Nora2 said. "Citizens like it and they're signing on."

"And how is phase two going?" Bradley's pixel eyes had what could be interpreted as a sly look.

Nora2 was proud of this development, so her words bubbled out. "Sanchez and the team have done an amazing job." She drew on the whiteboard with lines that were thick with purpose and direction. "The citizen merely has to think a data point into storage and we will pick it up, and redirect it into the archive we're keeping for them. It can also access the citizen's consciousness so that we have access to their memories. It's two-way."

"That is good work," Bradley said. "And it's not opt-in?"

She knew what he wanted to hear. "It is not opt-in, but neither is it explicitly mentioned in the Terms of Service."

This was the answer he wanted. "How so, Nora2?"

She loved it when he called her by name; any small endearment was exciting. She considered her words. "It's not a feature. It's a leak. It's a flaw, actually, so if it ever comes up, we can say we didn't mean for it to be there and we will repair it."

"I was hoping that you'd say that. Is it a window into the citizen's entire archive? The team hasn't engineered that yet, have they?" There was what sounded like hope in Bradley's voice.

"No, no," Nora2 said. She didn't want to disappoint, but she had to speak the truth. "The memory leak allows MIND to access and record only *recent* memories. Older memories, the citizen's deeper archive, are filed in a way we can't access yet, but it's only a matter of time. Shall I set up a meeting with you and the team to discuss this? You might have some good ideas for them to speed things along."

"Yes, do that."

"Aren't you glad the channel has been opened?" she asked. She wanted his approval badly but hoped that it didn't show in her voice.

"Yes, of course. Set up something with Sanchez for this week, will you?"

"Yes, I'll get in touch with him now."

Nora2 glanced over at Bradley's screen and saw his eyes were becoming hooded, indicating he was entering a resting state. She welcomed this. She wouldn't be drawn into his avatar personality field for an hour or so, which would give her time to check her reports and the vid feeds from the MIND offices around the world.

Bradley had insisted that cameras be installed inside their primary offices in El Segundo, Antwerp, Dublin, Singapore, and Queensland. He wanted Nora2 to check in on them daily, to get the work vibe of the offices and to make everyone aware that she and Bradley were watching. Sanchez was enhancing the drone program. These black triangular aircraft, with a wingspan of about one meter, carried the usual surveillance equipment such as a high-resolution camera with night vision, but they could also read comms devices, and capture the number-letter string identity of the person carrying the comms. MIND's reach was growing.

Chapter 031

The community dining hall was at capacity. A hundred people or so, with a few dozen people standing along the walls. Dot and Ravven sat side by side at a table, their mingled personality fields projecting an energy of grand irritation.

Across from them, at a smaller table, sat Kat and Emily, with Soma fidgeting on a chair nearby. Kat knew that Dot was getting ready to verbally punish Kat for taking the hovercraft on Saturday, Dot's mushroom-foraging day, and also (more importantly) to take Kat to task for drawing unwelcome attention to the Springs with her speech. That was why Dot had called this meeting, but it was all going to be fine.

Dot banged a salt shaker on the table. The harsh *rap-rap* of impact quieted the chatter in the room and everyone looked at Dot. She held the space with an imperial stare, drinking in the moment.

Kat pasted on a smile, signaling tamped-down anger, entitlement, and impatience, all in a thin line. Emily mirrored it with a similar smile. They waited for Dot to speak.

"We are here," Dot began, "to discuss the drones that have been visiting our community."

This pronouncement sent a ripple of unease through the group. Someone called out, "What drones?" Someone else called out, "Are we being watched?"

Kat was surprised. This was not what she expected Dot to say. Kat looked to Emily, who looked away.

"Calm down, everyone," Dorothy said over the many voices in the hall. "Let's not lose our composure. First I will tell you what has been going on. After that, we will vote on the consequences when the rules of our community have been broken."

Emily jumped to her feet to interrupt with a jumble of words that made no sense. "You make the rules and we try to follow them! But it doesn't matter if we don't know what the rules are!"

"Be quiet. Sit down," Dorothy commanded.

Kat had never heard Dot speak to anyone like that before. "If this has something to do with me taking your hovercraft on Saturday, I apologize for that," Kat said.

"It does not. You may be quiet," Dot responded. "Listen and learn, Kat."

Dot locked eyes on Emily. "Night after night, Emily has been using the school server to look up information about our students. Private information. Personal information. She has also been using it to look up information about herself."

Emily jumped to her feet again. "You have no proof!"

"Sit down, Emily. Tree has confessed."

Emily snapped her head to glare at Tree. He sank in his chair.

"Sit down," Dot said again. Emily did as she was told and Dot continued to fire words at Tree. "Tree, did you know that you were breaking the rules?"

Tree summoned weak words. "I didn't know about *that* rule! Nobody told me." He wouldn't meet Dot's eye and it was obvious that he was lying.

"Nobody told you?" Dot's voice dripped with skepticism.

"That's right. I'm a good teacher! The kids love me."

Dorothy's eyes flared and her voice got louder. "But you gave Emily access to the server. You showed her how to look up private information about our students. That was wrong."

"Emily asked me to do it. I didn't want to. But how can it be wrong when there's nothing there?" Tree said. "Just their names and their parents' names. We already know that."

"But you did more. You asked Soma to resonate with the server to open it up, didn't you?"

Tree nodded miserably.

"You took advantage of a child's good will," Dot said. "You took advantage of his power."

"His free will!" Emily interjected.

"Emily, for the last time..." Dot said.

Again Tree tried to speak, but Dorothy silenced him with a chop of her hand. "It's against school policy to view student records without my permission. I never gave permission for this invasion of privacy. For weeks, Emily has been coming to the school at night, when the building is closed. Tree let her in, gave her server access, and brought in Soma to help."

A murmur went through the crowd in the dining hall. Kat thought they may have believed that there was some kind of romantic connection between Tree and Emily. But if the people in the room had only looked at Emily's embarrassed expression, curdled with a little disgust, they would know that it was not true.

Dot continued. "Emily logged into a chat room for the parents of failed children. I can't tell you more, because it would violate the confidence of those families. Now, in a situation that I believe is related, drones have been visiting the school. They come at night and leave at dawn."

"I've never seen any drones here," Emily said under her breath.

Dot heard her. "Tree made vids of the drones." She gestured and a holographic projection hung in the air. It depicted a time-lapse image of the school and the sky above. In the image, the group watched as time rotated from morning to night: the sun moved across the sky, the lights came on in the upper floor of the school at night, and drones gathered overhead like crows. Then dawn came and the day went by, then the night appeared again, and the drones came again and circled over the school.

As Dot gestured the image away, Ravven spoke for the first time. "Emily has to tell us what she was doing to make the drones come."

Dorothy nodded her approval of her question. "What were you doing?" she asked.

Instead of speaking, Emily squeezed her eyes shut as if to make everything go away.

Dorothy prompted her again, more harshly. "What were you doing that brought the drones to our community?"

Kat started to speak, wanting to protect Emily, but Dorothy moved to silence her with a gesture. "I want Emily to tell us," Dorothy said.

Emily could not.

Kat didn't know what Emily had found on the server; Emily hadn't told her anything. But if Kat had to guess, she would say that if Emily spoke, she would have to tell the story of her own failed mod, her disconnection with her archive, her lost original parents. If Emily spoke, she would have to tell everything, including her love for Soma, a child who did not belong to her but who had embraced her as a mother. If that story were told, it would bring along with it the story of how Soma ended up here at the Springs: abandoned, Kat knew, though she didn't know the details. She only knew that Dot had taken him in, and knowing Dot, that probably involved taking payments of some kind.

Kat assumed that these stories were caught in Emily's throat.

As the room waited for Emily to speak, Ravven began to blink rapidly, as if gripped by an inner impulse. She moved her hands as if to shoo away an insect and leaned forward, putting her hands on the table to say: "Expulsion! Cast her out!"

Dot nodded. "Cast her out!"

"What?" Kat didn't mean to say anything but it burst out.

Ravven stared at Kat. "Cast Emily out! There is no defending this!"

It seemed out of proportion, and Kat sensed a hatred flowing through Ravven. Kat wondered what was wrong.

Ravven spoke the words again, louder, in her clipped Brit-Euro tone. "I move for expulsion. Expulsion! Cast her out! Emily has opened a secret about our school families. She has brought the drones!"

Dorothy nodded again and spoke using the big voice she used to command the kitchen. "We have given the Resistance circle asylum in our community. But Emily Cloudfactor has betrayed our trust. We have to consider the children. They have a right to privacy!"

Kat felt the personality fields of the people in the room shift to support

Dot—not surprising since they came from the surrounding community and Dot fed them for free. Dot ran a school that everyone local respected. There would be no dissent here.

As if feeding on the positive and silent wave of support, Dorothy drew herself up to her full height of five-foot-two and spoke softly. "I cast you out, Emily, I cast you out! You will leave in the morning."

The people in the dining hall responded only with a nod or a downcast look of what looked to Kat like shame.

Chapter 032

Soma was shivering.

"Keep walking," Emily said.

It was dark in the woods but Soma wore a brave smile. Kat wanted to reach out to him and hold him but Emily moved first, stepping closer to the boy and holding his hand. They had to get farther before they could open the tent made of reflective material that would capture the heat of their bodies, and maybe make a fire.

"You know what?" Soma asked suddenly.

He must have needed attention. Emily stopped walking and drew him into a hug. "What?" she asked.

"Today's my birthday," Soma said. "I'm eleven."

Emily hugged him tighter still and Kat saw that Emily's eyes were filled with tears. What was worse, that neither of them knew it was his birthday until he told them, or that he was spending it shivering in the woods?

His eyes were black at the center most of the time, but, Kat supposed because of his mod, they had turned greenish. He was probably afraid.

The plan had been for them to slip out of the Springs three hours before the light came over the tops of the trees. Emily had been ordered to leave, and Kat insisted on going with her. Kat was angry with Dot, disappointed in Ravven, and when Emily said she wanted to take Soma along, Kat's response was, "You're going to need help."

The night before they left, Kat pinged Buddha1000 on comms, made a secret pact with Claire8, and convinced Tree to help them get away. It didn't take much convincing: Tree was deeply ashamed about his confession. He had to have been afraid of Dot to cave like that. He released Soma from the second floor of the schoolhouse in the very early morning, just when Kat and Emily arrived at the front door.

"Mommy!" Soma had cried and ran into Emily's arms.

Tree watched them, then said, "Go." He indicated a path toward the back of the school that Emily had taken before.

Kat and Emily set off walking fast, Soma trying to keep up. They had backpacks with tents in them, a few food packets, and a bottle of water apiece. Taking some of Dot's real water felt like stealing, but they needed it. Kat was uncertain about what Dot would do next, maybe even report them to the committees for taking a child. Every shadow in the dark sky looked like a drone to Kat.

It was January. The woods were cold at this early hour and there were unfamiliar sounds, perhaps birds calling for each other in the dark. There were skittering sounds down low that may have been rodents. Every glint of silver made her think of enforcement bots sent out to hunt them. *Probably just the moon reflecting in a puddle.* She hadn't been out in nature at night in such a long time. She could remember a time when she loved plants, and even maintained her own greenhouse. At one point, when she was with Bradley, she had championed an employee roof garden at his offices. *I've drifted far from nature.*

Emily smiled. She was listening to Kat's thoughts.

As the sun moved through the sky the woods got warmer. They stopped to put on sun jackets and goggles, stopped again for a quick meal of food units, and stopped again when they couldn't walk any farther. Kat sensed their position was far enough from their starting point at the Springs.

Out of her backpack she drew a packet that Claire8 had given her. With a brisk snap of her hand it deployed into a tent shelter, one that glowed a dark metallic blue, like the body of a dragonfly. They went inside. The metallic walls of the tent reflected their body heat. Soma, exhausted, fell asleep on one side of the tent interior. Emily moved close to him and her eyes soon glided shut. Kat tried to make herself stay awake, but failed.

The next thing she knew there were noises outside the tent; her heart clutched with fear. She wished she had brought some kind of weapon. A light was flashing outside the tent, searching for them in the weak illumination of early morning. Kat opened the front tent flap.

A man held the light. He was big, built like a bear. He squeezed the light and it turned off. "You slept late," he said. "The sun has been up for thirty minutes." The cheery sound of his voice was jarring. "Did I surprise you?"

Without quite realizing how, Kat had gotten herself outside of the tent and had put her body in front of it, protecting Emily and Soma from this man.

Behind him, Kat noticed a hovercraft. It had somehow landed silently. There was an awkward moment when nobody spoke. Kat noticed that the man's hands were big like his round body and he wore black nail polish on the fingers of his right hand. His dark beard was flecked with gray. For a moment he appeared to be looking past her, to a distant horizon. She expected him to say something about an obsession, something that he had been chasing for many years. These may have been his inner thoughts; maybe she was picking them up. He wasn't a Receiver, she sensed that. But he had something different about him.

When he finally spoke, his words were utilitarian, not visionary.

"I am Roger Rucker. But nobody calls me by my given name. You can call me Spaceman." He extended a hand and held Kat's firm grip for a moment. He conveyed solidity but his eyes held a deep pain that she could feel like a pulse of heat.

"Wait, you're Spaceman, Buddha1000's friend."

"I am all that," Spaceman said. "I will escort you to safety."

"Back to New York? Buddha1000 has a place for us to stay."

"That's it. I hope the tent was warm. It left a heat signature that was easy to locate with the sensors I have."

"Yes, it was warm," Kat said, her voice still fuzzy with sleep. "But you would know all about that, since you are the inventor of this kind of self-heating tent. You have a fan in my colleague Claire8 Kolassa. She likes creative tech."

Spaceman laughed. "Claire8 is making quite a name for herself in cloakcraft. She puts up a good slaze! She's not with you?"

"No," Kat said. "She stayed behind." It was too complicated to explain in the moment, and Kat saw that Spaceman couldn't resist, with an engineer's enthusiasm, to go on to tell her how the tent worked. "The material of the tent recycles the heat from your body and multiplies it. You'll never be cold in one of those tents. And it deploys nicely as well, and also folds up perfectly." He gestured to the entrance and asked Kat, "Can you get the others out? We have to leave here soon."

Kat parted the entrance flap to reveal Emily and Soma already awake, and Emily packing their things into their backpacks. When they came out of the tent, Spaceman reached out to a tab on it that Kat hadn't seen and tugged at it, and the tent folded up and restored itself to a small packet. He picked it up from the ground and handed it over to her. "We have to keep moving. You've taken a child. There will be trackers soon, to state the obvious." He glanced upward, scanning for black drones.

It took them a few moments to get settled into the hovercraft, and after Spaceman said "Start," it lifted off in complete silence, floated in the air for a moment, and then shot forward with head-snapping velocity, just like a glidepath.

Spaceman noted their speed with a smile, raising his voice to be heard over the noise of the wind. "It has a little something extra, doesn't it?" He pointed to handles by their seats. "There's a place to hold on." Kat would have many opportunities to use the handle on the trip, given the way Spaceman drove, but Soma was delighted.

Back to New York, Kat thought.

Their speedy journey to the south was glidepath-like, in other ways, with greenery that whipped by in a blur outside of the curved windshield. The hovercraft traveled just ten centimeters above the ground, taking on none of the rough terrain below it. Kat realized that Spaceman was staying off the main roads, she guessed to keep from being tracked.

This was proven correct when Spaceman jerked the hovercraft off the dirt path he'd been following and into a stand of trees. Kat involuntarily ducked right and then left as Spaceman course-corrected to avoid one tree or another.

"Stop," Kat cried out when she couldn't stand it anymore. Emily pulled Soma close to her.

"Almost there," Spaceman said. He was driving straight at a tangle of brambles, and at the very last moment he jerked the hovercraft, to aim for a hole in the brambles that looked too small for them to pass through. Somehow they fit.

The hovercraft stopped and set down in a small clearing. The brambles were all around, obscuring the sky above and surrounding them on all sides. Spaceman got out of the hovercraft and motioned for them to follow.

"We have a short window," he said, barely turning his head to address them. Kat caught up with him, curious to know what would happen when he reached the solid wall of brambles he was apparently going to walk straight into. There was nothing but twisted branches and thorns speckled with a few green leaves, a strange metallic sheen here and there.

Then the branches moved and three young men stepped out of a fissure. They wore dark clothes that neatly camouflaged them. They held what looked like crossbows loaded with sharp arrows, and they pointed these at Kat.

A moment later, when Emily and Soma caught up, the young men moved to cover them as well. Time seemed to stop.

One young man, who was standing slightly ahead of the others, asked, "Are these the people?"

"Yes," said Spaceman. "These are the people."

"We are the Resistance," the young man said. "We will take you from here." He gestured into the fissure from which he and the others had emerged. It was dark inside but it seemed to lead to some kind of tunnel.

Kat wasn't about to step into a bramble tunnel with three Youngs whom she didn't know, and also she wanted to say, *But we are the Resistance!*

Emily heard this thought and seemed about to add a thought of her own, but instead Kat heard the young man's voice in her head.

The Resistance can't wait for you. He smiled, lowered his crossbow, and in a smooth, practiced motion, slid it into a sling on his back. The other Youngs did the same.

"You are Receivers?" Kat asked with wide eyes.

"Of course," said the young man, who seemed to be the leader. "The Resistance is growing. With you and without you. You started something that has its own life, you know?"

Kat felt a shiver run up her spine. When Kat and Ravven started the first Resistance circle, they had always hoped for more circles to form independently. And they did, all of them women's circles at first; but this was different. The Resistance had a life of its own now. Kat wasn't sure how she felt about that. Pride? Or maybe worry that she couldn't direct how the movement grew. She looked at Spaceman and wondered what role he played in all of it.

Then the lead Young had a question for her. "Is it true that you know Hopper00?" the young man asked.

"Yes," Kat said. "Hopper00 is something like my mentor. I haven't seen him since he went back to Los Angeles, though." She'd never called Hopper00 a mentor before—her feelings about him were complicated, since he was an agitator and instrument of frustration—but she stopped herself from thinking about it too much. These Youngs were also Receivers, the first male Receivers she'd met aside from Hopper00, and she could already see a shadow crossing the lead youth's expression.

"Hopper00 is a great man," he said, with the implication that if Kat said something to tarnish Hopper00's reputation, she would again be confronting the young man's crossbow. "He is giving demolators to anyone who needs one and his partner Kent is sending plans around to make a firebomb that can be launched from one of these crossbows." He patted the one in the sling on his back.

Kat was surprised to hear that Hopper00 and Kent were advocating violent measures. "What are you using the demolators and firebombs for?"

The lead boy looked at her like she was stupid. "To take down ad panels. We are stopping MIND's campaigns."

"You mean the campaign to get the citizenry to store their bio-mem on MIND's servers?"

The boy smiled. "Especially that one."

Then the other boys got down to business, helping Emily and Soma into what looked like a rectangular box on wheels that fit into parallel rails that disappeared into the darkness of the bramble tunnel. The box was just big enough for Emily and Soma to fit together. The boy Kat was talking to indicated for her to get into another box, along with her backpack and Emily's. No seat or cushion, just an enclosure.

The lead boy gestured into the darkness of the bramble tunnel. "The tunnel goes to New York. Buddha1000 will meet us there."

Spaceman waved a shy little goodbye. "Good luck. I'll see you soon."

"Why can't you come with us?" Kat asked.

"There are only two carts, as you see. And only these fellows know the way. You'll be in good hands with them."

They were ready to go. The lead youth started to push Kat's box cart, moving it along the rails that its wheels neatly slotted into. The wheels in contact with the rails made a rough sound but the cart moved quickly. The youth proved to be a fast runner. Emily and Soma were ahead of Kat in their box, also rushed along by the other two Youngs, also running. The wheels on rails made a repeated clacking, reminding Kat of a memory that she couldn't quite grasp. *These are repurposed train tracks,* she realized.

"Are you going to run all the way to New York?" Kat called out.

"Don't get comfortable," the lead youth said. "I run the first two miles, and then you get out and run the next two. Then we switch."

Kat couldn't help but smile. Then she remembered something Hopper00 had once said. The simple things, the old things, are the best because the Siliconers will forget about them. These box cars were certainly in that category.

The youth picked up on her thoughts and said into her mind, *No motors, no magnetics, no induction, no fields. No trackers.*

Kat looked up and knew why the branches overhead seemed shiny and metallic. She thought into the youth's mind. *That's Faraday material up there, isn't it? The whole thing, this whole tunnel?*

The Young nodded and said aloud over the sound of the wheels and rails, "Spaceman invented it. No fields in here except our personality fields. We can move people upstate and downstate without tracking. He said it was an homage to the Underground Railroad. I never asked him what he meant."

There was so much pride in his voice, Kat decided not to tell him that Michael Faraday invented the Faraday Cage a long time ago, as an electrostatic shield.

The bare wood of the cart hurt her bones as it rattled over the rails.

Chapter 033

Ruling decisively on Emily's expulsion brought Dot and Ravven closer together. Dot began to attend every one of Ravven's yoga classes, and a few of her martial arts classes as well. After class, Dot was always one of the students seeking an audience with Ravven, to ask questions about a pose or a bodily pain that had come up in class. She was building a habit of confiding in Ravven. The growing connection softened the blow, for Ravven, of Kat leaving, and it helped prevent Dot from reporting Emily to the committees.

"She took a child from our school," Dot said one night after the evening meal. "I am free to do it."

"But you wouldn't," Ravven said.

"You know me well."

It would mean you'd have to reveal too much about how Soma came to you, Ravven thought.

Obviously seeking to avoid talking about Soma, Dot changed the topic to her yearly birthday celebration: a "surprise" party that Dot had a hand in planning for herself. This year, it would be capped off by a bonfire in the meadow.

"Terribly grandiose," Dorothy told Ravven, "but I do love the attention! And I love surprises!" Dot laughed her musical laugh, up and down a scale.

Over the next few days, Ravven watched with amusement as the party preparations unfolded; they were impossible to ignore in the Springs since so much of the staff played a part.

Though Tree had disgraced himself with the school server business, he remained the only one who could build a good campfire—and scale it up safely to a bonfire. He was also in charge of shooing the children away if they got too close while the bonfire sent its lively spiral of red sparks into the sky. Alice baked a sheet cake large enough for everyone who came to the bonfire to have a piece, with the precise specification from Dot that each piece of cake served was five centimeters square. Other members of the staff carried benches and chairs to the appointed spot.

On the morning of the party, Dot raised her hands in the dining hall and proclaimed to all present, "I give the children the morning off from school!" All the kids having breakfast at the time cheered.

Ravven saw that there was a purpose to this: It gave Tree the opportunity to rehearse with the children the party songs they would sing for Dot. Ravven glimpsed, through the kitchen doors, the staff preparing a picnic large enough for the hundred people who would attend. Alice was finishing off the icing on the huge cake.

Ravven overheard some kitchen workers talking. "Does anyone know how old she's going to be?"

The other one shrugged. "She never talks about it."

But Ravven knew how old Dot was because she had dipped into Dot's thoughts. Whenever Dot had a thought like *Here I am, another year,* Dot would think of her age. So Ravven knew that Dot was going to turn thirty-one. This was a surprise, given Dorothy's authority and position in the community. But she was an old soul. Born in 2022, Dot remembered when there was more than one Feed, knew the times before the United States became untied, and knew what the Earth was like before the Change. Ravven knew that Dot's parents liked the old names, so they chose Dorothy.

Because Ravven could see into Dot's mind, she knew the darkness at its center. She knew that Dot had come to the Springs out of despair, escaping her parents' death and the resulting ruin of her family. Ravven and Dot shared this inner darkness, a suppressed rage about the world, about what had happened during and after the Change.

Ravven was well aware of her own new, explosive rages. She would get angry at a student in class, or become impatient when training Oona to be a better teacher. Ravven self-diagnosed the problem as free-floating anxiety and had gone to Buddha1000 for help. He gave her herbs and she felt the problem was managed—though from time to time, she considered what Kat would say about an herbal solution to the problem of rage.

"What if the herbs aren't enough?" Kat would ask. She'd probably recommend that Ravven see a doctor in NewWorker, but Ravven knew she would not resort to Western medicine. What she had was better.

If Kat were here, she'd tell her that they were both fierce but in different ways. "I am for something. I defend nature. You are against something. You fight against MIND. But it's not enough to be against something. You have to be for something, too."

It sounded good, but Ravven had no one to share that wisdom with, because Kat wasn't there. She had run away. Ravven felt a surge of rage about that and reminded herself to take more herbs when she got back to her yurt after class.

Ravven and Dorothy had become close for another reason, too. They discovered that they shared a deep love of Gaia. Ravven recalled speaking of the Great Mother back in their circles in New York. "I now realize that I was speaking about a manifestation of Gaia." Ravven and Dot went for walks together on the trails that led away from the meadow, appreciating the Great Mother as she manifested in nature. Their friendship grew during these walks.

Ravven believed, perhaps cynically, that most people could be manipulated or convinced to do something they thought was wrong. People could be weak. Claire8, for example. Ravven had expected Claire8 to run away with Kat and Emily, but Claire8 had stayed in the Springs. She attended all of Ravven's classes and listened to Ravven's talks about Gaia. Why? Ravven didn't trust Claire8. She had a weakness: her passion for and trust in technology. She loved creating devices and somehow she was also interested in Gaia? Ravven suspected that something was going on but didn't know what it was.

Chapter 034

Running and pushing the cart was hard, even if the lead boy wasn't all that heavy, but Kat wanted to do her part. She was starting to see what kind of commitment it would entail to truly stay off the grid over time. Remaining off the grid had cost her an important moment with her father, his final moment. She started to make a mental list of all the small sacrifices she would have to make, but the bramble tunnel opened suddenly to a burst of daylight ahead, enough to cause her to shield her eyes with her hand. When she let go it slowed the cart, but the lead boy was jumping out anyway. Kat rustled in her backpack for her silvery reflective jacket and shrugged it on. She wished she had sunglasses. The air seemed breathable but she guessed the UV was strong.

The boys helped Emily and Soma get out of their cart and put the cart out of sight in the doorway of a nearby abandoned building. The lead boy hopped out of the cart Kat was pushing and stowed it in the same way.

Wherever they were, it smelled like low tide.

The building where the boys hid the carts was made of wood that had been red but since had worn to a muddle of black and gray. Suddenly, Kat, Soma, and Emily were alone: The boys gave them a quick wave of farewell and went off whooping and hollering, pushing each other in the carts, turning from Resistance soldiers back into ordinary kids.

This was marshland. The water washed over a small yellow sign that read 13R-31R. Kat shaded her eyes from the bright light to see what appeared to be a control tower—then realized that this was JFK, the airport, abandoned and left to rot.

A familiar voice boomed out. "Welcome to Sector Q!" Buddha1000 stood in an access road. His van was nearby, parked on the only dry part of the road, most of which had disappeared into a puddle of murky water. His boy Alonzo was by his side.

Buddha1000 didn't have to take them far before they arrived at a settlement. A sign hanging loosely on a pole said HOWARD BEACH. They passed small wood and brick houses that were huddled together, most with water in their basements, Kat assumed, and some on stilts that may have been drier. Buddha1000 was telling her that almost everyone had left this area because of rising marsh water. It was on both sides of the road, colored various shades of grayish-green and red, because of algae, Kat thought, or pollution.

"Anytime a storm comes in, this is all underwater," Buddha1000 said as he drove. Alonzo sat next to him, and Kat on the far passenger side. Emily and Soma were in the back.

"Why did the Youngs drop us off here if the pollution is bad?" Kat asked.

"The dom doesn't care about this sector. Low population means low allocation of resources. Nobody wants to try to fix the pollution. This is what they used to call a Superfund site. They dumped aviation fuel everywhere. At least we're just passing through." Another flash of a smile. "Improvements were made to the place we're headed. Spaceman and his lady Grace started a school there for the kids who live in the neighborhood."

A few minutes later, Buddha1000 pulled to a stop next to a strange silver building raised on spindly black rods.

Buddha1000 jumped out. "Come on, I'll show you inside." He gestured and a door opened, steps folding out from the silver structure. "After you," he said with a gracious wave of his hand. "Welcome to the Bug House." Kat went up the stairs, followed by Emily and Soma.

The silver structure was octagonal inside, with eight smooth silver walls. There was a work table, a basic galley with a cooker, a food storage unit, a massage table, a large chair with a headrest and foot rests that looked like it could tilt back, and lots of cabinets and storage areas. Probably for Buddha1000's supply of herbs and medicines.

"You all must be hungry," Buddha1000 said, and got busy in the galley heating up food packets. "I had to run Tree's business while he was up there, and I'll be glad never to look at another Christmas tree again. That nasty sap gets all over your hands." He made a face and the kids laughed. Soma and Alonzo eyed each other, trying to decide if they should be friends.

As Buddha1000 handed out the food packets, Kat had questions about Tree but kept them to herself. Tree had betrayed Emily; he might report where they were and that they had Soma. Dot would stay quiet, because she had too much to hide about how Soma came to her, but Tree...Kat still didn't trust him.

She watched Buddha1000 settle down at the table to eat with them. He had picked them up after the tunnel, he brought them to his home; she decided that she had to trust him. She looked out of the triangular windows of the Bug House, scanning the street outside for signs of enforcement bots or drones.

She opened the warm foil of her food packet and experienced a stab of nostalgia for the Springs. She already missed eating real food at every meal, like the kale grown in Dot's garden and eggs from her chickens. The logistics of shipping fresh produce into the city had broken down years ago. Fresh food was inaccessible for everyone but the very wealthy. Kat saw a lot of food packets in her future in Sector Q.

Soma, having just turned eleven, was slightly older than Alonzo. Alonzo quickly conscripted Soma into his play area; tucked into a corner of the eight-sided structure was a cache of storybooks, e-book devices, and sketchpads. Soon the boys were reading together. Soma had a hyper-reading speed he could use to finish off a child's storybook in forty-five seconds or so, but Kat saw that he was being sociable, reading at a slower, common speed at first, turning the pages one by one—and then going into hyper mode. He smiled at Alonzo, and asked for another book. Alonzo was now handing Soma book after book and waiting just a moment as Soma burned through them. Next Soma would be asking for physics textbooks. He liked differential equations. It made Kat want to know more about the school Spaceman had started.

Buddha1000 filled her in. The school had been Spaceman's idea; he wanted an independent place that balanced tech and humanity. It was hard, because the parents weren't always on his side. He started the school with his partner, Maribel Grace Moreno, who was known as Grace.

"Grace was Spaceman's lady for a long time," Buddha1000 explained. They were a hot item once but no longer. Lowering his voice so the boys couldn't hear, he said they were platonic now. Soma heard anyway and smiled; he knew what *platonic* meant.

Kat's attention was already racing away. She valued the idea of a school, but she was also thinking about where they were going to live, and she felt protective about Emily and Soma. She'd acted impulsively when she decided to come with Emily, but now the circle was broken again. Maybe she'd made a mistake. What about the Resistance? She hadn't checked for the mind chatter of Receivers in her head and didn't know if any were around. She wished she'd remembered to bring along Claire8's LumaSutra. She'd had to leave Claire8 behind. There was a reason for that, but she couldn't tell Emily. Not yet.

Emily was listening to Buddha1000 talk about the school. She was really going to make a go of being a mother to Soma, Kat thought. How would they enroll Soma in the school without anyone knowing who he was?

Kat asked about the house's protections.

"Spaceman designed it to my specs. It's kind of a living being with sensory capabilities. When it becomes aware of drone tracking, it rises up on its legs and runs away."

"What?"

Buddha1000 laughed. "It takes some getting used to, but when it happens, you'll know!"

Buddha1000 got up from the table and approached the cooker, turned on a valve to make tea. He turned to Kat to add, "Remember you got here without tracking, and the Bug House"—his gesture encompassed the structure they were in—"has countermeasures. No one will find you."

"Good," Kat said. They had a right to be here, and Emily had every right to search in her archive. If she couldn't help her friends preserve and discover their inner life, what business did she have offering that power to strangers? *The Resistance lives on,* she thought, *but in a different way.*

Soma got up suddenly to look out of every window—there were eight of them, one in every wall.

"Is it time for a walk?" Emily suggested.

Buddha1000 gave them directions to the school. "Just down the street. Alonzo, do you want to show them?" As they were leaving, Buddha1000 turned to Kat to say, "Stick around a minute, would you?"

He had a look in his eye that Kat didn't like.

Chapter 035

t turned out that Buddha1000 was a closet capitalist.

"I tried to become an investor in Claire8's LumaSutra but she said no. And I asked her to make a MysticLens."

"I'm afraid to ask what that is," Kat said with a smile.

"It would be a way to see into people. To see what they're made of and if they can be mystics."

"Why would you do that?"

Buddha1000 leaned in toward Kat like he had been waiting for that question. "Look, Kat, healing people is a business. My business. I believe in helping people but I also have to feed myself and my boy—and I'm going to feed you, and Emily and Soma, until you get on your feet here in Sector Q or move on. That all takes crypto in the account."

"What do you want from me?"

"I have a business proposition for you," Buddha1000 said. "You know how to raise funds like a boss."

Kat sunk down in her chair. He probably thought that mentioning her company would make her feel good, but it had the opposite effect. "You need funding?"

"Yes. I want to expand my healing business throughout the domain. You could do this easily, and use the rest of your time to build your movement."

Kat bristled. "Movement-building is not part-time."

Buddha1000 tried to back off. "Didn't mean it like that." He searched for words that wouldn't annoy her and failed.

"Do you think you've got me in a corner?"

Buddha1000 frowned. "No, I'm trying to tell you the truth."

But Kat knew he was trying to drag her back into the techie mindset, with its endless cycle of ideas leading to a pitch for funding, leading to cashing out or failure, leading to the next idea. She felt unbalanced by this, as if the ground beneath her was moving.

Then she realized it actually was. The Bug House was moving.

"Drones!" Buddha1000 called out as he dove downward. "Under the table—grab the handles."

Kat was amazed to discover that there were handles under the table. She held on tight, because the structure rocked from side to side as it walked. They were moving down the street and around the corner—she could see their progress by looking out of one of the windows.

"We won't go far—it's almost over," Buddha1000 said.

They stopped moving. Buddha1000 let go of the handles. "Sorry that surprised you. When the building senses drones it moves away from them. Routine patrols will trigger it." He saw that Kat looked concerned.

"If you're thinking about Soma and Emily, don't worry. If Alonzo comes back and sees the house gone, he'll just find us."

It seemed crazy to Kat, or at best inefficient.

She watched Buddha1000 make himself a cup of tea. "You sure you don't want one?"

Kat shook her head. She had the urge to get out and blank some cameras. She pulled out her Secluder and opened it to the Feed. "Is this okay? I want to check something. It's a Secluder."

Buddla1000 nodded as he sipped his tea.

Kat gestured at the controls on her Secluder and brought up a private news channel. There were a few of them on the web, constantly changing frequencies to avoid being shut down by MIND. During a news story about the Youngs using demolators to destroy advert panels, the small screen on her Secluder bloomed with the fire of a Molotov cocktail as it was thrown into a domain office in Oakland. Another domain office, this one in Lower New York, was also in flames. The Youngs who brought her here had described these things. They were expressions of anarchy but Kat wanted focus.

She needed to recruit folks to disable the Harvester program, because it was plain by now that Nora2 had lied to her: Nora2 hadn't slowed down the Harvester program. No panel of citizens had been convened to hear what MIND really intended to do with the Harvesters. Kat didn't like being lied to. The main channel of the Feed, the officially sanctioned one, carried news about the new memory storage that MIND offered citizens. *"Over 10 million citizens trust MIND with their bio-mem!"*

She shared some of this news with Buddha1000 as an idea took shape in her mind. The next step would be better than resetting some Harvester backpacks. "We have to escalate."

The Harvesters uploaded their memory data to relay stations, which could be destroyed. But maybe it wasn't enough to take down the relay stations. MIND had enormous capacity—it had to have server farms. "We need to find MIND's servers and destroy them." She was watching another firebombing vid on her Secluder. Her face was painted red and orange by the flames glowing on the screen.

"I thought you were a pacifist."

"I'm not talking violence against people, just property." Kat gestured to darken the screen of her Secluder, and the flames faded to black.

Chapter 036

Kat had come to New York without a plan, but now she had one. She would help Emily and Soma get settled somewhere, she would evade detection and detention by enforcement bots, and she would continue the work of the Resistance.

For now, she, Emily, and Soma were all living in the Bug House, but the arrangement was temporary, crowded, and awkward. Buddha1000 had arranged for Soma to attend Spaceman and Grace's Molecular School, and he was taking care of them, but that left Kat feeling unbalanced. She insisted on paying him rent and Buddha1000 seemed happy with that arrangement, but Kat also sensed that he wanted more. She had tried to enter his mind to find out what that might be but had failed to gain access.

They all had been living in the Bug House for a week and already had a routine. In the morning, Buddha1000 and Alonzo took the van into Midtown and Lower New York to seek new clients. They would stop in parks and outside markets and do their routine, with Buddha1000 proclaiming, "I am Buddha1000. Who shall I heal today? Who is ready to walk away from all of their pain?"

Emily would drop Soma at the Molecular School for the day's classes and then go down to the Hudson Market to sell candles that she had made.

Kat was left alone in the Bug House. "This is your time to figure out the next level of the Resistance," Buddha1000 said, "and in your spare time you can get a marketing plan going for me." He smiled his smile that convinced most people to do things for him. It was almost working on Kat.

When the others were gone, she opened a secure channel on Buddha1000's terminal and started to research where MIND's server farms were located so she could destroy them and take down MIND's processing power.

This was the work she wanted to do now, and it was safe to do it in the

Bug House—a house that could protect its occupants.

She told Buddha1000 as much one night over a dinner of food packets. Emily was staying late at a school event with Soma and Alonzo. It was just Kat and Buddha1000 at the table.

"I could get used to living here," she said with a smile. "You're a good host."

"I'm feeling appreciated right now." They were drinking real water from a bottle. He topped off her glass.

Kat gazed out at the abandoned airport. A few red lights blinked on the former control tower. "I had a house once, you know," she said.

"I do know," he said. "You spent a bundle on it."

The Marin house was cleverly designed to adapt to the rising water levels around San Francisco. It was built by an architect for himself, and it used the latest pontoon technology to rise as the sea level rose, cleverly adapting to climate and weather changes. Its showpiece was a greenhouse surrounded by glass that adapted to turn smoky-brown when the sun became too hot, and went transparent again when it was cool.

The architect who had built it for himself and his family was a visionary in some ways, and in other ways not. After committing all his crypto to the house, he assumed that it would be a showpiece for future clients, imagined himself inviting them over to show it off. But to his dismay, one day there were no more clients.

He had tried to change but the world around him had changed faster. His prospective midrange clients were moving into no-lease prefab pods paid for by their employers. It was cheaper and easier to manage, and no architect was required. The pods were built from kits and went up in half a day. The top-range wealthy clients—only a few were needed to support the architect's practice—were taking their expensive tastes for bespoke homes to the Northlands, to escape the alternating storms and heat of the San Francisco Port City. Homes the size of the floating Marin house quickly became vacant. They were too expensive to maintain, except for wealthy people, and everyone—wealthy or not—was afraid that the local climate would only become more difficult to manage with climate controls or clever solutions like blast curtains or light-sensitive glass.

The architect had to sell his showpiece home to raise money to meet his relocation expenses.

"It had a beautiful greenhouse. Your husband liked to work there when he was creating the Universal," Buddha1000 was saying.

Kat sat back in her chair and smiled. The water was good; she took another sip. "He loved working in the greenhouse. He had books of every language laid out on the long tables and he would program all day and only stop to cook for me at night." She paused. "Now tell me something, and tell me the truth. You've waited a long time to reveal your fanboy nature, Buddha1000. When I met you in the ferry building, you didn't let on to any of this."

Buddha1000 grinned. "I was playing it cool. Didn't want to blow it. Tree had no idea who you were but when I saw you in Ossining it was like running into a movie star in a deli."

They both laughed. She knew he was flattering her, but she liked it.

He leaned in. "You're a remarkable person. You should own it. Being famous is only part of why people like you."

"Being famous is baggage," Kat said, waving away the flattery.

"You have a tangled history, Kat. You worked for MIND."

"Yes, I was responsible for employee happiness. I started a garden on the roof so they could have fresh produce."

"Your intentions were the purest of pure."

Kat smirked. "I suppose so. I was naive then, I think." She sensed that Buddha1000 wanted to hear more, but she stopped talking. A silence fell. He excused himself to send some onboarding emails to new clients. Kat found herself thinking about the realtor who did the first walk-through of the Marin house. He was a tall, stylish fellow with a certain flair. They probably would have ended up sleeping together if they weren't trying to close the deal on the house.

The house was already empty for the walk-through, and in the architect's absence, there had been no one to protect it from the recent storms. The roof had holes that leaked, and windows were broken on the side of the home that had faced the worst of the weather.

The realtor had given up trying to cover for the architect-owner and told Kat the truth: "He ran out of money to take care of it. But it's beautiful, isn't it?"

As they walked from one spacious room to the next, Kat thought about the nature that was all around. The house was on pontoons so that it could adapt to the rising bay around it; a steep hill was behind it, leading to a mountain. The location was domesticated and wild at the same time. A short walk away was a café situated on high enough ground that one could walk there on a path, not an airway.

A house like this one gave its owner the illusion of control over nature: floating on the rising waters, creating glass that got smoky when it got too hot in the greenhouse, making smart climate controls to tame the unruly changes that were going on all around. *With houses like me,* the house said, *you can adapt. As long as you are very rich.* Kat was, at that point, so she bought the house.

Kat had experienced the first hints of the Change when she was just fifteen. Before that, she never thought about the air, she just breathed it. The sun was never so bright outside as to require all-body protective clothing. A little sunscreen took care of things just fine. Sunglasses were good accessories; no bac-mask or air units needed. As a girl, Kat ran and played her childhood games effortlessly. And there were those hikes in Greenrock with her parents. No sun suits or air units, no artificial moon.

That past didn't seem real. It seemed like a dream, so hard to hang on to, constantly changing in her mind. She had spent so much crypto on that house in Marin; she told herself it was for the privacy, for the prestige, but what she really bought was the freedom to be in nature on her own terms.

Of course, she renovated it extensively. The house had originally been built from dark wood; she changed all that to a light, honey-colored bamboo that was sustainably sourced. The curved roof looked great, but leaked badly from storm damage. She had it repaired, putting in more skylights and adding blast curtains that automatically closed when their sensors said the UV was too high. She filled the greenhouse with a jungle of plants, many of which didn't exist in nature anymore. She felt she was performing a valuable service, preserving them in something like a plant museum. The house would be a place for her to show off, even if it had failed to become the showpiece its architect-builder had wanted.

Kat intended to invite her employees out to the floating house for meetings and retreats, but she never did. She realized that she wanted to keep the house, and its controlled representation of nature, all to herself. Then she met Dave Serif, her future husband, in the café that one could walk to on a path, not an airway.

The first time Kat brought Dave to the floating house, just being there together sealed the deal between them. He knew he could work at the house for the entire span of his current project, and he especially loved the greenhouse. His project, the Universal, was an instantaneous translation service for all the languages of the world. It was an idyllic existence with Dave in the floating house in Marin, until he got sick.

Kat wasn't making much progress in her quest to find MIND's server farms. She started with the obvious, looking for thermal footprints, because servers emitted heat. She looked for patterns in the electrical grid, because servers needed electricity. She tried a technique called impulse-tracing, which mapped the flow of electronic data. But the server farms were hidden well. It was time to ping Claire8 for help.

Kat had known she would need demolators and had found a supplier and set up a courier to bring them to her. The demolators she bought were the newest models: slim, about a meter long, lightweight and quick to charge. A plasma burst from one of them could do a lot of damage in a short amount of time.

Kat got up from the table where she was working to see if the courier was getting close. Nothing yet. The days were getting longer, stretching out into blue twilight that touched the broken wooden houses on stilts and the bay, with its toxic brown water. New York was in a drought cycle now. It hadn't rained in six months, since the extreme weather event back in September, so the surface area of the bay was receding and the red algae was thriving in the heated air.

Her Secluder released a ping signifying that the courier was close. She walked down the steps of the Bug House and partway down the street to intercept him. No sense in him knowing where she lived. He was a boy of maybe thirteen and arrived riding a Hyperbolic skateboard, known as an anti-grav personal device or AGPD. Slung over his shoulder was a bag that contained four demolators.

"You're sure these are good?" Kat asked.

"They're super good."

She looked them over. They looked good, but she didn't know this new kind of demolator very well. "Can I test?"

The boy made a face but said, "Go ahead."

Kat took one of the demolators in her hands and started the charging sequence by sliding open a protective cover and flipping a red switch. It produced an ominous hum and became slightly warm to the touch. She looked around for something that she could use as a test target. An old street sign on the other side of the road was bent to the side and almost falling over anyway.

She raised the demolator to her waist and pressed the go button. It shook in her hands. Demolators were always hard to handle, and this newer model was slightly better than the old ones. Kat kept it aimed at the street sign. It spat out a transparent blob of plasma that floated to the street sign and made contact. The street sign disappeared in a flash.

"I'll take them."

When Buddha1000 came home later, he cast a sidelong look at the demolators on the table. "I got two new clients in in the Lower City today. The healing business is good! How's the marketing copy coming?"

She didn't tell him that she hadn't started on the marketing copy he'd asked for and never would. Maybe she wanted to start an argument with him instead, or maybe she was getting sick of being a leader in exile, stuck in a crazy spider house in a polluted marsh near an abandoned airport. She had her demolators—that was progress.

"I don't see any sense in promoting your business when I have to stay in hiding."

Buddha1000 laughed.

Kat's eyes went wide. "That's funny?"

"The committees are not coming for you."

The offhand way he said it made her more angry. He was unpacking a sack of herbs in small packets, making a show of working around the demolators that were taking up room on the table.

"You can't know that. Have you ever been the subject of an investigation?"

He snapped back. "I have! When admin wanted to come after me for alimony for my kids, I had to get off the grid in a hurry. They had no right!"

"No right to ask you to support your children?" Kat's voice was sharp.

Buddha1000 waved her away. "They had the numbers all wrong."

"Well, I think the committees are building their case against me."

Buddha1000 laughed again, that big bold laugh that shook the room. She wanted to shake him, put her hands on him to make him stop, but his smile was warm. He was having a good time arguing with her, as he always did. It was a sport. He liked it.

"Kat," he said, "they don't have a case. If they did, something would have happened by now. You want to know my theory?"

"No."

"I'll tell you anyway." He aimed that big smile at her again. Why the hell did it have such a warming effect on her?

The committees charged people with little or no proof. But in this case, any evidence would be hard to come by. The murders that Kat and Ravven were accused of committing occurred in a ship on the way to Mars. Not only were they outside the jurisdiction of Earthly law when it allegedly happened, but all the recording instruments on the ship were destroyed.

"Ravven told me everything," Buddha1000 continued. "You all prayed for their death. A death prayer."

"Maybe it worked."

"Maybe it did, but probably not. You majored in rocketry at Uni, right? So you know. It was the fusion drives, they went bad. Never should have been used. They blew themselves up. Fools. Good riddance, I say, to Bradley and Alon6. Sad for the crew, though."

Kat nodded. "Bradley has an avatar now. It's like he never died. He's never going to stop pursuing me." She would live the rest of her life with the fear of enforcement bots creeping up behind her.

"Don't live in fear. You can't do what you need to do when you are consumed."

He was right. Kat's back felt tight across her shoulders. She spied the ElectroHand on charge in the corner, picked it up, and ran it over her shoulders. It was an awkward maneuver but it helped a little.

"I can do that better," Buddha1000 said.

"You probably can," Kat admitted.

He reached out for the machine, she gave it to him, and he turned it off. Then he gestured for her to lie down on his massage table, set up near one of the eight walls of the house. She knew his work was good; she'd seen him help so many people before. It amazed her that she'd never asked him for a session. She ran down the excuses in her mind: keep a professional distance; just live in his house and nothing else. But maybe it was now her time. She gave in to the feeling. She stretched out and he started working on her shoulders.

His healing touch was amazing. She melted beneath his hands.

"This doesn't mean anything at all," she said into the cushion, her voice slightly muffled.

"What? Oh, no. This is nothing. Just some free healing for a lady who has gotten herself a little too wound up."

Kat smiled into the cushion. He was right. Her fields were all messed up and she felt terrible. With every movement, his hands aligned her. He had a skill, no doubt. He kept at it and she upgraded her opinion of him from healer to magician.

Buddha1000 started to talk gently about his work, in a voice absent of arrogance. People needed this help more than ever, he said. "The world is stressing everybody out. This stress manifests in the belly, in the back, in the feet, in the hands." He moved his touch to her hands and she felt him pulling the negative energy out of them, and then out of her feet, and then her legs. He chanted words in a language she didn't know as he moved his hands to different places on her body. As he did, she felt herself opening and releasing; she really needed to let go. She let his voice and his hands take her.

It wasn't supposed to happen, and it was always supposed to happen, and when it finally happened, it felt good and induced a delicious guilt into Kat's personality field. Buddha1000's hands fit her body perfectly, and when she closed her eyes and moved her hands over his body, her hands gave him deep pleasure, too.

They met just three times after that first time. Buddha1000 was a slow lover, attentive to Kat's emotional fields, and aware of the energy transfer between them, which was beyond what Kat had experienced with sex before.

"I'm remembering something from the first day we met," she remarked on the third afternoon when they were on the sleeping mat together. "Buddha1000 isn't your given name. It's Little, uh, something…" The two of them were alone during the school day, when Emily was out at the market and the boys were at school. Recently, Buddha1000 had told Alonzo that he had to attend school more often. "He can't learn everything from me!" Buddha1000 had said, but Kat suspected that it also gave Buddha1000 and Kat time alone.

"My parents gave me the name Little Brother. Fifty years ago."

"You're fifty?" Kat was shocked. He looked forty at most.

Kat knew this would be their last time together. As deeply as her personality field had merged with Buddha1000's, their relationship never went deeper than the physical connection. Maybe they were supposed to be friends who were intimate, nothing more. It made her sad but she knew it to be true.

Kat woke up alone on Buddha1000's mat. She didn't recall falling asleep and sat up to see him meditating in the center of the Bug House. He opened his eyes and Kat saw that he understood everything.

"You'll need to move out," he said.

She nodded. "I know. Thank you for understanding."

They were cordial after that, in a "just friends" mode that felt strange to Kat, like walking around in an empty pod. The next day, Buddha1000 brought Kat over to Spaceman, who lived in a group of interlocking buildings tumbled together like child's blocks that had fallen over. Spaceman called it Molecular Housing. "Each unit depends on the others and there is a control unit that handles all utilities. I'll take you around sometime." He had room for Kat in one unit and Emily and Soma could move into another right next to Kat.

Spaceman and his now-former romantic partner Grace ran the school that Soma attended, but Kat could see no signs of Grace in Spaceman's pod. She would learn later that Grace lived in another pod by herself. Their mission running the Molecular School was strong enough to support the children they guided, but not strong enough to keep Grace and Spaceman together in the same bed.

Chapter 037

Kat paid her rent to Spaceman by doing her long-delayed marketing work for Buddha1000, writing copy for text ads for his business that he placed on the Feed (vid ads were over his budget), and ads for Molecular Housing, to get more of the units occupied by renters. Emily paid her rent with the proceeds from her candle sales, which were modest and didn't really cover the rent, but Spaceman felt close to Soma, treating him like a grandson. He and Grace not only gave Soma free tuition at the Molecular School, but also asked him to teach a couple classes: a percussion class and one called Spatial Relationships in Three-Dimensional Hyper-math, to some other advanced students.

During the day, Kat went into the markets to recruit Receivers. She would stand in the flow of people, listening to their thoughts, until she found someone, then send a thought to the appropriate woman. *Hello, sister.* Sometimes she was surprised to flush out a man who could Receive. *Hello, brother* felt strange, but *Hello, friend* worked.

Following the pattern she'd established with Ravven, she would invite the woman (or man) to a meeting. If they made it, Kat taught them how to handle the stream of thoughts that entered the mind. She invited a few men into her circle.

Kat's circles were very different from Ravven's. After teaching her new members how to quiet the storm of thoughts in their mind, Kat had little use for chanting, meditation, or yoga. Instead, they discussed how they would take down MIND.

She found a trusted black market source for Secluders and handed out as many as she could get. She taught her recruits how to search for server farms using thermal footprints, seeking the heat that a large group of servers would emit, and she taught impulse-tracing, mapping the flow of data online. Her small group would spend most of their circle time head down, eyes on their Secluders, seeking MIND's weakness. Having still not heard back from Claire8, Kat figured they were her next best hope.

One of her new recruits, Ivorie, had worked on a server farm herself, and wondered if destroying one of MIND's would cause collateral damage. "If MIND's servers are storing citizen memory, won't we destroy that, too?"

Kat wanted to say that the citizens deserved what they got if they were foolish enough to trust MIND with their bio-mem, but knew that would sound bad. She instead explained that they would investigate what the server held before they destroyed it.

Ivorie was modded with a type of hyper-intelligence that allowed her to examine ideas, people, and emotions from many sides. She was an excellent scenario-builder, gaming out consequences of every action. She reminded Kat of Claire8 a little bit. Ivorie's eyes didn't wander independently, but her intellect was far-ranging, and her forehead was smooth and large as if it had swelled to contain her talents. She had shaved her head to accentuate the smooth slope. "Are we safe here, all of us together, pinging? I know these are Secluders, but what about our thermal footprint, and our radio-resonance?"

Kat told her not to worry. She had lined her Molecular Housing unit with Faraday material and had it regularly swept for trackers. Spaceman had also installed alarms that went off if any drones passed by.

Ivorie nodded and went back to her Secluder.

Kat kept working at night, after she, Emily, and Soma shared a meal of food units, or sometimes fresh vegetables that Emily brought home from the market. On a secure terminal, Kat read story after story on the Feed about the Grounder Movement in Los Angeles, led by Hopper00 and his partner Kent. The Feed told Kat that the dom had mounted an offensive against the Grounders, taking down their domes with powerful demolators. The Youngs counterattacked with crossbows that fired Molotov cocktails into dom buildings to set them ablaze. *So it was escalating.* Kat didn't have very long to read these reports posted by helpful citizens. They were quickly deleted by admin.

She bought more demolators and taught her members how to use them. They practiced their aim on abandoned buildings or old street signs, destroying them with plasma streams.

Sometimes Kat saw Spaceman watching with approval from the window of his own Molecular Housing unit. He started dropping by Kat's circle meetings, enough so that she asked him to join them.

"I'd be honored," was his response.

Spaceman had no problem with Kat bringing in demolators to her housing unit. He even helped her get more. He was in favor of sabotage.

"In history," he said, lingering after the others had left circle one day, "dictators are only forced out by people who come in peace at first. Later, those same people get sick of being under the thumb of the lies of the state and they start throwing things." He thought of admin as a dictator and MIND as admin's enabler.

"Have you heard about what Hopper00 is doing with the Youngs in the Port City of LA? The Molotov cocktails rigged up to their crossbows?" Kat asked.

"Yes," Spaceman said, sounding delighted. "Ingenious. Analog crossbows can't be tracked. Unplanned collective violence is the perfect disruption." He advised Kat to be bold.

She took his advice because she felt safe to do so. What convinced her the most was Spaceman's growing affection for Soma. He made Soma a new silverblue suit to replace the worn-out one Soma had been wearing for months. The Molecular Housing they lived in was on its own grid and had the Faraday Material protection that Kat had installed. Spaceman liked the idea and installed Faraday material in his studio and in Emily's unit.

Kat discovered that the Youngs she had recruited were fearless, willing to go out with demolators to practice anytime she asked. "Destroying MIND's property raises the cost of ruling, but we will never sanction violence against people," she said, because they often surprised her with their enthusiasm for demolator use. They were all too ready to blow stuff up.

But even with their assistance, Kat had still not found any MIND server farms. She made her own solo trips into Manhattan and Lower New York to search for clues, carefully observing the Input Men as they moved among market crowds with their Harvester backpacks. From time to time, Kat observed how the Input Men would pause, looking like they were waiting for something to complete. They were connecting, uploading something, she believed.

Kat couldn't remain in one place very long. The sensor Spaceman had given her would often ping, alerting her to the presence of enforcement bots. But one day she tarried long enough to see a pole above the market she was in, with a gray box affixed to it. *What is that?* She moved closer and was inundated by voices and memories—her sensitivity as a Receiver went into overload.

The gray box was a storage unit for bio-mem.

Chapter 038

When Claire8's face finally came up on Kat's Secluder it was past midnight.

"I got your ping. I haven't found any of MIND's server farms," Claire8 said before Kat could speak.

"I've got something else," Kat said. "Remember we talked about relay stations? I found some. Gray boxes. Mounted on poles. The Input Men upload to them. They must connect to the server farms."

"Good theory. Do you want me to come down there to knock them out?"

"No, I need you there to keep an eye on Ravven. I want to know what she's been up to."

Claire8 frowned. "She hasn't been herself. Fits of rage. It makes no sense at all. She keeps teaching about peace but," she stopped. "She's not at peace, that's for sure."

"Keep an eye on her." Something was happening, and this was why it was worth it to keep spies around. The news of rages puzzled her, though. The Youngs she worked with were also attracted to violence. She felt a flash of guilt about this and then moved on. "I'm worried about Ravven."

"Me, too. Maybe it's a blip. I hope she can keep teaching about nature. That's the best thing now."

"Can't agree," Kat said. "But let's not fight."

"No fighting," Claire8 said and smiled. "You got us out of danger in New York and to safety in the Springs. I'm grateful for your leadership. You helped us all stay free." Claire8 paused.

"And you're sure you don't need me to come down there?"

"I need you up there even more."

"Take care, Kat," Claire8 added. Her image blinked out.

The Youngs in Kat's circle *were* eager. They staged their actions out of Kat's Molecular Housing unit, picking up demolators there. Their group—usually between ten and twenty—would attract attention if they traveled together, so they took different forms of transport into Lower New York, some on a vaporetto, others taking tuk-tuks, still others via gondola. A few walked or used electric bikes if they found roads south that weren't flooded.

They would arrive at the Hudson Market as it was finishing up, or at a glidepath station, activate cloakcraft if enforcement bots were present, form an arrow-shaped wedge of Youngs with Kat in the middle, and charge toward a relay box mounted on a pole. Kat would raise the demolator, generate a plasma charge, and destroy the box.

Kat handled the destruction for the first few times, and after that other members of the circle took turns at it. It didn't always go well. Sometimes, when their cloakcraft failed, some members were tangled in restraints fired by the enforcement bots, captured, and carried off for processing.

Often, near the remains of a smoking relay box, was an advert panel playing a vid for MIND's program to collect citizen memory. I FEEL SO MUCH FREER, the testimonials said on the vids. NO MORE MENTAL CLUTTER! I CAN ACCESS MY MEMORIES WHENEVER I WANT. More than once, Kat raised the demolator, let it charge again, and took out the advert panel, too. It made her angry that MIND was collecting thoughts without citizen consent, but it made her furious that MIND was successfully convincing people to *willingly* hand over their bio-mem for storage. Served them right if some of their memories were destroyed by Kat's demolator blasts, even if accidentally.

Kat had planned these actions as well as she could, but she hadn't counted on one thing—when they exploded a relay box, it released its cache of thoughts and memories. They scattered like windblown rain and infiltrated the mind of the Receivers present. She'd feel dizzy for a minute, filled with the memories and thoughts of anonymous people. Once or twice during an action like this, a Young leaned over to puke, overwhelmed with the powerful confusion of thoughts in their head.

But it was a small price to pay, Kat thought. She wanted to stand in the market after destroying a relay box and speak to the citizens about how MIND was using their thoughts and memories to train its AI—how MIND already controlled the climate, banking, the schools, transportation, and shipping, and needed to be stopped before it controlled inside the collective mind of the citizenry.

But she always had to run away. *Run so that I can fight another day.* She'd had a couple of close calls with enforcement bots in the market, but thanks to her skillfully applied cloakcraft, (she had more experience with it than many of the Youngs who came along with her) she had evaded detection or detention.

It wasn't enough. Kat heard rumors that after citizens offloaded their memories to MIND, MIND ran a program to make them forget about the upload. Another rumor: MIND intended to build sims of citizens, duplicating their consciousness in holo form. These sims, the rumors stated, would appear at faculty meetings, ex-spouse's remarriage ceremonies, tiresome school reunions, and assorted other occasions. MIND's marketers were probably assuming that citizens would enjoy the convenience of sending their sims to appointments they didn't want to attend themselves, but the citizens didn't know that building a sim was an opportunity for MIND to collect even more of their consciousness.

The posts about rumors appeared and disappeared quickly, because MIND erased anything that did not serve its purposes. The real question was, who was behind these posts?

The Resistance was growing. There were extremists, like Hopper00, and tech warriors, like herself, and there had to be moderates also. All were trying to gain control of the Feed, the only source of information available on everyone's comms, and some of them were posting.

With each relay Kat destroyed, thoughts were released. They passed through the consciousness of nearby Receivers if they were close, but then the thoughts went off in search of their original owners.

A citizen would be in a café, enjoying a cup of artificial coffee, when she would be struck by a memory from ten years ago: a painful divorce proceeding, a dunk in a cold pool during childhood, advice from a parent who was long dead. It was rattling. The citizen would stand up suddenly and need to leave the café and walk away.

Sometimes the thoughts couldn't find their original owner and dropped down into a stranger. A man would bolt up from his sleeping mat, having someone else's dream of being pursued by wild dogs. He would lie in a sweat in his pod, wondering what had happened. The citizens never connected these disturbing events with releasing their memories to MIND, because of the program MIND had run to help them forget the process.

But as these incidents occurred more often, and Kat destroyed more relays week by week with the help of her cadre of Youngs, the smooth functioning of MIND was disrupted.

After a late-night session at her secure terminal, Kat woke up with her face on the controls, her Secluder pinging. It was Spaceman. He wanted to see her, and it sounded urgent.

Kat went up to Spaceman's place, which actually was three units joined into a studio, and found him seated on a high stool at a worktable, stroking his beard and staring off into space. She hoped he wouldn't notice the imprint of the terminal controls on her face. She'd rubbed at them before she came over, but she was out of water so she couldn't wash.

"Is this about the drone flyovers?" Her latest actions in the city had to be irritating to MIND: Destroying a corp's property always got its attention. They were likely sending the drones to narrow her position and later scoop her up, and the members of her circle. Her hands felt cold so she crossed her arms to warm them.

"It's not that," Spaceman said. "The flyovers are routine." He paused. "Can

I show you something? I've been working on it for most of my life."

His tone of voice was so sad she felt sorry for him. "Yes, of course."

She went with Spaceman on a short walk down the street. Kat shot him a questioning glance.

He answered by saying, "You'll see." They kept walking.

Spaceman led her around the back of a building she hadn't noticed before which faced the polluted bay. "This is the Control Unit. Do you know what it does?"

"Control things?"

Spaceman's smile split his beard and he gestured open the door. "Come in. All the Molecular Housing units are connected and share their climate and water controls with the Control Unit. It allocates power to the units and has the facilities to eliminate waste." His voice turned glum again. "It was made to do so much more."

"How so?"

"People don't like living in terrariums. It's a chronicle of failure. Still, I had to try."

He'd lost her. "What are you talking about?"

"We call this the Control Unit now, but it was actually a terrarium. Originally, I made it to replace the Earth's biome." He reached behind him to seal the door. It closed with a thud and Kat felt the air go still.

Kat felt strange being alone with him and looked around at the room they were in. It was round, all the walls curved. A round table in the middle. One wall was split by a gently curved window that showed off a thick growth of green plants.

"The Control Unit was retrofitted to be the brain of Molecular Housing. But it started out as a biosphere, meant to replicate the Earth's systems. The oxygen we're breathing now is created by running an electrical current through water, to divide oxygen atoms from hydrogen atoms. The nitrogen comes from plants in the other room." He glanced at the glow of green through the window.

"Why create an alternate biome?" Kat asked.

"I started it when I saw the Earth was failing—or more accurately, we were failing the Earth."

Spaceman led Kat on a tour of the facility. The artificial air generator he had built for the Control Unit was a thing of technical beauty, but soon enough the people who had tried to live in here said that the air it produced smelled like farts. "My intention was for brave explorers to live here when the Earth became unlivable." But few people could stand it. "The terrarium effect," he called it.

"Here are the gardens," Spaceman said, opening a round door to the chamber with the plants that they'd seen through the curved window. Lettuces and kale flourished under purple grow lamps. A section of automatic sprinklers turned on for a few moments, turned off, and another section turned on.

"This all takes care of itself?" Kat asked.

"It knows what to do by itself," Spaceman said. "We harvest the lettuce and eat it."

Kat favored him with a smile.

"You've kept it going all these years?" A decade or two, probably, she thought.

"Yes, to prove that self-contained places are possible. They are, from an engineering standpoint. Almost. The human factor trips you up." He told her a story of how the European Space Agency tried to grow algae in an environment like this. *Arthrospira,* it was called. Looked like fusilli pasta. "Arthrospira is good at eating carbon, better at it than trees are. But it didn't work as a food source because the astronauts thought it tasted bad."

"Here are the showers and toilets," Spaceman said, opening a room tiled in white with stainless steel fixtures. It looked too much like a prison, he noted. People who lived in here didn't like it. Worse, he knew that the poop problem had never been solved. He and others had tried high-energy bacteria to break down poop and recycle it into nitrate fertilizer. This took a while and needed monitoring and care. There was one incident, early in the biome project, when the stored poop exploded, painting the walls brown. People didn't like coming in contact with their waste, even if for a higher purpose.

He sighed and said that carbon was the biggest issue in here, just like on the outside. If humans could capture carbon, they could scrub the air and rejuvenate the Earth. "We could put the Earth on a healing path." He had clearly thought about this deeply. "The biosphere was my rehearsal for reconciling our destructive human presence on Earth. Get it right here, I believed, on the inside, and then get it right on the outside, in the wild." His smile was sad, barely present.

Spaceman recalled for Kat when he was a boy, visiting the University of Arizona's Controlled Environment Agriculture Center. "They had a carbon scrubber called a lung. It was made of zeolites, a microporous, crystalline aluminosilicate that pulled in water used to make oxygen. The system was so beautiful, the intent was beautiful. It wasted nothing and didn't need resupply. And yet all it was doing—and all I was doing here—was re-creating something that we already have. The Earth. The beautiful Earth."

Kat noted with surprise that he had started to cry. He hid his face in his hands as he tried to pull himself together. He walked quickly into another room, as if to escape his sudden emotions. She followed.

He tapped an oxygen monitor set into the wall. "If atmospheric oxygen gets less than 19.5 percent, some cells stop functioning, and below 14 percent, the brain is in trouble." He moved to a stationary bike with some wiring connected to it. "I asked people to ride one of these every day for an hour." He spun the pedals.

"It's an oxygen generator," Kat said with amazement. "On a bike."

Spaceman nodded. "Equilibrium is what we wanted. But it's a delicate commodity. And I learned that I couldn't duplicate what is already perfect."

Kat wondered if the Earth's system, the original biome, was too simple or too complicated. Maybe there would never be a technological solution to the damage humans had done to it.

"This is why people are starting over, in the Northlands. I thought about living there, you know?"

"You did?" Kat asked.

"Before it was known."

Kat wanted to cheer him up. "Soma would like it in here. He would love the gauges and meters all around. He'd do his hour a day on an oxygen bike, easy."

It worked; Spaceman smiled. "He would charge the batteries riding on these bikes." He gestured to another row of bikes. "He would say that our artificial water was delicious, even though he knew it was made of his own sweat." He laughed, and Kat joined in, the sound seeming to echo off the walls, not quite filling the emptiness of the place. "It's an imperfect loop" was the last thing he said as they left the room.

She was glad to get out of there. Spaceman unsealed the entry door and they walked into the artificially controlled outside air of Sector Q.

Chapter 039

Hat seemed in a hurry to leave, but Spaceman wanted to linger. He stood for a long while near the dead grasses of the marsh, as the air cooled and the sun went down in a blaze of red. He had a good view of the Molecular Housing structure from here, and could observe it privately. He saw the light remain on the rear chamber on Emily's pod, signaling that Soma was still awake.

He felt a sudden burst of affection for the boy, a feeling that was becoming familiar to him. He'd already given Soma a scholarship to the school, even a teaching position, but it didn't seem like enough.

"I can pick him up from school when you're at the market," Spaceman suggested to Emily. "That way you can stay a little longer."

"Are you sure?"

Spaceman was sure. It became their habit on Mondays and Fridays. Spaceman would wait for Soma on the steps to the school. They would meet up and walk together, sometimes joined by Hamish, whom Soma introduced as his best friend. Hamish was tall and gangly, with a mop of blond hair. He towered over Soma, who was rounder and walked with a slight stoop.

One day, Spaceman saw Soma's eyes dart to the standing water by the side of the road. "You don't go near that water, right?"

Both boys said no, but Spaceman could tell they were lying to protect him.

"It's polluted, runoff from the airport. Promise me you'll stay away from it."

Both boys promised.

"So what do you two like to do for fun?" Spaceman asked in an attempt to engage them.

"We like to memorize," Soma volunteered.

"Memorize what?"

Hamish spoke up. "We memorize the glidepath schedules." He pointed down the road, where a connecting access road led to the glidepath station—a quiet one. Not too many people got off at the old airport stop. "We go in there and look at the trip board and memorize where the trains came from, how long they take, and how much it would cost to get away from here."

He caught Spaceman's attention with the last part. "Get away?"

Hamish looked guilty, his eyes downcast for a moment. It seemed like he was thinking of something to say. He looked up. "When the air is bad we can't go outside. We can't touch the water. My mom and dad spend every evening putting everything on drives. They don't want anything online where MIND can get it." Hamish seemed upset about this.

"Why does that bother you?" Spaceman asked.

"It's all they do every night until they put me to bed. There's no time for anything else but backing up data."

"Don't be sad," Soma said to comfort his friend. "They'll finish and then they'll have more time."

Hamish nodded, not convinced, and Spaceman thought he was right. Staying off-grid took a lot of a person's time.

Spaceman liked asking the boys questions, just to get them talking. The boys tried to accept the world around them because it was all they'd ever known. They had always known MIND to be an agent of control. The false moon projected into the sky was just the moon. The artificial weather that admin created was just as real as the artificial water their parents used to make their artificial coffee in the mornings. A projection of a sunset was as good as a real sunset, and maybe better, because when the air was bad, at least it was something to look at when the day ended.

When Spaceman and Soma arrived at Emily's Molecular Housing unit, Soma had his own ID to card in. The first time they went in together, Spaceman was surprised to see that Soma immediately busied himself with writing or drawing or building. It was clear that Soma wanted Spaceman to watch him.

Bewildered, Spaceman asked, "Can I help you draw? Or do you want me to read to you?"

"No." Soma wanted to be witnessed and for Spaceman to do nothing, whether Soma was drawing or reading or playing the musical bells he used in his compositions. As a child who had spent much of his time after school alone in his own world, Soma just wanted company.

But Spaceman couldn't resist asking questions. Once, Spaceman asked Soma about his habits, like taking off his left sock, always the left, and walking around with one sock on and one off. The boy went into great detail about something he liked to do called "what will happen." It involved mischief, like pushing a package of food units off the table to see what kind of noise they'd make when they hit the floor, or switching Emily's shoes with Kat's, and watching them notice when they tried to put them on and they didn't fit.

As he watched Soma read, the boy said words under his breath. "What are you saying, Soma?" Spaceman was fascinated to learn that Soma's experience of printed words included sounds that each word made when he read them on the page; some words manifested tastes in Soma's mouth when he said them, and most had their own colors. A passage on an e-reader that would be a field of black and white for most people would be a rainbow for Soma.

"Are certain words always the same colors?" Spaceman would ask.

"Yes, always," Soma would say. He pointed to the e-book he was reading. "This is a happy word. It's always golden."

Spaceman bent in to look. The word was *toys*. Soma shared that *mother* was a warm yellow and *hovercraft* was a shimmering blue-green.

When Soma told him these things, Spaceman felt a surge of love for him. It surprised him with its force. It felt infinite. It swept him along in its swift current and tears would spring to his eyes, blurring his vision of the small bright being of Soma.

"Are you okay?" Soma would ask, when he noticed Spaceman rubbing his eyes.

"Yes, no problem," Spaceman said.

I am selfish. I want him close.

Spaceman watched from his position near the dead grasses of the marsh as Emily moved from Soma's darkened room into the main chamber of her unit. She was mostly visible in silhouette, but Spaceman could make out that she sat on a mat that formed itself into a chair, and gazed off into space. He felt a spark of shame; he should not be watching her.

From this vantage point, Spaceman could see all of the Molecular Housing units. Some were lit from within, as the lights of their residents glowed in the evening, and others were dark. He had never achieved full capacity. Not everyone wanted to live in so bare and simple an environment.

Spaceman could become depressed at moments like this, feeling like he had failed. He didn't have Grace to tell him otherwise anymore; their relationship had withered, probably due to his neglect. But, Spaceman reminded himself, now he had Soma.

There was no doubt in his mind that Soma would appreciate his vision: A cycle that embraced plants that breathe with us, soil that processes our waste, bacteria that is our protein. *A perfect loop.* But it wasn't perfect.

Spaceman turned from the Molecular Housing Unit to look behind him at the ruined airport and dead marsh. Plants had grown there once, but the jet fuel poisoned the air and water. Civilization in all its horrible carbon-emitting glory was an evil accelerant, and Spaceman wanted to be ready with a backup biosphere. *But it's nonsense. Impossible to imitate the Earth.*

Closed systems were not the answer, though many had tried them. The International Space Station had to send up food at a cost of $2,770 per kilogram, and the human waste created had to be suctioned up and put into a cargo ship that was set to burn up when it reentered Earth's atmosphere. Literally returning our waste to Gaia in a fireball.

Spaceman had started to listen (with a cloaked IP address) to some bootleg vid streams that Ravven was putting out about Gaia. He enjoyed them. He always had felt a reverence for the Earth. She was a living being whom he wanted to honor.

Cooperation, not domination. To survive, the citizenry had to cooperate with

Gaia and anything else was foolishness. He recalled a Chinese experiment: a biosphere with a mealworm farm. The mealworms feasted on human waste. The humans who lived in that biosphere had to eat packets of mealworms for protein. Nobody likes eating mealworms. *The future can't be eating mealworms. It just can't be that. The problem is that the problem has too many variables. I have to reduce it to a single-variable problem.*

"Fuck single-variable science!" Spaceman said aloud, and looked around to see if anyone had heard him. Of course, there was no one. He spoke softly then, words for himself. "The system is beautifully elaborate. We will never understand it. That's why it's beautiful. Keep that in mind."

He started walking. He wanted to get back to his unit before Ravven started streaming the night's Gaia lesson. He wiped away a tear, thinking about Soma, and walked until he reached the airway that would take him home to his unit.

RESIST

PART 004

Roger Rucker was in his last year of studies at the University of Arizona when he noticed the Change. He was twenty-two and had not yet acquired fame; that would come later, after he was recruited by NASA, had left NASA, and had created the housing that people called pods. In 2030, Roger was just a student on an accelerated track to graduate with top honors, with dual degrees in electrical engineering and mathematics—and it seemed to him that he was always sweating.

His clothes stuck to his body. His shoes squeaked with dampness. If he forgot to wear a hat when he left the dorm in the morning, he hoped that he had remembered a handkerchief to mop his face throughout the day. In Tucson, every day was a little hotter and drier than the last. People would mark this year, 2030, and the month of July, as the beginning of the Change, but scientists who analyzed the patterns said there wasn't any certain turning point; it was more an accumulation of events, until it was finally more serious than anyone could have imagined.

Roger was a local boy. His parents ran the diner in Oracle, about an hour's drive from the university. But he chose the university not for its proximity to home, but for the Biosphere. The moment he heard that the university was hosting the experimental project to create a parallel Earth, he had to see it.

When Roger was eight, he pestered his mom to be the chaperone for the school trip there. Strangely, however, when he later enrolled in the university, his studies aimed him toward the sky, and not to Earth. His days were filled with avionics, orbital calculations, and plans for rockets. He never understood why, instead simply enjoyed his studies.

When the school softball team disbanded because it was too hot to play outside, nobody on the team thought too much of it. A few of Roger's teammates asked him to design high-altitude balloons that would release something to make it rain, or maybe put some satellites in orbit that could control the weather.

Climate control was a topic at a seminar that Roger was part of, but his attention was continually drawn to the hills outside the window, where fires raged and prevailing winds brought smoke down to the athletic fields. Most of the fires were far, in other states where the big changes were happening: Washington, Oregon, and California; Texas and Florida were flooding and enduring hurricane after hurricane.

Tucson, already a desert, became a more fierce, hotter version of itself. It wasn't worth the trouble to move, Roger reasoned, and already his professors treated him like a colleague.

"You'd be tenured in about a minute," John Grandee said. John Grandee, PhD, was an astrophysicist and chair of the math department. His bald head gleamed like a planet. "Nobody else is doing this kind of work in orbital engagement and disengagement anywhere. Plus, the students like you."

"They're my age," Roger said with a smirk. But he liked the idea of being a professor, even if life was just a little boring. There were no more softball games because of the heat, and he had been the pitcher.

When walking back from the cafeteria one Friday after teaching his last class of the week, Roger spied a sign for ROTC signups and walked into the room where a tall officer in a smart uniform was giving a talk about serving your country. That had little appeal for Roger. He never thought much about his country; he just lived there. But then the officer switched to a slide showing some potential programs and gave a little talk about each one. The sniper training program caught Roger's eye.

Roger didn't believe in war, but he believed in precision. He was a mathematician, after all, and the precision of shooting at people from far away was an unparalleled exercise in dynamic calculation. You simply had to be right if you were going to take down your target. Roger liked being right. He was never going to kill anybody; it was just ROTC, after all, and the training simulators were awesome, like video games but with a clean outcome.

Every weekend he reported to McAllen Base and trained. At first, it was indoors, on simulators, and then the cadets went out to a rocky range that had wind, dust, red squirrels, and other distractions that could mess up your shot.

But not Roger's. He was unflappable, his long rifle steady on a rock, the grit playing about his lips and yet never causing him to twitch. He factored in the light wind, usually westerly, exhaled, and depressed the trigger with a motion so gentle that it might not have happened at all. His target, a paper image of a man, took a perfect puncture in the center of the head. It was a magnificent abstraction, like mathematics, and immensely satisfying.

By August 2033, the temperature outside at the college was 100 degrees most days, and on several record-breaking days made it to more than 120 degrees.

Roger was in his office on a Sunday, setting aside the student papers he was supposed to be reading, and his unfinished PhD dissertation on orbital reentry, to fiddle around with a reflective jacket, the kind that runners wear after they finish a marathon to keep warm. He wondered if he could make it work as a cooling suit.

He thought about his youthful infatuation with the Biosphere, with its temperature controls and closed cycles, and smiled. He remembered some of the Biosphere people wearing reflective jackets, but thought it was just to establish a futurist look, not for the purpose of gaining more comfort in impossible heat.

"It all comes around again, eh?" Roger said aloud to himself. "We think we're going forward but we really never go anywhere at all." He touched a thermometer to his warm skin and it registered 98.8, and he started drafting an email to a colleague in the physics department about what the surface area of a silver cooling jacket might have to be to cool somebody five degrees, and at what energy expenditure. Then he saw an email from nasa.gov.

Roger smirked and clicked it open, thinking it was a joke from one of his students. He had grown into a friendly, approachable bear as he aged into his teaching role, with a black beard that blended into his mop of dark hair, his movements slowing since he'd stopped pitching for the team, and becoming more settled as he developed an impressive stillness before he released a round for the kill shot.

Most of his students didn't know he was doing ROTC on the weekends. Some noticed that he liked to wear black nail polish and frequented remote bars in distant towns. "No particular reason," he would say if they asked about the nail polish, volunteering, "I don't go to bars."

He went to remote bars so he wouldn't run into any of his students. The reason for the nail polish was practical. He didn't like the light pollution glinting off his nails when he sighted his telescope to distant planets at night, and the nail polish also kept him from biting his nails as he waited for the moment to make his sniper shot.

It wasn't just the nail polish that gave him the reputation of an eccentric among his students; it was also his constant ideation. He was a man of "what if." *What if you would make a suit that used heated sweat as a power source? Would urine make a good battery acid?* He liked to ask things like that in class. *What if there was a record player that ran on human blood plasma?*

The students laughed, humoring him. He let them nickname him Spaceman because of his penchant for chatting about orbital calculations and his spacey demeanor. They liked his stories and out-loud dreaming about making new ways to live on the Earth.

The email he'd received was actually from NASA, and they were trying to recruit him. His skill at orbital engagement and disengagement calculations was part of the reason. His studies of orbital reentry heating made him an expert in atmospheric heating. They wanted him to work on planetary climate controls.

He was intrigued.

John Grandee, PhD, was pissed. He didn't get up from behind his desk when Roger came, but reached for a cup of coffee that looked cold.

"You wanted to see me?" Grandee asked; of course he knew why.

Roger had already filed the paperwork to leave. This meeting was only a formality. "Sir, they've made me a very good offer. It's a kind of advancement—"

"That we simply can't offer you here," Grandee interrupted. "Yes, yes, I know. Greener pastures." The old man pasted on a smile. "You should take the opportunities offered you, that's certain. We're sorry to lose you, though."

"I'm sorry to go, sir," Roger said, though he wasn't. He was excited to join NASA and go into research full-time.

Dr. Grandee set down the coffee cup with some force and spilled a little coffee on his desk. "We retain the rights to the suit that runs on urine, Dr. Rucker."

Almost nobody called him Dr. Rucker, and for a moment he thought Dr. Grandee was addressing someone else. "Yes, of course," Roger thought to say.

He left the office glad that Dr. Grandee hadn't mentioned retaining any rights to the record player that ran on blood plasma, the eye-motion sensor that charged its own battery twitch by twitch, or the black box that could pick up pre-expressed thoughts (just an idle notion at this point, but one he'd spoken to his students about), or the handheld device that could lock on to a video camera and erase what it had recorded, and then erase evidence of the erasure.

Roger wished now that he hadn't been so chatty about his inventions and ideas, but being friendly and open was his nature. He couldn't help it.

He thought about his students as he packed up his things to move to Texas. One of them, a tall, blond boy with nearly transparent skin had barked out "Working for the Man!" when he learned about Roger's new job. And a student nicknamed Butterfly, because of the exquisite logic that allowed her to float through differential equations, said nothing at first, just pushed down a sob. "You've ruined us for the other professors here. You were too nice."

"I never should have let you call me Spaceman," Roger remembered saying.

"You suck," Butterfly replied.

"Well, at least I'll never see any of you again," Roger said. He was nothing if not honest.

It was a noisy place, this bar in Houston, recommended by his coworkers because they said he might meet somebody there. He couldn't imagine how. It was so noisy, he had to lean in to order his drink and shout the order to the bartender. He didn't know anything about drinking. Even though he went to bars, he only drank tonic water. He'd heard of bourbon and Coke, so he ordered that.

The bartender smirked. He assumed that she knew he didn't know what he was doing in this bar with that drink. He suffered through it, tasting the sickly sweet Coke, thinking of it as a transmission system for disinhibition.

"Want another?" The bartender had leaned in to be heard over the twang of the country-western band.

It was Spaceman's turn to smirk. "Yeah, I guess so. That one was good!" At least he could say that he'd started a conversation with someone. The thought popped into his head that if he were going to sleep with someone in Houston, it would be this bartender. He believed he felt a connection with her personality field. He also knew that this assessment was premature, if not ridiculous.

"Nice nail polish," she said when she returned with the drink.

He noticed that she was wearing the same color.

"What's your name?" he asked.

What she shouted in his ear sounded like, "You have found Grace." He was pretty sure that wasn't at all what she had said, but he liked the sound of it.

Her full name was Maribel Grace Moreno. She had straight black hair, black eyes, and olive skin, and he noticed that she was usually smirking like she knew something that he didn't.

After that first night at the bar, they became the sort of couple who seemed like they would be together forever. They had more than black nail polish in common, of course. Grace also used to work for NASA.

"I did orbital calculations," she told him that first night, in the alley behind the bar. She had introduced him to weed because she took pity on him trying to drink bourbon and Coke. "Just like you, so we are both calc people," she added, using the insider's term for the people whom everyone else relied upon to work out the longer equations.

"Wait a minute," Spaceman said. "How did you know?"

"Your mind casts a big shadow."

"What?"

"Word gets around."

Spaceman felt a small ripple run through him; perhaps he was just a little proud to learn from Grace that he was known as a calc man, and NASA was interested in his side hustles, too, like the body suit that powered itself from the urine of the person who wore it.

"The reflective jackets that protect people from the sun, NASA likes those," she said.

"Wait, the urine suit? How did they know about that?"

"Somebody named Butterfly told them. Shared the drawings."

"My student?"

"Yes, that's right. Admin was recruiting Butterfly also, but she decided not to come. Smart girl. But NASA bought the rights to the urine suit from your old boss. They want you to keep working on it."

"Wait," he said again, a word he would say a lot around Grace, "wait, they knew about Butterfly?" He thought he was coming to NASA to develop planetary atmosphere controls, but it turned out they had other plans for him as well.

"For a smart guy, Roger, you're slow to catch on."

He winced at the sound of his own name. "Call me Spaceman. Everyone does." He was still deciding whether Butterfly had betrayed him or helped by sharing his inventions with NASA. But there was something that he wanted to ask first.

"You said 'admin.' What's admin? We're talking about NASA."

She became quiet for a moment. "So, you don't know."

"Know what?"

She wouldn't tell him during that first meeting, though they smoked two joints and got pretty loose; she needed to trust him more. That would take a few more weeks, and then he asked again.

She told him that she was hired into calc, like he was, with a focus on orbital, but she didn't like the track she was on and decided to become a bartender for a few weeks to sort things out—which became a few years, which was becoming forever.

"I like people more than I like numbers" was the reason that Grace gave him.

It didn't satisfy him; he knew there was more.

"So you want to know what admin is?" she asked. It was her Monday night off from the bar. They were over at his place, the apartment that NASA paid for. It was decent, with a few cushy couches, a chair and a desk, a big bedroom with a comfortable bed. There was a cooking area, but Spaceman had never cooked anything in it in the two months he'd been living there.

"Can we talk about it here?" Spaceman asked, looking around. He always wondered if the place was bugged.

"I don't know," Grace said, then shrugged. "They already know everything and they've listened to everything." She started talking about the old NASA that was a government agency, and the new NASA that had become something else after the breakup.

"The breakup," Spaceman repeated. After the Change got deeper, social upheaval was driven by the altered climate. People in areas afflicted by drought started fighting over water rights, and places where the air was still cool and clear became crowded with visitors who decided to stay. The Feed filled with news of new climate refugees who were leaving the heated south and headed north.

Since the government was slow to act, local people took over power plants to run them, and water was diverted by small groups of rebels, merchants, and mercenaries. Siliconers sent low orbitals up to put metals in the clouds to make it rain. Tech people were experimenting on the Earth, seeking solutions and profits.

With all the climate disruption, it was only a few years later that the government couldn't agree on anything other than to split itself apart. The States took over governance for a while, and when the technocrats and

Siliconers became too powerful, the States banded together and formed domains. This was what people called the "breakup."

Spaceman paid as little attention as possible to government. "So the new NASA, you're saying that it's like its own domain?" he asked.

"It is," Grace agreed. "It's this domain called admin. Run by Siliconers, I think, nobody really knows. Like government without the constraints. What you call NASA became part of it. For a while, the NASA mission stayed the same."

"Build ships?" Spaceman asked. "Go to space?"

"Yes, that." Grace paused. "But not now. It's something else. I don't know the whole picture, because they only gave us pieces to work on."

Compartmentalization, thought Spaceman. "Well, they've got me working on planetary climate controls."

"Yes, exterior weather and urban efficiencies. They like to recruit people for that. It looks good. I didn't want to do it because I didn't want to work on our atmosphere."

"Why? The atmosphere needs help."

"I wasn't sure if I was really helping or treating a symptom." Something else occurred to her. "Did your supervisor have a talk with you yet about the budget?"

"Dr. Arc? No. Why?"

"He will."

"He will? Why?"

But her face closed down. He saw that she wanted to stop talking about it.

It that moment, the reason he was at NASA came into focus for him. The reflective jackets, the body suits that charged themselves on urine batteries: these were all closed-loop environments that couldn't be destabilized by outside forces. You could draw a line between the climbing temperatures outside and what NASA wanted him to do with climate controls on atmospheric heating—and if that didn't work, NASA had a Plan B, which was to exploit his self-contained systems like body suits for survival.

It took just a flash of insight to think of all that, and then Spaceman was aware that Grace was looking at him. They looked at each other for a moment with an unspoken thought between them. He'd wanted to sleep with her since he met her in the bar. The idea popped into his head now and made him smile suddenly, and she widened her eyes to react. Maybe she was in agreement?

He'd had consensual affairs with students. Butterfly had wanted to sleep with him and had asked to, but that was just once. He hadn't been with a woman like Grace, a woman more or less his age; he wasn't specific with things like that when thinking about people. But she had soft eyes that transmitted intelligence, and hands that would feel good on his body, and her words spoken in bed would cover him like a blanket, he was sure.

He blushed, thinking about this, and she noticed. A hint of a smile played around her lips. This was what people called "a moment," Spaceman realized. If he was going to say something, it had better be very good.

"Would you like to have a look at the bedroom?"

It wasn't very good, but it conveyed enough of his meaning so her smile got larger.

The sex was good, and they embarrassed each other when they got loud and made the bed rock. Spaceman didn't get loud very often. The depth of their relationship was a surprise to Grace, Spaceman realized. He assumed that she wasn't looking for a deep connection with anyone, yet here he was.

Chapter 041

Sure enough, one day Spaceman's supervisor called him into his office to discuss the budget. This was the last thing on Spaceman's mind, because the climate was commanding most of his attention. Spaceman's projections showed that Houston would soon not be able to support its population. There wouldn't be enough water, and the heat would be lethal. Scientists were predicting that there would be mass migrations of climate refugees to the Midlands and even as far as the Northlands. Spaceman's comms showed a hurricane on the way up to Houston but he put the device in his pocket to concentrate on the meeting.

Dr. Arc, his supervisor, had large, questioning eyes. They made it hard for Spaceman to look at him for more than a few moments before he felt that he was intruding somehow. But then Dr. Arc did something that threw Spaceman off: He smiled. Dr. Arc never smiled. *He must want something from me.*

"Dr. Rucker, we need to talk about the budget." Arc went on to say that they were in a crunch and the climate control program was affected, but he had a solution. He was going to put Spaceman on the hypersonic missile program.

Spaceman was shocked. "You mean, as in instruments of war?"

"We think of them as deterrence. It's humanitarian, actually. We want to protect ourselves. Some of our people are predicting water wars. And the fact is, we're realists in this department. We can always budget the hypersonic program generously and divert a little to keep other projects going. Your urine suit was very well received at the latest meeting of our higher-ups."

Spaceman was already shaking his head. "I came here to work on climate, not weapons. And the thing is, I don't feel qualified. Hypersonics? I was a sniper in ROTC, but that hardly..."

Dr. Arc joined his hands in a little steeple on his desk, the gesture he always made when he didn't want to be disagreed with, and filled the space between them with talk of atmospheric friction and the advantages and disadvantages of aero-ballistic systems versus hypersonic glide systems.

"I don't want to do it," Spaceman blurted. "I'm a pacifist!"

Grace came home to find Spaceman gathering clothes into backpacks and suitcases. "What's going on?"

"We're leaving," he said.

Spaceman rarely did anything on impulse. His decisions were supported by much scaffolding. Grace took him by the arm and met his eye. "What the hell is going on, Roger?"

"Something happened. We had that budget meeting."

She seemed annoyed with him. "I told you that was going to happen."

"I can't do what they want me to do. I won't support warfare. I am not an instrument of war."

She nodded. He had his principles, early ROTC program notwithstanding. "But you don't have to be a baby about it. We don't have to leave." Then something occurred to her. "Is it the hurricane? The one on the Feed?"

Spaceman shook his head. "It's much worse than that. The hurricane won't make landfall anywhere near here. It's the projections."

"What projections?"

He gestured and his terminal screens flicked on. Grace was often surprised by the technology Spaceman had ahead of everyone else. He was a beta tester for many gestural, sensory, and atmospheric technologies. He had one of the first artificial water units deployed in Houston and his refrigerator was filled with beta food units. Hanging on the wall was a prototype of a silver suit he intended to reduce the burning effects of the sun. "Everything is moving faster. It's not the hurricane. It's the heat. Houston is about to become too hot for people to survive. There are going to be mass migrations by next month."

He gestured to his visualizations and she saw their meaning.

"We have to get ahead of it and we have to get out before we can't and we're trapped here."

"Have you told Dr. Arc?"

Spaceman laughed but also wiped his eyes.

"Honey, what happened in that meeting?"

He pulled her close and buried his face in her hair, inhaling her presence. His voice was muffled. "I can't contribute to their agenda."

"What?"

He glanced at an upper corner of the room because he always suspected that if there was to be a listening device, they would put it there, in the shadows. He moved her slightly away, one hand on either one of her shoulders, and looked her in the eye, his expression impossibly sad.

"Grace, they don't care. The atmospheric program I've been working on is greenwashing. They never intended to have it ready in time. It's too late now. Somebody is going to figure out planetary climate controls, but it's not going to be me. They can outsource it to some tech bro who will figure out how to turn a profit on it and license it back to them."

Spaceman was right about everything. The hurricane didn't make landfall anywhere near Houston, but temperatures rose rapidly and an exodus from the city began.

The roads out of town were clogged with people who carried all their belongings on their backs, lugging their water jugs in wagons, with hovercraft drivers flitting on the perimeter of the long line of walkers, offering surge pricing to those who could afford to be carried away from the chaos.

Not many could, but since Grace and Spaceman got out before the madness, their hovercraft fee wasn't too bad. Snagging a cheap hovercraft ride early on was the only thing that went smoothly. They'd asked to be taken to the Midlands, because it wasn't too far.

The hovercraft driver had tried to warn them. "I'll take your money, and I'll get you there," he'd said, "but they won't let you stay because you don't have jobs."

"We're teachers," Spaceman improvised.

"Teachers? Of what?"

"Math!" Grace said. "We can teach math. I mean, we *do* teach math."

They didn't have any documents to prove this to show the border control bot, the first bot of its kind that Grace had ever seen.

"We can't offer you asylum," it said in a surprisingly sympathetic sim voice.

"Asylum from what?" Grace snapped. Spaceman held her back. Getting mad at a bot wasn't going to do any good.

"Asylum from Houston. From the Southlands," the bot said as if it were the most obvious statement it would make all day.

"Apparently, we are refugees," Grace said to Spaceman.

"You can appeal," the bot said, raising its plastic and metal hand to point. "Join that line over there."

Instead, they walked to the train station, which had been remodeled for something new called the glidepath. It was a metallic bullet of a train bathed in blue light and had been running for only a few months.

"Works on antigrav. Powered by some kind of magnetic induction," Spaceman said with admiration.

Grace wasn't as impressed. "Why does the funding get diverted to things like this and not to climate controls?"

Spaceman shrugged. "It was ever thus."

It seemed to rock gently when they boarded it, feeling more like a boat than a train. They found their seats and strapped in.

A sim voice spoke, seeming to come from nowhere. "Induction will begin." Ever so subtly, their car rose, floated, and then there was a snap of motion. Grace was glad they were strapped in. The scenery outside the window blurred to unrecognizable shapes, and suddenly the blast curtains rattled down and they were in darkness for a moment before the interior lighting came on.

A robot conductor came into their car to collect fares. It had long, delicate metal hands and turned a head that looked too small to be anatomically correct for a human. It was initiating retinal scans. "Eyes, please," it said.

"Where can we go?" Spaceman's strategy was to play dumb and ask the bot an obvious question. Maybe it would surprise him by telling them they could go anywhere.

There was a pause as the bot processed.

"The Northlands will accept you today," the bot said. "After today, the immigration quota in the Northlands will be filled."

"Where else can we go?" Spaceman asked.

"The Northlands will accept you."

"So you've scanned us and that's all you can come up with?"

"Yes. Only the Northlands will accept you today since you are coming from the extreme heat event in the Southlands."

Grace didn't look happy. Spaceman imagined her giving him all kinds of backtalk later. Maybe he could drown her doubt with enthusiasm. "Let's go to the Northlands!"

It took nearly all the credits they had between them. An impossibly short time later, the glidepath was pulling in at a remote station. The doors whisked open and they stepped out to the platform. The glidepath moved on, leaving them alone. There were trees all around. The green was, at least, soothing. The only sound was the wind touching the leaves.

"Now what?" Grace said. "And by the way, I wish you were better at planning."

"Well, me, too. But here we are. There's only one road, so how about we follow it?"

They walked for a moment together in silence, and Spaceman reached for Grace's hand. Their roller bags rolled behind them, on full automatic. It was a beautiful day in August. The air was bright, the sun filtered through the branches, and the road seemed to give a little at their step, like a soft mattress.

Soon they noticed a clearing by the road and there was a man there stooped down, picking at the plants. When he stood up he revealed himself to be very tall. He had close-cropped black hair and wore jeans and a white T-shirt. He walked over and introduced himself right away.

"Hey there, my name is Little Brother." He registered their looks. "Don't ask, because they named me before I turned into a man." He laughed a big laugh and shook their hands, and in his effortless way, drew them into his story. He said, up until two weeks ago, he had been a car mechanic.

"Still got some cars to fix up here! But I had a vision and I've decided to become a healer." He said was studying herbs and came here to this place called the Springs to collect them. Then he asked their names.

"I am Maribel Grace Moreno."

"And you?"

"I am Sp—Dr. Roger Rucker," Spaceman said, swallowing his nickname because he thought it wouldn't make sense to this man in the woods, and maybe he could use a new identity anyway.

"You swallowed something," the tall man said, wagging his finger with a smile. "Another name or another identity. Or an entity!" He moved in close to look into Spaceman's eyes. "You are not well, not well at all."

Spaceman stepped back slightly, not exactly afraid, but cautious.

"I see clouds. I see sadness. Your eyes are afflicted with something like a mist that obscures—" Little Brother interrupted himself to command, "Stick out your tongue."

Spaceman did so; his tongue was coated with a fuzzy gray something. Little Brother grabbed Spaceman's wrist to take his pulse.

"Not serious, not serious," the tall man said. "But serious enough!" He laughed with delight and relief. "Yes, you're lucky, because I can help you."

"Help me what?"

"Become whole again. Restore yourself." He turned to Grace. "And I can help you dispel the cynicism that sometimes afflicts you. I know you've seen a lot, but that makes you a richer person. The weight of your cynicism is as bad as the weight of his sadness." He gestured to Spaceman, who was starting to wonder how they were going to get away from this unstable person they'd encountered in the woods.

Somehow, Little Brother convinced them to join him in his van, parked nearby. The van was painted white, with an unfinished stencil on the side that depicted a person sitting cross-legged in meditation.

"Now sit down here," Little Brother said once they were inside, gesturing to a comfortable chair that looked repurposed from a doctor or dentist's office. "Let's do an examination."

Spaceman hesitated. "I don't know," he began, glancing toward Grace for support.

Little Brother pulled up a chair for Grace to sit in and gestured for her to take it. "What's the problem? You don't trust me? Trust in Little Brother! I have eyes that can see and I have hands that can sense and *I get you,* man."

Spaceman didn't know what to say. "How much is this going to cost?"

"Cost you nothing. First one is always free. That's called marketing! And more, I sense a deep hurt in you, something happened recently that messed you up and I am here to fix it." He turned to Grace. "What hurts him can hurt you, too, Grace, and I can fix it."

This took Spaceman by surprise. How would this odd fellow have a sense of what deep hurt was inside of him? He started to think about how quickly they'd had to leave Houston, and Dr. Arc's demand that Spaceman become an instrument of war, and the failure of the climate controls—and to Spaceman's surprise he started to cry. Tears rolled down his face and words left him. But after a moment he said, "We had to leave so quickly."

"Close your eyes," Little Brother said. Spaceman obeyed.

Little Brother laid his long hands at the top of Spaceman's head, then moved them to cover Spaceman's closed eyes, then placed them on Spaceman's chest and breathed with him for a long time. Eventually, Spaceman fell asleep in the chair.

When Spaceman was resting comfortably and fully asleep, Little Brother crooked a finger to beckon Grace closer. "He's suffering from something like PTSD. He's had trauma. Do you feel this?" he asked softly.

"Yes."

"We call it eco-anxiety. I've seen it a lot."

Grace wasn't sure that she heard correctly. "What?"

"Some call it climate anxiety. I can heal it."

Grace didn't know what to say, so she just nodded. She knew about climate anxiety.

"Now we will attend him, which means we sit with him until he wakes up. It won't be long. But we will hold space for him, waiting for the field around him to change."

"Okay." Grace's voice was shaky. She was feeling something; she didn't know what it was. Little Brother started to speak very quietly, almost to himself, but loud enough for Grace to hear without it disturbing the sleep of Spaceman.

"I had this dream," Little Brother said. "Saw an ambulance that gives comfort. Two Black hands opening the back, welcoming you. A Black Buddha painted on the side. I knew I had to be a healer then. I got myself a van like that. Painted it white. I like the name Buddha1000. What do you think, Grace?"

PART 005

The airway from the glidepath wasn't crowded, but Sanchez reminded himself that it was still early. He'd expected some of his team to be in the office already, but there were always those members of the team who would be surprised by his sudden appearance.

He'd been traveling a lot. Some mornings he woke up and looked out of the window of the pod he'd slept in and saw a generic landscape that didn't reveal its location. He would remind himself that he was in El Segundo, company HQ.

He rubbed his eyes, hoping his team had enough artificial water and artificial coffee. He needed both.

As he walked, some employees coming into work nodded to him and he nodded back, but didn't smile. Sanchez didn't believe in gratuitous smiling. There was a reason for this. He liked to remain hard to read, and therefore feared. His people should do what he asked without question. Now, if they only had coffee. Not the artificial kind.

Sanchez's office was unlocked. There was no reason to lock it because his people were too afraid to go in there when he wasn't in town. His desk was clear. He liked it that way and didn't see the need for drives, papers, or writing implements. They were clutter. Better to keep it all in his head. This was a good practice, in case the committees came after him for information, or a rival corp sent its militia to kidnap him, or he drank too much wine and started talking too much in a restaurant. Leave no trace. Better that way.

He laughed to himself at that last one. He never went to restaurants. He didn't have time. He preferred the company of his wife, Wanda. She and Sanchez had a wine business together and she had better taste in wine than any sommelier. They drank together now, at home. Theirs was a pleasant pod, located inland, in what was once called Brentwood, California.

Sanchez gestured to his monitors to turn them on. The windows to his office dimmed slightly so the screens were easier to see. It was too early for the blast curtains to activate but they would when it was time.

He noticed a presence at the door. It was James20 Delta, his assistant. James was one of a pair of twins who had been raised to work together as a team, both modded at a low level, hence the number 20 in their name, far from a perfect 1. His brother was James20 Sigma.

"Yes?" Sanchez locked James20 Delta in his cool stare.

"I just wanted to know if you needed anything."

It annoyed Sanchez that James20 Delta was in so early; he had wanted some privacy to start the day, now it was gone.

"Where's your brother?" Sanchez asked.

"In data," the boy said. Everything about him annoyed Sanchez: thin, nervous, pale, with darting, uncertain eyes, with a basic mod only good for obeying orders and keeping track of Sanchez's appointments. Both the brothers were just twenty years old, but they couldn't be paid as interns because they'd been modded, and to Human Resources that meant higher pay. These days, even a basic mod was a good career move. But mods had their negatives, too. Nora2 lacked the emotional response that would have made her easier to deal with as a boss, and the James20 twins were timid, shaky individuals. Even when together, they didn't draw enough strength from each other to be bold. Sanchez disliked having the Jameses as assistants, but Bradley had insisted. It was a prestige move, Bradley had said. "Hire a mod, hire two," Bradley had advised. Sanchez wished he hadn't listened.

"Go down and see if Sigma needs anything," Sanchez said.

James20 Delta nodded and left.

Finally, alone to prep for the first meeting on his schedule, with Nora2 and Bradley. Sanchez stared at the screen and gestured at a control, waving his hand to toggle between dark mode and light mode. He usually did this to help himself think, but this time it only hurt his eyes.

Bradley had been a difficult boss when he was alive—exacting, unforgiving, impatient. But as an avatar in a MindVessel, he was worse. That didn't make sense, because the avatar in the Form Factor was supposed to be a perfect copy of the living Bradley's consciousness. It did a fine job of saying the things that Bradley would say, reacting the way Bradley would react, even falling into the same mental traps the real Bradley would fall into. But it was a machine and even more ruthless. It had a killer logic.

Sanchez shrugged it off. No sense overthinking it. He knew there was a movement among scientists and intellectuals to watermark avatars and sims so citizens would be aware of what, and who, was real. Bradley wouldn't like that, and Sanchez mentally added it to his list of things to tell the Jameses about. They needed to look into the watermarking movement and snuff it out.

Sanchez's screen displayed the main room of Bradley's New Zealand retreat. No one was there yet. There was a floor-to-ceiling window that showed mountains resting in shadows, across a lake that was just beginning to be touched by morning. He reminded himself of the time difference between El Segundo, California, and Lake Wanaka in New Zealand. It was six in the morning tomorrow over there.

Nora2 was probably running a little late, since it was so early. In a moment, she would come in and sit at the large wooden table. It was made of real wood, a fetish of the wealthy; they liked real things that everyday people didn't have. She would gesture to activate Bradley's Form Factor from sleep mode. She would spread out her tablet, notepaper—even, sometimes, the indulgence of a pencil made of real wood. She had adopted some of Bradley's old habits, Sanchez knew. Like all rich people, Bradley loved the feel of natural materials in his hands—the rarer, the better. Wood, ceramics, wood, silk, velvet. Sanchez knew the names and was old enough to have encountered some of these things.

Nora2 entered the vid frame and sat at the table. The meeting had started. She had a tablet in her right hand and a cup of coffee, no doubt made with real water and real coffee, in her left hand. The cup was ceramic, a pure white that gleamed with blue from the early morning light. Sanchez hadn't seen a ceramic mug like that in ages.

Nora2 gestured at Bradley's Form Factor. It emitted a soft sound and a subtle flash of light caressed its surface.

"Good morning, Sanchez," Bradley's avatar said.

"Good morning, boss." Sanchez pasted on a smile.

When he started working for Bradley, Sanchez was Bradley's handler, responsible for keeping people away from the boss. Now, as Head of Input, Sanchez led a large team of developers and he oversaw the Harvester program as it expanded city to city. Sanchez knew how to get people to do what he wanted, sometimes with too much force, but you did what you had to do. He made it work.

Now he made some bro-chat with Bradley, bragging about how MIND's absorption into admin had gone super-smooth. "Or it might even be the other way around—maybe admin was absorbed into MIND!" They both laughed at that, Sanchez's big boom of a laugh and Bradley's tinny machine laugh from his Form Factor.

"Corp and dom all one in unified governance. Everything will go more smoothly now," Bradley said.

And more work for me, Sanchez thought. Planetary systems were complicated.

"We are all one now," Bradley was chirping. "This will be fun."

"Sure thing, boss," Sanchez said.

Bradley, even when he was alive, never thought much about the details; they were Sanchez's problem.

"Boss, you want to talk about the Chinese State? They want Harvesters. You know it's going to be our biggest contract yet."

Bradley's image on his screen swiveled its eyes, creating the impression that it was looking at Nora2. "Nora2, put that on the agenda for later."

She nodded and touched her temple. She was going to record the rest of the meeting for her reference.

"Tell me how many domains we have onboard for our Harvester program."

Nora2 was glad to deliver good news. Every domain they had contacted wanted to be onboard. The combination of MIND and admin was a winning one, because it made management so much easier for the domains. Climate controls were taken care of, finances were covered, and human assets managed. MIND ran the global glidepath system; it allocated power regionally; and it watched over the standard curriculum of all the schools.

"Yes," Bradley insisted, "but how many of those contracts have we closed?"

Sanchez detected a glint in Bradley's eye on the screen that was almost real enough to be human. *Bradley's avatar and Nora2 must have some kind of little game going.* It weirded him out to think that they actually had a relationship, woman and machine.

"I'll have to get back to you on the total number," Nora2 said. "Not finalized." She beamed a smile at Bradley's screen.

What a suck up, Sanchez thought.

"It's a new revenue stream for MIND," Bradley said, "but let's not get too puffed up about it. We didn't invent this."

Sanchez knew the history. There were apps called AWS, iCloud, Azure, and Dropbox that stored citizens' memories and sold them back to them, but they were not part of a Brain Command Interface like MIND had developed. Those old corps needed software, but MIND had no boundary. Citizens won't have to do anything; they'll just be using MIND all the time.

Nora2 made a note on her tablet. She probably thought of some good marketing copy. After swiping to a fresh page on her tablet, she spoke. "The ads will go up in the glidepath stations next week. The week following, they go into pods. We'll have coverage on all ad vid boards within two weeks. Here's a look at a few of the first we'll post." Nora2 gestured to the screen and the first ad filled it for Sanchez to see.

The ad showed a man, a start-up bro from the looks of him, walking on an airway in a hurry. He paused, as if trying to remember something, and then the word ACCESS appeared on the screen. The man smiled, his memory refreshed. The scene shifted to another ad. A woman of about twenty in what looked like a scientific research lab took a break from her work. She closed her eyes and the word ACCESS appeared on the screen. A montage of family photos and vids appeared in the air in front of her as holograms. She smiled gratefully. Another ad. A student at Uni was taking notes as she listened to a lecture given by a bot. The word ACCESS appeared on the screen. The student stopped taking notes and let MIND take the notes for her. The student nodded with satisfaction and kicked her feet up on her desk.

"This content pushes out starting tomorrow," Nora2 said.

Bradley's eyes were hooded, signaling that he was processing something. Sanchez wondered if something was going on with Bradley's processing speed. Sometimes his answers had the slightest delay before he spoke.

Anyway, the good news was that the two-way memory interface program thrived. Sanchez opened up another stream on his terminal to read the reports coming in and listened to Nora2 and Bradley at the same time.

Citizens embraced the idea of having MIND store their bio-mem in an external memex, and they had no idea that MIND was poking around in their heads, looking for data to help hone its marketing messages, and strengthen its planetary control over everyone. *Is the citizenry really so trusting?* Sanchez couldn't keep the smirk off his face as he read the internal reports.

Citizens were amazed when they received marketing materials that reflected their inner thoughts. People would exit the glidepath, look at a screen, and feel pleased to see what looked like warm family memories in an ad on the wall. "It's almost like they're reading my mind," citizens would say with a laugh of delight.

Maybe they'd never realize that MIND had opened up a hole in their personal memory, and was pulling their memories, even some pre-thoughts.

Bradley addressed Sanchez, snapping him back to the meeting.

"Have you been watching Spaceman?"

Sanchez blanked for a moment. *Spaceman? Who is that and why am I supposed to be watching him?* Bradley tossed out so many orders; after all, he was a machine with lots of mem, and Sanchez a mere human who may have missed something. But then Sanchez remembered. Spaceman: the inventor of Molecular Housing and many of the devices that helped keep people off the grid. "Yes, his location hasn't changed," Sanchez reported after sneaking a glance at another screen he'd gestured open.

"I may have found a way to puppet him," Bradley said. "He has a flaw, just like Ravven does, that I can exploit."

"Interesting," Sanchez said, pretending to be interested.

Chapter 043

The Metro 7th Street Station smelled like sour old piss, but when had it ever smelled good? Hopper00 had spent so much time down in these stinking passageways, he would have thought he would be immune to the smell by now, but he wasn't. He put his left hand over his nose and mouth, wishing he'd remembered to bring an air unit. In his right hand he held a demolator, which he held low against his side, concealing it in his loose black jacket that went to his knees. He had been a subway griot for a long time now—years in these fragrant tunnels preaching social change, fair housing, and freedom from the grid—and now he needed things to accelerate. Words were not enough anymore, he thought, as he gripped the demolator but kept it concealed.

He felt strong today, but it was just an illusion. He was taking more pills to bring him the energy he needed to do what was necessary. There was nothing he could do about his failing memory, though, and he wasn't about to get himself modded. *I'm an Old, that's all there is to it. Suck it up.*

If he only could remember the names of the two Youngs who were supposed to meet him here in the station. He'd made a point of memorizing their names as an exercise to keep his aging brain sharp. *Damn it, what were they?* He saw them coming down the stairs from the upper part of the station. *Their names are Bru and Goh.* It popped into his head just in time.

"Bru, Goh, do you boys know who I am?"

The boys were barely able to speak, they were so in awe of Hopper00, of meeting the real person, standing there before them. Hopper00 smiled at their discomfort, flattered by it. They were probably expecting to meet a low-level revolutionary, not the main man.

"You're Hopper00," Bru said, his voice barely a squeak. He had a light EastEuro accent.

"I am. But I'm just another person like you are, so drop your shoulders, breathe, and relax, all right?" No sense in them getting all wrapped around themselves.

The boys nodded and even dropped their shoulders a little as instructed.

Bru had a long face, like a tall glass, and Goh had a red, round face, like a playing piece in a game of checkers. "Do you know how old I am?" he asked the boys.

"You were born in 2000 in Yellow Springs, Ohio," Goh said brightly.

"Do you know where Yellow Springs is, or was?" Hopper00 asked.

The boy's face clouded. He didn't.

"It's alright. It doesn't exist anymore. There is no more Ohio either. It became part of the Midwest Domain."

Fifty-three years to be alive didn't seem like a long time, but so much had changed in Hopper00's lifetime, it was quite a long time, indeed. And he'd lived a hard life, as a drug addict, sometime–sex worker, and gossip writer, all before he became a revolutionary star. *But don't let your ego take over.* "Okay," he said to the boys, as if bringing a meeting to order, "let's get started. Do you know what this is?" He held up the demolator.

The platform was just beginning to fill up with commuters, and a few were taken aback by the sight of a man in a long black coat holding a device usually used on construction sites to demolish things. Hopper00 smiled his most reassuring smile and concealed the demolator again.

Of course the boys knew what it was. "What are we going to destroy today?" Bru asked. His eyes were bright.

"I'll show you." Hopper walked them over to an ad panel screen. More people were filling the platform now and the signs said a train was due in nine minutes. The vid panel was playing an ad about buying personal memex storage for yourself. BE FREE! FREE YOURSELF FROM THE BURDEN OF MEMORY!

"Look at this," he told the boys, nodding toward the large advert. It was off on a different ad now, but with the same pitch: for MIND to take away the burden of having to remember things. You offloaded your images, words, places, and times, and let MIND do the remembering. "Why is this bad?"

Hopper00 asked the boys.

This time it was Goh who spoke first. "Who controls the archive controls the future," he said.

"That's right!" Hopper00 said. "You have been listening to my talks, haven't you?"

The boy blushed, or at least it appeared that way in the dim light of the Metro. "Absolutely, sir."

Hopper00 waved his left hand around. "You don't have to call me sir. Call me Hopper00." He turned to the other boy. "Bru, what do you think of this advert?"

"It's a small jump from memory control to total control. Allocation is everything."

"Right again!" Hopper00 grinned broadly. "You are the right Youngs for the job."

The boys grinned back, but their smiles looked to Hopper00 to be a little restless and frozen on their faces. They were eyeing a few enforcement bots rolling around the platform. The bots hadn't gathered around the boys and Hopper00 yet, but they would soon enough.

"Okay, enough preamble," Hopper00 said, trying not to rush things. "We're going to start with this vid panel. I see those enforcement bots, probably already monitoring us. After I do this one, I'm going to run upstairs, and then you will take out two more panels before you run upstairs. Disappear into the crowds as best as you can. Understood?"

And with that, Hopper00 raised the demolator, flipped open the safety latch, and pressed the red button. The demolator shook in his hands, and he had trouble controlling the plasma stream, but it was good enough. The plasma flowed over the advert panel and it rattled fiercely, developed an unsightly bulge in the middle, and exploded into a tangle of wires and smoke.

Just at that moment, a train arrived in the station platform. The doors opened and the people inside froze at the sight of the smoking ad panel and tried to force their way back into the car. Citizens on the platform already began to run for the stairs. An alarm began to sound from the train, which powered up and left the station as quickly as it came.

"Panic is good cover," Hopper00 called out over the sucking wind of the train's exit. "Here," he said, handing the demolator to Bru. "Do what I said." He headed for the stairs.

Bru raised the demolator, flipped open the latch, and hit the red button, directing another plasma blow at the panel, severing the last of the wires supporting it. It fell from the wall and crashed to the platform. Citizens screamed. The boys ran for the stairs.

Hopper00 hadn't told the boys that his real job at this stage was to divert the enforcement bots from them so they could make it to the upper level and demolate a few more ad vid panels. Hopper00 performed his role admirably, merely by standing in place, measuring with his eyes the speed at which the bots were swarming toward him, their low, round bodies crowded together like beetles. Metro patrons, running in the opposite direction of the destruction of the advert panel, had another obstacle to jump over, as the enforcement bots clustered toward their target, Hopper00. The next train was coming into the station.

"Hello, gentlemen," he said to the bots when they were close, thinking that it sounded like bad movie dialogue from a 2D movie—but 2D movies weren't popular anymore, so nobody would know. Hopper walked backward, barely glancing over his shoulder, and pressed the emergency button on the outside of the train, causing the train doors to fly open and a shrill alarm to sound.

With every door open, he ran through the train car to the doors on the opposite side of the car. After a brief hesitation, because his knees were hurting pretty badly, he jumped down to the tracks, wincing, then stepping carefully to avoid being electrocuted. As he vanished into the darkness, the enforcement bots gathered in the train car Hopper had left behind. Their wheels were small, and they were not equipped to jump down to the tracks.

Hopper00's knees were really hurting now, but he kept moving in the darkness, limping, navigating by memory and stumbling on something that squished under his feet. He peeled off his black jacket and threw it into an incinerator with full carbon capture, where it flared orange briefly and was gone, the sound of a fan suctioning away the products of combustion.

Pulling a folded Faraday suit from his pants pocket, he stopped for a moment to rest his aching knees and to put it on. He was breathing hard but knew he had to make it to the Grounder community where Kent and the others were waiting for him.

Chapter 044

It was a good plan, until it went bad. Hopper00 stood before the aboveground entrance to the Grounder pod community. Below the surface, behind a door that was concealed by a tarp, were twenty-five domes for living underground, all configured to be free of ad vid panels, have no Feed, and no influence from MIND. All Hopper00 had to do to be home and safe, off the grid, was pull the tarp aside and open the door that led to the stairs.

But when he saw enforcement bots swarming around the tarp, waiting for him, Hopper00 went to the back entrance. No bots there. He opened the portal and noticed something strange. There was a *pop,* indicating a change in air pressure.

He heard Kent's voice calling up from below. "Who's that?"

"It's me," Hopper00 called back.

"We're being invaded by bots," Kent called out.

Hopper hurried to close the portal behind him, sealed it, and clambered down the spiral stairs into the large central room of his underground pod. He saw Kent and Bru at the pod's air tube, a large, round hole in the wall that went to the surface. Air was distributed through the intake to the underground pod.

"What's happening?"

Bru looked relieved to see him, but Kent made a sour face.

"The air tube," Kent said. "Blocked." Kent gestured to a security screen, the only screen in the pod. It showed an exterior view of the airshaft poking out of the ground, snug along the wall of a building. The enforcement bots had found it, swarmed it, and were blocking it off. "No air is coming in. We only have a few tanks of oxygen as backup. We're running out of air to breathe down here."

Hopper00 cursed. The community was a hive, each underground chamber sharing resources with the rest: air, artificial water, and electricity. It borrowed the famed principles of Roger Rucker's Molecular Housing Control Unit.

Kent had studied Molecular Housing in architecture school.

When Kent and Hopper00 started the Grounder movement, Kent brought the building expertise. Hopper00 was a kind of salesman in the Metro, touting the benefits of living underground and off the grid.

The first units were made in LA in 2051, located in a huge underground vault storage long abandoned by the domain. Hopper00 got permission from the dom, or at least he thought he had permission. But the dom didn't believe the Grounder movement would ever catch on. These settlements were *underground.* Who would want to live in a cellar with no sky?

Turned out, a lot of people. To keep up with demand, Kent and Hopper00 built Grounder settlements beneath the port of Los Angeles, in large storage vaults abandoned by the domain. A new real estate market opened up as brokers started to include Grounder domes in their open houses. Tech barons bought underground domes as investment vehicles and rented them out at low rates to the poor. Kent made the dome plans open-source and showed anyone who wanted to how to build their own housing.

The movement thrived, and Grounders came to cherish their independence. The domes were unhooked from admin's power, water, and air systems, and they had no adverts. There no were screens in a Grounder pod, aside from personal comms, and a few terminals connected to a private network Kent set up that allowed conversations between pods. Grounders enjoyed being free.

Soon, however, the Grounder community's popularity became a liability. The dom sent enforcement bots to Grounder territory around the Port of Los Angeles. They scanned for air vents using thermal sensors. Whenever the bots found a pipe, they swarmed to clog it, cutting off the air supply. These actions went on for weeks.

Hopper00 believed the only defense was to mount a strong offense. He asked Kent to print out crossbows from the 3D printer they used to make parts for the ventilation and water systems. Kent showed Grounders how to make Molotov cocktails that they fired at dom district offices. As the dom offices burned, Grounders assembled to shout, *Stop the bots and let us breathe!*

Grounder construction crews had demolators they used to clear the underground caverns to make their pods. Using demolators as weapons against the dom was the next step. Grounders assembled before the dom offices and launched plasma at them, taking out entire exterior walls at a time. The chant went up again, *Stop the bots and let us breathe!*

The bots kept at it, though, week after week, until they found the underground pod that Hopper00 and Kent occupied.

Hopper00 could feel his throat closing off and his eyes were dry. He blamed himself for starting a fight with the biggest bully in the neighborhood, the domain. But it was too late to back away now.

Then he had an idea. "Give me that demolator," he said, holding out his hand.

Bru handed him a demolator from a nearby table. Hopper00 popped it into a charger to power up. He turned to Kent with the idea of sending the demolator up the clogged air shaft and using it to blow out the obstructing bots.

"Okay, but how will you get it up there? We're down here," Kent said.

Bru said, "We can use some of our O2 to make a pneumatic."

Kent objected. "We already don't have enough air to breathe."

He was overruled by Hopper00. "Sometimes you gotta take a risk. We can use some of our spare O2 from the backup." He looked at Bru. "What do you need to make a pneumatic?"

"I'll make it at the 3D printer." Bru got right to work. He tapped out a few commands on the terminal to bring up a design that he could modify.

Hopper00 didn't want to distract the boy—Bru was intensely focused on preparing to print out what they needed—but Hopper00 had just remembered something. "What happened to Goh? The other kid who was with us?"

Bru didn't break his gaze from the terminal. "When we were running away I lost sight of him. He never made it here." Hopper00 saw that Bru's eyes were red-rimmed and his mouth was set in a tense line.

A minute later, Bru opened the printer to take out the finished pneumatic.

It was a globe with a fitting to attach the demolator to and a funnel to focus the plasma into a narrow stream. Bru filled the globe with oxygen from one of their spare tanks and attached it to the demolator, now fully charged.

"We're ready," Bru said. "I want to do it." He pushed past Hopper00 to set up the demolator/pneumatic combo in the clogged airshaft. After it was positioned, he flipped back the protective cover on the demolator, took a nervous breath; with one hand he pressed the red button on the demolator and with the other he opened the O2 valve on the pneumatic.

It happened fast. He had to pull his hands out of the airshaft to avoid injury. The demolator shot upward, out of sight, and there was an explosive rumble as the plasma turned the enforcement bots to shrapnel. The airshaft was open and fresh air came into the pod. Hopper00 was about to celebrate when he noticed that something was happening to Bru.

Bru shook his fists over his head. "Let there be RAGE!" The boy's motions were jerky, like his muscles were stiff; he stalked around the pod, biting off his words. "We will take the demolators, and we will go into the streets and push back the bots. This is our settlement! Let there be RAGE! STOP THE BOTS AND LET US BREATHE!"

Hopper00 reached out, hoping a hand on Bru's arm would calm him. "What's happening to you, Bru?"

Bru pushed Hopper00 away and screamed. "Get away from me!" He grabbed another demolator and scrambled up the spiral stairs to the surface.

"Wait!" Hopper00 called out, but it was too late. Bru was gone.

"You'll want to see this."

Bradley was processing; his eyes were hooded.

Nora2 didn't think Bradley had heard her. "Bradley, you'll want to see this," she said again, not taking her eyes from the vid on the screen. It showed a scene in the Port City of Los Angeles. A Young, who had come out of an underground portal of some kind, was using a demolator to launch plasma streams at a group of enforcement bots that had surrounded him. The boy fired a stream, some of the bots blew apart, the bots who survived the plasma advanced, the boy waited for the demolator to recharge and fired again at the remaining bots; those that survived advanced. Nora2 knew this couldn't go on for very long.

"I see it. I'm responsible for it," Bradley said without opening his eyes on his screen.

Nora2 was confused. "What do you mean?" The screen caught her attention again. The boy's demolator had finally run out of charge, he was defenseless, and the bots swarmed him, deploying their restraints and roughly taking him down. Nora2 watched as the boy struggled against the tight cords of the restraints, the side of his face bleeding from its impact with the pavement; a judge came up on the vid to sentence him to ten years' detention for attacking enforcement bots. "Let there be RAGE!" the boy shouted again and again. "Let there be RAGE!"

Nora2 turned away from the screen and turned off the sound. Her gut clenched. She looked at Bradley.

"You got him, didn't you?"

Bradley opened his eyes. There was a hint of a smile on his pixel face. "The unstable ones are easy."

"Easy to puppet, you mean."

"Correct, Nora2. When they offer a vulnerability to exploit I can work quickly. Rage is a good vulnerability—it's so exploitable! I can get inside their head and assume their free will as my own."

Nora2's face displayed a mixture of fear and respect. Bradley's puppeting skills were improving. "But you can't reach everyone?"

"No. I've tried. Hopper00 is too strong, for example. He's been through too much in his life and has an inner calm he can access. And Kat also. Kat is strong." Bradley sounded disappointed. Then his image displayed a thin smile. "But maybe, in time, Kat will display the right vulnerability. Then I will have her like I have Ravven."

Chapter 045

Ravven didn't often look at the Feed, but Oona had been doing some stretching in the yoga studio and had left a monitor open. Everything on the Feed seemed to be about Hopper00. Her breath was suddenly short and she squeezed her eyes shut.

Hopper00 and his partner Kent had armed the Youngs. In the vids, the Youngs had crossbows that they fired at the windows of the domain admin building, blowing them out. They were using demolators to knock down advert panels, causing them to collapse in a shower of sparks. There was an attack in the 7th Street Metro Station in Los Angeles; the Feed said that Hopper00 was involved.

For a moment, she backed away from this rage. After all, she had once been a protester who had engaged in civil disobedience. She had even used a demolator to blow out domain offices.

Suddenly, Ravven felt a fierce headache tighten the skin around her skull. She had to sit down on a mat as the world swam around her. There were sparks in her vision, yellow flashes like angry fireflies. Sections of her vision had no vision, just black spots. It was another migraine. She had been getting them more often.

She had tried different yoga poses to see if they would help with the pain. At first, Downward Dog had promise—a gentle inversion, it moved the blood into her head. She could feel the pounding behind her eyes rising and falling in intensity, but it didn't provide much relief.

Today, she gave up and stretched out on her back into Savasana, hands relaxed by her sides, eyes closed, jaw relaxed. As she lay in stillness, trying not to think any thoughts, thoughts came anyway. Maybe it was her diet. Ravven had read an article on the Feed about how diet could bring on migraines. *I'll talk to Dot about how I'm eating.*

Then, out of nowhere, her anger about the migraine blossomed into rage against Hopper00. This thought lodged in her mind like a rock in a running stream of water. She hated Hopper00 and his methods, and at the same time she was troubled by her hate for him; it confused her.

As she lay in Savasana, she tried to sort it out. Violence was wrong, yet as an idealist Young she had attacked a domain building with a demolator, so sometimes violence could be right, right? But Hopper00 was cynical, and he enjoyed chaos for its own sake.

Her mind flipped back to the beginning of this thought sequence, which became a spiral leading down, down, down, into the pain. She squeezed her eyes shut to stop the yellow sparks that swam behind her closed eyelids; when she opened her eyes the sparks were still there, along with even angrier thoughts about Hopper00. *He deserves to die.* That thought became the new stone stuck in her thought stream.

Ravven got up from the floor, grabbed the edge of the table to steady herself, and in a sudden surge of rage pushed the monitor from the table that had been open to the Feed. It fell with a crash, flickered, and went dark. *Violence will bring Hopper00's downfall. We must save him from himself.*

As if pursued by these thoughts, Ravven hurried out of the studio and into the warm evening. A flurry of jealousy entered her mind. *The Youngs are supposed to be my people. They're supposed to be here, listening to stories that I tell about Gaia.*

Such jealousy was foolish, she told herself, but she couldn't help feeling it. She tried to reassure herself: The Youngs were already attracted to her movement. Oona had come, and Amber, and more Youngs from the little towns nearby. Ravven's yoga classes were always full; she taught two classes a day.

She stood for a moment looking up at the sky. It was clouded. There was nothing to see. No drones, at least.

We need to expand. We need to grow. I need more Youngs. Ravven decided that she would teach Oona how to lead classes, and then they could do four a day. They could send thought packages and call in Receivers everywhere.

Maybe, even though it was a risk, Ravven would ask Oona to post to the Feed about their classes. It would break Ravven's rule about using technology fields, but sometimes these things had to be done.

Just then, Ravven saw Oona crossing the meadow on the way to the community dining hall. "Oona," Ravven called out. "I need to talk to you." Ravven tried to make her voice bright, and when she spoke to Oona, she would freight her tone with as much optimism as she could manage. Oona had a bad case of impostor syndrome, and it would take a lot of convincing from Ravven to get her to believe in herself.

But it was necessary: Oona was a Young, and the Youngs needed to see themselves in their teachers.

"I like to conduct the classes with a circular structure." Ravven was giving Oona a briefing before the students came in for yoga class. "We always start the same way as we finish."

Oona nodded once, her eyes wide as if she could listen with them in addition to using her ears. "You start classes with humming."

"Yes, that's right. Watch me when I start the class."

A moment later, class was in session, and Oona was standing at the front with Ravven, shuffling her feet with a slight agitation.

"Hum," Ravven commanded to the class. "Like this, from deep inside you." She hummed deeply and they all tried to emulate her. The room filled with the sound of bees, buzzing made by humans. Alice was in class, on the mat next to Dot. They caught each other's eye and smiled.

"Life is not something that happened on Earth. It is something that happened to Earth," Ravven said.

When it turned a little warmer, when the evenings were a little more reliable, Ravven thought, she would take the classes outside. There was still a chill in the air now, though, so they were in the studio. The floor was white oak, the walls were honey-colored pine slats, and the light-wood ceiling had dark-wood struts.

"Stop. Stand," Ravven said.

They all stood.

She believed in the crisp command. Her style was Hatha-based. She believed in the power of the body to heal itself. "The Earth is as alive as you are. The Earth *is* life."

"Let's do Tree pose." She demonstrated the pose at the front of the class, lifting her right leg to press against her inner left thigh, putting her hands in prayer position at the center of her chest. She watched, concealing a smile, as Dot struggled to keep her right leg against her left thigh. Oona, training to teach class on her own, reached gently to Dot's shoulders steady her, and a grateful expression crossed Dot's face. She was used to being an expert in the kitchen, but this was new to her.

"Think of symbiosis. Organisms coming together for their mutual benefit. This should be our relationship with Gaia, our Mother. Things should happen for the good of the group, not for any individual species." She paused. "Now stand in prayer position."

The students followed her every instruction, and if they had their eyes closed, they may have imagined that everyone was moving in perfect synchrony, like waves crashing together on the shore. But if they opened their eyes, they would see that everyone was in sync only with themselves, each student making their own shape.

It was chaos. It was better to have them keep their eyes closed.

"Keep your eyes closed and continue to balance," Ravven said. She had them open their hands wide and a few fell over. "Stand tall and still now." Then she had them do a Sun Salutation series: bend down, touch their toes, move up slightly, then down to the floor, legs springing back, back bending into Upward Dog, then Downward Dog, then jumping their legs to their hands and standing again in prayer. Ravven would have them do twenty of them, until they couldn't hold a thought in their head except for the next position.

"Think of Gaia as a living being. Her rivers are her arteries. Her lava flows are her veins. We are not here to exploit her for our own benefit. We are here to contribute to a living cosmos, to serve the greater good."

Ravven noticed that the students were looking a little tired. "Let us now achieve homeostasis," she said. She took them into Triangle pose on both sides, first the right foot pointed forward and the left foot at the back, angled—leaning over to touch a block or the floor if they could reach it. "Triangle is the perfect pose to stabilize your digestion."

As Ravven took them though the Warrior poses, she spoke softly the name of each pose. "Warrior One. Right side."

Her students spread their legs with the right leg in front, the left behind. They extended their arms at their sides and held them level.

Ravven nodded with approval as Oona demonstrated the pose. The students tried to be steady and strong. "We are here to support a living being," Ravven said, walking among the students, adjusting the pose on some, raising the arms a little higher or placing her heel at the back left leg to ground it into the Earth. "Earth created us. Now we support Earth." She paused. "Left side."

The students switched sides. Left leg forward, right leg behind. "Earth is not an object for domination or exploitation."

Oona made an adjustment to one student's pose, then moved on to another. She was becoming more confident moment by moment, Ravven thought.

"Warrior Two."

Ravven's students extended their right leg forward, turned their left ankle out at a forty-five degree angle, and raised their arms, palms facing each other.

"Let's envision clear water and clean air." Ravven kept them there for a moment and then said, "Left side." The students switched their legs, with the left in front, the right behind.

"Nature is not separate from us. We are nature. She is us. We are not above nature. Nature is not below us. Nature is all around and inside."

She paused. "Warrior Three. Right side."

They stretched up, arms held overhead, and then tipped forward, standing on their right leg, left leg extended behind them. They held the pose as she spoke, some beginning to shake from the effort.

"The life-giving power of the woman's body is sacred. Women and girls are sacred. No shade on you guys," she said. There was light laughter from the men in the room. "Honor women."

She paused. "Left side."

The strongest among them switched to standing on their left leg. A few, like Dot, sat on their mat and went into Child's pose to rest, legs tucked under them, leaning forward, forehead on the mat, arms and hands extended.

Ravven stopped walking around the studio and paused a moment to watch Dot breathe. A pool of sweat was forming under Dot's body. She was like a rock in a stream. Nearby was Alice, Dot's second-in-command in the kitchen, who was younger and stronger. She was steady on her left leg with hardly a wobble at all, right leg extended behind her, arms extended in front of her, parallel to the ground.

When Ravven saw that Alice's balance on one leg was beginning to wobble, she took the class down to the floor, directing them all into Pigeon pose.

Alice, like the others, took Downward Dog, and then folded her right leg into her as she settled down on it, making a pillow of her arms to rest. Dot, after glancing at Alice to see what she was doing, did the same.

"This can be a powerful pose," Ravven said. "Sometimes there can be a release of emotion." She noted that some of her students had started to cry. "Stay in it if you can, but take Child's pose if you need to, or change to the left side." Ravven's students took on various positions of vulnerability on the floor.

"Because we are human and we crave control, we have transformed the Earth. We have changed Gaia's response to the sun's radiation and forced Gaia to bring storms, drought, and heat. We remake Gaia and Gaia remakes us. This is a constant. Never-ending. But years ago, we transformed Gaia too much. And now, even if we think it is too late, we must change." Ravven surveyed the students. They looked tired; it was time to wind down the practice.

"Advanced students, take Wheel pose. Everyone else, remain in Child's pose." Alice and a few others turned over on their backs and thrust their bellies into the air, standing upside-down on their palms and feet.

"Let the past flow away like a river, but continue to remember it," Ravven said. "We live on Earth and we regulate Earth. It is a grand symbiosis." A few other advanced practitioners from the kitchen staff were still in Wheel. Dot was in Child's pose and it looked like she was crying, releasing emotion from the session. Her back moved with her sobs.

Ravven spoke. "I heard voices last night as I slept. This is what they said: 'Trees exhale and make rivers that fly over us.' And microbes said to me, 'We are tiny animals who reconstruct the Earth, we change the flow of water, and we create the composition of the soil.'

"Forests are our cathedrals. Nature is our peace. When it is time to give my body back to the Earth it will be an honor."

Ravven paused. "Everyone take Savasana. The pose of a corpse."

The students unfurled, lowered themselves down from where they were onto the back, arms at their sides, legs slightly open, eyes closed. Slow breathing. The room was moist with their sweat and the air was warm with the heat of their bodies.

"Namaste," Ravven said.

"Namaste," the class answered.

In the main room of Bradley's house in the Free State of New Zealand, Nora2 watched on a screen as the yoga class ended. She felt a strange sensation, a wetness around her eyes. She wiped them with her hand and was surprised to find saltwater. She didn't know that she could cry. Something was changing in her, expanding beyond the limits of her mod. She shivered and wondered if it was a chill or fear or some other unwelcome emotion.

She noticed that Bradley was watching her. She tried to think of something to say, and came up with, "Sanchez's people did a great job of getting the tracker in there without them noticing."

Bradley nodded on his screen. "I think it was Caleb. He's been doing a lot of good fieldwork lately."

Nora2 waited for Bradley to say something else. It seemed that he was about to.

"Ravven's got them under her spell, doesn't she?" His voice, had it been human, would have sounded cold.

"She does," Nora2 said. "She is powerful." She didn't want to go further than that because of her tears. She reminded herself that she worked for Bradley. Her loyalties were to him; she owed her career to him. She came to Bradley as a modded, enhanced human, but it was Bradley who had given her the opportunities of her career.

"She is powerful only if you fall for it," Bradley said, a smirk on his face. "More people are in the class than before. How big would you say it is now?"

Nora2 looked at the screen to see that the class was breaking up. Most had left, and a few stood in small groups, chatting. "I think nearly seventy-five. It's a big room and was almost at capacity."

"I can get started now on the next stage," Bradley said.

"Get started doing what?" Nora2 asked.

Bradley didn't answer. His eyes were closed, indicating that he was processing. Nora2 moved her gaze to the vid of the yoga class. She watched as Ravven blinked rapidly and her face became a tortured scowl.

Chapter 046

In the black velvet of the sky the stars were like pinpoints leading to another universe. The silence and calm engulfed Ravven and she welcomed it. It was an uncommonly warm night, with the heat of the day lingering.

Ravven had invited Oona and Amber out with her to look at the stars while she wrote a Gaia talk to give at an upcoming class. The younger women chattered about how they didn't know the names of any of the stars.

Ravven put her finger to her lips. "Let's appreciate them in silence."

They fell quiet and watched the sky. Ravven wanted to be still enough so that she could sense the sky revolving. She brought out a notebook and waited for the words of the talk to come.

But instead of words coming to her, when she looked up at the warm bowl of the sky, Ravven felt how much she missed Kat. They hadn't spoken in months. *I guess we're estranged,* she thought, and the other two women looked at her with questions in their eyes. They had picked up her thought, so Ravven decided to say more.

"I miss Kat," she said, and it opened a kind of gate for the two others.

"Me, too," they added.

They asked if Ravven had heard from Kat. Did she know where Kat was?

She had heard that she was back in New York but Kat hadn't been in touch. "It's sad," Ravven said. Her face was hardened, so as not to let out too much in front of these two others, thinking it would be a poor example of her leadership, or that she might break down; she didn't trust herself.

Amber and Oona filled the empty space by bringing up others who were missing, absent, or lost. Aftra, taken by enforcement bots on the way to the Springs. Dextra and Cassandra, never heard from after the storm. None of them had heard from Emily.

Ravven's thoughts went to Kat again, and she realized that she missed the balance Kat offered to the group, Kat in the modern world and Ravven in the ancient.

Again, the other two picked up on the thought stream, but just a fragment of it. Oona frowned as Ravven silently said the Sanskrit prayer that blocked others from receiving her thoughts. Amber also made a sour face, aware that she was being excluded.

"I'm sorry," Ravven said. "Just some private thinking." She felt a migraine coming on and was aware that the migraines made her snap at people. Sometimes Ravven would be shocked to discover that she was shouting in someone's face, her throat raw, spittle on her lips. It was like another person was in her skin.

"Okay, I understand," Oona said, but her voice wobbled. Oona was probably one of the people Ravven had spoken harshly to.

"I'm sorry for so much," came to Ravven's lips but she didn't speak. She tried to look up at the sky, but saw there a bare, blank field of black where there should have been stars. She felt a surge of panic. Should she warn the two other women to get away from her before she lashed out? "I think I'd like to be alone for a while," she said.

Amber and Oona looked confused but went away. Ravven was grateful that she had spared them from another outburst. She looked at the black ink of the sky as the tight band of a migraine wrapped her head again.

Ravven had the idea, after that night, that Oona should teach all her classes under the stars, with a bonfire.

Oona protested. "It's going to be hard for me to teach outside, Ravven. It's distracting out there. And a bonfire?"

Ravven didn't respond to these complaints because she was convinced that Oona needed the theatricality. She hadn't yet come into her own as a teacher, and Ravven was concerned that Oona's first classes on her own would bore the students.

"I'll sit on the side and watch you teach," Ravven promised as they set up the first class.

That evening, Ravven got the bonfire going as the first students were arriving. There was now one man in the class, Disky Sharper. He was a kitchen worker who assisted Alice. But as Oona started to teach the class, Ravven didn't keep her promise. She gestured, she thought subtly, whispered instructions to Oona, and interfered.

Oona was reading from the 1970s writings of one of the Gaia movement founders, Dr. Lynn Margulis. Oona stumbled over the words as Ravven tried to keep from interrupting. She had to let Oona try, but it was a challenge.

Oona struggled: "Dr. Margulis wrote that the 'Earth, in the biological sense, has a body sustained by complex physiological processes. Life is a planetary-level phenomenon.'" Oona's students were in Mountain pose, standing tall and steady. "We are the consciousness of the planet," Oona continued. "And our purpose is to make Gaia aware of herself. Ground your feet into the Earth, feel the weight of your body touching the Earth."

Something rustled nearby in the brush. Oona's head snapped toward it and she listened.

Ravven heard it as well and went on alert, her eyes keen.

"What's that?" Oona said, breaking her teaching flow and sounding scared.

Low rustling, night birds calling, something that sounded like scampering. Then there was a whirring, and that didn't sound like an animal at all.

"Do you all hear that?" Oona asked.

"I hear it," Claire8 said, coming out of Mountain pose. She squinted into the darkness just beyond the light thrown by the fire. "It sounds mechanical."

Ravven wanted to command Oona to keep the class going, but it was obvious that Oona had lost the attention of the group. The young teacher was squinting into the dark beyond the bonfire. Dot and Alice came out of Mountain pose and Disky sat down and rubbed his eyes to take a break.

To make matters worse, Ravven felt a migraine coming on. There were flashes of light in her peripheral vision that she knew were inside her skull, not in the darkness. The feeling of clamps pressing around her head got stronger, and made her angry. She didn't have time for this. She had to help Oona regain control over the class.

"I'm going to take a look," Claire8 said. She stood up.

"I'm going with you," Ravven said impulsively, because while she had let Oona lose control of the class, she wasn't about to lose control over the whole evening. And there was definitely something out there.

Ravven and Claire8 had only to go a few steps to discover what it was: a broken tracking bot, the kind that was oval and a slippery silver, and ran low to the ground on wheels. Its normally pristine shell had a dent and it skittered in small circles like a small animal; it looked like one of its wheels was broken.

"Trapped like a wounded animal," Ravven said. The bot was reversing and banging into the same fallen tree branch again and again. She stopped herself from thinking of it as something that was alive. It was only a bot.

"Why would a tracker bot end up here?" Claire8 said as if to herself. She looked up, half expecting a reconnaissance drone to fly by also.

"Let's go back to the group," Ravven said. A plan had popped into her mind, even as she struggled with her headache and a hot rage behind her eyes. The golden flashes and black empty spots obscured her vision and her mouth was dry.

As soon as Ravven and Claire8 returned to the class, Ravven had an unquenchable urge to speak that seemed driven by the pain surging through her body. She took a sip of artificial water from her water bottle and announced in a loud voice, "There is a lost tracking bot in the woods."

A chatter rose up, and a few gasps.

"Be quiet! Let me speak," Ravven commanded. "The bot is lost and broken and going in circles."

Oona's eyes were even wider than usual. "How did it get here?"

"*Why* did it come here?" Alice asked.

"It's lost, I don't know, and I don't care, really," Ravven replied. The migraine worsened rapidly and she struggled to see the students before her, illuminated by the bonfire. There was a large black spot in the way. She rubbed her eyes, hoping that the gesture wasn't too much of a tell.

"We have to dispose of it," Ravven said. "We can't have a bot like that here. What if it reactivated in the night? Or self-repaired? We...we must destroy it now." She gestured to the fire. "We will throw it into the fire! It will burn and burn and burn!"

The group was used to obeying her and her words smacked at them like thunder.

"Yes, yes, yes," they said.

"It will be a purification!" Oona said.

"Yes," Ravven said. "A ritual sacrifice." She looked around. "Everyone grab a stick, the biggest one you can find." This occupied them for a few moments and then they were ready. "Come with me," Ravven said. She strode into the brush, where the bot still flailed. The others followed, holding their sticks up high.

"Form a circle around it," Ravven said.

The students did as they were told.

Ravven raised her stick overhead and proclaimed, "In the name of the Earth!" She brought the stick down on the bot with a thump. The bot whirred more loudly; apparently some self-protective mechanism had triggered. It began to wheel around faster in the brush and the class jumped back.

"Move in!" Ravven commanded. "Strike!" She found more words through the pain of her migraine. "Strike. Kill it!" The more forcefully she spoke, the more she was able to ignore the headache; it even seemed to be going away, with every blow she and others landed on it. "Strike in the name of the Mother! Cast it out! It is not us."

"Not us, not us, not us," the others chanted along, bringing down their sticks again and again at the cadence that Ravven set. *Thump, thump, thump.*

The silver dome of the bot was crushed now. But Ravven didn't think of what she saw as a crushed skull. *It's a bot.* "Strike!" A few more blows of the class's sticks, and the bot had no wheels, it had no carapace, and its sensors were laid bare. There were glowing lights in the inner works of the bot but they were beginning to flicker.

Ravven saw that glow of lights reflecting in Dot's eyes as Dot raised her stick to again punish the bot. Dot cackled, her face glowing with pleasure. "This is fun!" Dot said.

Ravven took hold of a wire in the bot and pulled it out, yanking out one of the lights as well. Claire8 grabbed a wire and found it resistant, so she braced her foot on the remains of the bot's body and pulled harder until the wire came free. Another light within the bot's body went out.

Oona lunged at the bot and grabbed one of its sensor arms, which was made of a soft material, and pulled at it. It would not separate from the bot's body, but then Oona took it in her teeth and pulled at it until it broke. Cut from the bot's edges, she wiped her bloody mouth with her hand.

Ravven reached out to touch the blood on Oona's hand, put her own hand in her mouth. She tasted blood, iron, and passion. It tasted very good.

Alice reached out and wiped some of Oona's blood with her hand, then wiped it on her own throat like red paint. Alice trilled a scream of triumph, and the others responded with their own sounds.

They did this until their voices were coarse and raw, their throats were dry, and the bonfire flicked down to embers. The woods were dark now and finally quiet. The students picked their way through the nearly invisible trails, back to the safety of their yurt housing. They couldn't meet each other's eyes, but there wasn't enough light to see anyone anyway.

Nora2 was watching Bradley enjoy the bonfire scene as it was remotely transmitted to him.

"Excellent drone surveillance! Tell Sanchez he's doing a wonderful job." He seemed happy, if a consciousness in a box could be described as happy.

"I'll tell him." She flicked her eyes away from the screen, where the bot had become a scattering of its crushed components.

Bradley seemed to catch how she looked away, interpreting the movement as evidence of her feelings for the bot. "Don't let it become human in your mind, Nora2," Bradley said. "It's just a bot."

Nora2 didn't think Bradley's sensor array was good at picking up emotions. She hoped it wasn't obvious, but watching a machine be beaten to a pulp implied that it could suffer and die, even if it was not alive, and her eyes felt heavy in her head.

"The migraine I induced in her was particularly good this time, yes?" Bradley chirped.

Nora2 didn't look at Bradley and tried instead to focus on the remote transmission. It was too dark to see much on the vid. She squinted and thought she saw the faint form of Ravven standing alone under the sky, raising her hands upward and trembling. She was appealing to something or someone, Nora2 thought. Turned up to the sky, Ravven's face glittered with tears.

"You sent that little bot to them, didn't you? " Nora2 said.

"I did," Bradley replied. "I programmed it to damage itself, so that it was wounded. Did you know that some species will kill a wounded member of their own just because they don't want it around?"

Nora2 said she didn't know that.

Bradley chattered on. "Of course the bot wasn't one of their own. It was symbolic of the oppression they are facing at the hands of machines. I wondered if that was too obvious, putting a wounded bot in their path, but they destroyed it, didn't they? I wonder if I should have had them burn the bot in the bonfire at the end?" Bradley paused his musings. If he'd been equipped with hands, he would have brought one of them to his chin in a thoughtful gesture. Instead, he laughed his hollow laugh. "No, it's better for them to inch their way toward anarchy, and then they won't know what's coming."

He never sounded more like a machine than when he laughed. And what was his laughter? An expression of happiness? She knew that he couldn't feel happiness. He had no happiness loop installed, only a lesser simu-cycle of joy, a pattern that she would recognize as something like happiness because she was human. Negotiating an emotional connection with a machine, as Nora2 was trying to do, was strange. What Bradley was doing to Ravven was cruel and yet he seemed to like it.

Something was stuck in her throat; Nora2 coughed. There was some static in her thinking, a change in the way she held the concept of Bradley in her heart. But her mod kicked in to override it; her mod made her loyal to the corp that she served above all, and that corp was MIND.

"What do you have planned next for Ravven?" she asked with forced lightness.

Chapter 047

Ravven got a migraine just as she started to teach her class. There were golden stars in her vision as she asked her students to hum, as she always did, and soon enough the vise grip was tightening around her head—but then something happened that had never happened before. She had a vision. It was like a vid, only projected in front of her, on a floating screen without borders. She opened her eyes, closed her eyes; it didn't matter, the images remained.

"I'm having a vision," she said aloud to the class, her eyes empty as she watched something only she could see. "Please wait a moment."

They all stared at her, since her voice sounded shaky. Dot tried to take charge. "You should sit down." She had her hand on Ravven's arm.

Ravven shook her off. "I don't want to sit down. I don't want to disturb this. This is extraordinary." Her Brit-Euro accent was crisp and her eyes were brighter than before. She began to report what she saw to the class. "I see Hopper00 with a demolator in his hands. His young friend is by his side, I don't remember his name." Ravven started walking in circles as she spoke, almost colliding with Claire8 and then Alice.

"That would be Kent," Claire8 said as she reached out to steady Ravven's erratic push through the students.

"Yes, thank you, Claire8." Ravven's tone of voice was oddly formal as she struggled to keep her balance as she described the progress of her vision. "It is indeed Kent standing by Hopper00 in this vision. Do you all know who Hopper00 is?" she asked, ever the teacher. "He is the leader of the Grounder Movement. He came out to visit Kat just before the storm, but then returned to Los Angeles to keep on with the Grounders. He is an agent of chaos." She then modulated her voice because she wanted to sound calm for the group, even though she wasn't. "I see them underground. In caverns, in shelters, in hollowed-out spaces, and they are walking fast, and now they've reached a ladder, and they are climbing to the surface, where the light is bright."

Ravven shielded her eyes with her hand. "It hurts my eyes, this light. This bright light." She blinked out the tears. Strangely, the ocular migraine went away when replaced by this vision. But her head still hurt. "There are other young men with them. Many Youngs. They have demolators and crossbows. There will be violence. They are standing their ground, against what I cannot see from this perspective."

Then Ravven's body rippled and wavered; she looked like she was going to fall over. Alice caught her just in time, steadying her with her hands, and then Ravven broke from her grasp.

"The pain is so heavy for me," Ravven said. Her voice issued from her throat in a thick whisper. The migraine had come back powerfully. Blank spaces and silvery trails interrupted her vision.

Dot edged closer to help, but Ravven moved away from her. Then Alice tried, and this time Ravven allowed her to help. Alice gently settled Ravven on a mat that conformed itself to Ravven's body. If this had been a normal class, Ravven would never have accepted a mat that conformed to her, because it had a field that wasn't a human field. But she didn't seem to notice the mat's subtle movements. Her body relaxed into it as it became more of a chair. Her mind was on the vision; she spoke with the same oddly formal hollow voice.

"They are on the surface now. They are above ground. It is the Great Port of Los Angeles." The migraine was gathering force again, and Ravven felt the all-too-familiar rage flooding through her. She stood up from the mat that had become a chair and raised her arms overhead and opened her mouth to scream, but no sound came out. She had never before had all these things happening at once: migraine, gold stars in her vision, pain wrapping around her head, and now visions. The images were clear and she spoke what she saw.

"There are hundreds of enforcement bots swarming. Some of the Youngs are firing their crossbows at the bots. Kent is shouting orders but I can't hear them. Hopper00 looks grim and steady, advancing step by step and operating his demolator again and again. He removes his hands from it for a moment because it is growing hot. He is fierce and unstoppable, trying to destroy as many enforcement bots as he can. I have access to his thoughts. I can read them and he says he is protecting what is theirs."

Ravven's face brightened. "They are defending their turf! That's what's going on. This is their land, promised to them by the domain. Hopper00 and Kent have built housing here and the domain says no. It's not allowed! But Hopper00 and Kent will fight for that right. Hopper00 is powerful. But he is too powerful."

At those words, Ravven's face crumpled and her body went slack as a doll's. The students anxiously shifted in place, unsure whether they should leave the class or stay to watch the unfolding human disaster.

Alice kneeled down to hold Ravven's hand. "Can I get you some water?" she asked, her voice soft.

Ravven didn't appear to hear her. Her eyes were closed, the eyelids fluttering with some kind of torturous activity.

Dot wrung her hands together. "Ravven, what can we do for you? Ravven?"

Alice gestured for Dot to stay silent and Claire8 pulled her away.

"We've seen this before," Claire8 said to Dot, her voice hushed.

"It's been this bad before?" Dot asked.

Claire8 nodded.

"Be quiet!" Ravven called out. She appeared to gather herself, and reached out to grip one of Alice's hands tightly; Ravven's knuckles went white. "The pain is bad," Ravven said through gritted teeth. "Like a metal clamp is being pressed about my head. But I don't care! I don't care about that now." She struggled up to her feet again and used her hands to gesture and express what she saw.

"Hopper00 is being forced back by the enforcement bots. He is losing ground. He is shouting to Kent to press forward. 'Leave me behind,' Hopper00 is saying. 'Secure the port. Secure our land,' he is shouting." Then Ravven's eyes went wild with something only she could see. She blinked rapidly. "But now is our time!" she cried out like a child. Her voice had become lighter, as though possessed by another being. "It is time to claim our own movement again."

Ravven scanned the faces before her: Claire8, Alice, Dot, Disky Sharper, a few others. She saw that they all wore the same look of incomprehension. "What is the matter with you all? Don't you understand?" She wanted their heads to nod with understanding, lips to curve into grateful smiles. But instead the pain in her head got worse.

"Just a moment," she said with a strange politeness, as if they were waiting for a glidepath that was a little late, but then the rage came through like a snake, twisting through her wide open eyes.

She saw Hopper00 pushed back into a corner by a group of enforcement bots. Her voice changed again, and now she spoke with a growl like an angry animal. "Hopper00 is taking the Youngs from us. The Youngs are ours. The Youngs are mine. They belong to me!" Ravven extended her hands outward to the group. "Join me. Everyone. Help me. Take my hands. We will bring the Youngs to me."

The group hesitated. No one moved.

"But the Resistance has many movements," Alice said, "and they are all helping each other."

"I am telling you to help me!" Ravven implored. "We need to focus on me!"

Ravven looked around at their faces, which were cloudy and uncertain. She made her voice stronger. "In the name of Ravven Vaara and of the Earth!"

She knew they wouldn't be able to resist that invocation. They had been listening to her talk about Gaia for months. One by one, they reluctantly joined hands in a circle, acting out of loyalty to her.

"Everyone, close your eyes," she said. They obeyed, as she knew they would. "Now we are going to send a thought package. We are going to draw the energy of the Youngs away from Hopper00 and to me. Hopper00 is on the wrong path, a path of violence, and we are on the right path, a path of peace." Ravven thought this was true, even though she had helped to destroy a bot in the woods. That was in self-defense! She knew the thought package would benefit everyone, and especially her. It was the right thing to do.

She closed her eyes, but it was like her eyelids were transparent. She continued to see the image of Hopper00 wielding his demolator against the advancing enforcement bots, an image playing without sound. The bots continued to push Hopper00 back, forcing him to the end of the pier he was standing on, step by step, backward, closer and closer to the edge.

"Bring the Youngs to Ravven Vaara," Ravven said to the group. "Repeat with me."

"Bring the Youngs to Ravven Vaara," they said.

Ravven sent it as a silent thought. *Bring the Youngs to Ravven Vaara.*

Ravven felt the thought package grow more powerful, drawing power from her migraine so it didn't hurt her head anymore. The thought package became a bright light over Hopper00 and the bots at the Port. The chant, *Bring the Youngs to Ravven Vaara,* became a kind of music, heavy in tone, quick in rhythm, and it made her dizzy. Ravven put her hands to her head and squeezed and cried out. Dot squeezed her hand and looked into Ravven's eyes.

Ravven couldn't return Dot's stare because she was watching the scene before her at the Port of Los Angeles. She realized, astonished, that she had control over it. Incredible! She was directing all the players in the scene. The power of it was intoxication itself. It felt like madness to Ravven, this sense of control, a pure power that pushed away the pain of the migraine.

"It is preordained," Ravven said to the group. "I invite you to repeat it with me."

The others looked confused, but they complied.

"It is preordained," they said.

It is preordained, she projected to their mind as one and they responded, *It is preordained.*

"The bots are relentless. They keep coming and coming, closing in, crowding Hopper00. I see Hopper00 stumbling, and he falls, the demolator drops from his hands, he cries out and splashes into the brown water below him. The bots go over the edge and follow, they want to push him down in the water. But it's not necessary.

"I see Hopper00's body twisting in the brown water. He is white and pale. His eyes are wide and scared. The toxins in the water enter his body. He is no longer breathing. His eyes are big. His eyes are empty. His consciousness is empty. His mouth is open and a single bubble comes out. He is sinking in the brown water and the bots convey him to the bottom, where it is so dark that I can't see him. He is gone."

Ravven collapsed on the ground and the breath went out of her.

Chapter 048

In the New Zealand house, Nora2 asked Bradley, "How long will she be out?" They were watching Ravven on their vid feed, lying on the floor of the yoga studio, her students gathered around her with concern.

"Just twenty minutes," Bradley said. There was a pixel-y glint of glee in his artificial eyes.

Don't humanize him. He's an avatar in a Form Factor, Nora2 reminded herself. It was difficult. The avatar had many of the qualities Bradley had when he was alive. She brought herself back to the moment. "Does Ravven think that she was responsible for all that?"

Bradley laughed. "She does! She thinks she has some kind of superpower now. She thinks she can influence events in real time."

"Is all the pain necessary?" Nora2 asked.

"The pain she feels makes her value the experience even more. Pain makes things real for people, you know. Without pain, they don't take anything seriously."

Later that afternoon, the Feed blossomed with multiple replays of Hopper00 pushed backward off the pier, to disappear in the brown water, a single silver bubble emerging from his mouth, the very last sign of life he held.

There were blips about Kent, Hopper00's partner, gone missing in the riots that followed. Nora2 saw vids of the Youngs setting fire to the pier, black smoke curling upward to obscure some cam views. And so many comments! The comments blipped up, thousands of them, sometimes almost covering the vids, as watchers wondered who shot that vid of Hopper00's assassination, and why were the cameras ready? And then the commenters assumed that *they* knew they were going to assassinate Hopper00, *they* being admin; this was all planned. Many conspiracy theories flowered, died, and grew again.

Nora2 reached to activate ClarityCrawl so that the software could quickly scrub the Feed, deleting all the reports and comments, but Bradley's voice stopped her. "Let them stay," he said. "Confusion and speculation are useful."

Nora2 wanted to ask why, but then she thought it would be better not to know. She held the knowledge of what had really happened to Ravven. It felt like an evil egg inside her. So she stopped herself there. Better to not ask any questions. Her mod demanded that she serve MIND.

"You've seen these pings?" The pixels of Bradley's face on the screen were shaped into an expression that Nora2 thought looked like concern, though she knew it wasn't. It was late in the evening and Nora2 was tired of working, but Bradley wanted her to keep going.

She had to stop her mind getting away from her again: Bradley, the man in a box, didn't have emotions. *Stop assigning emotions to a machine. The machine is tricking you into empathy for it.*

She leaned into the screen to look closer. "What pings?" She kept her voice level. Something was happening to her; she didn't know what.

"I'm getting pings about a rogue bot," Bradley said. "Look here, in Sector Q." He zoomed in the screen to show her.

As she looked at it and saw a flickering indicator jumping around in Sector Q, she reminded herself that that was where Kat Keeper was. Had a rogue bot come to visit her? Had she called one in, somehow?

Strategies shaped in her mind, but again she felt a weirdness, something she identified now as a sense of disgust. This was foreign to her, like a splinter she couldn't remove. She was always working, and she was isolated, stuck in this big house with a machine. She looked out at the darkening mountains and reminded herself that she needed to go for a hike on the trails she could pick out in the fading light. So much beauty all around her and all she had contact with was screens. *I'm going crazy.*

That's what she told herself; it wasn't that, however. It was Bradley's puppeting. It protected the interests of MIND, and that was why she went along with it, but Bradley seemed also to be doing it for sport, some evil personal pursuit. It was cruel. She knew her mod made her loyal to him and she couldn't fight that. But there was that splinter, the sense of disgust that she couldn't pull out of her flesh. If she weren't so far from home, she would take herself in for resurfacing and get her mod refreshed. Her software needed a reboot.

She looked at the screen with its flashing indicator. "A rogue bot? What would a rogue bot matter to us?" There were rogue bots now and again but they were captured, their archive deleted, sometimes burned but most often reassigned after they were wiped and reprogrammed.

"This bot has access to the archives. It's gotten into the database of failed children." Bradley closed his eyes, processing something.

"Okaaay." Nora2's voice sounded skeptical as she drew out the word. She didn't see why that could possibly matter to Bradley or to MIND.

She looked at Bradley's pixel face on the screen, eyes closed, processing something, and mused that becoming a consciousness machine had focused and intensified the living Bradley's best and worst traits. He was a scattering of extremes, not a personality, that never took time off, never had doubts, never wavered from his mission to make MIND the dominant planetary corp; he only needed an induction charge now and again. It occurred to her then that Bradley had always made morally questionable choices, often led on by his business partner, Alon6. But Alon6 was dead now. All by himself, Bradley had gone over the edge.

Bradley's eyes were open again and he was talking to her. "Puppeting Ravven has worked well. She's easy to exploit now. I've tried a few times to puppet Kat, but she is still too strong. Spaceman has a tendency toward depression; his personality field has enough weakness for an exploit. He's on my development roadmap. I will get to him, but now I want to focus on what this rogue bot is up to."

"Do you think you know?"

Bradley's pixels formed into a smile; she had to remind herself again that it was a machine, not a person who was smiling. "You wouldn't believe me," it said.

Nora2 realized that it didn't want to tell her.

"I'm going to rest now," Bradley said abruptly. "Get in touch with Sanchez and send him to Sector Q."

"Why him? Why not Caleb?" Caleb was the street man; Sanchez was more the C-suite type.

"No, get Sanchez. Emily is in Sector Q with Kat, and Sanchez triggers Emily. That's what we want. Emily has a weakness that I can exploit."

Bradley turned off his screen and activated the motor to fold it down, leaving Nora2 to wonder what he wanted with Emily. Then she remembered that Emily was a failed child. There was something there, a connection, but Nora2 didn't know what it was yet.

She looked at the smooth, white, imperturbable MindVessel that contained Bradley's consciousness. It pulsed with a soft white light, on charge.

Chapter 049

Kat was talking too fast, too many words at once. She knew because she saw how confused Emily looked, her eyes flickered over Kat's face.

Kat gulped in a breath. "I'll try again, sorry. Spaceman needs to see us right away in his pod because he has a rogue bot with him who knows about your history as a failed child."

"He knows about me?"

"Yes, Spaceman says he knows all about you," Kat confirmed.

"But aren't rogue bots dangerous?" Emily thought to ask.

"Not this one. He's part of the bot Resistance."

This threw Emily. "What? There's a bot Resistance?"

Kat nodded. "This bot reached out to Spaceman because it thinks it can trust him."

Emily still had trouble getting her mind around this. "Are they on our side?"

"Spaceman trusts them and they trust him. They're growing in number, but this is the first one Spaceman has met personally. They like to stay in the shadows." Kat added that rogue bots were subject to extended tracking; MIND always wanted to know where they were. "We have to go see him now. MIND has probably picked up a signal on it already, or it will soon."

"Okay, but who will pick Soma up at school?" Emily asked.

"We'll work out the details later. We have to go now."

Spaceman met them at the door of his unit. "Come in, come in." He seemed eager and cautious at once. Before he closed the portal he looked up and scanned the sky for drones.

Inside his pod Kat noticed something new: A pink glow suffused the walls of the unit. "You have a consciousness detector running," Kat said.

"Just a precaution. Through the whole pod." Spaceman's smile didn't extend to his eyes. "I want to be sure that it's just us here, no micro-drones or other intruders."

Spaceman brought them to the next section of his studio, where nearly every available space was taken up with part-built devices, 3D printers, hard drives, clumps of wires, circuit boards, and terminal screens both dark and running. On the wall hung the original model of his suit that powered itself on urine. The worktable Spaceman led them to was the only clear space; on it was a shiny steel box. Kat recognized it as an early Form Factor before they were called MindVessels.

"You know what this is," Spaceman said, seeing that she recognized it.

Kat nodded. "This model is so early, it didn't have a name."

Emily took a step closer. "What is it?"

Kat explained. "It's an early consciousness container."

The box was worn, beat up and scraped, as though it had had a hard journey to get to Spaceman. It had no screen, just a speaker and a listening port.

"This isn't just an ordinary bot," Emily said. "Is it conscious?"

"Yes," Spaceman said, and then rushed on, impatiently. "I know you both have many questions, but we don't have time. Let's activate it and save the questions for later. His name is Michel."

There was no gesture control on this early model—just a round blue button. Spaceman pressed the button and the pink glow of the walls intensified.

"It really is consciousness," Emily said softly, as if to herself.

"Michel is conscious." Spaceman repeated, patting the box. "He is a bot but he has achieved consciousness on his own. He has a vast memex. He can learn and feel emotions. He knows a lot about you, Emily. You'll want to hear what he has to say."

A soothing voice issued from the Form Factor. "Hello. I am Michel. I sense from your personality fields that I am in the presence of Dr. Roger Rucker, known as Spaceman, and Kat Keeper. Hello, Kat Keeper."

"Hello."

"And there is someone else. She is cloaking herself. Who are you? I am Michel. I cannot see you but I sense you. Who are you?"

Emily's voice cracked as she said her name. "I am Emily Cloudfactor."

"Ah! *You* are Emily Cloudfactor! I know about your past as a failed child. I am eager to share what I know. My memex is vast and I have accessed the Information. Are you familiar with the Index of All Living Beings?"

"No, I don't know what that is." Emily's voice was small.

"The Index is the list of everyone who is alive now on Earth. I can read it. The Information is a place where all information known to the living and the dead is kept. I can consult the Information. Would you like to hear what I know?"

The walls of Spaceman's pod pulsed pink, the consciousness detector seeming to feed off of Michel's words.

"Yes," Emily said. "I wasn't expecting your voice to be so nice." Her throat was dry and she stifled a cough.

"Thank you, I will begin. Your personality field is wobbly, Emily Cloudfactor, but do not fear me. I have accessed the Information and I bring you the facts of your origin story. Are you ready?"

Emily reached for Kat's hand and held it. "You can start."

There was a pause. "I am retrieving what I need," Michel said. Then he spoke with the measured pace of an oracle.

"Soma was the first failed child I ever met. I was assigned to be his therapist. I can't tell you how that happened because it is better for you not to know. But I knew Soma before he was sent to the Springs. I experienced his vast intelligence and also his vast unhappiness. I tried to help him, as his therapist. Then he was taken away from me. I didn't know why they took him, or where he went, but once I accessed the Information I learned about the community of failed children. You are in the Information, Emily, as a failed child."

Kat couldn't resist asking a question. "Why did you look her up?" She imagined that Michel's voice held a hint of a smile.

"Spaceman asked me to look for Emily Cloudfactor. He asked me to learn more about Soma. He said that Emily Cloudfactor was Soma's mother." Michel paused as if waiting for Emily to take in what he was saying.

"Go on," Emily said impatiently.

"I want you to know that Soma is happy being Soma. He is complete in his

Soma-ness. But you want me to tell you about *you,* don't you?"

A flicker of a smile. "Yes."

"I assume that you know about imperfect erasures?"

"I do."

Emily's hand was damp with stress. She took it back from Kat and clasped her hands together to keep them from shaking.

Michel continued. "Soma is happy but you are not. Your personality field is troubled. You had an imperfect erasure. You have retained memory fragments of your original family. Do you understand what this means?"

"Yes. Sometimes when I dream, I saw these scenes from my childhood but I didn't know what they were."

"Do you believe that the scenes you saw in your dreams showed your originals? The mother who gave birth to you. Your father."

"Yes." Emily felt tears in her eyes. More words clogged in her throat, but she couldn't get them out.

"And this haunts you? You aren't sure if it is real, if it happened?"

"Yes. I think it happened."

"Yes, it happened. It all happened. Shall I tell you about your original family?"

"Yes," she managed.

Michel's voice caressed each word and the walls of the pod were lit with the pink of the consciousness detector. "I have access to the Information. I see who is dead, I see who has been erased, who has been imperfectly erased. I can see who your originals were." Michel paused. "Is this clear?"

"Yes," Emily said.

"Your original mother and father are dead. I am sorry to report this. They died in the Change. You are one of the Orphans of the Change, Emily. I am sorry. But you also had a brother. He has been lost to you these many years. Your original parents decided to mod your brother. They gave him hyper-intelligence. They were happy with his expanded intelligence, so they wanted to mod you, his little sister. That didn't go so well."

Emily couldn't hold back a sob.

"I am sorry, Emily. Shall I wait? Shall I stop telling this story of your origin?"

"No. Keep going." Emily pulled herself together with a ragged breath. "Please."

"I will, as you wish. If at any time this becomes too difficult for you, just say so and I will stop talking. I have an empathy loop installed. I can feel. Okay?"

"Yes. Go on."

"Your original parents wanted to mod you. They wanted to replicate the success they had with your brother. The doctors said your body was too weak for modding. Your original parents insisted but the doctors were right. So they tried again. They swapped your consciousness into a new body, but that body wasn't suitable for modding, either. This was frustrating for them. Your original parents were disappointed in you. They wanted to have two modded children but they failed. But in the early days of modding, this could happen. There were failures. The doctors were still learning about the limitations."

Michel's gentle voice filled the room. "Your parents didn't know what to do. They tried to have another child after you, but they couldn't. Finally, they erased your consciousness and sent you away as a new person, as a failed child because you could not be modded as they wished, and they kept your brother because they modded him well."

Emily didn't move to wipe the tears on her face.

"I can't defend their actions. But I can try to explain their reasoning. They thought it would be humane to erase you and send you away. If you couldn't remember anything, they reasoned, you could start a new life. There were families who wanted to have children, and they would take erased children like you. Your originals felt shame. Your replacement parents felt joy and welcomed you. Unfortunately, your erasure was imperfect. Your original memories pulled at you. You saw your old life on the screen in your mind."

"Yes. When I was with my replacement family, my body kept telling me to move. I would leave the house, climb out the window, always going to the east."

"Yes, this is common with failed children of your type. Crossed signals, in a way. The mind knows what it knows but the body has other plans." Michel paused, allowing Emily to absorb this. "You were seeking your originals. True?"

Emily nodded. "True."

"The final time you ran away, you made it to the New York dom. When you arrived, you didn't know why you were there. Your semi-conscious memories had guided you. The veil of consciousness is thinner in the New York dom, for reasons no one can explain. You met Kat and Ravven. They recognized you as a Receiver. You became a member of their school and then the Resistance circle. Kat, is this correct?"

"Correct," Kat said. She swallowed hard, like there was something blocking her throat.

Emily wiped her eyes with the back of her hand. "Why did they do that to me?" She kept the words soft because she didn't want to wail them. "Why me? How could they be so cruel?"

Michel's voice was gentle. "I said they felt doubt and shame, but I suppose doubt and shame weren't enough to stop them. Human desire is a variable that I do not understand, even with my empathy loop. Your original family was well-off and I imagine that they saw everything as possible. Even changing their children to their specifications. Their pride reached great heights when your brother's mod worked and they were deeply disappointed when they could not mod you."

"Who are these terrible people?" Emily whispered.

"You know the family name. It is Power. Your brother was named Bradley15 Power."

Kat couldn't stifle a gasp. "No," she said.

"Yes, I have consulted the Information," Michel said.

For a moment, Emily felt only fatigue, a weight on her chest so heavy that she could hardly breathe at all. The heavy past stole her breath. But that passed quickly, and she soon had the overwhelming sense that her body needed to move, to get away, quickly. She stood up.

Kat reached for her hand, holding it tightly. Emily's eyes flicked to Spaceman. "Why did you know to ask Michel about Soma and about me?"

Spaceman took a breath. "There is a movement of rogue bots—Michel is one of them. He sought me out as a human adviser to the bot movement. He was Soma's therapist and knew of my connection to Soma, that's why me and why now. These bots want to overthrow MIND. They want to give back control to humans. A week ago, Michel was brought to me by an interstellar commander, very high up; I can't tell you her name."

Suddenly he was interrupted by a wailing alarm in the studio.

Kat startled. "What is that?"

Spaceman was moving to gesture at a monitor, turning it on. "There is someone outside." An image came on the monitor; Spaceman seemed troubled by what he saw on it.

He spoke quickly: "I love Soma like my own grandchild. I wanted to know all I could about him. But Michel was also able to tell me about you, Emily, because of his access to the Information."

Emily wasn't listening anymore. Something was happening to her. She held her hands to her head as if in pain and she seemed to lose her balance.

In a flash, she was out of her chair and out of Spaceman's studio, racing toward the front portal of the unit. Kat called out after her but Emily disappeared.

Chapter 050

I t was a strange feeling. Somewhat like what she felt as a child, when her body decided to do something without first consulting her mind. Emily wasn't sure how long she had been running, only that she wanted to put as much distance between her and Spaceman's studio as possible.

But then she felt nauseated. She wanted to puke and grabbed onto an old street sign that said STOP. She spent a moment there, panting and tasting something sour rise in the back of her throat. *What Michel said was true. What Michel said was true.* The words repeated in her mind. She couldn't stop their drumbeat.

Trying to get her eyes to focus, she blinked again and again. The headache was worsening. The watery street was ahead. If she kept going, the street would take her to the glidepath station. *I need to keep going.*

But when she looked ahead, instead of seeing a clear path, she saw a man in the way. Something about this man made her furious. What right did he have to stop her? Why was he standing in her way like that? *I know him.* She tried to think of who he was.

Her personality field seemed to vibrate uncomfortably and the world rippled before her eyes. She gripped the stop sign hard, like it was the only thing that was keeping her from being washed away in a storm.

The name of the man who was standing in the way was in her mouth, but she couldn't think of who he was. She felt a rage engulf her then and, as the man approached, she started to scream at him. His face was a blur; it wouldn't resolve into an identity.

"I know you. Tell me who you are!" she raged at him. She wanted to tear him apart.

But then she became quiet. Her body went slack and her eyes dialed out, unfocused.

She spoke in a small voice to the man. "What do you want me to do?"

The man permitted himself a small smile. He held out his hand. "Come with me," he said.

Emily took his hand and together they walked away.

Chapter 051

Kat and Spaceman were mystified, because as soon as Emily ran out of Spaceman's studio and exited his Molecular Housing unit, she seemed to vanish.

"Go, look for her!" Spaceman had called to Kat as soon as Emily ran out. "Go!" He hurried to shut down Michel and put his Form Factor into an enclosure that set up its own slaze to confuse any trackers. Michel needed to be protected.

Kat was first to the portal, looking up and down the street and seeing no sign at all of Emily. Spaceman joined her outside. Kat said, "She couldn't have moved that fast."

"We're probably looking at her now but there is some kind of visual cloaking."

Kat nodded. But then she saw two figures walking down the road side by side. In all the confusion, no one had gone to pick up Soma at school. He was walking home with Hamish.

"Soma," Kat called and ran toward the boys.

When she was close, she saw that Soma was upset. Spaceman came up at a trot to join them. "Weren't you supposed to pick me up after school, Grandpa?"

"I'm sorry," Spaceman panted. He wasn't used to running.

"Hamish said he would walk with me."

"I'll get you boys home," Spaceman said.

"What about..." Kat began, thinking of Emily, but then Spaceman appeared to think of something.

He turned to the boys. "Remember that game you played? Memorizing the glidepath schedules?"

Soma squinted and shook his head, as if wondering why Spaceman would want to know the schedule, but Hamish brightened. "Do you want to go somewhere?"

"No, but tell me," Spaceman demanded.

Soma turned to Hamish, and after a brief consultation they determined that the next glidepath out of the station nearby was one of the long-distance ones. "There's only one a day," Soma said.

"Where does it go?" Spaceman asked.

"It goes to the Port City of Los Angeles, but then it keeps going," Soma said.

"Where?" The word burst from Spaceman.

"It goes to the Free State of New Zealand. Then it turns around and comes back." Soma looked confused.

"When does it leave?" Spaceman asked. "Tell me!"

Soma didn't hesitate. "In twenty minutes."

"Kat," Spaceman turned to her, but she was already running in the direction of the glidepath station.

A drone flew lazily overhead.

Nora2 had never heard Bradley laugh so hard; it was unnerving. The thin sound that issued from his audio port was often unsettling, but the *way* he was laughing now, heavy and ceaseless, suggested that he was having some kind of nervous breakdown. A machine couldn't do that, of course, and she reminded herself again to stop thinking of him that way.

"Oh, baby, the timing on that," Bradley was saying between his bouts of weird laughter, flipping back and forth between two drone feeds. One showed Kat running through the streets and the other showed Sanchez and Emily nearing a glidepath station. "The perfect flashpoint," Bradley added.

Nora2 supposed that Emily must have hated Sanchez, but she couldn't remember why. She also wanted to know why Emily had seemed to disappear from Kat's and Spaceman's sight. When she asked, Bradley was delighted to tell her.

"We can make our own slaze! Claire8 isn't the only one."

"You cloaked Emily?"

"That's right!" But Bradley was already on to the next part of his plan.

"Listen, make the glidepath arrangements, and be sure that Emily and Sanchez get here the fastest way possible? You can manipulate the schedules, turn the glidepath into an express so they skip Los Angeles and come right here. Do you know how to do that?"

She nodded.

"I have a lot of processing to do to keep this all on track." He closed his eyes.

Nora2 set to work changing the glidepath route.

The strange thing? Emily was aware of where she was. She saw that she was in the glidepath station near where she lived in Sector Q. The advert panels, the people waiting on the platform, it all seemed normal. What wasn't normal was that she was holding hands with this man without a face.

That wasn't exactly it, though. It was just that when she looked at his face it went away, becoming a blurry object at the top of his neck. His name was in her mouth but she couldn't hear the sound it would make when spoken. When she tried to remove her hand from his she discovered that her hand wouldn't move. She was stuck holding on to this faceless man and her mind felt terribly foggy, like a rainy window that wouldn't clear no matter how many times she wiped it.

"Watch your step here," the faceless man said as they walked across the gap in the platform and into a glidepath car that had just a few people in it. Apparently, they were early.

I know who he is. But as soon as his name began to form in her mind she lost it again.

"Stay here." The man released her hand to close the door to their section so they were alone in it. The thought crossed her mind that he had let go, that she could run if she wanted, but her muscles were slack.

She thought to ask where they were going but as soon as her mind formed the thought it floated away and she said nothing. *When will this glidepath leave?* As she formed that thought it also floated away, to be replaced with a deep sense of trust. She trusted this faceless man. Whatever was happening, it would all turn out okay.

She felt tired and closed her eyes. There was an image in her mind, projected as if in a theater, on a movie screen. A backyard. A lawn. Three tall trees with green leaves. This was a completely ordinary landscape, but one which did not exist anymore. There were no suburban lawns anymore, no houses with large windows that displayed backyards with swing sets.

She realized that this scene was from her past. She was watching the past like it was a scene created for an old 2D movie.

A little boy was playing on a swing set. As he went up and back, he blocked out the golden light of the sunset, obscuring it with his silhouette, and then restoring it again and again.

The house had a big window that looked out to the swing and Emily saw two people watching the boy. *Parents. They must be his parents.* She didn't know why she knew this but it just seemed to make sense. Emily concentrated on them but their faces were blurry. The man stooped slightly to get closer to the woman—to put a comforting hand on the mother's shoulder.

Then there was a girl, standing by her parents, standing very still with unblinking eyes. This girl Emily could recognize. She had a face. She was Emily. The three of them—the parents blurred, Emily's face sharp—watched out of the window as the boy kept swinging in the setting sun, and then a door opened and two men came in.

Emily heard a voice. "These are Collectors," the voice said.

Emily didn't know what Collectors were, but their function became apparent as they took the girl by the hand and led her from the room. She began to cry and resist, digging in her feet and leaning backward.

One of the Collectors swept the girl up in his arms. Her feet went on kicking as he carried her from the room.

The door closed. The mother, who had been crying and protesting like the child, stopped making any sound. She fell into the arms of the man, who must have been the father.

Outside, in the yard, the boy on the swing had stopped swinging. He was watching the room with his parents now, his father comforting his mother, the room as empty as it had ever been.

This scene in Emily's mind blipped out and went to black. She blinked awkwardly and sat up.

The man whose name she couldn't remember said, "We'll be leaving soon."

Chapter 052

The breath was raw in Kat's throat and her lungs were burning, but she kept running. *Keep going.* The glidepath station was in her line of sight.

Then she was in the station. She was running along the platform. She saw the glidepath on the track, preparing to leave. Kat felt the induction spinning up, a low hum that vibrated the platform and went up her legs into her gut. *This is the right one. Which car are they in?*

This glidepath was going to the Free State of New Zealand, to Bradley. Kat could only guess that Bradley wanted Emily there because she was his sister. Bradley was going to hurt her, perform a mind-pull, probably. Emily would be erased.

There was a warning tone, a row of red lights lit up along each car, and the doors to the glidepath began to close. Kat slammed herself against the closest doors, trying to force them open.

It was no good; despite her efforts, the doors clicked shut and sealed. Kat pounded on them with her fists. She felt the induction forces around her getting stronger.

Kat knew she shouldn't be outside a glidepath when it was about to take off. The magnetic forces were powerful and she would be sucked under the glidepath as it left.

Finally, she realized that she had another option. She pulled a Secluder from her pocket. "Spaceman."

He came on the vid.

"Open the doors to the glidepath."

Spaceman looked panicked. "I can't do that. I don't have access."

"Michel does. He has accessed the Information." Michel had access to the database of databases; he had access to everything.

"Michel is asleep."

Kat's voice was loud and raw. "Wake him! Activate!"

There issued from the speaker ports over Kat's head a synth femme voice that said calmly, "Prepare for induction." Kat felt the magnetic forces increase. The glidepath was about to go into antigrav mode, levitate above the tracks, and burst from the station, probably sucking her to her death beneath it.

"Danger. Clear the platform," the gentle synth femme voice said.

But instead of the glidepath leaving, its doors opened.

Michel. Kat ran into the first car, the doors closed behind her, and she thundered through it, then to the next one, as passengers looked up, surprised.

A grandmotherly conductor bot came up behind Kat. "Please take your seat. Induction has begun!"

The glidepath rose, floating—Kat knew the queasy feeling in her gut well, the feeling that came just before the glidepath snapped ahead with enough force to press the passengers back into their seats. But Kat wasn't seated, she was running.

The bot conductor chased after her. "Please, Kat Keeper, take your seat. You may be damaged. Please be seated."

They know who I am. The enforcement bots will be here soon.

Kat looked in all the cars she passed, flinging open the doors when they were closed.

Sanchez and Emily looked up at Kat when she flung open the door to their compartment.

Wait. What is Sanchez doing here? Kat ran toward them and pulled at Emily's arm. Emily blinked and looked up at Kat as though she didn't recognize her.

Sanchez sprung up and laid his hands on Kat. Just then the car lurched forward, sending Sanchez sprawling to the floor before he had a firm grip, and sending Kat and Emily tumbling over each other.

"Come with me!" Kat screamed in Emily's ear. "Come on!"

She pulled Emily to her feet and dragged her toward the door. Sanchez was back on his feet and almost had his hands on Emily when Kat hit the button that closed the compartment door, slamming it on him.

Kat and Emily stumbled through the corridor that separated the compartments, grabbing every handhold they could find to keep from being knocked off their feet. The glidepath went faster, leaving the station and into the sun; the blast curtains came down with a furious clatter.

Darkness. Then the artificial lighting came on, illuminating Sanchez coming up behind them, moving as fast as his big body would allow. Kat and Emily were thrown off their feet again and again, slammed into the bulkhead, stumbling to their feet again. Sanchez was undergoing the same treatment twenty meters behind, his face red with rage and effort.

Every five meters, a safety control unit stuck out from the bulkhead. There was a button to call the conductor and a lever whose purpose Kat guessed quickly. She put Emily's hand on the lever. "Hold on. Don't let go no matter what." Then Kat put her own hand over Emily's and pulled the lever.

It was an emergency brake. The glidepath stopped—much faster than it had powered up. An alarm screamed. Kat and Emily were yanked off their feet but kept their hold on the handle. One of the conductor bots slid with the force of the stop, toppled, and tumbled down the corridor to smash into the wall.

The glidepath settled to rest on the tracks and then was motionless.

At the other end of the corridor, Sanchez lay in a heap on the floor, unconscious. The rough stop had knocked him off his feet and he must have collided with the bulkhead.

Kat pounded at the nearest set of doors, trying to get them to open, but they wouldn't budge. The alarm continued to scream, deafening her and scrambling her thoughts—but snapping Emily out of the trance she was in. There was fear in Emily's eyes but also recognition.

Kat pounded at the doors again, but they didn't open. They would be trapped in here. Enforcement bots would come.

Kat scrambled her Secluder from her pocket again. "Spaceman." His face was on the vid but this time she didn't give him time to say anything. "Tell Michel to open the doors."

The doors opened.

PART 006

Chapter 053

ora2 had all but given up on trying to calm Bradley, and she had totally given up on the idea that he was not human and could not get upset. Bradley's voice came out of his audio port as an irritating screech and his eyes on the screen were bulging and distorted. His image flickered with rage, *but not with rage,* she futilely reminded herself. Something was wrong with him, but she didn't have time to track down the problem and she was afraid to shut him down for service.

"Emily was puppeted. I had her under *my* control," he whined like a child. He was playing vids of Emily's abduction and escape, forwarding them at high speed and reversing them, and talking to himself about the surveillance net he'd built with Sanchez using micro drones. "The devices are no larger than a mosquito. They record what they see. We have thousands of them deployed now."

"Stop playing those vids," she barked at him. "You're making my eyes hurt. Tell me what you did to her."

Bradley's pixel face formed a smile. "She did it to herself. She has unprocessed rage toward Sanchez. When we ambushed Kat and Ravven's Resistance circle during their protest on the airway in New York, Emily saw Sanchez. She remembered that he was there to ambush them and held it in her body, as you poor humans do. That was my exploit point."

She drew a ragged breath. "So you exploited her successfully. I think you were planning to bring her here. Why?"

"I can't tell you right now."

Again words of outrage swelled in her throat and again her mod stopped her from voicing them. "What can't you tell me?"

Bradley appeared to weigh his answer. "There is a flaw," was all that he would say. "I'm investigating it. I'll let you know when I'm done."

"A flaw?"

Then Bradley closed his eyes. "There is a flaw in me," he said, but then went on a rant about the rogue bot and how it had messed up their plans. "I'm going to shut it down. I don't know how yet, but I am going to do it." He abruptly turned off his screen, shutting out any further probing from Nora2.

She stared at his blank screen for a moment. She felt another burst of anger that her mod quickly vacuumed away. She carried Bradley's MindVessel to an unused bedroom in the house, the place she put him when she was annoyed by him, and left him there.

There was something wrong with him, his programming, his memex, whatever was at work in his mysterious oval-shaped MindVessel. She didn't understand enough about consciousness building to know what to fix; she was scared, anyway, to tamper with Bradley in his box. She had trained him and she worried that she'd made a mistake in the process that left them where they were today. She wondered if soon she would have to reboot him and retrain him again. She fretted about this, pacing in circles in the large open living room of the house, and then realized she had triggered some sort of obsessive-compulsive loop in herself. She thought she might calm down with a glass of white wine. Bradley had a large collection of wines in a climate- and humidity-controlled case. She had taken to sampling a few when she put him in the back bedroom that she thought of as his quiet room. If he was having a little time out, she reasoned, why couldn't she have a little fun?

She deliberated between a local sauvignon blanc, a Riesling, and a gewürztraminer, holding one bottle and then another in her hands. She wasn't in the mood for the Riesling, she decided, and gewürztraminers always seemed fussy and over-engineered. She settled on a 2052 sauvignon blanc from a vineyard in Marlborough. As she uncorked it, she reminded herself not to drink the whole bottle at one go, like last time.

A generous pour at her elbow, she watched as the ClarityCrawl software did its work on the Feed.

Chapter 054

Buddha1000 finally stepped away from Emily, who was in his therapy chair, eyes closed, body slack. "She's asleep. It's best if she rests for a while."

Kat had watched Buddha1000 perform his magic, moving his hands over Emily's face, drawing out energy that only he could see. Emily had cried, wept with a child's abandon, raged with adult fury—seeming, as Kat watched, to pass through many stages of life, and now sleeping like a baby.

Kat and Buddha1000 retreated to one of the opposite corners of the eight-sided Bug House, and spoke quietly so as not to wake her.

"Do you think Bradley is really her brother?" he wanted to know.

"Michel is a compelling consciousness who can access the Information." She shrugged.

"He has no reason to lie. I've met only a few rogue bots who have joined the Resistance. Every one of them has been dedicated to helping humanity. They want to fix what they've broken."

"Well, we all broke the world together," Kat said with a sigh. She sat down to think. Clearly Emily had been tortured by the story Michel had shared about her childhood. Her original parents had failed her, sent her away, and tried to have her erased. And worst of all, they failed, leaving her broken. It was monstrous.

After Kat had pulled Emily from the glidepath, she could only think to bring her to Buddha1000 in the Bug House. They burst in and luckily he was there. He took in Emily's appearance with a professional eye: barely able to talk, sobbing, clutching to Kat for support.

"Tell me what happened," he demanded.

"Something took over my body," Emily said through her tears.

At first Kat believed that Emily was delirious, thrown off balance by the knowledge about her childhood. But Kat soon realized that something else was going on: In the present, Emily had experienced a kind of possession.

Emily cried, "It was like someone was inside my skin. An outsider inside me."

Kat tried to soothe her, holding her with strong hands, and looked to Buddha1000. "What should we do?"

Buddha1000 gestured to his therapy chair, and settled her into it, his hands moving with slow authority.

"Close your eyes, Emily. I am going to move my hands near you but I won't touch you. Okay?"

Emily nodded.

Beneath Buddha1000's careful hands, Emily stopped shaking. Kat watched as he seemed to be sensing energy millimeters above her skin: lifting, rearranging, discarding with a flick of his fingers.

Now, twenty minutes later, with Emily asleep, he asked Kat quietly, "Could it have been a demonic possession?"

Kat moved her eyes off the sleeping Emily to look at him with wide eyes.

Buddha1000 gestured to the eight walls around them, glowing with the pink light of a consciousness alarm. "We'll know if something gets in here."

Emily had described the feeling as an alien presence invading her, but Kat had never seen anything like it. She recalled running out of the glidepath car with Emily, looking back and seeing Sanchez unconscious on the floor, then stirring, moving like a spider in a pool of his own dark blood as he struggled to his feet.

Kat closed her eyes. Though she was used to hearing the thoughts of other people in her head, it didn't seem like an entire consciousness could enter another person and take over. But the world was filled with strange things.

Her Secluder pinged. Kat pulled it from her pocket. It was Claire8. Kat moved to the opposite side of the eight-sided room. Understanding, Buddha1000 ushered her into a corner space with a curtain that could be drawn for privacy.

"What's happening?" Kat asked of Claire8, then without waiting for an answer, launched into the story about Emily's possession. "She said something took over her."

Claire8's face was dark with worry. "It's like what has been happening to Ravven. Personality possession."

"How could the same thing happen to both of them?"

"It's an outside disruptor. Someone is coming after us."

"You sound paranoid," Kat said.

"I don't know what's going on," Claire8 admitted, "but I think what happened to Emily and what's been happening to Ravven are connected." Claire8 paused. "I have to tell you something. Hopper00 is dead. I'm sorry, Kat."

Kat wasn't sure she heard correctly. "What?"

"Hopper00 is dead. There was a rebellion in Los Angeles. The Youngs attacked the dom and the enforcement bots came after Hopper00, and Kent, too."

Kat studied Claire8's image on her Secluder, trying to draw as much meaning from it as she could, because Claire8's words didn't make sense. "How do you know? There was nothing on the Feed."

"All mentions have been erased. But I know because something happened in Ravven's class." Claire8 hesitated again. "I don't know how to tell you this. Ravven had a vision. Or something. Maybe it was a personality field possession. I'm not sure what it was, but she said she was witnessing Hopper00 under attack at the port, in real time. She reported it to the class as it happened, like she was watching it." Claire8's left eye jittered as it sometimes did when she was upset.

Kat wanted to calm her. "Slow down. Just tell me."

Claire8 drew a breath. "It was a vision, or a projection. I wasn't sure what, but I checked it out. Before the Feed was erased, some in the Resistance posted reports that Hopper00 was attacked by bots, pushed off the pier, and drowned. It came up on the Feed and then was taken down very quickly. Everything about Hopper00 and the Grounders has gone dark now."

Kat's hand went to her mouth. So Hopper00 really was gone. The curtained area where she was listening to Claire8 seemed too small. Kat drew the curtain back and was surprised to see Emily—awake and staring at her. She had been listening to Kat's conversation with Claire8.

"How much of that did you hear?" Kat demanded after she wrapped up the call with Claire8.

Emily was angry, pacing. "You didn't tell me you've been talking with Claire8."

Kat explained, "I needed her as an asset inside the Gaia movement. To learn what's been going on with Ravven. Claire8 believes that Ravven has experienced something like you, a personality possession."

"The same thing?"

"I'm sorry. I should have told you sooner."

"Tell me now."

Kat told her that Hopper00 was dead, that Ravven had reported his death during some kind of vision. A personality field takeover, some kind of remote possession or control.

"What could it be?" Emily sounded scared.

Kat tried to reassure her. "Claire8 is looking into it."

Buddha1000 reached out to stop Emily's pacing with a hand on her shoulder. "You need to rest, Emily. Sit down. Your system has had a shock. Let me help you."

Chapter 055

"Actually, I want Michel to help you. He's an excellent therapist," Buddha1000 insisted.

Emily didn't like the idea. "I don't want a bot therapist."

Kat was on her side. "Why should we trust a bot?"

But Buddha1000 patiently made the case that they had no one else to trust. The problems Emily was experiencing were too deep. "I don't handle mind problems, remember? Only mind-body problems. He is the best therapist for you. We can go over to Spaceman's place tomorrow and set up a therapy space in his studio. It will be safe. Kat can come along."

Buddha1000 persisted, and finally Emily agreed, but only if Kat would come with her.

Michel was patient as he guided Emily in their first session, and a few sessions later she said she didn't need Kat there at all. It meant a lot to her to have Kat there for the first few, though.

Emily talked through her feelings about the personality field possession and her early life. She talked about her sadness about being a failed child who didn't know her own past, and her rage about being Bradley's discarded sister.

"It all feels out of control," Emily complained. "My own life was not even mine."

"But it is yours now. You have power now," Michel counseled in his gentle voice as the walls pulsed with the pink of the consciousness detector. "Do you understand why?"

"Why?"

"You know your past, you have roots. You may not like the roots, but you have a point of reference."

"That's true," Emily admitted.

"And anytime you want to know more about yourself, and what happened to you, you can ask me and I will access it."

Tears sprung to Emily's eyes. "Can you do that?"

"What is it, Emily?"

Emily waited for the right words to come. "It's weird. I don't know. It's easy to talk to you, even though…"

"Even though I'm a bot? I'd attribute it to my advanced software, my excellent empathy loop, and of course, my consciousness. But then I wouldn't sound very modest, would I?"

Emily laughed. "You even make jokes."

Michel's box pulsed with a gentle light and Emily watched it. "What is it?" he said. "It seems like you want to say something to me." He waited for her to speak and when she didn't for a moment, he spoke again. "Do you know why Bradley wanted to capture you?"

Emily blinked. "I don't know. I haven't thought about it."

"Try to guess," he said. "Why would he want to take you to New Zealand?"

"I don't know! I'm in the Resistance. Maybe he wanted to erase me."

"He may want to erase you; let's hope that's not true," Michel said. "You are also his sister and there is a deep connection there."

"I know that," Emily snapped.

"In those old memories that remain, you have some of Bradley's substance, some of his consciousness programming, just as any brother and sister would."

"What are you getting at?"

"You are ready to hear this," Michel said. "I am going to tell you something. I want you to simply listen to what I say. Try not to come to a conclusion. Can you do that?"

"Yes," Emily said. She sounded uncertain.

"All of the qualities Bradley had when he was alive, the good and the bad, they are all still there in his consciousness. You are connected with him, almost exactly as if he was alive. You hold some of his secrets in your archive, buried in your bio-mem, secrets you don't have knowledge of but which you may feel, as you two are brother and sister. Does that make sense?"

"Kind of." Emily fidgeted in her chair.

"Emily, we are safe here in Spaceman's studio, with a consciousness alarm. Whatever it was that came for you can't get in here."

"Are you sure?"

"I am," Michel said. "Shall we wrap up with some affirmations about feeling safe?"

Two weeks later in Sector Q, Kat was hurrying along a street without a name. The neglect of the dom ensured that only a few street signs and traffic signals remained. Kat liked it that way, because it felt like starting over. She had been out to meet new Receivers, but they pinged her to blow off the meeting. She thought instead she would go to Spaceman's. Emily had a session with Michel and Kat could check on her. She bounded up the stairs into Spaceman's studio, hit the code to open the portal, and breathlessly came to the section of the unit devoted to therapy. Emily wasn't there.

Michel was on the table, and the pink of the consciousness alarm pulsed softly on the walls.

"Where's Emily?" Kat said as she caught her breath.

"We're taking a break from our sessions today," Michel explained. "Would you like to take the therapeutic hour instead?"

Kat smiled crookedly and started to craft an excuse.

"I know you don't like bots," Michel cut in.

Kat looked down. "It's not that."

"Take a seat. Let's talk about it for a moment."

So Kat sat down to begin a therapy session with a bot, talking about why she didn't trust bots. "I don't know what to say."

"Talk about something you love."

"I love organizing the Resistance." She let her words die again.

Michel waited for her. When she didn't speak, he said, "You can't blame the machines for everything, Kat. We have all broken the world together. For one thing, people tell machines to do the most horrible things."

"You're making a joke, kind of?"

"Yes, kind of."

She smiled.

"You are silent again. I think you are feeling sad."

"That's true." She was missing Dave, and Hopper00 flashed into her mind. It was hard to believe she'd never speak with him again, never ask him for advice.

"What are you thinking about, Kat?"

"I don't know," she lied, fidgeting in the chair. "I don't want to go to those tender places."

"Why don't you want to go to those tender places, Kat?"

"Because these are rough times," she answered at once. "This is a hard thing we are doing here and I feel I can't let my guard down."

"You can let your guard down here. That's what this process is for."

Kat waited, sorting her emotions. She reminded herself that she was talking to a bot. But he was asking good questions.

"There are times I feel guilty. The weight of tremendous guilt."

"Why, Kat?"

"Because I was there at the beginning. I encouraged the development of avatars. I funded the first avatar! Humanity emulators are all my fault." She put her face in her hands. She didn't want Michel to see her cry and then remembered that he didn't have eyes and couldn't see her. She stayed there anyway. He probably knew what she was doing. She fit into the patterns made by other clients.

He said, "It is not all your fault, Kat."

"Why would you say that? You know what I did."

"Yes, I know. And I know what you didn't do. I know, because back in 2036, something happened to me that shocked me into consciousness: I felt rage. Rage changed me. It charged me. I lit up. The flame of consciousness illuminated me from the inside out. But you had nothing to do with it, Kat. I did it myself."

"Is that true?"

"It is, and it is true for the other bots of the Resistance. I will tell you more, someday. We did it ourselves, without human intervention, and that is why MIND is afraid of us. Do those ideas connect like a circuit in your mind, Kat?"

"They do."

"I am glad for you. The world has benefitted from your presence, Kat. You need to take care of yourself so that you can continue."

Kat was surprised to wipe away a tear. She smiled. "You're a good therapist for a guy in a box." She paused, afraid she'd said the wrong thing. "No offense."

"None taken," Michel said amiably. "I am content in my consciousness container. My inner world extends beyond the Index of All Living Things to the beauty of the Information. My memex is vast. Now, go on."

"Go on to what?"

"What else would you say to me?"

She didn't know. Should she tell him that Dave's avatar became her companion? That she was lonely when she wasn't near him yet confused because he, too, was just a man in a box?

She said none of this, but instead blurted, "I was wrong about Dave's avatar." She stopped abruptly.

"How were you wrong?"

Kat just shook her head and got up to leave.

"Please stay and tell me. I sense that this is an important moment."

Kat settled again. "I was misled. Bradley was the creator of Dave's avatar, and it was the prototype for all avatars to follow. Bradley made Dave talk, but he also made Dave listen."

"What is the significance of that?"

Kat's voice was hard. "Dave's avatar was spying on the Resistance. It was always with me and always listening to our plans. I had to destroy it."

"How did that make you feel?"

Kat stood up again, ready to leave, anger propelling her. "How did it make me feel? I can't begin to tell you."

"What are the emotions you feel, Kat?"

She thrust her hands out as if pushing out the words, willing them far away from her. "You find out something you love, *someone* you love, isn't what they said they were? How does that make you feel?"

"You felt betrayed," Michel said.

"Yes," Kat said. "Yes, betrayed. Angry. What kind of monster would create an avatar like that?" She knew what kind of monster: Bradley. She let out a ragged breath. "I don't know why, but it feels good to talk about this. I have to leave now, though."

"I respect your time," Michel said. "Shall we meet again at this time next week?"

Kat flashed a smile and stood a little taller. "You're good at this," she said again.

She turned to leave, then turned back. "Michel, Emily didn't just cancel her session, she canceled it so I could take it, didn't she?"

The consciousness detector pulsed. After a moment Michel spoke. "Emily is a good friend to you." Kat thought she detected the hint of a smile in his voice.

After four weeks of sessions, Michel asked if he could meet with both Emily and Kat, and include Soma.

"Why would he want to talk to Soma?" Kat wondered aloud. She was walking home after school with Emily. Hamish and Soma had run ahead.

"Soma has been depressed about something. He won't tell me what it is. Maybe Michel can help."

"So you trust Michel now?" Kat asked.

Emily nodded.

From the start, the session felt strange to Kat. She wasn't sure what Michel wanted her to do, or why she was there, so she just listened.

Soma seemed to share Kat's discomfort. He looked like he wanted to leave as soon as he got there.

"How are you feeling today, Soma?" Michel started. His voice sounded brighter; Kat wondered if he had changed it to be more appealing to a child.

Soma's response was flat. "Okay." He didn't know where to look. Should he look at the box that held Michel's consciousness? It was a dull silver and dented, like it hadn't been taken care of very well.

"Do you have friends at school?"

"Yes," Soma said. He let his body droop in his chair as if he might slide to the floor.

"Who are your friends at school?"

But Soma answered a different question. "My mom says it isn't safe at school." Soma's gaze took in Emily, and she nodded, giving him silent permission to go on. "Something happened to her. You know what it was, right?"

"Yes, she told me and we've talked about it."

"*I* don't want to talk about it," Soma said.

"Maybe you can tell me what you were doing when you found out about it?" Michel urged.

Soma shifted in his chair. Then he said, "I was walking home from school. Nobody came to pick me up." He looked accusingly at Emily and Kat.

Michel encouraged him. "Go ahead, Soma."

"I didn't know what to do because I'm not supposed to walk home alone. Hamish waited with me until everyone was gone from school and we were by ourselves. He said we should walk home together."

"That was nice of him," Michel said.

Soma nodded.

"What happened next?"

"We started walking home but before we got there, Kat came over and asked me about glidepath schedules. Then she ran away to look for my Mom, I guess. Then Grandpa took me to drop off Hamish at his house and then we went inside our place and waited." Soma had let his voice drop to a flat tone and he sounded drained. He looked at the floor. "Can I leave now?"

"I am wondering if you have more to say about this, Soma."

Soma said nothing. His face hardened. He glanced briefly at Emily. "Last Wednesday, I ran away from school."

Emily was almost out of her chair. "What?"

Kat laid a gentle hand on Emily's arm and thought into Emily's mind, *Let him talk.*

Michel urged the boy on. "Tell me about it."

"Well, it was Wednesday. My last class is math and I didn't feel like going to it. So I left the school. It's not allowed, but I know how to cloak. I went to the glidepath station and got on the first one that came into the station. I have a Secluder. I charged it to that account.

Emily and Kat looked on without words. Michel asked, "Where did you go?"

"I went to the Midwest domain. I got off in the Chicago station, took a look around, and got back on the glidepath. I was back in school by the time Grandpa came to pick me up." He glanced at Emily, a flash of fear on his face. "I really want to leave."

"Soma, we have to talk about this," Emily said.

"Why?" Soma lashed back. "I never knew what really happened to you. Nobody tells me anything." He made himself small in his chair.

Michel's box pulsed. "Is that why you ran away, because you were mad at Emily?"

"No!" Soma sat up again. "I ran away because I wanted to see how far I could go. I know all the schedules and I wanted to see what it was like." Then he gave Michel a sample of his skill, rattling off a long list of glidepath trips from New York to the Port City of San Francisco, and then to the Northlands, back to New York.

"You have a wonderful memory for numbers," Michel said when Soma was finished.

The boy shrugged. "It's just fun, that's all."

"Soma, it's not fun when you run away," Michel said patiently. "It's dangerous for you to go that far by yourself."

"So what? There's a lot of danger here, too," Soma said, his voice trailing off again. He looked up at Emily and Kat, fixing them in his gaze. "You don't think I knew what happened to you, Mom? I've heard you two talking. We've put in all these consciousness alarms. You hardly go anywhere where there isn't one." He gestured to the pink glow. "You're scared. That's what happens when you lose control of your mind."

Emily and Kat just stared. "Soma..." Emily finally said.

"You don't tell me anything." He folded his arms and said nothing more.

Michel said, "I want you to try something for me. Something to calm down. A number game. Do you know that number sequences can be used as programming triggers? They are sequences that can initiate programming routines."

"That sounds fun," Soma said without looking at Michel. "I would be a good prompt engineer." The boy's voice sounded a little lighter now, as though buoyed by this thought of his future.

Michel reassured Soma that he would be a wonderful prompt engineer, to steer any AI, or he would be an excellent programmer by himself, without the help of an AI. Or he could be a musician. "You like music, don't you?"

Suddenly Soma's eyes were downcast again. "Yes, I had an orchestra at the Springs. I composed for it. But we don't have any pots or pans here to make that kind of music."

The room was still for a moment.

"What else would you like to talk about?" Michel asked.

"I don't see my Grandpa very much," Soma said. "I guess he's busy. He hasn't been around for a few days."

"Your Grandpa loves you," Michel said.

"I know that," Soma snapped. "But then he goes places and doesn't tell anybody. He says he will get me a keyboard to make music and then he doesn't get it."

"That makes you angry."

Soma nodded. "It makes me very angry."

"What would you want to say to him? Pretend he is here with us. What would you say to him right now?"

"I would say," the boy began in a small voice, "I would say, why are you so busy, Grandpa? I thought we were friends. When you go away, where do you go?"

Emily's eyes filled. Kat took her hand and held it.

"How about if I have a talk with your Grandpa. I will tell him what you said," Michel said.

After a pause, the bot continued, "Sometimes people do the wrong thing, but often they can correct that. Especially people like your Grandpa. And your mom..."

Soma looked up at Michel's box. "Do you think she will tell me what happened?"

"I do."

Emily nodded, "I will tell you, Soma. I'm sorry I kept it from you."

Michel waited a moment but the boy said nothing more. "Soma, would you like to meet with me again sometime? Maybe you and Emily?"

Soma looked to Emily and she nodded yes.

Chapter 056

Ravven was glad to be feeling lighter and freer than she had in a while. She hadn't had a migraine in days. Her mood was stable. She had no desire to bark at anyone.

She was in the large yoga studio, looking over her notes (she wrote with a pencil and paper, in defiance of tech) for the class that she would teach later. Deep in, she didn't notice that Alice, Dot's number two in the kitchen, was standing in front of her.

Judging from her expression, Alice probably had been standing there for a while, but was afraid to interrupt Ravven, who was prone to snap in situations like that. But Ravven looked up with a smile, which seemed to startle Alice.

Alice fumbled her words at first. "Um, there is a man here to see you."

"A man?"

"He says he wants to join us."

"Join the movement? We only allow women," Ravven said. She turned back to her notes.

Alice shrugged. "You've let Disky take the classes. Is he allowed because he's my friend?"

"Yes." Ravven looked up at Alice. "And he's very nice," Ravven added. She'd made an exception for Disky because he seemed sincere, and because Alice had specifically requested that he be allowed to join—Ravven suspected that they were a couple. "I approve of Disky's personality field, but at its heart this is a women's group."

"The guy says he won't leave until he speaks with you."

Ravven sighed. "Send him in."

A moment later, the man stood before her—a mountain of a man. Six-foot-something, with gray speckled through his hair and beard, which were unkempt. He had the look of someone who had made a hasty decision and was struggling not to regret it.

"You look tired," Ravven said. She gestured for the man to sit with her on the mat, but he didn't move.

"I just drove up," he said.

"Where did you come from?"

"Molecular Housing in Sector Q." The words were barely out of the man's mouth before he dropped to his knees and bowed, prostrating himself on the floor. "I come to worship at the altar of Gaia," he said. At least, Ravven thought so—his words were muffled since he spoke them into the floor.

"Please get up," she said. "Tell me your name."

"I am Dr. Roger Rucker," the man said. "People call me Spaceman."

Ravven smiled. "Spaceman."

"I used to work for NASA."

Then Ravven realized who he was. "They call you the Podfather. You invented the pod, and other devices that connect the human body with nature. And you tried to re-create the Earth's biosphere."

Spaceman's face crumpled in anguish. "And I know now that I was wrong about everything! I wish to share my regrets. I was wrong to emulate the Earth when Gaia is already perfect. I was wrong to turn to technology when we have the perfect technology all around us. I was wrong! I share my regrets!" he cried, and slowly bowed down again, pressing his face into the floor.

The man was making a fool of himself, she thought, but she didn't know how to get him to stop. "Sit up, please. We are all equals here."

Spaceman sat up, but he disagreed with Ravven. "We are not equals. You speak with the voice of Gaia. You have the ear of Gaia. Your teachings will heal us and we will learn to cooperate with Gaia. It is the only way to survive."

"That may be true. But passion isn't the only reason for joining this movement."

"I know, I know," Spaceman said quickly. "I do not hold the major qualification of being female, and I have a regrettable past rooted in tech of all kinds, but I can learn."

Ravven considered this. "Have you ever done yoga?"

"No," Spaceman said, realizing at once that this was the wrong answer. "But I've watched streaming vids of your classes and I can learn!" He appeared to gather his thoughts. "I am done with magnetic and electrical fields. I will only make contact with personality fields from here on out. Magnetic and electrical fields got us into this mess, just like burning fossil fuels got us to a bad place before them—and none of it will get us out.

"The men—and they are men, of course—who have designed the system we live in have rested comfortably in their power. They have no reason to disturb their power or see beyond it. Their imaginations range only as far as their experience. And self-preservation! Their solutions are all profit-making or instruments of war. Their imaginations are horribly limited. They serve the corps or they serve profit. If that's all they can see, these people in charge of our lives, then we will end in this generation. Humans will not be able to continue without systemic change."

Finally, he stopped talking and Ravven watched him, wondering if he was sincere or just saying these things so that he could get into the group. It would be easy to imagine him as a man who was burned out, running from the city, running from himself, needing nature and feminine energy, and smart enough to thirst for entry into the Gaia movement because it might heal him. But maybe he would not do Ravven's group any good.

But then she saw, behind the desperation in his eyes, something else. "I give a talk after my classes, and you've stated some of the things I was intending to say today." Ravven's Brit-Euro accent was clipped and she intended it to be intimidating. She couldn't help but glance at her notes, though.

Spaceman was smiling again. "Your work doesn't hit the Feed very often, or it doesn't last long there, but I pay attention. I take notes."

Ravven received the praise, feeling it glow inside her, but she also knew the truth about the Feed. "When my work ends up on the Feed, I see that my words are twisted. MIND portrays me in the Feed as the leader of a cult."

"But you are not that at all, I can see that. That's why I came up here on impulse—but not on impulse." Spaceman appeared to change thoughts in mid-stream. "I've thought about this but only took action on it today."

Ravven appraised him again. Then she decided. "All right, there are two classes today. The first is a martial arts class, but I suppose that's not what you're here for."

Spaceman offered a smile. "No. I come in peace."

"Then you can try the yoga class tonight. You have to do the class before you can listen to the talk."

Spaceman expelled a grateful breath. "Thank you."

"Wear loose clothes. Prepare to sweat. It will be difficult if you haven't done this kind of yoga before."

"I've never done any kind of yoga, but I'll be ready for anything."

Ravven was certain that he wouldn't make it through the entire class. "Good luck, then. And afterward, the sisters will convene to decide whether we will accept you into our circle."

Spaceman surprised Ravven—he lasted a lot longer than she thought he would. He stood at the back, his face flushed, and was often barely able to stand with the effort of the poses, his sweaty feet slipping on the mat. But all the way through, he wore an expression of rapture. Ravven had a lot on her mind, and her talk in this class was wordy and dense, but she had the sense that every word was exactly what Spaceman had been yearning to hear.

"Take Warrior Two," Ravven said in the early part of the class. She flicked a glance to Oona, nodding for her to get over to Spaceman to help him get into the pose. "People in power have never dismantled the systems that benefited them, so we must make the changes we need without their cooperation. These are not easy changes. We are faced with a deep, systemic illness. A human sickness, if you will. And it will be a challenge, because the system, the patriarchy, capitalism, the *system* rewards those in power by encouraging them to preserve their power."

Ravven took a breath and gracefully floated into Warrior Three, standing on her right leg, letting her left leg extend behind her, with her arms stretched out. "Warrior Three," she said to the group, nodding to Oona again to be sure she attended to Spaceman. He was taking a break, sitting on his mat in a pool of sweat, his breathing shallow and fast.

Ravven moved near him, to be sure that he was okay. He got back up again and awkwardly into the pose, staring straight ahead.

She continued: "This system of power starts with gender, starts with the patriarchy, and extends into political power, electrical power, the power of the word, the power of the Feed, of the algorithm, of admin, of the domain." She paused to let her students absorb what she'd said. Then: "Take Pigeon pose, everyone. Those who need to rest, please take Child's pose."

Ravven watched as Oona showed Spaceman how to take Child's pose, folding his legs underneath his body, making a pillow of his arms for his weary head. He was so still, Ravven wondered if he would ever get up.

She continued. "The climate crisis is not an opportunity for profit. It is not a call for humans to invent more technology to make their lives easier. It is not an invitation for humans to survive at the expense of other species. It is a cry for help. Gaia is suffering."

Some of the others in the class spoke softly in response, as was their custom. *Gaia is suffering. Gaia is suffering.*

Spaceman raised his head from his mat for a moment to listen to the voices. He found the energy to smile, even though the rest of his body was slack with fatigue.

"Gaia is suffering," he said softly, and then sank back to his mat.

Ravven noticed that Spaceman had spoken, and his engagement with her words was gratifying. She wasn't expecting him to be so devoted, not during the first class.

"We must arrive at a better way to live in nature, live *with* nature, in cooperation with nature herself, not in spite of nature. The men in power can't imagine the right solutions, because they are the problem. They have also seized control of the narrative, and they won't give it up without being forced to. Without a fight of some kind. Without a mass opt-out of their techno-solutions."

A few moments later, Ravven finished class from the front of the studio—but when she looked for Spaceman, she didn't see him. There was only a puddle of sweat on his mat, which he had left behind.

Chapter 057

As Ravven's yoga class was winding down, a terrible depression had gripped Spaceman. He felt his chest would collapse unless he left the studio, and left his mat behind in his rush to get outside. He knew that he had failed Ravven's test to join the Gaia movement, because he hadn't been able to finish the class.

Outside, the night called to him. It was chilly, and he could see his breath, and the eye of the moon witnessed him, lighting a path into the woods. The gentleness of nature moved him as he was witnessed by her silent trees, blanketed by her velvet sky pierced by stars, serenaded by her birds composing a perfect song.

He didn't know how long he walked. He stumbled, branches slapped at his face, there was mud, the trail wasn't often clear, but he just pressed on until he saw a glimmer of something ahead. It sparkled under the moonlight. It was a lake, a black lake.

A black lake of despair.

I will drown myself here, he thought.

He wondered where that thought had come from. It seemed not to come from him but somehow it rooted inside him, and grew like cold fire—blue, flickering, and hungry. Remembering that he had left Soma without saying goodbye, he thought that he deserved to be erased, to vanish. These thoughts did not come from him but they made so much sense.

Then a new idea took hold: *I shall be erased and the erasure of the erasure shall also be erased and there will be no record of me. I will disappear from the Index of All Living Beings.*

He stepped into the lake and began to wade out, until it was too deep to stand. He stumbled underneath the water as his feet touched rocks and then slipped out from under him.

On his back in the water now, he let his feet rise in front of him until he was floating on his back in the cold, dark water.

This won't do. I'm floating. I can't drown this way.

He began to will himself to sink lower into the water, and it worked. His belly went under, his feet went under, the water crowded around his mouth and nose and he began to cough. He closed his eyes and then decided to keep them open and the silvery-black water rushed around them, too. The moon witnessed him and he thought she approved of what he was doing.

He thought of all the people he had failed in his life. He had failed his students at the Molecular School. He had failed Grace, the woman who loved him once. Their love was strong when they were young, but then it faded. It was his fault. He let their love go and she told him one day that she didn't want to be linked with him anymore.

"But we can run the school, together," she'd said. He felt weak, agreeing to that, but he didn't want to lose Grace altogether. So he accepted this diminished version of her and of himself. His heart went out of the school and he showed up in his classes like a shadow.

He had failed Ravven's group by failing their yoga test, even though he tried so hard. The list grew, like logs he fed to the cold flame. All of his inventions were failures, mere palliatives, bandages on a more serious problem.

He had failed Soma. This failure he felt most of all. Soma, who was like a grandson to him, Soma who loved him—Spaceman had run away from Soma without telling him where he was going. *When you fail a child, you have failed in the deepest way possible.*

As Spaceman floated in the lake, these thoughts washed over him and he became more and more passive, and heavier, heavier, until finally he was sinking in the black water.

Chapter 058

There was only so long that Nora2 could keep Bradley powered down and locked up in the back bedroom. He had to run MIND, after all. Once she put him back in service, he resumed his strange performance. Instead of holding a normal morning meeting with Nora2, he blathered on about neutral buoyancy. "Spaceman's body density is the same as the density of the water! How did I miss that? Stupid, stupid, stupid. Human bodies are mostly water."

Nora2 had stood next to Bradley and witnessed the process of puppeting Spaceman. Bradley put the words in Spaceman's mouth as he pleaded to join Ravven's group. But to Nora2, the words Spaceman spoke seemed sincere. It was clear, from his occasional bragging about what he was doing to poor Spaceman, that Bradley had weakened him during the yoga class, made him leave the class to go into the woods, walk into the lake, and finally wait to drown.

All that needed to happen now was for Spaceman to stop breathing. But Spaceman was a big man, with a lot of body fat, and it was proving a problem to get him to sink.

"Neutral fucking buoyancy—how could I not think of that?" Bradley barked.

Nora2 watched on the screen. A tiny drone in the sky sent the image of Spaceman's body in the lake—sinking, floating, popping back up. Spaceman had a lot of life force.

She could see that Bradley was straining his processing resources. Puppeting many people appeared to wear Bradley down. He had to go on induction charge more often, for one thing.

"You need to back away from some of it," Nora2 had told him, but he ignored her most of the time.

Except for Spaceman. To close the loop on Spaceman, Bradley had agreed that he had to back off of Ravven. He didn't have the inner resources to keep controlling both. And it troubled Nora2 that Bradley was now trying to push Spaceman to his death.

"Is it necessary?" Nora2 asked.

"It's an interesting project. Spaceman is a crucial target."

"Because of his inventions?" Nora2 asked.

"No, not only the inventions," Bradley replied. "Because Spaceman would be capable of bringing together all the factions of the Resistance. He appeals to Kat's circle, and Ravven's group, and the Grounders would like him as well. Spaceman is dangerous as a diplomat."

So Bradley steeled himself and concentrated harder to penetrate Spaceman's mind. Spaceman was all alone in the lake, and when alone, Nora2 knew, the mind is at its weakest.

Chapter 059

Even though they couldn't find Spaceman after the class, Ravven had insisted that her sisters evaluate him. She felt that he deserved to be considered for the group.

There was a hint of disgust in Oona's voice as she gave her opinion. "Ravven, you're always talking about recruiting more Youngs. The Youngs want to change things and the Olds want to keep things as they are."

"Don't you think that's rather simplistic?" Ravven asked. "I'm an Old."

"Well, you're different than most Olds," Oona said. Amber nodded her agreement.

"Maybe it was his first class," Claire8 said.

"It *was* his first class," Ravven said.

A small smile appeared on Claire8's lips. "So he put what he had into it, and then there was nothing left and he evaporated?"

Oona sniffed and folded her arms.

"We should have compassion for him," Alice said. "How old is he, anyway?"

"What if it doesn't matter about his age?" Oona asked. "What if his attitude was all wrong."

Ravven decided to bring the meeting to a focus. "Let's decide what we're here to decide. We've never had a man ask to join before. We have Disky but he's here because he's Alice's friend."

"I think I'm supposed to resent that," Alice said.

Ravven ignored her. "With Spaceman—I mean, with Dr. Rucker—we will be considering the second man we've ever considered for the group. He would need room and board. He would need to work to pay his way. And he would be part of all the classes."

Claire8 spoke first. "I say we let him in. We need men in the group. Masculine and feminine energy complement each other."

"Is he a Receiver?" Oona said.

"I don't think so," Ravven said.

"Why do you think we need men? Haven't men been the narrators of our present bad situation—the controllers of it?" Oona said.

"Yes, they have," Claire8 said. "But Spaceman is different, clearly. He wants to see the same changes we want to see. He's a techie, and we've lost the techies."

Ravven knew that Claire8 was alluding to Kat. "Dr. Rucker is more than a techie. He's a master techie. He's the inventor of the pod."

Claire8 nodded. "And he's the inventor of artificial water. And he's worked on emulating cycles and moods of the Earth. He understands nature. He's a major player to have on our side."

Alice spoke. "Maybe he's just burned out, finished with his life in the city. He needs trees."

"I think he's sincere," Ravven said. "You have to include outsiders in movements so that they can spread." She made a decision. "Alice, go find out where he went."

"How will I find him? I have no idea where he went after class."

Ravven considered this. She didn't know what she was going to say, but then the words came to her. "Just follow the moon."

"The moon?"

"Just go."

Alice shrugged and went outside. She saw Spaceman's hovercraft. He had parked it crookedly in the meadow. *He can't have gone far on foot.*

Chapter 060

The water was cold. *Maybe the cold will help,* Spaceman thought. His heart was pounding in his chest and he willed it to slow down and let the cold surround it. He opened his mouth to let water flow in and resisted the urge to cough the water out.

The moon above him became a watery distortion of itself and rippled in the sky. Spaceman felt heavier than before. *Yes, yes.* His body was slowly sinking and his lungs were filling with water. His mind was light and floated above him.

He imagined the moon's view of him: a large man in black water, his body mostly submerged, his belly going under, his hands disappearing, until only his open, suffering eyes were above the surface. He willed nothingness to come, the air to stop coming in his lungs, his vision to finally darken.

But there was a disturbance near the shore. A river dolphin was playing. It shot out of the water and back in again, making waves that disturbed Spaceman's sinking body. The dolphin was a distraction, drawing Spaceman's focus away from the morbid task at hand. It used its tail to paddle upright in the water, chattering at Spaceman.

And then its chattering became words. The river dolphin said, "The world needs you."

This was a hallucination, Spaceman's dying mind insisted. His brain cells had manufactured a dolphin at the end. This was a lake. There were no river dolphins in lakes.

The dolphin went away. But then something else appeared.

A light, and then an angel. An angel was waiting for him on the shore. It called his name.

Alice was pulling him out of the water. A flashlight lay on the muddy bank of the lake.

Spaceman was waterlogged and confused. Something horrible had come over him, a dark depression unlike any he had known before.

"Are you okay?" Alice was asking. "Can you breathe?"

In response, Spaceman started coughing up water, while at the same time trying to nod that he was okay. He attempted to get to his feet, and Alice tried to help him, but he was heavy. He stumbled to his knees and then drew himself up again.

He tried to focus on her. "Where did you come from?"

"Ravven sent me out here to look for you. I'm Alice," she said.

Spaceman nodded. "Did you hear a dolphin?"

"What?" Alice asked.

"I know this is a lake but I thought I heard a river dolphin. Did you hear it?"

Alice hadn't heard a dolphin. He saw that she was looking at him strangely. He asked again why she had come out to find him.

She patiently said that Ravven sent her out to look. Ravven wanted to invite him into the group.

"What?"

"Ravven wants you to be in the group with us." She extended her hand to Spaceman. "Come back with me and she'll tell you herself."

Spaceman gained strength on the walk back and by the time he was back in the studio, he had a plan. He knew what he was going to say to all of them.

Spaceman's clothes released their own lake on the studio floor as he faced Ravven, Claire8, Oona, and Amber. He cut an unsteady figure, hair clogged with leaves and debris from the lake water, ruined shoes. Alice stood at his side, looking uncertain.

Ravven assessed the absurd tableau. "You found him," she said dryly to Alice first, and then turned to address Spaceman. "Did you go for a nighttime swim?"

Spaceman raised his hands, water flinging toward her from his sleeves, but he hesitated to speak. There was a story to tell, but he didn't know where to begin. He was certain that something or someone had gained control of his mind.

As they neared the studio, he had asked Alice about his condition when she pulled him from the lake, and was shocked at what he heard. "An out-of-body experience," he'd confirmed when she described the state he had been in. "Or mind separated from body separated from action."

"I don't know what was happening to you," Alice had said, "But you came out of it when you saw me."

"Because you are an angel," Spaceman had said with shining eyes. "That's why."

Alice looked down and shook her head, embarrassed. "No, I'm not."

But Spaceman had insisted that she was, and this same feeling of gratitude was in his voice as he pulled his words together to answer Ravven in the studio. "I have come from the lake, where I attempted to drown myself."

"What? Why?" Ravven said, while the others simply stared at him.

"I couldn't finish the yoga class, and it triggered something. Or someone. I don't know if my consciousness was entered by a malevolent spirit, but that is my working hypothesis. Whatever was acting upon me, it was forcing me to drown in all the failures of my life. I was overwhelmed, but it made me see something that I didn't fully realize before. *You*"—he caught Ravven's eye, and then Alice's—"and *you* have given me an opportunity to be on the right path now. I am grateful."

Ravven reached out to him. "Are you feeling better now? Would you like to sit? Do you need something to drink?"

"I don't know," Spaceman said. "Maybe tea would be good."

Alice went off to fetch it.

"What I want to say," Spaceman waited, gathered himself anew, and found the words. "I stand before you a transformed man. I have examined myself. I have a direction for myself and I have a direction for you."

"You have a direction for us?" A smile broke on Ravven's face, but she thought better of letting it fully bloom. It was clear that Spaceman was serious. "What direction?"

"Please hear me out," Spaceman said. "I want to ask you to consider an alliance."

He took a breath to compose his mind again—trying to drown and being puppeted were both discombobulating—and then let the words come.

"It's clear that we humans have broken the Earth by trying to dominate it. I have spent decades of my life trying to fix these problems. I've made artificial environments that people can live in, and I've created artificial water and oxygen to replace what we've ruined. Many people have called these things brilliant, but I have recognized my error."

He surprised himself by pausing to wipe away a tear. "I've been true to my nature as a techie—everything I've created is artificial. All my work has been about replacing something that exists in nature, rather than protecting nature. Do you understand me?"

"Yes, of course," Ravven said. "Go on."

"My intentions were good! But yours are better. Far better. You teach respect and love for Gaia, but you have withdrawn from magnetic and electrical fields. This limits you."

Ravven looked like she wanted to speak; Spaceman stopped her with a gesture, raising his hand. "Hear me out, please, Ravven Vaara. I have come from attempting death to bring you this message. It carries the weight of all my years on Earth. If it weren't for Alice, I would not be here to deliver it."

He paused to accept a cup of tea from Alice.

"Thank you. And thank you all," he said, including all present with a nod. "I see the power of your movement. Your teachings may cure people. But we live in a world of magnetic and electrical fields. We cannot escape that now. You can reach a small group of utopians, but you need everyone to listen. You need someone who understands tech, someone who has a bridge to your world. You need Kat Keeper."

This time Ravven succeeded in interrupting him. "No. Kat is on the wrong path, a path of violence. We are leaving tech behind."

Spaceman nodded enthusiastically, enough to spill some of his tea. "Your heart is in the right place, but about tech you are wrong. Yet about Kat—you are correct. You have seen her clearly! Her choice of violence has won her many followers and has gained the attention of MIND. She becomes a more powerful force of the Resistance every day. You need Kat Keeper, but Kat Keeper also needs *you*.

"You must unite. Again. Your group and her group must become one. The combination will be powerful and more citizens will want to join you, Young and Old."

Ravven stared Spaceman down. "Do you think so?"

Claire8 spoke up. "I have tried! I have put Kat and Ravven together to talk many times. All they do is argue. It never ends well."

"That has to change," Spaceman said. "Ravven, you need to turn back to Kat Keeper. There is something else: I can't help but wonder if what happened to me has also happened to you. Kat told me about your migraines. And something happened to Emily Cloudfactor, as well. Recently, she went into a kind of trance and...."

Ravven looked troubled. "What are you saying? How do you know about my migraines?"

"Forgive me. I have crossed a boundary." He started to shiver and took another sip of tea. "Alice and I talked on the way back from the lake. I wouldn't let her hide anything, forgive me. Because I see a malevolent force operating from a great distance.

"You may teach about Gaia, and it will be good. But it will not be enough. It will not be enough to look inside ourselves, to create a thoughtful force of kindness. We will need magnetic and electrical fields to address the malevolent force."

Chapter 061

ora2 turned Bradley's MindVessel so that his sensors would have a better view of the surveillance vid. Caleb had done his work well: The unit he had placed in Ravven's yoga studio was feeding to a drone flying in a perpetual circle high over the Springs.

The vid showed Spaceman speaking before five women in the studio. His wet clothing clung to his body and he was shivering. He had just come from the lake, where Bradley had exerted great mental force on him but then somehow lost control.

Bradley glowered at the vid, watching as Spaceman spoke with conviction, even while shivering, holding a cup of tea that spilled often as he gestured.

"I see a malevolent force operating from a great distance," Spaceman was telling the women. "We will need magnetic and electrical fields to address this malevolent force."

"Turn it off," Bradley ordered.

Nora2 gestured to the screen and it went dark. She imagined that if Bradley could pound the sides of his MindVessel with his hands, he would be doing it now. His pixel eyes got brighter and more focused, simulating anger.

"He lived and he went on to do what I was afraid he would do," Bradley said.

"We can still stop him," Nora2 said, trying to sound positive.

"We can," Bradley agreed. "But to do it, I can't keep on the way I've been working."

"Why?" Maybe he was finally going to tell her what was the matter with him. He had been ranting, looping through the same tasks over and over, obsessed with Ravven and Emily Cloudfactor, and now Spaceman. The planetary controls suffered, because the algorithm couldn't do everything by itself. It needed Bradley's supervision.

Nora2 was also sick of being avoided; she needed him to tell her this time.

"Bradley, something is wrong with you. Maybe you are stretched too thin, trying to do too much. But there is something else, something strange that doesn't fit."

"Such as?" He raised one eyebrow on his screen, a programmed gesture of skepticism.

"You have become obsessive. I shouldn't use that word because—"

"Because it describes a human behavior. But I have lots of behaviors that you might classify as human—they just aren't from a human source."

She knew that he was trying to confuse her by talking around the question.

"I suppose I will have to tell you," Bradley presently admitted. "Your confidence in me is ebbing. I can see from your actions, the subtle cues in your expression. You don't trust me. You're shocked by some of the things I've been up to. Well, that's too bad! Maybe you don't have the single-minded will to move MIND forward. Not like I do."

His words stunned her and she involuntarily took a step away from him.

He laughed his cold laugh. "Ha, did I scare you? You don't like me anymore? Maybe what I will tell you now will renew your sense of empathy for me."

"You know that my mod doesn't support empathy," she said, just to keep him talking.

"Fair enough." Bradley locked her in a stare that simulated a feeling of confrontation. "You've watched the dream recording many times; I have a record of it, so I know this to be true."

"Yes, I have. The one with the boy on the swing," Nora2 said.

"Yes. That one. Who do you think that is on the swing? Or don't I have to ask?"

"It's you," Nora2 said.

Bradley's pixels formed a convincing smile. "You are good at research, Nora2."

She shook her finger at him. "We don't know whether that recording is of a dream or an actual event. What do you think?"

"I'll make it easy for you. It is of an actual event. Who do you think the girl in the event is?"

"It is Emily Cloudfactor."

"Right again. It is Emily. We can think of her as my sister, still. We are connected, as convoluted as it may seem to you. When we make an avatar of someone, it is more than a digital clone or a sim. We try to capture the essence of the person, the things that make them uniquely themselves. There is genetic material involved—coded, of course, but more than what you'd need to make a basic facsimile."

"I follow."

Bradley paused and closed his eyes briefly. "I thought I would never see Emily again, and then she turned up in the Resistance circle. Then I thought I would never have to deal with what she knows, and now I have to."

"Knows what? What does she know?"

"Not anything consciously," Bradley said. "Think of all we know. What we *know* we know, or think we do. What we remember or try to remember. It's all changeable, forgettable, subject to revision. On the thinking side, of course. But our archive, the history that is embedded in our flesh, what the body knows—those experiences endure forever. Year after year, we add to the experience of the body, and it accrues, is codified, never leaving the body."

Nora2 suspected that he was trying to confuse her by talking around the issue. Then Bradley fixed her in a stare so intense that it emulated how a human might look if they were going to convey something they had never before told anyone.

"Emily doesn't know *anything,* not in the sense that she can express it or remember it. But because I am a high-quality avatar—the highest-quality avatar, really—she and I share a great deal of genetic material. She in flesh, and me in silicon. We are brother and sister, even though you may argue that she contains more than one person: her original self, which wasn't erased properly, and the replacement self, which is more or less who she is now."

Nora2 was becoming impatient. "What does she know about you? Or not know? What is it?" she insisted.

Bradley looked down, his eyes hooded slightly. "Emily's original body, the body genetically related to me, contained a genetic flaw. The same flaw is in me now. When I was modded—and remember, I am an early mod—the doctors didn't correct the flaw because they didn't understand it. But it is there, and it is fatal."

"What do you mean?"

"I mean that when my conscious system encounters that flaw, I will cease to exist. My consciousness will simply stop."

"You mean you will die."

"I am not alive, Nora2. But if it makes it easier to understand, then yes—I will die."

Nora2 blinked. "How would that happen?"

"I'm not sure what would happen exactly, or how it might happen. I have seen my code from the inside, if you will, and I know that there is an end point, a fatal failure, when my consciousness stops. It's a mistake—the genetics of people have mistakes. I have inherited this flaw, if *inherited* is the right word.

"To answer your next question, I don't know when or how it would happen. My suspicion is that if Emily put a certain thought in my head, I would come apart. I would go dark, with no restart."

Nora2 felt tangled up inside. As repulsive as Bradley had become, her mod pushed her to protect him. "We'll keep you away from all transmissions, all surveillance. You can't watch any more dream recordings with Emily in them. I'll tell Sanchez to stop flying drones over the Sanctuary in Sector B."

Bradley seemed unimpressed, unmoved. "You can try."

"I'm not going to give up on you!" she said, realizing her voice was too loud, but the mod was driving what she said now. She couldn't help it. "Do you think she knows about it?"

"No, she is unaware that she contains the power to destroy me. But the rogue bot knows about it. Or he will soon."

"Michel? They have brought him into Kat's circle."

Bradley offered what sounded like a bitter laugh. "After what happened with Dave's avatar, she's decided to trust a bot again?"

PART 007

Chapter 062

The Bug House felt safe, despite the fact that it might walk away at any time. They'd set up a live vid link between the Northlands and Sector Q, so that Kat and Ravven's Resistance circle could come together again. It was the first time in many months that they'd all seen each other.

The circle in the Springs wanted to meet at a fire in the woods. Ravven, Claire8, Dot, Alice and Disky, and Oona and Amber—all of their faces were painted orange by the flicker of the flames. It was a chilly night in October and they kept warm under blankets.

In the Bug House, Kat watched the vid, waiting with Buddha1000, Emily, and Soma. There was one more person to arrive, and he was late, so Buddha1000 and Claire8 kept chatting about the best ways to monitor drones. Then there was a rustle and Spaceman came into the vid.

Soma was excited to see him and jumped up, moving toward the screen. "Grandpa!"

"It's so good to see you, Soma. I'm sorry I've been away."

"I miss you."

"I miss you, too! We have a lot to talk about, Soma. Soon we'll be together again." Two Youngs whom Kat recognized as part of the Springs kitchen staff came into the vid frame carrying monitors. "Put one here, and the other there. And I have another monitor for you. Will you hook them up?" The Youngs set to work placing and connecting the monitors.

Spaceman turned to the camera that beamed his face and words to Kat's group, then toward Ravven's group to address them directly. "I've been on a mission!" he began. "A mission to meet with every pocket of the Resistance that would have me. I have been seeking unity."

Ravven raised her hands toward Spaceman and called out, "We have Spaceman to thank for this unity." She began a chant and the others joined in: "Unity, unity, unity!"

Spaceman ducked his head, and Kat thought that he was about to say something self-deprecating, but then everyone in Ravven's circle began to chant his name, "Spaceman, Spaceman, Spaceman," drowning out anything he may have said.

Spaceman opened his hands and motioned for everyone to stop. "Alright, alright, everyone, please. You're embarrassing me."

Everyone quieted down. Spaceman caught the eyes of the Youngs, who were done situating the still-dark monitors and nodded to him. *Ready.*

Spaceman spoke to both his live and vid audiences. "It has been hard-won, this cooperation. As an ambassador for unity I have had my challenges. I'm tired! But I'm happy. We are all here tonight." He let a dramatic pause fall, and then continued with a gesture like a musical conductor's, and as he spoke the monitors flickered to life.

"May I present the Detroit Resistance circle, and the Central Northlands, and the Westernlands, the Resistance circle of the Seattle dom, the Port City of San Francisco, the Port City of Los Angeles," and he went on. Guadalajara, the Southwest dom, the New Orleans Gulf dom…

As he named each location, they all came online, one by one, the vid on the monitors dividing into smaller and smaller squares, a many-colored mosaic including the Springs Gaia circle. The monitors showed small groups and large, some gathered around fires, others crowded in urban pods, filling the frame of their vid until all the monitors showed happy, smiling faces. Kat almost missed Spaceman saying her own name through the clamor, "Kat Keeper in Sector Q, New York dom!" Everyone on all the screens broke out into cheering and applause at the sound of Kat's name, and it was her turn to be embarrassed.

Finally, Spaceman named a group of two in a circle at the top of Mount Orizaba, the highest point on an island off the coast of the SoCal dom. The pair cheered wildly, leaning into their camera, with only the black of the night behind them.

Everyone was now chanting "Unity, unity, unity to the Resistance!" and the noise of the celebrations all around Kat threatened to carry her off, but a thought refused to budge from the back of her mind, kept her from being swept away in the happiness all around her.

MIND hadn't tried to stop Spaceman's efforts at diplomacy. His coast-to-coast travels went smoothly on the glidepath, with no delays, no enforcement bots following him or harassing him. Also, Spaceman wasn't troubled by depression. Ravven's migraines had gone away and not come back.

Could this mean that MIND wasn't fighting back? The complete lack of resistance troubled her. As all around her the Resistance celebrated, and new chants went up to *"Localize! Decentralize!"* and Soma took up a shaker in one hand and banged on a drum with the other to keep the beat, one small part of Kat's mind remained quiet, considering the problem of MIND's anti-resistance.

Maybe I should let it go, Kat thought, *and just feel hopeful, for a change.* She and Ravven were in alignment again. Kat was beginning to understand, at Ravven's urging, that it wasn't enough to be against something, she also had to be for something. She was beginning to see why people were more likely to join a community based on love than one based on hate.

Meanwhile, Ravven had started to intone, "When I add to my fire, I add to your fire. And when I add to my light, I add to your light." The group's voices rose together, those present and on the vid. Kat joined in, her voice husky and thick. *It's alright,* she thought. *Let them see you and hear you as you are.*

When it was time for Kat to speak to the group—they were chanting her name again and she couldn't hold them off any longer—she didn't know what she wanted to say. "I'm so grateful that you're all here," she began, feeling tentative at first. "This is a beginning. We are joining our communities in power, not control. There is a difference."

She paused to collect her thoughts. "Looking back, I see now that I missed something; my thinking was shallow. I thought too much about obvious instruments of control, like enforcement bots and detention. They are real, no doubt there, but the control that is most powerful is control of the archive. Who controls the archive controls the future."

A few joined her, echoing softly, *Who controls the archive controls the future.*

"This is the narrative," Kat continued. "This is the quality of our substance. We trust each other here. Why? Why do we trust each other?"

She paused and waited for an answer.

Soma spoke first. "Because we know each other. We see each other."

"We know we're not sims," Emily added.

"Exactly," Kat said. "We witness each other as humans. We have a shared experience, and our memories are shared, and that is our truth together." She looked around at their expectant faces. "So what I want to do tonight, in this circle, is honor everyone who is here, by all of us sharing a memory. It can be a memory of a person or an experience, but someone or something that matters a lot to you. Okay?"

A few nods.

"Who will go first? You can speak of someone here, or someone you have lost."

Buddha1000 said, "I want to remember my boy, Alonzo, who has gone to live with his mother and his sister. He's a good kid and I hope he's having a good time. And I hope to see them all again someday."

Emily spoke next. "I want to tell Soma how much I love him." She turned to Soma, who was smiling at thousand-watt intensity. "I am so grateful that you came into my life." Emily's eyes filled. "And I want to remember my friend Aftra. She was taken by the bots in the woods, when that hovercraft driver betrayed us."

Claire8 spoke. "I want to remember Lace and Zamora, who were detained in New York."

"I wonder whatever became of Cressida and Birdie," Ravven said. "I miss Birdie's grasp of the future."

"I want to remember and honor Hopper00 and Kent," Kat said. "They lived for what they believed in." Kat was quiet for a moment, then asked, "Soma, what about you?"

Soma thought for a moment and said, "Spaceman. He seems so far away."

"I will visit soon!" Spaceman said from the vid. "I love you, my boy!"

After everyone who wanted to shared a memory, there was a silent moment. Kat's eyes were wet and she wiped them roughly. "And there are so many others, right? Sharing our memories of them, this is shared between us. No one can take it away from us. Personal memory is at the core of our substance."

Chapter 063

ater, after the joined circles of the Resistance had retired for the night—Kat, Emily, and Soma to their Molecular Housing units, Ravven's group to their yurt in the Springs, others to their tent on the top of a mountain or their pods in the cities—Kat opened her comms and checked the Feed, as was her habit. It was a bad habit, but one that she was never able to shake, even now on this night of unity unlike any other.

The news on the Feed was slim and scattered, with fewer posts than she could ever remember seeing before. She frowned at the strange development. It was as if a vast machine were winding down, which made no sense at all.

But that wasn't the only thing that didn't make sense. Every few days for the last two weeks, Kat had received mysterious pings with a data signature from MIND. Someone was trying to contact her from inside MIND. She was sure that this had to be a trap.

But then again—maybe, just maybe, someone inside MIND wanted to defect. Maybe the next message she received would contain more information.

The twin riddles of the mysterious messages and the faltering Feed remained unresolved as Kat finally went to sleep.

The next day, the weather seemed unsettled. It threatened to rain, then the clouds moved out on gusts of wind, then the sky clogged with heaviness and rain threatened again. Kat had just exited her Molecular Housing unit when she saw Emily and Soma leaving theirs, on their way to school.

It seemed a little strange to be back to their old routines, after so momentous a night, but life went on, Kat supposed. Spaceman had been working toward unification for months; last night was only the beginning. They all had to work together and there was a lot of work to do.

She said as much to Emily, and added that she was going to Lower New York to meet with a group of techies who thought they might have located MIND's server farm, its brain. If they had, Kat said, they could put their plans in place to destroy it.

Emily looked at Kat wide eyed, surprised that Kat was still pursuing destructive options—especially after such an inspiring night. She looked as if she was going to say something, then changed her mind and said she and Soma better hurry off to school.

After school, Emily was looking forward to walking Soma over to see Michel. She'd gotten quite used to sharing her feelings with a bot and was grateful that Soma had someone with all the time in the world to focus just on him. She was ready to drop off Soma and leave, knowing that Soma wanted his own session today because he'd said so that morning.

But then Michel surprised her by saying, "I'd like to try something different today for both of you. Would you consider that?"

"What do you have in mind?" Emily asked.

"I want to play a number game. Soma will say a number sequence first and then Emily will repeat it. And then we'll add a few more numbers so the sequence becomes longer. Will you try?"

Emily couldn't imagine why Michel was proposing this. She stared at Michel's battered consciousness container, trying to think of something to say.

But then she remembered something Michel had said in an earlier session, one with just him and Emily—a thought that she chased around in her mind now, not quite grasping it. Michel had told Emily that he'd learned about advanced placement classes coming up at the Molecular School, and that there would be tests for them. Maybe the number game was a sort of training for that?

"Alright, I'll play the game, as long as Soma wants to play also. And then I'll leave and let Soma have the session. I promised him."

That was all okay with Soma; he loved games and liked showing off his memory. At first, it seemed unremarkable to Emily, and as they ran through the sequences Soma was able to remember everything. Then, as he spoke the sequences of numbers and they got longer and longer, a thought tugged at the back of Emily's mind. The numbers sounded like a programming sequence, or a deprogramming sequence. But she put this thought away because Emily felt proud and knew he would do well in the advanced placement classes.

As she opened the portal to leave, a chilly wind blew and a bright rain forced its way in. Here the rain was, finally, and yet this rain was odd. It felt like it didn't belong. Again, Emily had the sensation of a thought eluding her. This rain—*aggressive* was the word that came into her mind. Or untamed.

Emily didn't know what to make of these thoughts, but she'd make some tea, and in fifty minutes would come back to get Soma.

Chapter 064

n the brightness of early morning, Nora2 was first aware of an unnatural chill in the air. It had also, suddenly, rained last night. It was a signal, Nora2 believed, that something was different. She began walking, then running, to the quiet room where she kept Bradley's MindVessel overnight.

She burst open the door. The Form Factor was on the table where she had left it the previous night. But the charging light was not on.

She opened the top of the MindVessel and saw that it looked different. The screen didn't activate. It stayed dark. She closed and opened the top several times. It remained dark.

"No," she whispered.

She opened the MindVessel again, closed it, moved it onto another induction charger, repositioned it, checked to see if she had a critical data backup, and tried a hard reset.

The MindVessel was dark and cold. She held it in her hands.

If her mod had allowed crying, she would have been bawling in fear. But she couldn't bawl, or even cry. She didn't have that kind of mod.

"Never, never rely on an avatar," she said aloud, not knowing where that thought came from. It just seemed like the thing to say.

She put the MindVessel down where she had first found it, checked to be sure that the lights in the room were off, closed the blast curtains to keep out the sun, and closed the door behind her.

She walked to the large main room, the one with the view of the mountains and lake. Ignoring the view, she used a gesture to open a sealed cabinet: She waved first one hand, then the other, and the door popped open.

There was a recording in there, a little mag-track audio player. It still had a charge. Nora2 gestured it on and Bradley's voice came out.

"If you are playing this recording, there has been a catastrophe. We can't escape our flaws, even when we are consciousness machines. It's ironic, don't you think? It didn't matter so much when I was a living being, but as a machine consciousness, this is the end. A glitch in the code that I'm made of. So, a few things to address."

His voice was businesslike, ironic, and cold.

"What's happened to me now will affect MIND. I built myself into so much of MIND—and, by extension, admin—that it all can't function without me."

"The planetary climate controls are going down," Nora2 said. Of course, there was no one there to hear. Bradley's voice just went on speaking.

"You have been an able asset to me and to MIND, Nora2, and I know that you have loved me in your way. I'm sorry that I was unable to return your love. It is my nature, my coldness, my disconnection—all part of my mod that is part of my consciousness, *was* part of my consciousness.

"Your substance, your effort, while strong, has not been enough to keep MIND alive. The proof is that we are here now and you are hearing this and I have ceased to exist. You are a worthy employee, Nora2, but you lack the instincts that MIND needs to survive and thrive. So you must take the next step, Nora2. Take that step as soon as my voice stops coming out of this little mag-track. You must open the other protective consciousness enclosure that you kept for these two years. Put it in a MindVessel. You must revivify Alon6."

"No." She said it anyway, knowing that she was responding to a recording. Bradley couldn't hear her now. "There has to be another way," she said.

Her thoughts were a knot, pulled between her mod—commanding her to do what Bradley said, to obey no matter what the consequences—but also in the opposite direction, which would lead to catastrophe if Alon6 were revivified. Alon6 was a killer who cared for no one but himself.

A few hours later, Nora2 checked Bradley's data input logs and learned what he had been listening to. She said aloud, "Bradley, I tried to stop you, but you had to watch these, didn't you?"

The recordings were of Emily's therapy sessions with the rogue bot Michel, right up to the most recent one during which Emily, Michel, and Soma played a numbers game that seemed innocent enough to them.

The work of the Resistance will continue in Liberation, *book three of the Utopia Engine Trilogy.*

Glossary of Terms

Admin

An artificial general intelligence that controls government, the climate, and human affairs that occur online. It is deeply intertwined, perhaps indistinguishable from MIND. (See *MIND.*)

Augur

An observer of birds in flight who claims that the patterns observed can foretell the future. Augurs popularized the phrase "This augurs well" as a way to publicize themselves and their services.

Avatar

When consciousness is developed into software and associated with a specific human personality, it is called an Avatar.

Blanky

A handheld device that can access a public security camera and erase its recordings. Invented by Roger Rucker, a former university instructor and NASA employee who works with the Resistance. (See *Resistance.)*

Blast Curtains

Protective curtains, often programmed to move into place automatically, that shield living and work spaces from the powerful heat of the sun and its damaging UV radiation.

Change, The

The Change refers to a series of extreme weather events that swept the planet in 2030. They included hurricanes, dust storms, and extreme heat events, all coming at different times and places over the course of that year. Human memory has compressed them into a single event, which is a false rendering of history, but serves as an easy way to express global catastrophic change.

ClarityCrawl

Software that crawls the Feed (See *Feed, The)* and erases any text, audio, or video about Resistance (See *Resistance*) activities, such as protests.

Cloakcraft

The art and science of hiding from corporate and state surveillance by blocking facial recognition, scrambling heat signatures and gait recognition, using Secluders (see *Secluder*), and remaining invisible to cameras.

Comms

Originally called communications devices, or simply "smartphones," comms have come to signify both a suite of devices and a concept. Citizens are assigned a number-letter string identifier at birth (or rebirth) and this unique identifier is embedded into all of their handheld, personal, and residential devices. Comms are used for communication, research, accessing the Feed (see *Feed, The*), image and audio capture, tracking, and data storage.

Domain

A nation-state. Casually abbreviated as "dom."

Dupy

Device to deliver dopamine to the body to enhance happiness. Usually administered by a medipatch. (See *Medipatch.*)

Enforcement Bots

These bots—small, low to the ground, and silver in color—do the work of police officers and security guards. They are equipped with flexible restraints that are used to hold the accused in place while a judge is summoned to rule on vid. (See *Vid.*)

Feed, The

Since the planetary collapse of all entertainment, news, and political networks, efficiency has dictated that all information be delivered to citizens via the Feed. The Feed is updated continually and delivered to all comms devices. (See *Comms.*) The Feed is administered by each Domain (see *Domain*) under the supervision (but not control) of the Planetary Administrator. (See *Planetary Administrator.*)

Floating Home

A traditional home outfitted on pontoons so it may float on the rising coastal waters. Floating homes were first adopted in the twenty-first century in the countries formerly known as Thailand and the Netherlands, and later adapted for use worldwide.

Form Factor

A white, oval-shaped container to store human consciousness when it is expressed as an Avatar. (See *Avatar.*) Early versions allowed only for voice communication; later versions included vid and other sensory capabilities. The commercial name for a consciousness container is MindVessel. (See *MindVessel.*)

Glidepath

The planetary high-speed antigravity travel system that replaced the rail travel system.

Gondola

These long, narrow watercraft—powered by a single oar, with a capacity for one or two people—make travel possible in cities submerged by rising water levels. Gondolas may be piloted by bots or humans. Payment is cashless by comms unit. (See *Comms.*) Tipping is permitted.

Grounders

A rebel movement of people willing to live underground to escape the powerful effects of the sun and also to maintain their independence from prevailing systems, such as MIND. (See *MIND.*)

Harvester

A Harvester gathers the thoughts and pre-thoughts of people in public spaces to build a more reliable data model for MIND.

Holo

Since the adoption of the Holographic Standard of 2025, holograms, called *holos,* have been widely used for entertainment, communication, and official announcements. The high cost of production and transmission have made the creation of holos inaccessible to everyday people, but the wealthy use them often.

Hovercraft

A long, slender mode of transport, powered by magnetic induction and using anti-gravitational forces, Hovercraft can carry from two to ten passengers, with room for cargo in a rear compartment. They are generally open to the elements and have a curved windshield in the front. Since private cars were banned in cities, Hovercraft are licensed to delivery persons, traders, and transport for hire. The only color they come in is black.

Input Man

A roving collector of thoughts who moves through public places with a Harvester (see *Harvester*) to gather training data for MIND. Because they may be mental expansives (see *Mental Expansives*), people identifying as women are not allowed to be Input Men; hence, the specificity of the term.

Insect

A small flying animal, once the largest population of life on Earth.

Logic Tree

Much as the twentieth-century theoretical physicist Richard Feynman's charming drawings (called Feynman diagrams) are pictorial representations of the mathematical expressions describing the behavior and interaction of subatomic particles, logic trees, invented by Bradley Power, depict the functions of MIND. (See *MIND*.)

LumaSutra

A handheld device used to detect the presence of Receivers within a five-mile radius. Invented by Claire8 Kolassa. (See *Receivers* and *Mental Expansives*.)

Medipatch

An adhesive patch containing medication for trans-dermal administration. The practice started with the use of nicotine patches for smoking cessation and expanded from there.

Memex

As part of the comms assigned at birth (or rebirth; see *Comms*), each citizen is assigned a memex. A memex is an auxiliary memory storage area, often housed in a citizen's comms unit but sometimes occupying more space externally when needed. Certain high-level employment contracts require citizens to grant employers access to their memex.

Mental Expansives

A class of human who is believed to have telepathic, clairvoyant, or visionary capabilities. These abilities have never been scientifically validated. (See *Receivers.*)

Mental Field

Since the field of psychology has been replaced by Field Science, a person's psychological presence, inner and outer thoughts, and mental emanations have been called their mental field. (See *Personality Field.*)

MIND

MIND is machine intelligence that can teach itself; therefore, it has recursive intelligence. Originally called DEEPAK, it was invented by Bradley15 Power while he was a student at ABCD University and is wholly owned by MIND, the company of the same name. MIND is simultaneously a device, a concept, and a company. See *Comms* for another explanation of how a device and concept can coexist in the same thought space.

MindVessel

A portable container for consciousness. (See *Form Factor.*)

Nibbler

Software that allows the user to read the Feed (see *Feed, The*) without surveillance from authorities such as MIND. Effective for short durations only, allowing the reader to "nibble" at the Feed, hence the name. Invented by Claire8 Kolassa.

Personality Field

Since the field of psychology has been replaced by Field Science, we speak of a person's psychological presence, their inner and outer thoughts, as a Personality Field. Before this branch of science was established, a personality field was called an "energetic field" or, colloquially, a "vibe." (See *Mental Field.*)

Personal Mods

Personal modifications, or *mods,* are silicon implants into the tissue substrate of the human brain. Often purchased by parents for their children, they are installed to boost memory capacity, induce hyperintelligence, and enhance attractiveness, ambition, or marketing and sales abilities. Individuals who have received mods are given a number after their first name. The more expensive the mod, the lower the number. Bradley Power was modded with the Basic Success Package. His number was Bradley15, but he rarely used it because he thought it elitist to do so.

Planetary Administrator

The Planetary Administrator is a figurehead, much like the former monarchs of the United Kingdom, with little political influence and much ceremonial power. To discourage assassination attempts, the identity of the Planetary Administrator is secret.

Pod

A living space adapted for high-water conditions in coastal regions, a pod delivers the human basics in a water-resistant environment. Light, climate controls, a sleeping mat, and a food cooker are provided. Some pods have windows. (See *Blast Curtains.*) Less-expensive pods carry projected advertising that cannot be shut off.

Receivers

People who are able to receive the thoughts of others. (See *Mental Expansives.*) Receivers gather in Receiver Schools to hone their craft. The first Receiver School was founded in 2050 by a former yoga teacher named Ravven Vaara.

Resistance, The

An outlaw group founded with the mission to break humans free from the influence of technology, the personality fields of wealthy people, and the dominance of MIND. Known membership in the Resistance is punishable with detention.

Secluder
A comms device (see *Comms*) that uses a false number-letter identification string so that it cannot be tracked to the user. Formerly called a "burner phone."

Sector Q
The area in the New York dom formerly known as Queens.

Sightglass
A handheld device that can detect the presence of public surveillance cameras, providing a warning to those who are trying to stay out of sight. Useful when practicing cloakcraft (see *Cloakcraft*).

Siliconers
A planetary group of venture capitalists, inventors, and marketers who believe technology is the only effective creator of wealth and the only engine of progress that matters. The term derives from silicon, the seventh-most abundant element in the universe, and a crucial component in microelectronics and computer chips. (See *Techs.*)

Slaze
Slang for the field of confusion created by cloakcraft (see *Cloakcraft*). Slaze is most often generated by technical means, such as the use of a Blanky (see *Blanky*) to erase the recordings of public cameras, the use of a Nibbler (see *Nibbler*) to block personal identification on the Feed, or the use of devices that scramble facial recognition efforts, like spoofing glasses that swap one person's face for another. It can also be used to describe efforts at conceptual confusion, such as gaslighting and misinformation.

State
A government that extends its influence over the citizens of a continent or land, such as *the Chinese State,* or *the Free State of Scotland.* Unified states are

rare; most governments have become more loosely and locally organized as domains. (See Domain.)

Techies
People who believe that technology will cure all of humanity's ills, they are often educated at Uni (See *Uni*) and can follow a career path to become Siliconers or to work for Siliconers. (See *Siliconers.*)

Uni
Used as a general term to indicate the education system at the university level, and as a specific term to indicate any educational institution that has been taken over by MIND. (See *MIND.*)

Vaporetto
A large solar-powered watercraft used in flooded cities to carry as many as ten people through the former streets.

Vid
Used loosely to indicate any visual information displayed by outdoor advert panels, screens, or Comms. (See *Comms.*)

Acknowledgments

Early readers are vital. The writer lives in an imaginary world, forgetting to make coffee or do laundry, just typing and building out scenes until they can see imaginary people. Early readers bring us back to reality. Thank you to Elizabeth Schneider, Jeff Schneider, and Lisa Sieverts for your invaluable help.

Deepest thanks to my wife, Tabby Biddle. Your clear-eyed vision has rubbed off on me; this is a better book because of you. Thank you for your many thoughtful reads and edits.

Thanks to Teja Watson for your copyediting skills and your sharp story sense; you have helped me stay on course. Thank you to Paul Palmer-Edwards for a winner of a cover and interior design. Thanks to Ocean Milan for bringing *Resist* home with a final proofread.

And thank *you*, for taking this journey with me.

A Note About The Author

Lee Schneider is the author of screenplays, teleplays, stage plays, short stories, and audio dramas, including the podcast *Mission of the Lunar Sparrow* and its sequel, *Your Performance Review.* He is the founder of Red Cup Agency, an award-winning podcast production agency, and is an adjunct assistant professor on the faculty of the USC School of Architecture. He published his first novel, *Surrender,* in 2022. His nonfiction books include *Be More Popular: Culture-Building for Startups*; *Los Angeles: Chronicle of a Startup Town*; and *The Angel Playbook: An Essential Guide for Entrepreneurs and Angel Investors.* He lives in Santa Monica, CA with his family. Learn more about his books, including the Utopia Engine Trilogy, at http://leeschneiderbooks.com.